Y0-CPC-990

I DIDN'T See This Coming from MY FAMILY

Niecy M.

authorHOUSE®

AuthorHouse™
1663 Liberty Drive
Bloomington, IN 47403
www.authorhouse.com
Phone: 1 (800) 839-8640

This book is a work of both fiction and nonfiction; as a result, reader's discretion is advised. Meanwhile, as in all fiction and nonfiction, the literary perceptions and insight are based on experiences of the imagination. All the characters, location, names, incidents are pure coincidence and merely a product of the Author's foreseen abilities and/or used as fictitiously.

Published by AuthorHouse 10/31/2017

ISBN: 978-1-5462-1530-1 (sc)
ISBN: 978-1-5462-1529-5 (e)

Print information available on the last page.

DEDICATION

This book is dedicated to my Father, H. C. Morton better known by Pimp and Boss man by family members and close friends. Rest in Heaven. In my opinion I felt that my Dad left us too soon. I felt that my dad's work wasn't finished even though he suffered greatly with multiply illnesses. Selfishly I still wanted him to continue being among the living with us. I did not like seeing him go through so many fazes from; the agony of different pains, his tiredness from sleepless nights, watching if not taking him to and from the emergency rooms, and lastly, seeing a huge array of prescribed medications he was taking daily it was a lot to bare. Truthfully speaking I wanted him to somehow miraculously heal without having any more pain. Instead, our Lord and Savior saw differently and called my dad home to rest internally. My father, a hilarious wise man had hella wisdom with charm. He was extremely humbled but gracious. He was a jokester who often tested us kids with his knowledge by saying some awkward shit like 'how do you spell A.' this would puzzle us kids. My Mother; on the other hand, would ignore all of us during these quizzes and say 'yall kids figure it out'. My siblings and I would discuss among each other many ways in how to spell the letter A other than using the actual letter A. We could never figure it out!

Contrarily, my dad was a quiet man who was known for his smile. He had many accolades from Ministering for the Lord to being a truck driver. He often sat back and observed others before giving his honest opinion. He could literally tell if someone was being dishonest by using his southern instincts. My dad always critiqued my siblings and I friends especially the male friends whenever they visited. Dad could always spot a player like no other. Once one of my sisters ended her relationship and developed a new one. My dad met with the new guy and his overall perception was and he said 'she went from shit to hell…damn!' The man was a riot! Those were the best times.

As an adult looking back on my childhood from my memory bank I wanted to covey the most vivid, the most outrageous and the most unapologetic events that stood out to me as a child while enforcing my self-knowledge. There were many questions that needed answers. It was executing truth verses lies that were told to others by my family members as I listened. My family and I were a few steps behind with society but we eventually caught up with the world ending with some of us making hurtful decisions and choosing sides to be on. I learned the value about trust and betrayal within love which exhibits various attributed about feelings.

However, in life we make choices and say words that sometimes can't be taken back. It's always wise to be respectful in how you approach a person because you would want to be treated with respect yourself. So in saying that, I say this that every culture exemplifies difference in lifestyles which can sometimes become alarming. I saw a lot as a child which helped me mature at a young age. What I witnessed within a three week span in New York most would have had taken years to manifest in the country of Oklahoma. My lifestyle immortalizes hidden truths that were covered up by the least possible person within the family. I latched on to my favorite Auntie who was nearly a shadow of protection and knowledge to me but deep down she was battling insecurities. She took the time to explain her many encounters of doubts of self-assurance on a daily bases while trying to fight for respect. She blamed her insecurities on some of her siblings who made it known they disapproved in how she was built making her feel like a failure. This girl was self-absorbed until she discovered the difference between a man and a woman and because of this comparison I watched our family fall apart.

CHAPTER 1

Adventurous as my childhood was living in the South, I can truly say, that I enjoyed being raised in an undissipated lifestyle given to me by my parents J. W. and Geraldine White. Over the years during the early sixty's I indeed, witnessed first-hand an array of personal life style changes linked to experiences resulting in; dramas; love, secret sex scandals, betrayal of the heart, and witch craft. I matured quickly in those days at a young age. The atmosphere on our farmland was fast pace, unpredictable, unsettling and mind boggling.

Aa result, I will take you on a ride into many life's changes of events that left an everlasting dent or while some would say a scar in my life and. Here's my story.

CHAPTER 2

I was thankful school was over for the day. I couldn't wait to be dropped off at my Auntie Eisha's classroom. My teacher, Mrs. Waller often walked me to meet my Auntie in her last period class after school. Upon reaching my favorite Auntie I immediately noticed something different about her. I couldn't pinpoint it right away but, from her appearance something about her demeanor was out of bound. The sadness upon her face was noticeable; almost, as though she had been crying in school all day. I stood there next to my teacher not wanting to let her hand go; because I knew personally when Auntie Eisha's mood shifts all hell breaks loose. She had a tendency in taking her anger out on any one that was near her. I knew what to expect from her from previous circumstances and I really did not want to be her punching bag all the way home. She had a quick temper that was sometimes obnoxious with a bit of sarcastic in it. I use to think maybe she acted this way because she was the baby among her siblings. She regularly had tantrums which pretty much got her, everything she wanted; her way. Undoubtedly, when Auntie held her hand out to retrieve me from my teacher's hand, she said 'come on So-soo' and snatched me away from my teacher's hand. My head jerked I looked back at Mrs. Waller who saw that, and should have said something to Auntie Eisha, but she chose to ignore us by looking at the floor making me secretly yelled underneath my breath 'bitch call my Momma'!

In addition, our daily routine Monday's through Thursday's consisted of my teacher Mrs. Waller who walked me to meet Auntie Eisha in her last period class. She was schooled in the next building over where both the middle and intermediate students went to up till the eighth grade. On this day my Auntie's demeanor after school that day made me watch her every move. She gathered her books; I mean she was slanging those books on top of one another, than she tried to yank her raggedy Ann purse only to realize that the belt strap was wrapped around the chair. This mild set-back infuriated her even more, nevertheless, causing her to make a huffing sound, and at the same time wouldn't you know once she unwrapped her purse this brod snatched me once again by the arm! Do you know once we got outside to walk our two mile stretch home this heifer nearly dragged me about a quarter of a mile! When I screamed her name to stop pulling me she then stopped, looked down at me and said 'So-soo I did not realized I was pulling you'. Her mind was set on something heavy. Hell bout time we made it home from school my Mother saw us walking abruptly. She ran off the porch to meet us then grab me by my upper shoulders and said 'Sofay what happened to you, were you in a fight'? I said 'Huh Momma'? Before I knew it I just busted into tears. Momma said 'look at you Soo' I did not know that my ribbons on my hair were untied and hanging loosely on my pony tails, my hair looked as though someone ran a rake through it, my culottes' skirt was lopsided, I had one shoe on because Eisha would not slow down for me to go back to retrieve my other shoe that slide off my foot. Momma said 'now Sofay tell me exactly what happened'. After, I told her how Eisha was looking in school and acting funny again Momma did not let me finish. She grabbed my hand as we walked passed the men on the front porch saying to me 'Momma's gone take care of this causz ain't no bitch gone be yanking my baby all the way home in this hot ass heat'. Granddaddy looked up from playing cards with his longtime friend gossiping Mr. Johnson and yelled out 'what in the God's name is going on now'? Momma yelled back 'your baby girl is at it again being grown and out of control'! Momma did not have much tolerance to evil when it came to the family especially me and Daddy. She walked right up to Auntie Eisha's face and said 'now looka here little girl this is your last damn time that you will scare my baby by pulling her hair and thangs'. Eisha looked at both of us with a dumb look on her face. Oh how I desperately wanted to say to Eisha no I did not say that! Well we all knew how my sweet Momma always had a vivid imagination which automatically triggered her to add on unnecessary, but additional untrue drama to make the story juicier. I knew very well not to interfere with Momma's conversations. I learned early on to stay in a child's place. Momma did not play with me she would pop me in the mouth within a heartbeat if I attempted to interfere in any of her conversations without being spoken to. Momma always said 'you speak when spoken to'.

Consequently, I always stayed quiet when I really wanted to voice my opinion. My opinions usually did not matter because my Mother did all the talking for me even though that did not stop me from talking underneath my breath.

CHAPTER 3

However, Auntie Nitta the second oldest was walking pass us. She stopped and asked what was going on? Momma said 'your baby sister tripped my baby making her fall out her shoe'! I was humiliated! I wanted to roll myself to the shed and just stay there for the night. Auntie Nitta looked at Eisha than took her by the hand and they walked on the farmland looking for my Grandmother – Gramz's who was near by picking blueberry for that night's dessert. Before, reaching Gramz, Nitta whispered to Eisha to open up and tell us what was bothering her. Gramz's turned around to see; me, Momma, Eisha and Nitta standing around her. She then said 'what yall cherrins up too?' Nitta said 'Momma I do not know why this child of yours got all these different attitudes and taking it out on us this needs to stop'. Eisha stood there like a zombie and did not bulge when asked questions regarding what was wrong with her, instead, she started crying; sliding down onto the ground. This drama occurs whenever she thinks everyone is ganging up on her. Momma shouted to Eisha 'girl if you gone fall down don't hold the tail of your skirt to cover your butt on the ground, just fall your ass down like a normal person would'. Daddy walked over just in time to hear Momma's outburst and nudged her in the armpit with his elbow meaning to be quiet. Auntie Eisha paused from crying for a moment. Somewhere in the back of her mind that humiliating joke Momma just said did not sit well with her. This forced her to say 'shut up Geraldine and take care of your own busy husband'. I thought Huh? I was clueless in hearing that statement somehow or another the siblings knew what that statement meant including Momma who grasped for some air then she shut the hell up. She looked at daddy who stood there looking up into the sky weary with his eyes bulging out the sockets. Next thing I knew Momma stormed off. Truthfully speaking, it was no secret that my Daddy with several of his brothers hell maybe even Granddaddy had philandering ways with many women in town. I once asked daddy what hoe meant? He said 'Soo-so stay in your place'. He was never able to answer any of my sexual questions it may him uncomfortable. He would stare at me, clear his throat, and act like he was choking on something before saying go sit down somewhere. When he turned his back that's when Eisha and Nitta (if she was not painting her eyes black) would explain to me the meaning behind those unfamiliar adult words.

Meanwhile, Gramz's had just about enough of both of the exchanges and bickering of words so she shut them all down by screaming at the top of her lungs saying 'everybody shut the fuck up' throwing a balled up fist into the air. Like in a cartoon animation all of them dropped their heads like soldiers shutting up one by one.

Anyway, before I knew it, the area where we all were standing seemed to have drawn attention from the visitors and the remaining siblings. Who by then, made their way to where we were standing and immediately started asking 'who did what-what happen-what's wrong?

Ironically, this was certainly not out of the ordinary to have a large amount of people standing around because we kept visitors throughout the day at the farmland. I just don't recall the visitors being so concern nor involved with our family drama or maybe I never paid attention until now. The visitors were friends of my Dad along with his siblings. We had Granddaddy's longtime friend's ole gossiping Mr. Johnson, sickening Mr. Brown and old man Martin who visited daily if not every other day. Their wives were Gramz's friends. Mr. Johnson who had no glue to what was going on jokingly said 'alright suggar nobody messes with my baby cause I'll shot that sucker down' Laughter exploded, ironically, any other time, Gramz would have replied back by saying 'ol go sat your gossiping ass down some where Johnson' but this time she did not respond back. Even my Dad J. W. took notice to say 'Momma you okay you didn't say nothing to Mr. Johnson' it was like she was hypnotized staring blinkingly into Eisha's eyes. Gramz's was thinking back to when Eisha started this tantrum shit. She was used to Eisha normal tantrums of; whining, pouting and loud outbursts but none of us was prepared for this new fond of tantrums that consisted of; pushing and shoving, rolling her eyes, storming off during conversations it was too much. Hell, I was the baby and I knew better to not act like that! To make matters worse many who were standing there clueless began laughing silently just concurring up shit without a clue. I'm not sure if their laughter was geared towards Eisha or geared towards Momma for storming off or maybe the laughs were geared for both of them. I could not tell yah which one but it was starting to become irritating. Eisha begin looking at everyone standing there laughing and became so frustrated that she blurred out 'all yall miserable asses can go to hell' I didn't know what she expected behind that statement because all she got were more laughs.

Truthfully speaking, she was right misery does Loves Company. By this time, Gramz's was boiling over with anger she could not take any more shenanigans from Eisha who still would not say what was bothering her. Gramz's decided she would beat it out of her but as soon as she tried to reach for her neck Granddaddy walked in between them. He blocked Gramz's stretched out hands and said to his wife 'Olivia leave her be'. Eisha get up off the ground and gone on up to the house I will be up there later. Whew Eisha dodged that beaten! It is a good thing Granddaddy came between them because Eisha would have been swollen for days from being whipped and nearly strangled by her Mother.

Likewise, my heart fell looking down at my sweet Auntie with her legs crossed on top of one another on the ground. As she got up off the ground she gained her composure but looked bewildered mostly from crying. She looked angrily at those that were laughing then turned up her top lip and gave them the middle finger causing some to bend over with laughter. I did not understand why she would do such a thing she was already the center of attention. I guess it was the brat in her that was being unleashed. I silently laughed and thought Eisha always gives a show when she's put on the spot. I looked over at Gramz who by this time stood there shaking her head left to right. I then looked back to Auntie Eisha relieved to see she started getting her dignity intact by; straightening out her skirt, and fixing her hair. She began to walk I immediately grabbed her hand and we walked back uppa yonder to the house. She looked down at me and I tried to encourage her by saying 'Auntie you are my favorite! Eisha took a deep breath paused then said 'So-soo I love you sooooo much! That was my way of apologizing for telling Momma she dragged me home from school earlier in the day. I thought to myself if only Eisha had not dragged me home none of this would exist.

It just so happened, on our way to the house Granddaddy was standing directly in front of the house making those that were still laughing at Eisha to stop. He said 'that's his child and enough is enough'.

Apparently, Momma, with both Auntie Nitta and Camille apparently didn't get Granddaddy's memo to leave Eisha alone because they were still giggling having a good ole conversation. They eyed us as she and I walked passed them. Eisha tried to ignore them but somehow she just couldn't. She screamed out saying 'what cha looking at? I wanted to scream out those same exact words, but looking at momma I didn't want her to give me that ass whipping look, so I looked at the ground as we passed by them. But you better believe I cuss all of them out underneath my mouth.

CHAPTER 4

Then there was Mr. gossiping Johnson sitting on the porch with everyone else looking peculiar and unsettled. Auntie Eisha and I looked straight at the front door ignoring those on the porch. Luckily for us Uncle A.J. was standing directly in front of the door as if he was waiting for us to go inside. He opened the door and said 'yall gone on inside and freshen up'. He slammed the door behind us and we heard him going in hard on his friends. Eisha was relieved knowing the family had her back she had a slight smile which made me smile.

Finally, we made it to the bedroom sweaty we both were. Eisha fell on top of her bed relieved to breathe under the homemade fan. I laid next to her rubbing my foot while humming a song into the fan. My one foot was still hurting from being dragged in the dirt and stepping on rocks I asked Eisha when would the foot pain go away? She did not know but rose up from underneath the fan to massage my foot. We were both still hot and sweaty so Auntie Eisha decided that we should go ranch ourselves off with cool water. She went to the window and called James Junior to bring several buckets of water from the well so she and I could take a bath. He obliged and had Uncle Floyd to help him bring in the water.

Meanwhile, she and I waited patiently for them two to fill up our home made tub which was adjacent to the back bedroom that my parents and I shared. Funny though, if you looked at our house from the top of the windmill; it looked like a Crayola box of colors. There were so many adjacent rooms added onto the house that from the outside it resembled a colorful maze.

In contrast, Granddaddy and the boys continued throughout the years building rooms and making everyone comfortable. Another room! Baebae shouted out. Uncle Marshal said 'yes Bae we need to be inside bathing so Dadday and I decided to build a tub with another toilet'. They used all sorts of; lumber, cast iron, pile wood, cement, boards, pipes and everything else that was needed. It took them days if not months to complete this project. I was more eager than anyone else because I was tired of the barrows we used to bath in and besides I enjoyed telling my friends that we had an indoor tub.

Moreover, the tub was in a room of its own. Gramz's had decorated it so pretty she was determined to make this room her sanctuary for peace and quiet. She was so excited that she implemented a plan to decorate the tub room. She purchased multiply pieces of linen fabrics and used her sewing machine to make these beautiful long types of curtains that hung from the top of the tub rails and hung low on the floor like a wedding dress train. There were new wood chairs which were built by the hands of Uncle Floyd. He placed one chair near the tub while the other chair was in front of the window for Gramz's; for when she would sit, look outside, and hum songs while picking vegetables but drinking a cup of moonshine. Uh huh I saw her trying to be slick by using a coffee cup instead of the drinking glass for the moonshine. Gramz's believed in improvising and wasn't quick to throw anything away. There was extra material of linen left over so instead of trashing that material she made matching linen chair covers. I have to say; once everything was in place the tub room could have been put in a magazine.

Finally, my goodness both Uncle James Junior and Floyd were finished filling the tub with water. Once we left from underneath the fan it seemed like the sweat was fiercely running down our backs. I could not wait for that cool water to hit my body. Auntie Eisha said 'come on So-soo take your clothes off,' nothing was out of the ordinary with her saying that. She took off her blouse but left her shorts on. Again, this was not out of the ordinary. I climbed into the tub like an old lady relieved to remove the sweat off my body and to remove the remaining residue of rocks that were hidden underneath the skin of my toes. We both were silent for several minutes then Eisha did the unthinkable. She got the wash rag and roughly started bathing me with the soap bar splashing water everywhere. I thought 'uh-oh here she go again acting crazy'! She pulled my leg into the air to wash it completely ignoring my other leg. Before, I could respond she pulled me up from the water by my arm to say stand up. By this time, my heart was beating a mile a minute. My body trembled uncontrollable and honestly, this was the longest bath of my life. I told her Auntie it's okay I know how to bath myself. Truthfully speaking, I didn't know what had gotten into her but I didn't want to stick around to find out what was next up her sleeves. One minute she's sweet as pie but within seconds she turns into an uncontrolled maniac like she's rushing to complete a race. I was so confused. I did not comprehend those mood swings which were scary at times and this was one of those times I was scared.

Finally, this devil left me alone so I could bath myself. It was so hard to explain how she flips personalities like she did. She sat there on the edge of the tub constipating like she was studying something silently making me wonder was she cracking up. I could tell she wanted to say something but she didn't know how to explain it. All I know is I didn't take my eyes off of her as I continued bathing myself. Moments later she said 'get out the tub Red' I nervously climbed out the tub looking at Eisha hold the towel to dry me off. She dried me off and then said the unthinkable. Auntie said 'Sofay I got something to tell you and only you'. I asked what is it then she paused once again.

In the meantime, I became delirious thinking to myself of all the times nobody is in the house. Where is everybody? Any other time somebody would have walked through the house by now.

Nevertheless, Eisha took a deep breath and shared with me that our good family friend Mr. gossiping Johnson had been messing with her. My stomach fell even further away from my intestines I had simultaneously forgotten how she tried to bath me just that quickly! I said 'Eishaaaa what'!'

As a result, I did not understand why she did not share this hidden secret with Gramz when asked moments earlier. I didn't know what to say so I kissed my Auntie on the cheek very thankful that she did not do anything else to my precious body. She went on to explain with clear but precise details about her encounter with Mr. Johnson. This little secret thing started two months ago with him being playful with her. Clearly, no one and I mean not one of my fifteen Aunties or Uncles ever saw him being playful with her. She cohesively struggled but giggled trying to re-iterate her sexual experience. She and Mr. Johnson would meet behind the shed at night when everyone was sleep. I said 'the stinky shed'? Remember we were in the country without street lights. He wanted to use the shed as a hide away. The shed was approximately ten or more yards away from the house way towards the fields. The shed was a cooler storage for the meat that was hunted. No one would have expected nor been able to smell any scent of sex floating in the air. I mean what was smelled was the blood from the animals that were; hunted, killed, cleaned and skinned for food.

Contrarily, we as a family were not lacking in the food department. We rarely went to the grocery store for food because my Grandparents had everything both inside and outside the farm. We had fruit trees, cows including goats for milk, chickens for eggs, pigs, hogs and other animals for meat. We had a rooster along with several horses. Also there were different acres of vegetable which was how Granddaddy made his financial living for the family. He was a farmer. He grew the crops then separated them into piles dividing one for the household, and the other piles were sold for profits. This was a three to four day weekly process with help; from all eight boys, Granddaddy's two brothers and various friends. There were a lot of pipes directly on the side of the shed with a homemade sign that said 'watch the pipes'. I had a tendency of running around and through the shed area causing Granddaddy to have a nervous attack. He was afraid my foot would get caught in between the pipes and maybe get cut off. That was his way of scaring me into playing elsewhere on the farmland.

Anyway, I was stunt to learn that Mr. Johnson was bold enough to have had touched my Auntie on our property. She said 'when they would meet he would already be charged up'. She would be dressed in her pajamas eagerly awaiting his arrival. Those two had secret codes they used whenever Johnson would want to see her at night. I on the other hand, was stud to hear that Eisha would even go this far let alone with him of all the people in the world.

Likewise, I did not see a good outcome with this situation because all of my family members had some what of split personalities with doing the unthinkable. Eisha went on to describe explicit details into what took place between them two. I sat there frowned up trying to absorb what she was saying to me because she was teaching me something here. At first, she didn't let me get a word in because I could not get pass certain words. I said 'umm' stopping her midway. Auntie Eisha said 'So-soo let me finish telling you wanna know the meaning of these words…right'! Then she went into a descriptive dialog of the meaning speaking in a way that I would comprehend. Eisha continued on by saying once she experienced woman hood he never gave her enough time to catch her breath before continuing on. From all of that she was in heavenly bliss flying into Orbitz. I had to stop her again, I said 'Eisha you lost me with that. I said it's ok because I don't know how to follow along with what you are describing to me. Auntie Eisha was red in the face from laughing at me. She said 'Red when you get older you will appreciate a man loving you then she broke out smiling. I was beyond studded I did not want to hear any more of this crap it was too explicit for my ears. Now remind you dammit that she was just five years older than me making her fourteen. I was mortified because I did not know I had female parts that move. I was not familiar with sex at all then again maybe I was. My parents and I shared a bed. Whenever there were two pillows placed between us I pretty much knew what was about to take place. Hours prior to bed I would sometimes hear Daddy tell Momma Geraldine get ready for Jimmy tonight causz we gonna wear you out! Momma always whispered to daddy saying J.W. be quiet before Sofay hears you. Funny though, the next morning some would have thought that I was the one having sex from my looks because of; my baggy sleepy eyes, wild hair and excessive yawning. Gramz's took one look at me and knew instantly her child and daughter in law were at it again. She often said to my father 'J.W. why don't yall make So-soo a palette on the floor she's getting to big to sleep with you two'. Dad would just shrug his shoulders. I personally, thought it should be a permanent palette from the way these two who fucked like rabbits.

Besides; I learned from using my imagination, hearing, and not seeing my parents having sex. I heard sounds smelled odors and heard Momma silence screams of oh it is so good bababee. So in hearing Auntie Eisha's sex rundavoo with Mr. gossiping Johnson it really was nothing new to me but quite alarming knowing she was acting grown with a grown married man, who had a family living four miles away from us.

Realistically, I thought only Momma and Daddy did the who'd-chee-coo at night. I didn't know other people did that type of activity and I certainly did not expect Eisha to have such an experience at such a young age. From the look on my Auntie's face, it was priceless I did not know whether to scratch her eyes out or open up the window to scream for help. Ooowee I was beyond perturbed with both Eisha and Mr. Johnson. How could a friend of the family stoop so low in being nasty with a child?

CHAPTER 5

Henceforth, I was seeing fire being put on Mr. Johnson's juicy lips, thin neck and pop belly. Strangely enough, Eisha also revealed that she blamed Mr. Johnson for her sudden change in personality. He wanted to end their affair because he didn't want her to fall in love with him. Whereas, Eisha didn't want to end the affair she wasn't ready to let him go.

In fact, she couldn't concentrate during the day because of her wild imagination. Mr. Johnson told her all this jive she didn't want to hear before ending this secret affair. For instance, he said she was too good for him. Firstly, he was the one who initiated this ordeal and secondly, truth was I think he grew tired of her and had already moved on to the next young thing. Oh how I wanted to kick this man! I didn't realized that seconds if not minutes had went by because I was hearing the crickets outside. I heard Gramz making her way into the kitchen to start cleaning the food she was about to prepare for dinner. She had the girls Auntie Gwen, Baebae, and Monee to help her. I peeked outside through the window to see it was getting dark but not pitch black. People were still outside, however; I was relieved that Eisha was in the house away from Mr. Johnson. As I got up off the floor to put my clothes on Eisha slowly took off her shorts and underwear like she was in a daze and got into my bath water. When I glanced at her it looked as though she was about to cry. She had one arm over the tub with one leg out the tub just ah twirling staring into space smiling. When I saw that smile I hurried even faster putting my clean clothes on to run outta there quick, fast, and in a hurry! Thank goodness I made it out of that room safely leaving Eisha in her own world. I was so caught up in a whirlwind of thoughts that I didn't know if I was coming or going. Within those last few minutes I re-hashed what Auntie Eisha had said to me and I was spelled bind. Man what was a child my age to think? I was to think enough to go tell on both Eisha and Mr. Johnson nasty asses. I made up my mind while walking through the kitchen that it will only be right to tell an adult. I was so mind-boggled that I didn't hear Auntie Gwen said to me 'hey baby girl supper will be ready shortly'. I heard her but then again I did not hear her. Gwen stopped looked at Gramz who said to me 'So-soo go out there and tell Earl to come in here to light this here stove up so I can start cooking'. I kept walking without saying anything. She turned around putting her hands on her hips to say Sofay White did you hear me gal? I said 'huh' Gramz sarcastically repeated back what I said; she said 'huhhh', huh what? I said 'mamm' she said 'mamm what' then I said 'yes mamm'. Gramz then said 'girl get your red narrow tail outta here and go do what I say'. So I went out the door to search for Uncle Earl to rely the message. Once I got outside on the porch I thought I was seeing things. It's was him that bastard Mr. gossiping Johnson who should have been hiding miles away from us but instead, he was sitting there in the flash gossiping about some lady's coochie. I wanted to scream out as loud as I could I hope you not talking bout my Auntie Eisha's coochie but you know I couldn't say that so the only other option to get back at him at least I thought was to spit on him. My goodness, what was I thinking! Because that's what I did spitted at Mr. Johnson and ran off the porch. I did not look back but heard Granddaddy say what the hell! I ran straight to the shed covering my nose because of the blood smell. I wanted to see any type of signs of sex I didn't know what to look for but somehow or another; I needed to investigate where Eisha and Mr. Johnson had been having oral sex. I did not see any signs of a blanket or any forms of body prints carved into the dirt so I sat there at the locked door weary and out of breath. Suddenly I saw images of a tongue and I couldn't make out the face of the person hell I didn't know if it was me or Eisha so I hurried and tried to delete that from my imagination and began rehearsing what I was going to convey. I wanted to be cohesively clear on what was told to me by Auntie Eisha. The last thing that could happened from my story was to be compared as an emanate person like my Momma.

In addition, I was indecisive in whom I would tell first. I went down the line of sisters:

Camille: -uh-uh- She would stab him on the spot

Faye – hum mm- She would reason with him before sic'ing the hounds on him

Antoinette - uh uh- She would try to wrap him around a tree

Gwen - uh-uh- She wouldn't be able to see him from the tears streaming down her cheeks in trying to read various scriptures from the Bible

Monee – naw- She would not be able to see straight from the moonshine

Nitta- maybe- Nittaaaa she would sum it up with a blink of her painted black eyes and all

Bae bae naw- Just plain ole crazy

Nonetheless, I named my Uncles excluding my dad:

_R. L._ - nope- He will yank his front teeth out with his bare fingers

James Jr. – nope- He would pull him down the road with the horse whip

Earl –nope- He would hang him on the wind mill

Floyd ?? po Floyd??

Marshal- nope- He would drown him in the well

Chester –he'll follow him home and that would be the last of him

A.J. – maybe- AJ heyyyy he IS a chain saw freak who loves experimenting

Goodness gracious this was more complicated than I expected. I went over the list once again. To make certain the right Auntie or Uncle will make Mr. Johnson put those lips away for good. Miraculously, I just realized Eisha did not say it's our secret don't say nothing to nobody or did she? Either way I'm saying something I want to make certain he never use Eisha again….oops he didn't use her, geez! I'm acting like Momma. He bruised her pudgy-pie, no he didn't…uh-rah-uh he raped her darn-it he didn't do that either oh I don't know what to say because she *liked it*. I got to think…think Sofay think I can't think from suddenly becoming overwhelmed. I knew there will be consequences and repercussion. A friendship of over forty years ruined because of lusting a youngin. Goodness gracious, the battle between the White's and the Johnson family has just begun. It was getting darker and I heard someone calling me. Lord and behold it was Auntie Nitta oh no! well hear I go my voice started stuttering and all. Auntie Nitta come quick! She ran to me quickly without hesitation saying oh Lawd what's wrong with my baby! When she reached me I started crying. She said 'now wait a minute baby girl firstly, whatcha crying for and secondly, why you spitting on Mr. Johnson like that'? I said 'Auntie I'm so fairous I don't want to get into trouble but it is about Eisha'. Nitta said 'Eisha! Baby girl the word is furious'. She said 'So-soo take your time think about it first then tell Auntie what it is'. I took a deep breath and before I knew it the words just floated out of my mouth I told her everything except for Auntie Eisha experimenting on me. I told her how; Mr. Johnson ended their affair and where the affair took place. Nitta stepped back three steps looked down on the ground and said 'Red are you sure they did it right here on this spot...right here'? Her mouth dropped with shock; she grabbed the hem of her skirt to wipe away the dark make-up from around her eyes, then she wiped the sweat from her forehead, and then she covered her nose. I have to say she looked human without all that black makeup running from under her eyes. She said 'my God that explains why he looks so suspicious whenever Eisha is around'. His whole persona changes drastically. She said 'one day while applying her make-up she thought she saw Mr. Johnson blow a kiss to Eisha but he did it so fast that she thought she was seeing things'. From that point on Nitta said 'she started paying close attention and even told A.J. to start paying attention as well'. I said to myself I chose the right two people to handle this situation hooray! Nitta said 'Soo you did nothing wrong by telling me' and hugged me. She lifted my chin up wiped my eyes and said 'Auntie gone take good care of this don't you worry'. Do NOT say nothing to nobody you hear me Sofay you hear me? I said 'yes mamm'. She said 'my po baby sister what was she thinking'? Come on let's go inside the mosquitos are hungry tonight so, she grabbed my hand and we went through the tub room door into their room.

CHAPTER 6

To top things off, Auntie Nitta, Eisha, Faye and Gwen shared a bedroom together with two twin beds and one full size bed. It just happened to be that Eisha was lying on her bed alone. Nitta scanned the room and the boy's room which was across from them to make sure the coast was clear to talk. She ran back into their room looked and said to Eisha with a three step dance 'well little Miss Missy we no longer a virgin huh'? Eisha instantly stopped twirling her one foot in the air then rose up from her bed and said 'I'm still a virgin'. Auntie Nitta said 'Eisha I heard all about it from my baby Sofay and you lucky she did not get ahold of Momma Nor Dadday or else you would be skinned alive'. Eisha did not say anything just starred at Nitta. Moments later, Nitta surprisingly ran and jumped onto Eisha's bed wrapped her arm around her shoulders and said 'tell me all about it baby sis and don't leave nair detail out'! I on the other hand, was afraid to move from my spot. I knew in my heart Eisha was angry with me for telling Nitta but fortunately for me she was not. She held her hand out for me to grab; I grabbed it. Before I knew it, she pulled me towards her then placed me on top of her lap. She held me tight as Nitta conveyed to her everything that was said from me.

Likewise, I wondered after that, had I told Nitta her sister used me as a Ginny- pig in the bath tub earlier that day, I wondered the outcome.

Nevertheless, the two sisters continued to converse together answering each other's questions and even prayed by asking for forgiveness from our Lord and Savior. Eisha cried not because of the ordeal but because Mr. Johnson was finished with her according to Auntie Nitta. From prior experiences with several men in her life, Nitta knew right away that Eisha and Johnson runavoo was more pleasure for him. He took full advantage of her innocents and vulnerabilities as a youngster. She couldn't blame it all on Johnson because Eisha was a willing participates only out of curiosity. Nitta's observation was Eisha was curious but innocent in wanting to feel a man. She learned sex education hands-on instead of learning the bases from family or school. Regardless Eisha was still a child of God's. Nitta was furious but she decided that she would not hurt nor discourage her baby sister any longer about Johnson's male ego.

Instead, she focused on helping her sister move forward and to be prepared but receptive to criticisms once this news linked out. Eisha said 'from hearing about oral sex from other girls in school she wanted to see what it felt like.'. But after looking at his thang she said 'I couldn't gather my nerves to let him inside of me'. Actually, I couldn't let him near me it looked so nasty and I…I… I just couldn't let that stuff touch me. He was angry and started huffing and puffing. I just couldn't go along with him and his request. Nitta replied 'thank you sweet Jesus you did not go all the way with him because he has done enough damage to you as it is. Eishhhh I hate to say but umm I think because you were not willing to do what he asked of you that might have been the reason he lost interest in you. I'm just saying maybe that's his reason.

CHAPTER 7

Subsequently, everyone started making their way into the house to wash up for supper. The usual loud talking began to overshadow both of my Aunties conversation. Granddaddy made his way to the girl's room searching for me. Upon seeing me sitting on Eisha's lap, with my head on her shoulders he just stood there looking and said 'now I see my grandbaby I was about to whip your ass for spitting on Mr. Johnson'. Nitta jumped in to intervene and said 'oh no Dadday, Red was getting sick so she spit the vomit taste out her mouth and it so happened to land on Mr. Johnson'. Sofay meant no harm you know she got manners. Granddaddy said 'yell you show right Nitta'. He walked up to me and lifted my head to look closer into my eyes. I quickly began rubbing my eyes fiercely so they could turn red. Granddaddy did not go for that con he said' look up baby' and I did. He said 'you know Nitta saved your ass causz ain't a damn thang wrong with cha'. Do it again and I'll have Olivia beat your ass you hear now'? I jumped and said 'yes Sir'. I could never fool Granddaddy but honestly he's never whipped me he always threatened me or threatened to get my Dad or Gramz to do the whipping. Being the first and only grandchild I basically had my Granddaddy wrapped around my fingers. Before he left the room Gramz made her way into the room saying So-soo what did I tell you to do earlier before I could respond; Granddaddy said 'Oliver this baby suddenly got sick and she said 'oh Lawd child my baby done got sick'? Granddaddy put his arms around Gramz's shoulders and maneuvered her to walk with him. He looked back at us; me, Nitta and Eisha and winked his eye with a smile.

In contrast, I said 'damnnn' Nitta looked at me with a smirk and said 'what Sofay'? I said I won't be eating dinner tonight let alone that good smelling blueberry pie because Gramz is about to whip up her healing potions for sickness. That meant soup and several types of homemade remedies. Both Aunties laughed I did not because I smelled those good ole collar greens with turnips, chicken and dumpling, bar-b-que chicken, fried chicken, potatoe salad and really all of my favorite foods. Momma came to the door of the room to say 'Sofay yall come on and eat' Nitta said 'ok thanks sister n law we will be right there'. I looked at Nitta's face and she looked like she got ran over by a bull just from talking with Eisha for those minutes. She said 'one more thing I got to say is Eisha you are never to; I mean never ever deal with a married man or a man living with his woman. It will leave you heart broken or maybe even create a disastrous situation with that woman.

As a matter of fact, now that I'm thinking about it that night several weeks ago did Mr. Johnson blow you a kiss? Eisha said 'yes he did'. Auntie Nitta said 'girllll you don't know Eisha but I was up all that night pondering if I was gonna wake you up or not to ask that question'. When you thought I wasn't looking I was. I've been watching you heavenly ever since that night. But what's blowing my mind is how you got pass me at night to go meet this man? Eisha responded by putting pillows in her bed when she left, she puffed them up like a body some kind of way making it seem that she was still in bed when she wasn't. Auntie Nitta said 'I wished I was a man to beat him down to his socks'. But I will maintain my composure and so will you. This is our secret for now, us three; me, you, and Sofay. Eisha swallowed long and hard knowing Nitta is really a no -nonsense evil type of woman who believes in revenge! The two ladies with me dragging behind them joined in with the family to eat supper. I could not get into the kitchen fast enough before Gramz's walked up to me to feel my fore head then my throat. She said 'you don't feel hot you feel normal'. We not gone chance it So-soo come on over to the stove I made you some soup with bread and brewed up some cod liver oil. I also got mental soaking on this here towel so you can sweat out what's in yah. I said 'yes mamm' and told her awh Gramzzzzz I hate that hot cod liver oil I can barely swallow it down. Do I have to drank that? She said 'girl don't sass off get over here now'! When I looked at Gwen she made a sad face but slightly smiled. I didn't think anything under my breath about her because she meant well. I was instructed by Momma to go and lay down in our bed after sipping my soup. Nitta stepped in suggested to Momma to let her watch me for the night. Momma looked at daddy, he said 'sure'. Normally when I'm sick I take full advantage of the catering services that all of them give me. I lay in bed all day and everybody take turns bringing me food, liquids, homemade cakes and that's when Gramz's is a little leany because she don't force me to sip on that cod liver oil. I usually lay there watching TV while Eisha raddle off the latest gossip within town. My father is quite worrisome during my sick times because he can't stop kissing my cheeks nor checking up on me. It's Momma who make him stop and tell him to go back to work.

In the meantime, I went back into the girl's room to climb into Nitta's bed I was exhausted it was a long hot day and truthfully speaking I was starving. After supper, the girls cleaned the kitchen then everybody slowly left the kitchen for their beds. The boys gathered the trash and used a bucket with a lid to store the trash for the morning. We all were settling down to rest. I went to my Grandparents room to say good night. Gramz wanted me to sleep with her but Nitta insisted she would be responsible for me so everyone could rest peacefully. Once I climbed into bed Gwen rose up from her bed smiling she said 'Sofay come here, come over here for a second' when I went to her bed she moved the covers and there was that night's dinner including a slice of blueberry pie. You don't know how delighted I was to eat that food. As I was eating Auntie Eisha came into the room smiling and eating another slice of pie saying 'Sofay I prepared your food for you and don't be alarmed because Nitta told Gwen everything. I rose up saying 'huh' because Nitta specifically said tell no one. Nitta came into the room observing us all and said 'So-soo it's okay let me explain Gwen knows because I couldn't keep this to from her. When you get older in life you will know who you can trust to not tell your business. Gwen is not a gossiper and can truly keep a secret. Auntie Gwen said 'So-soo you are too young to be this involved with grown people businesses'. We are not trying to confuse you but we want you to be aware that there are vicious people in the world. That's one reason why we keep you near one of us at all times just like Granddaddy kept all sixteen of us near him especially us girls. We are a huggy- kissy kind of family. We got each other's back daily and that's why we teach you to stand up for yourself. I'm so very proud of you Red for stepping up for Eisha. Had you not Mr. Johnson would still be taking advantage of her. Listen, Red we don't want to go to jail for murdering someone who is taunting or harassing any of us and that's why we teach you right from wrong and sometimes revenge. We want you to be cautious outside of your surroundings. I can stand strong in saying the WHITE'S are a loving connected family with back bone.

In addition, So-soo, look at the Johnson's. His kids bicker and physically fight each other all the time in public. Look at Mrs. Johnson who boldly rips her middle daughter down with insane lies secretly whispering to others in saying that Tisha is molesting her younger daughter. I guess she figured if she speaks people would automatically believe her since people are under the impression that family don't lie on one another. The devil is a lie I've seen and heard Mrs. Johnson speak these lies saying Tisha is a man. She is ever so wrong Tisha may have broad shoulders but she's one hundred percent a full fledge woman with a beautiful golden smile. She is truly attracted to men I know that for a fact! Shit I've seen her twice coming out the witch doctor's house and I know she's there for one reason and that's to kill her unborn child. Like I said 'I know for a fact she ain't no fucking man'.

Coincidentally, we don't know what goes on behind closed doors but from what I gathered Mrs. Johnson has an evil jealous spirit hovering against her flesh and blood Tisha. I was never aware of a Mother who bridge gaps and keep her children divided among each other. Gramz's said 'she was floored when she went over to visit Mrs. Johnson one day and she watched her literally tell each child what the other child had said about them causing; all kinds of hate, sibling rivalry and division among her kids'.

Your Grandmother-Gramz's said 'Mrs. Johnson is full of

wickedness'. Her house is a true theory of a house divided won't stand because of the hatred she has for her younger daughter. Maybe that's why Mr. Johnson is here daily if not every other day advoiding the atmosphere he helped build, a house of darkness. Georgis Johnson is just as involved with the bickering between his kids because instead of disciplining them he chooses to turn a left eye meaning he ignore their fights and don't step in to teach them respect nor how to love one another.

In fact, have you've ever noticed Sofay that Mrs. Johnson has limited her visits with Momma? I said 'yes'. That's because Momma don't relate to her nor is a guppy to help in sabotaging that girl's credibility…it's sad…poor Tisha. As for us, Church and Momma's prayers are what keeps us humble with encouragement Sofay. We don't tear each other down because Gramz won't allow it; instead we turn our burdens over to the Lord'. I once read from Power of positivity where it suggests *"the bad people give you experience, the worst people give you a lesson and the best people give you memory.'* I said 'ok Auntie' trying to keep from falling asleep. Truthfully speaking, I actually had one eye opened and one eye closed saying to myself dog-gone-it are you finished yet! shit as sleepy as I was! I managed to look over at my Auntie Eisha who was looking more relaxed and relieved. Her skin tone changed it had lightened for some reason. I hope she's preparing herself for the next chapter in life.

CHAPTER 8

Likewise, out of all my Aunties again, Eisha was my top favorite with Antoinette following behind her.

In fact, when I observe physical bodies I have noticed that all the White girls were either stocky or shapely with either thick hair or a combination of naps blended in with thin curls. To me Eisha's body was the shaped of an adult woman who works out doing exercises. She always demanded attention by sashaying around the house wearing her older sister's jewelry, clothes and high heels. She loved entertaining everyone with her many accolades from sewing rags into an outfit to cooking in the kitchen with Gramzs, or drawing unique artwork. She was definitely multi-talented. Eisha was like a second mother to me not because we were five years apart in age but because she always took her duties as my Auntie as a badge of honor.

And truthfully speaking, at one point I think she started believing that she gave birth to me. She treated me like I was a Barbie doll by always matching my clothes before school completely disregarding the clothes that my Momma had already laid out for me to wear. She would carry me throughout the house on her hip until my Grandma would shout out put that lanky red headed gal down. Then Eisha would laugh, put me down only to grab my hand as we both walked throughout our farmland.

In fact, it was Gramz who nicknamed me both So-soo and Red. She chose Red because of the color of my shoulder length hair which none of them could part straight for ponytails except for both my Momma and her Momma Grammy. All my Aunties tried to comb my hair but somehow they had the hardest time parting my scalp for pony tails. Whenever, I looked at Nitta, Camille, Monee and Baebae's hair I always thought they all had curly hair.

It just so happened, my Aunties would pour water on top of their hair before leaving the house in order to stay cool. Once the watered dried and they perspired from the heat, honey, and those curls would ball up into scattered knots that looked curly but in actuality they were naps. Auntie Camille always said 'a perm won't do for her because she sweats too badly'. The sound of the comb going through their hair was like popcorn popping or grass being raked. I really tried not to laugh because I did not want to hurt their feelings. From Momma's reaction she could have cared less about their feelings.

Subsequently, I developed my second nick name So-soo also from my Grandmother – Gramz's. She said I was always hard-headed making her repeat herself twice if not three times when she told me to do a chore. She said 'I worked her nerves when I didn't listen', ha-ha, hey, what can I say. Gramz's would say this girl child just don't listen worth a damn, I bet if I get that switch on her high yellow tail she'll listen to me then. Boy I tell yah, it was something about even hearing the word switch it made my skin crawl. My Gramz's was a no nonsense type of lady who could care less what anyone else was doing or saying, when she told any of us to do something she wanted it done instantly. That basically meant to drop whatever it is you were currently doing and do what she says.

I on the other hand, could have care less what was being told for me to do because I was too busy trying to keep up with my Aunties who were either entertaining their guests, or courting boys. Whenever those little timid boys entered the farm for one of my Aunties; you could have heard thunder roaring with Granddaddy and his boys who raved angrily with resentment against them without even knowing many of their names. It was hard for Granddaddy to accept the fact that his girls were turning into both young ladies and women. Those boys didn't have a chance with any of my Aunties' which was hilarious. Once, visiting the farm Simon a nervous but well-mannered boy who lived four miles from us had just started courting Camille. He was nervously there to take Auntie Camille out on a date. Camille is the oldest daughter who had much attitude. We found out later, Simon was cautious with the men of the family because of their reputation. My Uncles were known for beating the shit out of people that crossed them. He wanted to stay on good terms with the family and didn't want any little obscurity to interfere with dating Camille. I remember seeing Simon standing there clueless on the road. He was pacing two steps forward then he would turn around to head back then stopped just to turn back around towards the house to stand still in that same spot on the road. I instantly busted up laughing knowing this boy was petrified. I would count to myself- one, two, three and off I ran out of breath towards the shed to tell Granddaddy a nappy headed boy was there for Camille. Granddad often had hearing problems but I guaranteed you in that moment that built up wax in his ears opened wide when he heard the words boy and Simon because he marched out that shed with a machete in his hands from skinning a hog. There would be blood on his trousers; his shirt would be hanging off flying in the air as he walked in a fast pace, and he would be cussing up a storm with some of his sons touting behind him. They all would rehearse what they were going to say upon reaching Simon. Simon looked up from staring at the ground and saw Granddaddy with the boys approaching him. He began sweating bullets and his belly apparently began to make sounds. Granddad and the boys were standing on the road with Simon. They slowly started circling him, finally after what may have seemed like forever for him, Granddaddy said 'son what parts of this here county you from'? Simon stuttering couldn't find words; furthermore he was hypnotized with that machete that was glistering from the beam of the sun. As he tried to talk there was a strange sound coming from either his throat or his stomach. Within seconds, Granddaddy realized what that sound was. Within a bleak of an eye, Granddad and my Uncles were bended over with laughter realizing that was not a sweat aroma flooding in the air but more of a shit aroma. Yes, Simon did number two on himself. My dad had a soft heart and tried to make them leave him alone. He walked him into the house to wash up and change into clean clothes.

However, Auntie Camille was heated up with anger when she found out Simon's mishap and called her self-snapping on everyone that made fun of him doing number two on himself. She couldn't get pass the fact that he could not hold his bowels and furthermore, she didn't want to pursue the date any longer with him. To make matters worse, Auntie Camille had not a clue that my dad with three of his brothers were going to chaperone her on that date. Upon hearing this news Auntie Camille was outraged she was orange in the face. She was angrier hearing her nosey brothers would tag along on her date than anything else. It wasn't funny, but then again it was when Simon came out the house with Chester's clothes on Camille looked at him and shouted ulll I'm disgusted! she kept repeating out loud what grown ass man shits on his self? Suddenly my eyes widen I remembered something and I whispered to Gramz's. Gramz looked at me then smirked she said 'that's not nice Red' she covered my mouth with her hands before I blurred out Auntie Camille who are you to talk? I see your panties when doing the laundry with Gramz's. Truthfully speaking, out of the entire girl's dirty underwear's Gramz had to scrub her panties twice. Gramz often said 'to Camille girl your thang down there is like knives, I can't seem to get the soul of your underwear clean'. Camille always smiled and said 'Momma'!

Ironically, when Camille would get up from a chair I never sat behind her causz I didn't want to catch whatever it was that stained her underwear's to attach and stain my underwear's. I guess that's why she always kept her legs cocked wide open fanning herself down there.

CHAPTER 9

Moreover, it was always some type of amusement or drama flowing around the farm. There were talks between some of my Aunts who have nothing better to do and occasionally they're conversations pertained to Auntie Eisha's shape or appearance. Like I said earlier Eisha was a pretty girl who was shy and always smiling. They poked fun at her shape as she walked. Her walk was something she was working on to control. Her walk drew added attention that she didn't like. Her sisters made it no better with the stupid riddles they would sing once she entered the room. It was nerve racking to see and hear them act silly towards her. At one point Eisha would raddled back putting her sisters in their places but lately she just stands there saying nothing. So I call myself defending her in saying Nitta I know you ain't talking looking like a witch on a broom with all that black make up under your eyes. She would reply back saying maybe I'll whip up a spell and put it on you then your walk can resemble your Auntie's. My father would walk in every time and catch her talking smack to me causing him to say Nitta I wish you would. Keep talking to Sofay like that and see what I'll do to you. Thank goodness, my Daddy had my back. He would then tell Nitta to go find something constructive to do instead of picking on me. What she didn't want was for me to tell my Momma who had a short fuse for ignorance. Momma would have definitely checked Nitta, Baebae and Antoinette for wasting time when the baskets of apples needed to be; washed, peeled, sliced and cooked for the pies.

Nevertheless, my father was under pressure in being the oldest son. He had a heavy responsibility in being; a son, a father, a brother, a nephew and a husband. He was grown with a family and still at home with his parents. My father was so ready to move out into our own place but my grandmother had a whole on him. I could never understand how he cussed out his siblings and anyone else but was never able to stand up to Gramz's his mother it didn't make any sense to me.

CHAPTER 10

Moreover, my Gramz's was definitely the lady of the farmland. She was sassy with a genuine heart. She was God fearing and often quoted scriptures or verses from the Bible. I remember her always correcting her depict of me when I was hard headed. Instead of saying 'you nappy headed heifer' like she often said to her daughters when they misbehaved; she would call me by my full name 'Sofay Camille Antoinette Gwen Faye Monee White' when I heard thattttt! Babaeeee I took off running because I knew I had done something awful that I was not supposed to do. Gramz's would say let me at her! You ole red headed yellow heifer' and sure enough Eisha would be right there sniggering and running with me to help find a hiding place. During those moments I would try my hardest to say out loud a verse from the Bible "Mo peal pons is against me" Auntie Eisha would say no So-soo that's not appropriate right now just run. After what seemed like hours from hiding in our hiding place from Gramz, Eisha would say gasping for air then say now So-so you only say that verse when someone is trying to bring harm to you. Momma is not bringing harm to you, she's just gone whip your red ass for pouring that moonshine in the chicken's food-look how they acting going berserk with feathers and busted eggs everywhere. You know better girl! Eisha went on to say from what I remember, the verse says *No weapons formed against me shall prosper* though I don't remember the name and verse in the Bible I'll have to ask Momma later on. Eisha said 'you only use that verse So-soo when you are in trouble or in harm's way'. I told her hell Eisha this is harm's way Gramz gone whip my ass and leave; all those damn red whelps on my legs, back and butte girl those burn like hot pins. Auntie Eisha said with a smirk 'you shouldn't have done it girl'.

Anyway, I didn't feel like hearing anymore of her logics so I said okay.

Eventually, the atmosphere calmed down. Auntie Eisha and I tip toe back into the house, my routine was to find Gramz's and give her the biggest hug and kisses to make her forget why she wanted to whip me in the first place. My hugs sometimes worked with both her and my Granddad. Granddaddy always said 'Red you gonna learn right from wrong but somehow he always, always and I mean always practically melt in my arms when I hugged him to say I'm sorry.

On the other hand, Gramz's would give me a hard time. Eisha would say Momma she was trying to say the weapon verse and couldn't get it right. What Eisha was doing was trying to soften her up as a way to distract her from whipping me. Then I would reach up to kiss her on the cheek and say Gramz's I can't remember the verse please help me batting my eyelids. She would smile saying oh really now! Come on over herr Red and sit on my lap let me see that particular verse is in Isaiah 54:17 where it says: *No weapon that is formed against thee shall prosper: and every tongue that shall rise against thee in judgement thou shalt condemn.* As Gramz's recited that verse Ms. Missy was lighting my butte up using her hand to whack me. I mean she was hitting me hard making me shout out ouch. I have to say, I liked those whacks better than those switches whenever she did get a whole of me. Funny though, when she was adamant about whipping my butte, do you know, she made me go to the bushes to pick my own branch so she could whip me. (Can you believe that?) I remember the smallest branches being the most painful ones. Eisha would say don't get the skinny ones they hurt the most So-soo (my nickname). She said 'get the medium size one or the biggest switch cause they break quicker and Momma would get to frustrated to continue on whipping you'. I paid very close attention.

Meanwhile, my Uncles and my Daddy weren't so receptive to my con of hugs and kisses because they had to clean up the mess in the chicken coop and what a mess it was. I felt it wasn't my fault that I couldn't tell the difference between moonshine and water. I always wondered why water tasted that way; furthermore, I always wondered why Granddad along with his sons Marshal and James Jr. would walk lopsided at times with orange eyes after drinking what I thought was water. The three of them along with our neighbor Mr. gossiping Johnson and sometimes old man Martin would make that moonshine in the wee hours at night. I couldn't tell you how they made it; my Aunties and I were not allowed near the men when they were making the liquor. I do remember them using corn from the field, molasses and what I thought was a bar of soap which later on I was told was yeast.

In time, I would notice the more the men drank that moonshine the louder their speech became. Their conversations would at times become a stampede match where they were all standing in a circle pointing at one another shouting who was right or wrong. I couldn't make out what was being said because of the distance but I bet cha it involved a whole lot of cussing. From their looks I could tell they were all intoxicated from the way they were staggering and wobbling just trying to stand up. The men started shoving one another I guess they were ending the party but decided to return back to their original spots and continue on with their argument. It was funny to watch them from a far in my bedroom window. When Gramz would notice the time how late it was and the how the dogs were barking she would go and awake my Dad and Uncle R. L. to go out there and shut that drinking down. Once the boys went out there they would practically get cussed out for breaking up their good time. My Dad literally would have to run behind and drag Mr. Johnson home by his belt on his pants because he never wanted to leave. Dad said 'Johnson would be slopping from his mouth as he tried to speak I don't wanna go home! Dad would ignore him and pick up the pace faster to get him home quick.

Meanwhile, Uncle R. L. would be left alone to handle his drunken brothers and Father. R. L. would demand his brothers to straighten up and walk to their beds but Granddaddy on the other hand, gave him a hard time. Granddaddy would threaten R. L. if he didn't take his hands off of him he would skin him alive just before tripping on his own feet. I tell yah, when potent moonshine was on the surface those observing the drinkers were in for a good time. The morning after, is another round of laughs. I would laugh so hard. Momma said 'Sofay never laugh at people when they at their lowest it's not Godly'. I couldn't stop my laughter especially after seeing all those mosquitos' bites on Granddaddy's face, neck, and arms. He would be in the kitchen justa; scratching, fussing, and cussing because he couldn't control the itching. Ha-ha, family!

In contrast, when I think about it, my Gramz's was more than a trip. She often needed some me time for her self-meaning everybody including Granddaddy needed to give her space and quiet time to be alone. She would sit in the tub room with the doors closed; humming songs, knitting blankets, drinking her cup of moonshine, or she would just sit there in peace observing nature through the open windows. I really didn't like it when Gramz's spent time to herself away from everybody in the tub room. She was definitely missed during those moments and truly needed. I only realized what her time alone meant as I grew older. She was always being called by one of her children throughout the day which at times got on her nerves. But, being; a wife, a Mother, a mother in law, and the best Grandmother in the world we appreciated her for being who she was and what she meant to all of us. Baebae decided that we all should give Gramz's one day off a week for being everything to us. We certainly didn't know how detailed Gramz's ran the household until we all pitched in to take over her daily routines. The older siblings chose Saturdays as a day off for Gramz. I didn't mind but everything was so particular with precise details from getting up at 5:00am to start chores and pick but clean food for three meals. It was tiresome! Somehow or another Gramz's didn't sit in the tub room all day she couldn't be still she was so used; to moving around, delegating duties, and being the woman of the nest. So I see exactly why she needed a little boost in energy from drinking moonshine after handling an entire farm with kids, a husband and grandchild anybody is liable to drank. She always said 'yall gone drive me to drank!

Even though, I have to say that my Grandmother wasn't always a saint and neither were many of my Aunties. For some reason, they kept the moonshine near the water. There were many separate cups of that moonshine sitting throughout the kitchen. I always seem to get a whole of Gramz's cup, hell; she was the one that told me it was water! When I first drank that liquor; I nearly chocked, it was hot going down, I regurgitated, the taste was like rubbing alcohol or something dead. From that taste, I figured it was some type of liquid for the chickens to grow, so I feed it to them. Not knowing they would act up in that way with all; the chaotic fighting, plucking of flying feathers, laying eggs, and I mean it was a sight to see! My mother would be angry at the family for leaving the moonshine laying around the kitchen meanwhile, my Dad would be angry with me for picking up food or drinks lying in the open without being covered up. All I can say is that they confused me a lot while growing up.

CHAPTER 11

Miraculously, I had enjoyed watching Auntie Eisha change and transform her ritual routine of fantasizing to be with Mr. Johnson to being a kid once more. She started sewing again making all these neat clothes from skirts to pants. She made matching outfits for; me, her and Gramz. She and I dressed alike going to school, Church, and even just hanging around the farm. She had Uncle Marshal to reset and bring out her drawing materials and easel to start back painting again. Eisha's healing was great at least I thought! Out of nowhere she joined the Usher board in Church Gramz's was so happy to see that but in reality she was still secretly healing from her rundavoo with Mr. Johnson. The lust she once had suddenly resurfaced in her memory causing a hostile rage.

I mean, after all, Mr. Johnson continued on visiting Granddaddy like nothing was wrong. In fact, even Auntie Gwen's rage slightly intensified as she saw him but she tried to keep her rage in clock nit toe.

On the other hand, I can't say the same for Nitta who did not want to hear any sorts of reasoning or forgiveness in the matter of Mr. Georgeis Johnson. All she saw was anguish with revenge. She was persistence in ending it all, her way. Exhausting as this was my Grandparents were still clueless to what was going on behind closed doors. The more I looked at Mr. Johnson my heart felt for him I would see him either walking down the road or sitting on our front porch mingling with the fellows. I know Granddaddy noticed the change in atmosphere whenever, he was around.

Consequently, Nitta's rage had grown tremendously over these past two months causing her to say unhuman acts of violence.

In addition, from those acts Nitta started expressing when and where her first beat down for Mr. Johnson would take place which not only frightened Auntie Gwen but forced her to involve the reminder sibling's. Gwen felt her sibling's needed to know this secret from the past several months. This pressure took a toll on Gwen which, reflected in her to instantly cry at the drop of a hat for everything. Auntie Gwen was indecisive in which sibling to start with so she started with Uncle A.J. She tried to tell him the ordeal between Eisha and Mr. Johnson and how it has now affected her and Nitta. It took a lot to keep him from getting his chain-saw. Poor Auntie Gwen wasn't masculine enough to hold A. J. down she had no choice but to call out to Uncle R.L. to help her.

In fact, A. J. was so out of hand with sharpening his chain-saw blades that he and R. L. literally began to wrestle. Nitta made it no better upon reaching them both she influenced A. J. to run up on the porch to beat Mr. Johnson's ass. Why did Nitta say that because all hell broke loose! Uncle R. L. ended up screaming for James Jr., Chester and Earl making them change their route from going out into the field to work but instead, they went running towards R. L.'s direction. From his voice they knew it was something wrong. Chester asked what the commotion is about. A. J. shouted what Gwen revealed to him about Eisha's rundavoo and instead, of the four of them staying calm they all went berserk over this news and each one was trying to run towards the front porch one by one. Uncle Floyd saw his brothers and immediately ran over and demanded to know what was going on. I didn't know what to do in between crying my damn self and wishing I had never said anything to anybody about Auntie Eisha's and Mr. Johnson's rundavoo. R. L. said 'hey, hey, what the fuck mane! Ah we got to quiet down and start moving in that direction. I don't want Momma and Dadday to hear us. I looked into the corn field and luckily I saw both Daddy and uncle Marshal walking out the field getting ready to separate the corn into piles. Daddy came out the field to re-call his brothers he thought maybe they didn't hear him so he came out to look for them. As Daddy was walking towards his brothers I ran towards him. When he saw his brothers shoving one another he thought they were fighting and called back for Marshal to come quickly. They both started running in A. J.'s direction. I have to say it was so much land that it seemed like it took nearly an hour just to reach my Father. I literally had to stop running just to catch my breath then I continue back running towards my Daddy. The closer I had gotten the more I feared for Mr. Johnson after all, he was still there on the porch visiting Granddaddy.

Finally, I got within close proximity to my father and Marshal. My Daddy was too consumed with looking at his brothers from a far he might not have noticed me bend over gasping for air but luckily he did notice me. He stopped running; looked at me and said 'Sofay what you doing running towards me like that'? Out of breath I said 'wait Daddy…Uncle Marshal' my goodness Marshal was like wait… wait for what? At first it looked like he was gonna ignore me but thank goodness he re-thought about it and walked back towards me and my Dad. I said 'yall Mr. Johnson was freaking Eisha behind the shed and I told Auntie Nitta'. Both brothers mouth dropped! Uncle Marshal said 'you've got to be kidding me'. He said 'J mane I told you something was going on with Eisha's ass'. Daddy said 'Sofay who told you this shit'? I said 'Auntie Eisha' both brothers' looked at one another knowing that I was telling the truth. Daddy said 'got damn mane, got damn; he picked me up as I wrapped my legs around his neck then he and Marshal continued on running towards their sibling's direction. Again, thank goodness the fields were so far and beyond apart that my Grandparents hadn't heard the cussing and all the rages that were floating into the air or else they would have been right in the mix.

However, upon reaching the sibling's Daddy went straight for A. J. to pin him down with Earl and R.L.'s help. A. J. was definitely some kind of crazy he never learned or at least he tried not to learn how to let stuff go he took everything personally and offensively. Neither Gramz's prayers nor Granddaddy's threats triggered his mind set into accepting Faith by not bringing harm to people. He was truly a hard head bull. I couldn't tell you how long it took but things semi started calming down until Auntie Eisha came out the house. She came out to pick peaches that Gramz's told her to pick. She saw her siblings standing there yards away from her. It seemed like they all suddenly stopped what they were doing to look directly in her direction. Eisha thought that was strange so she headed in that direction miraculously no one bulged from their spot nor said anything. When she got closer to them her instincts moved in quickly and she knew they all knew about her ordeal with Mr. Johnson. My heart pounded a mile a minute. Uncle R. L. said 'so what up sis'? Nitta said 'Eisha don't start that crying and carrying on I want you to know that we all know except for Momma and Dadday'. And we gonna keep it that way A. J. said. Eisha's eyes were so watered she looked like a faucet I started walking toward her only to be stopped by Uncle Chester who told me not to move. Gwen's started tearing up saying Eisha you have a purpose to go on and do well in life. Daddy said 'Gwen be quiet'! He said 'Eisha we all want to hear from you; when, where, why, and how this all started'. Eisha slid down to the ground looking dumb found. I thought thank goodness Momma wasn't standing there to see Eisha sliding down to the ground ain't no telling what she would have said to her this time. Poor Auntie she was silence for several minutes. She looked up at everybody standing there and began to speak. It all started in the tub room. I was bathing got out the tub and walked onto the added space outside (which now days is called a patio). She said 'she decided she wanted to air dry instead of using a towel to dry off'. She had no idea Mr. gossiping Johnson was back there. She sat there on top of the rail to dry off. A. J. screamed out that bastard! Eisha paused. She continued on saying 'he made a noise which caught her attention causing her to stand straight up and reach for the towel to cover up her boos and pudgy-pie. She asked who's there because she knew it wasn't any of her brothers. She knew none of them would have never hid they would have demanded that she go put some clothes on. Earl said 'since when anybody goes back there as much company as we all have here'. He knew she was back there I just feels it, mane he knew she was taking a bath! Chester said 'hold on mane let her finish'. By this time the tears were rolling down Eisha's cheeks and she continued on in saying he came out from his shadow behind the tree because at first I couldn't make out who that was he said 'hey sugga it's me Mr. Johnson'. Eisha said 'she was shocked and got off the rail looking for her towel'. Mr. Johnson grinning said 'wait don't! No need to cover up you is a beautiful caramel stallion of a woman'. He said 'good Lord Eisha you are more beautiful clothes less than with clothes on'. Girl looking at you, you got my heart skipping a beat. He then started wiping off sweat from his forehead and neck with his handkerchief. Uncle Chester said 'that mother fucker he went in on you making his way inside of you'. Daddy said with the most evil look I've ever seen on his face' let her finish'. Hell I was becoming more afraid than ever for this man. Eisha said 'the more he talked the more he eased his way onto the stairs then he sat on the rails grabbing her towel off the rail'. A. J. tried to run towards the front porch where Mr. Johnson was sitting thank goodness his brothers including Nitta tackled his crazy ass down to the ground. Baebae was walking home; she looked over into the yard and saw us she immediately walked toward us. Upon reaching us, she shouted out 'ah shit what done happen'? I don't recall who filled her in but somebody did. Uncle Floyd walked towards Eisha to pick her up off the ground and held her tightly. He told her to hold it together and stop crying. Poor A. J. was a wreak he shouted to his Sibling's 'Im'ma pulled all those fucking windows out and put bricks in them. He was standing there the whole fucking time I'm telling yall he was standing there lusting after her with his foul smelling breath. He was waiting for the perfect time to make his move on my baby sis. Mane I'm telling yall. Oowee when those curtains are pulled back you can fucking see directly into the tub room mane.I.I..Im'ma kill him. Nitta said 'no you not A. J. you not gone kill him'. Firstly, Momma would want to know why you putting bricks in the window for and secondly, this news would devastate both our parents we will never tell her nor Dadday about this, it will destroy them and we all know Dadday would be the one to kill him. R. L. stepped up to say 'ok Eisha you told us how this started but when did he lured you into getting inside of you. He didn't get inside of me with his thang Eisha said. Baebae said 'whatttt! And looked at each of her brothers'. It tripped me out how all the siblings standing there where either; in shock, in disbelief, outraged, or just didn't know what to feel. Eisha, in the back of her mind somehow knew the law would be involved but then again, that didn't affect her during that moment. Whenever there was a potential case against a White the victims almost never come around to testify nor point them out forcing the law to leave us alone and close the case. We were known for; torturing people, bruising people, and even sending some for an overnight hospital stay. Those that were injured kept their mouths shut.

Nevertheless, R. L. said 'Eisha back up in your story you said he made his way on the steps then what'? Eisha went into extreme explicit moves that were performed on her. Eisha paused again but this time she knew she had her sibilies undivided attention so she asked yall mad at me? Gwen said 'no, no honey no we are far from being angry with you we love you unconditionally'. Nitta said uh-mm Gwennnnnn! meaning please be quiet. Eisha said 'I'm so embarrass and I even went to Church to repent my sins asking the Lord for forgiveness'. Yadi-ya-ya don't start with that bible shit A. J. said. Eisha knew to finish the story she had to be courageous after all; she knew she was within a matter of inches her damn self from being skinned alive by her brothers. She said 'yall want me to finish'? No one said a word. They all just starred at her. Eisha felt the coldness and cleared her throat to finish with her ordeal. Ok, ok, okkkk that's enough of this shit Uncle James Jr. said then he started walking and got railroaded by his brothers then A. J. tried to rush pass them and got tackled once again. It took seconds before both James Jr. and A. J. semi calmed down. My father shouted out I don't believe this shit mane this ole school player wouldn't stop until he got her cat and here I go…her cat? Daddy said 'Eishh baby girl you fell for it when you backed up against him'. He knew you would be putty in his hands that bastard! Chester said 'naw mane it's when he eased his way up on the stairs to sit on the rails that got me. He said 'see, he was strategizing how to make his move on you prior to this'. He was standing under the shade behind the trees knowing he wouldn't be seen because of the beaming sun. I'm telling yall he's been in that same spot plenty of times to know how she operates. He waited for the perfect time to make his move he knew we boys wouldn't be around he knew that we would either be; in the field working, or coming home from school, or hanging out with our friends. He knew you ladies would be home setting up to cook or settling down from a long day. How many other sisters has this mother fucker watched hiding back in his shadow? From what it sounds like he musta stepped on a branch and lost his balance trying to stay quiet. He thought he was cleaver until you heard his clumsy ass. Wait hold the fuck a minute James Jr. said 'this low down ass hoe molested my baby sis and still continues to stop by here like nothing has happened'? All I gotta say is he got extra hits coming from me Im'ma blow his front teeth out and that's for damn sure'. Earl said 'that's enough Eisha we don't need to know every step we pretty much figured it out once you said how it got started. See Earl my Dad said, 'I just said we gotta stop keeping friends on the property. Our sisters are turning into women and I got my baby around here seeing all this shit. Everybody was quiet looking at one another. At that point there was no hope for Mr. Johnson he was good as dead. The conversation shifted into ways to harm him. Most of the brothers were still in disbelief in Johnson's boldness to continue on visiting. What tore A. J. up was that he still spoke to Eisha knowing that he secretly molested her. The brothers discussed all kind of tortures from cutting his tongue out to tying him up around a tree my goodness their ideas of revenge were treacherous that lead into what some would call a subliminal state of revenge. Uncle Floyd said 'ok yall we got to be careful not to; tell Momma, Dadday, NOBODY and Nitta I mean nobody'. Baebae you fill Camille, Antoinette, Faye and Geraldine in on what's going on. This is our family secret and it will be handled as that. Floyd continued on and said 'Eisha what you gone do is make a date with Johnson's funky ass'. You will stay calm. No teary eyes and none of that motherfucking crying when you approach him. You gone do whatever it is you do to get him behind that shed tonight! Eisha shook her head side to side saying no, no, no, noooo; I'm not gone do it! Floyd said 'oh yes you will do it and I'm not playing'. Eisha eyes were larger than a saucer she knew it was useless not to cooperate so she shook her head meaning ok. A.J. stepped up to her saying 'girl you had one more time to say no and I was gonna smack you into kingdom come then run up on that fucking porch and kill Mr. fucking Johnson. We all knew A. J. would follow through on what he said. I looked over at poor Auntie Gwen I think she cried the entire time everyone was gathered around. My gosh this rundavoo was more serious than I thought. I was trying to remember but I couldn't remember if Eisha ever said to us girls about the towel incident…hum…that was the first I heard of how this all got started. I thought silently to myself why she didn't tell us that part. You couldn't pay me to utter one single word during that moment. Daddy said 'ok everybody back to what you were doing. Keep it cool say nothing and Eisha after tonight this bullshit ends permanently do you hear me girl? She said 'J. W. it's already ended'. My Aunts and I begin walking back towards the house with Eisha and Marshal walking behind us. Nitta asked Gwen-hey Gwen do you recall if she ever told us how all this started. Gwen said 'naw I don't, she never volunteered all of that information to us like she just did for the boys'. Nitta said 'that's what I was thinking'.

CHAPTER 12

Inadverterly this man; was unaware of what was about to take place. Ironically, we all pretended that Mr. Johnson did not exist as we walked back to the house while Uncle Marshal was walking and prepping Eisha on how to maintain her dignity without being obvious. He told her to program herself into thinking her secret still remains the same with just her and Mr. Johnson knowing. The closer we got to the house the more everyone seemed to have scattered into different directions. As nervous as Eisha was Marshal whispered 'show time' into her ear before departing into the field. She walked straight pass him sticking her tongue out her mouth like she was licking her lips while eyeing him. That was their usual signal for them to meet that night. As he managed to straighten his composure by clearing his throat he crossed his legs with a curious look on his face. Eisha proceeded into the house and did not look back. She nervously proceeded to the kitchen forgetting about the basket of peaches. Gramz said 'damn it girl where's the peaches'? with all that was going on Eisha had forgotten about them causing Gramz's cooking schedule to be delayed. Gramz's said 'I told you got damn it! nearly two hours ago to go and pick those damn peaches'. What were you doing to not do what I say? Eisha started stuttering 'Mamm' Gramz said 'get your ass out of here and go get my peaches Eisha White'! She said 'Antoinette go with her'! They left going through the tub room door to retrieve the baskets but come back through the front door. Mr. Georgeis Johnson jumped when he saw Eisha a second time within the last thirty minutes. His cigarette lighter fell out his hand. Eisha put her basket of peaches down on the steps and bend down to pick up his lighter and placed it in his hand slightly running her thumb finger on his palm and whispered same time, same place. He couldn't reply back because old man Martin was sitting there along with Granddaddy playing cards. Eisha nervously did not look back for fear she would have surely given it away. As the hours went by dinner was finally prepared Gramz's and the girls made; candied yams with marshmallow, smothered pork chops with onions, fried pork chops, neck bones with onions, mash potatoes, sprouts, string beans along with corn bread, macaroni with cheese and peach pies for dessert. Gramz's cooked like that maybe three to four days weekly if she's wasn't tired. If she's tired it would be something simple like; beef stew with carrots, onions, garlic, potatoes or soup with homemade bread with vegetables. My goodness my Grandmother was a beast in the kitchen. Everything was cooked from scratch she didn't believe in can or frozen foods. She always implemented special seasoning and various sauces that she used on the food which gave it that added touch of greatness.

As far as I am concerned, the boys were anxious for night fall to arrive because Uncle A. J. continuously asked what time is was like a broken record.

In addition, most of the siblings maintained their secret throughout dinner with normal conversations with each other. Except for Eisha she was jumpy and couldn't quit sit still. She picked at her food and watched that clock for dear life I felt bad for her.

In fact, I refused to even look in Auntie Gwen's direction for fear she was crying. However, the girls cleaned the kitchen while the boys put the usual trash in the usual waste barrels. Still in the back with the trash my Daddy was the mediator who facilitated the plan. He and Earl decided it would be best if A. J. didn't participate because they wanted Mr. Johnson alive.

Meanwhile, back in the kitchen Eisha was pacing back and forth wanting to know which specific brother was going to do what once they reached the shed. None of them told her their plans in fact, they kept it to themselves. For me, I definitely wanted to know every freaking move on who was going to do what. I didn't get that opportunity because Momma made me go to bed. I was restless and couldn't sleep knowing this beat down on Mr. Johnson was hours if not minutes away. I dozed off and didn't realize it until I woke up around five in the morning to use the bathroom. I laid there on my side of the bed with Momma at the foot of the bed listening and watching Daddy undress to get in to bed with us. I rubbed my eyes to get a better look at him as he spoke in details from hours before. Momma rose up eagerly saying J. W. noooo you didn't! Daddy said 'Geraldine this fool ass Negro showed up just as jolly as ever Marshal and Earl were standing there on one side of the shed while Floyd and Chester was standing right there in the door way of the shed. He didn't know I was walking directly behind him following his every step he made. He couldn't see me. He was my bull's eye target I mean he didn't know I was less than four steps behind him…ha-ha…man I just wanted to dive on him but I didn't want to spoil it. Eisha's ass didn't mention when they met she had already unlocked the tub room door and used that door to leave the house instead of using the front door. Geraldine how in the hell she got passed us is what I want to know. Momma said 'J. W. leave it alone their secret love affair is over'. I wanted to say 'it's not a love affair he never went inside of her with his thang but you know I didn't say one damn word'. Daddy continued on by saying this fool was ten minutes early with his shirt unbutton wide open pimp walking. Wait, wait let me back up. Cleaver as Floyd is…did I say my brother is bad! Floyd facilitated the plan for Eisha to stand directly in front of the window as if she was waiting on him dressed in her panties and bra. The curtains were open with the light on. When Eisha saw him she opened the door to whisper go on ahead I got to go back in to turn the light off and besides Georgeis you early I'm still getting ready. Georgeis said 'some mumble jumbo bull shit then he went on towards the shed and that's when I started following directly behind him. The closer he got to the shed the more he sang Eisha's name like he was little Richard or somebody. When he turned to open the shed door Earl grabbed his hand and said 'why hello their Georgeis' I know he may have shit on his self. Marshal had grabbed both of his arms and bends them backwards behide his back causing him to say now wait a minute. Georgeis screamed out what yall doing? That's when Earl, Chester, and I made our presents known. Chester stood in his face and said how long you been fucking my baby sister? Georgeis said 'what'?

Marshal repeated the word what! four or five times before punching him in the neck. Momma asked 'did he scream out? Daddy said 'hell yeah he screamed out like a girl'. I asked him mane why Eisha out of all these fine sisters out here explain to me why Eisha. Momma asked did he answer you. Daddy said 'naw and that's when I just dived into his face. He tried to swing back but missed that's when I whipped his ass even harder. He managed to say some shit about I'm like yall Father what will James Sr. think of you boys for jumping on me. Earl said 'not a mother fucking thang and punched him in the eye'. He said 'it will be in your best interest not to involve James Sr. if you want to continue living'. Earl went on to say to Georgeis 'niggar stick you're fucking tongue out! I couldn't laugh even though I wanted to especially when Earl changed his voice sounding like a girl he went on to say oh Georgeis porgies pudding pie sucked the girl and made her cry. Huh nigguh you like little girl's yeah, yeah then he punched him in the ribs and said 'If you ever use this here tongue of yours on any of our sisters I would rip every vain, every muscle out'! Earl made him stick his tongue out further then sliced it. Mane if A. J. crazy ass was there…he would have probably clipped that motherfucking tongue right outta of him. Chester had to stop Earl if not his tongue would have been on the ground. I stood there looking at Johnson vomiting, crying, and holding his bloody tongue. That's when we all begin elbowing and punching him. After hearing that I suddenly had a case of diarrhea and flew to the bathroom my stomach couldn't take it. Once I returned to bed Daddy was in bed next to Momma still talking. The last I heard was my Daddy, Earl and Marshal carried him to the road and left him there crying, bleeding and full of pain.

CHAPTER 13

After, the beat down by my Uncles and Daddy, Mr. Johnson seemed to have vanished from the scene. Granddaddy and many others began wondering where Georgeis Johnson was; he was missed from playing cards and telling those outrageous sex stories. My grandfather had decided to pay him a visit. Once Granddaddy returned home he was sad. He waited until dinner time to explain to us why his longtime friend had stopped visiting. Dinner was the usual atmosphere with the menu that night being; meatloaf with sauce, mashed potatoes, string beans, green peas, liver with rice, black eye peas, corn bread, fried chicken and spaghetti. The desserts were chocolate cakes along with coconut pies.

However, Granddaddy didn't have an appetite he kept thinking about his friend Georgeis Johnson. He said to Gramz's 'Olivier I went by to see my buddy earlier today'. He been in the hospital he was bandage up with small swellings here and there on his body. His tongue got stitched up making it a little hard for him to talk. His chest was wrapped up from a chip bone I asked him what happened and he said 'he finally got caught up with one of his sweet thangs husband'. From the looks of it he beat him bad. Nitta's sarcastic ass blurted out 'that's what he gets'! Granddaddy stopped talking and cut his eyes at Nitta to say what the fuck you mean that's what he gets? That man is almost damaged. Nitta said 'Dadday I'm sorry but he's always talking about some girl or woman's coochie it was bound to happen'. Granddaddy said 'well I tell you what Nitta when he starts to come back over here cause he's coming back I want you to go the opposite direction so you don't see Mr. Coochie man'. Georgeis ain't never done nothing to you or to any of yall for that matter. Gramz's said 'Nitta your mouth will get the best of yah you hear me heifer learn to shut the fuck up when you hear of somebody's bodily injuries it's no joke'. That man has been here for this family during our struggling times. He always flirted with women with some old bull talk. I hate that his past done caught up with him. Chester jumped in and said 'Dadday you can't be mad at Nitta she telling the truth bout Mr. gossiping Johnson'. The man is a piece of work. Too bad he got beat down like that and besides, I can't help but think what if it was one of my sisters that he licked their private parts? Eisha damn near jumped out her skin. Chester continued on looking the opposite of Eisha whom he saw jumped. He decided to focus on Camille and said 'what if it was Camille'? Camille jumped in saying hold it now! Johnson would never have a chance with me because Simon is my guy. Daddy said 'yeah, yeah, yeah good ole pooping Simon' then everyone laughed'. Granddaddy said 'son you just said something here but I wouldn't have to think twice bout Georgeis fooling around with any of my babies causz he knows I would kill him with my bare hands'.

At that moment, you could have heard a pen drop on the floor with everyone looking at each other for validation or some sort. Gramz looked at my Momma with a curious look on her face. For some reason, I think Gramz had an incline to something going on but she couldn't figure it out.

Nonetheless, that ass whipping secret remained among the White children and I'm pretty sure it also remained a secret with Mr. Georgeis Johnson.

CHAPTER 14

Indeed, this was certainly a moment of curiosity. So much has transpired since that night I slept in the girl's room. Through it all, Eisha had begun to slowly make progress in cutting both tides and that gravitational hold that Seemed too had resided in her Soul. She pulled herself together and kept pulling until every relinquish thought of Mr. Georgeis Johnson was completely removed from her existence.

So much for that, it was the holidays coming up including Floyd's birthday. Auntie Camille and Antoinette thought it would be a celebration for Floyd considering he didn't have any potential criminal charges pending against him nor has he been jailed for his usual one night stay. They felt Floyd deserved this birthday celebration because he changed for the best. He worked so hard in the fields helping Granddaddy and staying out of trouble with the law.

Moreover, he too was a hard head bull like his brother A. J. But when I think about it, Uncle Floyd periodically got into trouble but his weakness was for the ladies. He was known as a heart throb meaning he's broken a number of hearts with a vast array of women in the area. I got to give it to him he was a good looking middle height man who stood at five eleven in height he was built like an inflated mickey mouse. He had light funny color eyes almost like three different colors in one, his hair was cut low exposing his sandy red curls, he wore his shirts fitted revealing his muscles, and he was also known for opening up car doors for ladies as he passed them by in town. We didn't have weights or exercise equipment's at that time.

Instead, all the boys got a daily work out from; running from field to field, lifting hay, fixing the tractors, climbing the windmill, and organizing the crops which consist; of pulling, stretching, bending and excessive lifting.

In addition, Uncle Floyd's latest fling was this chick named

Karrie. She was funny looking different from the other ladies he brought to the farm. My aunties and I often laughed at the sight of Karrie because in her mind she thought she was fine as wine but in actuality she was dead ugly. She stuck out more than the other ladies that courted Floyd. I didn't see the attraction with them two so I asked him did he noticed how ugly she was. Uncle Floyd told me Red looks aren't everything it's what's in the inside that counts. So, me being me, I had an inquisitive question to ask Eisha she was nowhere around so I went to Auntie Camille with this one and asked her what that statement meant it's what's on the inside. She said 'Red your Uncle is attracted to her personality and not her looks cause we all see that she's far from cute or pretty. Her Soul is real far from masquerading to be someone she's not. Floyd likes how she keeps herself clean and fresh. She works at the hardware store. She finished school and she has dreams that she want to fulfill. He enjoys their conversation together by talking to each other and not at each other. They've discovered so much in common with what they like and dislike. They respect one another by not bringing their past relationships into what they are trying to build as a couple.

Surprisingly, many in town were flabbergasted knowing that Floyd would even consider Karrie as relationship material. Rumors had it that Karrie's reputation was to hit it then quit it. She was known for being a one night stand. After a while I think the rumors had an effect on Floyd because for days he would be sad mopping around the farm barely speaking to anyone because of Karrie's past choices and all the rumors that surrounded around her. His friends were coming down on him for developing a relationship with her. They felt Floyd should have left her as a one night stand and moved on to a real woman. He kept saying how ironic that he was dating Karrie now suddenly no one wants to see them together. Truth of the matter was Karrie was promiscuous and Floyd was starting to believe the rumors. It was Auntie Nitta who told him she did him a favor by sleeping around with so many men in her past and current because now he knows where he stands in her life. What he didn't know and it was brought to surface is how so many of his friends also had a piece of her. He was semi ok with knowing about one friend but when all these other friends popped up with stories he couldn't take it and decided he couldn't marry her nor continue on in the short term relationship.

Ironically, prior to the rumors Nitta tried to tell him to not get too caught up in having a life with Karrie because she was known to be loose under the skirt. Floyd originally brushed Nitta's advice off as being mean and jealous.

Funny though, Auntie Antoinette was dating Karrie's brother at the time and saw several men at their house for Karrie. When she told Floyd he was in shock. He was hurt but said 'he rather be hurt then be a fool in love with someone who was loose and didn't cared about him'. Nitta said 'she was using him for his money' which may have been true because they were always out doing something in town or in Oklahoma City he was buying her clothes and shoes quite often.

Finally, Uncle Floyd made the decision to leave Karrie's loose ass that night and unfortunately, the next day he was in town and subsequently, who did he run into? Yes Karrie and her secret fling Keith. Floyd said 'at that moment he re-hashed every rumor, every gossip pertaining to her and knew everything he heard was the truth'. He walked right up to her and planted a kiss on her lips and told her to take care. Karrie was speechless. She tried her damn-ness to explain that the dude was a friend. Floyd just starting walking away from them. The dude felt disrespected and shoved Karrie out his way as he proceeded to walk in the opposite direction. She Looked at Keith but went after Floyd calling his name to slow down so she could talk with him. How I know this information was from Auntie Nitta's best friend Sybil who was on the same street and happened to walk out the grocery store just as Floyd kissed Karrie on the lips. Sybil was about to speak to both of them until she realized that Karrie wasn't with Floyd but the guy Keith. She couldn't get to Nitta quick enough to tell her what she saw in town.

Certainly, Auntie Nitta couldn't hold water meaning she couldn't hold a secret let along gossip. She was nearly out of breath telling her sisters Gwen, Faye, and Monee about the news regarding Karrie and

Floyd. Floyd kept it moving after that he was done with her. He was too busy saving his money to build his own house on the farmland. He was in town that day meeting an associate who was teaching him how to build furniture.

Apparently, Karrie never had a man leave her before nor spoil her. She couldn't accept the fact that she was dumped it hurt her pride.

In fact, she stooped so low as to start stocking him; he ignored all her attempts and told her it was over once again. This girl refused to give up. She literally came by the house daily knowing Floyd was in the field. She sat there for hours even into the night fall. It was funny because instead of using the front door he used the tub room door to enter our home. Monee would go on the front porch purposely teasing Karrie and saying shit like he still ain't made it home huh; knowing perfectly well that Floyd was already in the house relaxing, watching television or eating. Karrie then said 'I don't know why he's blaming me for being with someone else when he's not a goody two shoe himself'. Monee said 'girl did you forget he just saw your ass in town yesterday with Keith Mayberry? Monee continued on to say Karrie I read just yesterday from this script from Daily wisdom where it says: *To change a behavior, we must address the thinking that produces it sometimes people pretend you're a bad person so they don't feel guilty about the things they did to you.* Karrie said 'what you mean Monee'? Monee said 'girl if you gone be a player walk in the footsteps of a player. You know this town is too small and everybody knows everybody business. Answer this why wouldn't you think it wasn't going to get back to all of us hell you are so messy with these men. The men you've been with gossip more than medusa. Monee said 'apparently Karrie, you've already forgotten that Antoinette is dating your brother…tick tock! Karrie looked dumb found and said nothing. To show you how out of bound this chick was the next day she planted a sit on the porch again. Momma, Eisha and I returned to the farm from shopping for presents and decorations for both the holiday and Floyd's birthday, we ran into Karrie sitting on our front porch. She spoke then asked Momma if she could check to see if Floyd was home. Momma told her no she's not getting involved and preceded into the house. I asked Momma why she was so mean. She said 'Sofay when couples are feuding they start involving other people into their mess. They choose a person who they want to nit-pick for all sorts of personal questions about their ex. They start explaining how the relationship ended and who was at fault. They want you to help them to get back with that person by any means necessary. I've learned over the years to mind my own damn business because many times that couple eventually patch things up and blame you for telling what you saw the other mate doing. Sometimes those break ups makes the relationship stronger as well as it could also break it permanently. See baby, relationships can; be sticky, misleading, sometimes not trust worthy then again with the right person a relationship can be the best thing that ever happened in your life. That's why when gossipers in town tell me about your Dad sometimes I investigated it for myself for truth whereas other times I confront him for the truth. Either way it leads to an argument. Baby Love is a powerful thing it will make you become; paranoid, confused, do crazy things like hiding behind bushes, or doubting yourself and it can make you insecure. From my experience with your father love can be painful or it can be the most joyous but unexplainable feeling.

Even though, Karrie and Floyd's relationship has been less than six months me and your Auntie Camille confronted both of them about their personal behaviors and endeavors. I've personally seen both of them with other people on dates and your Dad was the one who told me to stay out of it. I told Floyd about seeing Karrie on a date and all hell exploded with me being called a mellower. So now I don't get mixed in it and I don't give out any information'. I said 'oh ok.' Momma took the bags of balloons, party ribbons, and other decorations out to the barn passing up Karrie. She asked Momma again Geraldine is Floyd in the house? Momma said 'girl I done already told you don't ask me shit about Floyd J. White! And she continued walking to the barn.

Meanwhile, the boys were setting up the tables outside. Gramz's had sewed cute party material together for table cloths. We had already started blowing the balloons up until Uncle R. L. came in and said 'I see yall forgot about the air pump in the barn we can use it for the balloons'. Camille laughed and said 'hell yeah we forgot' I don't know how R. L. said and took the bags to the barn to finish with the balloons. The next day was the celebrations. The kitchen was covered with food and drinks everywhere.

Furthermore, Gramz's, Grammy, the girls, Gramz's two sister-n-laws, along with both Mrs. Martin and Mrs. Brown were in the kitchen laughing it up and going over recipes to cook which gave me and Eisha a break from helping and mainly getting in their way. We never had to worry about Momma preparing food because I honestly don't think she knew the difference between water and melted butter. My Momma couldn't cook a meal worth nothing. She always kept everybody company in the kitchen and watched how they cook. Gramz would always snicker with laugher looking at Momma telling me So-soo you gone learn how to cook and that's exactly what she and many of my Auntie taught me. I literally had to stand right next to Gramz or an Auntie as they showed me the ABC's of cooking. I learned how; to separate, clean, and season the food. I learned the difference between healthy meat verses spoiled meat by examining the meats from the shed. I looked at both sides of the meats, I smelled the meat, and looked for redness and not white or any other unusual colors in the meats. As far as the chickens you see, my Grandfather would go into the chicken coop and yell for Gramz's to come out and pick out which birds she wanted. Once she did that Granddaddy would grabbed a chicken by its neck and cut it off with that giant machete knife. Blood would gush out through the empty head. The chicken walked headless for minutes before completely dying off and falling to the ground. Honestly that was detrimental to see as a child but I got used to seeing that. Any hoot, from watching my grandmother I learned how to pluck feathers off a chicken which was awkward and yucky in the beginning of learning. She taught me how to soak those naked chickens in lemon water for several minutes before she cut them down the middle to remove the insides. She always put the gizzards in their own pile to also cook along with the chicken. After that I would cut the chickens into pieces; two breasts, two wings, two drum sticks, two thighs and that was a job. It wasn't just one chicken there were four sometimes six chickens I had to pluck then cut up to cook and it was tiresome.

In fact, I also learned how to soak greens in salt water to get the earth worms and grids off then wash them several times. Gramz's did the chopping and always went behind me to make sure nothing dark was floating in the water of the greens. I learned the difference between turkey necks and ham hocks which many of us ate with hot sauce. I learned how to clean fish by putting newspaper on the table. Secondly, I used a sharp pointed knife to Chelsea down the scales which seemed to pop off flying everywhere except for the newspaper. I then cut the fish down the middle to remove all the guts, anus and other parts. Then thirdly I soaked the fish in lemon juice to help remove the taste of the ocean water. After that Gramz's took over. My goodness after helping in the kitchen many days I would be tired no one said that cooking would be easy in fact it wore me out. I usually lay on the bed afterwards or I would go sit on the porch with everyone else. Momma always said to tell both my Gramz's and Aunties thank you for taking the time out to teach me how to cook.

CHAPTER 15

However, it was getting closer for the celebration to start. I saw Granddaddy walk into the tub room so I went behind him. He moved the chair in front of the window and just sat there looking out at everyone. After several minutes I asked him what he was doing. He turned around and looked at me smiling to say come here baby girl. I have to say I loved our one on one time together without anyone else interfering. Granddaddy said 'Red you will grow up one day and the one thing that makes me proud is knowing you've learned from the best'. I want you to be one of those renaissance ladies where you are capable to handle it all and not be helpless dragging behind a man. I want you to have back bone that can stand the test of time. If need be you will know how to improvise and make well doing in your circumstances. I don't want you to be a punk nor easy but to be able to stand with wisdom and have stability in knowing you got courage. I want you to use the skills you've learned to carry you throughout life successfully. That's why Olivia stays on yah to listen and to do what she tells yah to do. She teaching yah that you got to pay attention, understand, and ask questions if you don't get it. From now on I want you to stop being in a rush to hang with your Aunties. I want you to start paying more attention to your surroundings for example when I see yah walking home from school Red I want yah to start looking behind yah self sometimes it don't hurt to see whose back there walking behind yah. If you ever in an accident you would be able to remember something or someone to tell. Yes indeed, baby I want yah to listen with both your eyes and your ears. Repeat back what's being asked of yah so you can complete the tasks. This is for yah own good cause Granddaddy ain't gone always be around. I stopped him and said 'Granddaddy where you gone be'? He said 'baby one day we all gone be in this place called Heaven'. My body gone shut down and I won't have no more worries I'll be resting. I squeezed my arm around his neck tighter I didn't want to hear he's gone be resting I needed him here forever.

In addition, I shared with Granddaddy how Reverend Haystack talked about transition from life in Church. I wanted to know if that's what he was talking about. He said 'yes baby'. Granddaddy said 'nothing is given to you for free in life you got to get out there and earn it honestly'. I'm so proud of my boys even though every now and then a couple of them may get into trouble with the law. But those boys know what hard and honest work entails. Yes I know A. J. maybe out there in town acting a got damn fool but remember there are always two sides to a story and maybe even three sides. More than likely in between those three sides; the truth lays in there somewhere. He stretched his leg I was sitting on and said 'Red have I ever told yah that you are one of the best things in my life! You the first Grandbaby and there is nothing more precious to hear is you saying 'Granddaddy' it makes my heart melt. When you bat those precious eyes when yah lying or when your ass is being hard headed I look at yah but could never whip you when you needed it.

Indeed, Sofay have I ever told yah when you were born me and Olivia was so pitiful we got on the kids nerves and you weren't even hear yet? I said 'no granddaddy' he went on to say Olivia had meetings with her friends and n-laws asking questions on what to name yah. She had me to add that room back there for you but it turned out to be for you and your parents. We wouldn't and didn't want yall living no other place but right here with us. Olivia round here crying and carrying on asking me; where yall gone live, who gone cook and take care of you. She was being worrisome and worked all of our nerves. When you was born Sofay, Olivia pushed your Grammy to the side and took over the waiting room. I think she forgot she didn't give birth to your Momma making Grammy (Geraldine's Momma) angry. Boy those two women I mean your Gramz and Grammy are like mud and water. The hospital nearly put us out before your birth because of them bickering but thank goodness for my brother Uncle Junior's wife who was a nurse there. She saved us three from getting put out by the law. When it was time to name yah, both your

Grandmothers had all these crazy names they wanted to give yah. Those two bickered about that! It was your Dad after he recovered From fainting in the delivery room that named yah. Yeah, hee-hee, my son was so anxious for your arrival he nearly stopped breathing. Red, when he saw you coming out your Momma's womb he fainted sliding down on the wall unto the floor. The nurses left both the doctor and your Momma to tend to your Daddy. They thought he had died right there in the delivery room until one of them saw him breathing that's when they put that sniffing salt under his nose. When we saw him being rolled in a wheel chair into the waiting room our hearts skipped a beat we didn't know what to say or do. It was the nurse that told us What happened hee-hee….my boy! When J. W. was fully concise he asked what happened and we told him heehaw. After sitting in the waiting room the nurse said 'we could go into your Momma's room'. When she opened that door! Geraldine was holding you. I had never seen so much beauty in my life and Olivia agreed with me. Your Momma laid in that bed justa glowing and smiling while kissing on yah. J. W. broke down crying and couldn't believe he missed your birth. Both your Grandmothers were teary eyed. I stood there proud to be alive to witness my first Grandbaby. Shortly after that, a nurse came in to check on yah and Geraldine then another nurse came in with your birth certificate to write your name on it. I was relieved both your Grandmother's stayed quiet during that moment. We all looked at your Dad for an answer he was the one that named you after my girls. Sofay is your Grammy's middle name. If there was more room on paper your Dad would have had all my girls' names on it. He said 'her name is Sofay Camille Antoinette Gwen Faye Monee White'. Before he continued on with the story Gramz's came into the room to say James baby we waiting on you and Red come on outside. Granddaddy rose up from the chair and kissed Gramz on the lips and said 'Olivia you mean the world to me and I love yah to the moon and back'. Gramz playfully hit him on the shoulders blushing and smiling and saying ol James. She said 'James it brings me so much joy to see you talking and teaching our chillrens and Grandbaby about self-knowledge'.

She said I just read from this here book that's been laying around something about self-knowledge where it says: *A good life, is when you assume nothing, do more, need less, smile often, dream big, laugh a lot, and realize how Blessed you are'*. It pleases me that everything we planned forty years ago has become our fruit of labor. Granddaddy smiled with his hands over Gramz's shoulders saying who bought that book? I'm hearing more verses from what seems like daily readings. Im'ma have to sit down and read it one day. Oh Olivia I'm just sitting here with Red reminiscing back into our past and at the same time I'm teaching her about growth. I was waiting to tell everybody at once about a permanent contract deal with this headquarters that run a chain of grocery stores. I'm still in disbelief about it. It seems like a dream Olivia. Gramz silently screamed with excitement and gave Granddaddy the biggest hug. They both stood there looking into each other eyes for several minutes. Granddaddy expressed how he was nervous with the deal because he wasn't familiar with all those legal terms, acronyms or contracts. Gramz said 'that they will pray over it and she would get Grammy, Camille, Faye, my Momma and Uncle Junior to help him understand and absorb all the legal terms and negotiation that he will be up against. The last time Granddaddy signed legal paperwork was when his Daddy was still alive about forty five years ago. My Great Granddaddy fought long and hard for this farmland that we all resided in. He would be proud if he was alive today to see all the renovations that's taken place over the years. Gramz wiped Granddaddy's eyes and told him she was so proud of him. She grabbed my hand and Granddaddy's arm and we walked out the tub room door to join in the celebration. We walked out onto the outside and marveled at how well everything looked. The back yard looked like a County fair except there were no rides or clowns but plenty of decorations with a cotton candy machine. Goodness gracious, there were; barrels of beer, moonshine, Kool-aide, sweet tea and soda pop. Auntie Antoinette was the DJ playing those oldie but dusty music. There were a whole lot of tables lined up in one row with the cotton candy machine in the middle of the tables. A little to the side were more tables with chairs full of games and playing cards.

We kids had our own games of choices to play on the opposite side of the game tables. We had pinned the tail on the donkey, we played the apple bucket game where Grammy filled a bucket of water with apples. She covered our eyes and we had to use our teeth to retrieve an apple from the bucket. It may sound boring but we had a blast playing it.

In addition, some of that good food consisted of everything from; Baked turkey, fried turkey, dressing, chitterlings, mac and cheese, sweet baked beans, fried alligator meat, roasted duck, roasted pig, greens with cha-cha, turnips with Ruther bagels, sweet corn bread, fried corn, chicken in dumplings, green bean casserole, green beans with white Potatoes, sweet ham, candied yams, red beans with rice, and potato salad. There was so much more food and desserts that I can't remember it all. The desserts table had; banana cream pies, pumpkin pie, sweet potatoes pies, lemon pies, 7 up cakes, pound cakes, rum cakes which the rum alcohol was used and a slight dap of moonshine, yeah I saw Baebae when she slipped that in (though us kids weren't allow to eat any rum cake), there was blueberry pies, strawberry upside down cake and so much more.

However, I loved seeing everybody mingling, smiling, dancing, and getting alone. We had so many people that I got lost in the crowd. I saw Uncle Floyd standing there with his friend Melvin and I immediately glued myself by him and begin looking around for Auntie Eisha. Someone nudged me and it was Karrie she greeted me then hugged me while Floyd looked at her and said nothing. He waited several seconds before asking her what she was doing at our farm. She said 'she just needed to talk with him'. Floyd said 'damn Karrie what's with you why the fuck you can't keep your legs closed'. Karrie just looked at him then me which made me think and wanted to say to her 'I don't know why you staring at me cause I'm not the one loose under the skirt'. You can't imagine how I was itching to say that alone with 'mum huh I heard Nitta and them talking bout your butte but you know I couldn't say that either. She finally stopped staring at me then grabbed Floyd by his belt and said 'she wasn't gonna let him go until he talked to her'. Uncle Floyd gave in and said 'to

Karrie hold on let me find my sister-n-law so I can give her So-soo'. We both searched for Momma or any of my Aunties but didn't find anyone. We did see Gramz but I told him I didn't want to stay with Gramz because she would put me to work by cleaning up behind everybody. Uncle Floyd said' ok baby'. When I turned I saw Uncle A. J. talking to the law. Once Uncle Floyd and I reached A. J. we were relieved to see them chatting and laughing. We found out the law was driving pass and it was A. J. who flagged them down for an invitation to join us. Floyd spoke and said to A. J. 'watch Red I'll be back for her shortly'. I stood there still searching for Eisha instead I saw my cousin Glorie who I called out too but Uncle A. J. made me stand next to him. His conversation with both of those Officers was out of the ordinary. This fool was trying to convince them to hire him. Officer May laughed saying now A. J. why would we hire you when we've been trying to nail all these potential charges against you. Officer May said 'admit it A. J. it was you who beat Charlie Ray into a coma right'? A. J. laughed and said 'now Officer May why would I implicate myself to hear-say'.

Nevertheless, this was a conversation I could do without listening to because it wasn't juicy enough.

Meanwhile, I looked and saw the back of Auntie Nitta walking on the path towards the lake which was approximately three miles away. I was trying to understand why she chose that time to vanish from the party scene. I told Uncle A. J. I had to use the bathroom knowing that was my only escape from him. He said 'wait So-soo' and I took off running towards the path where Nitta was headed without looking back. I ran past a flock of people who started calling my name I didn't even stop running I had to see and be with Auntie Nitta. Little did I know Auntie Baebae was one of those people calling me and she dropped what she was doing to follow me. Man, I had to stop several times to catch my breath and to see the distance between me and Nitta. While running, I kept hearing my name being called the further I went out on that trail the more it started looking scary. I suddenly remembered what Granddaddy had said earlier during our one on one conversation when he said 'Red when you walking stop sometimes to look behind yah to see what's back there'. I don't recall why I stopped running. But when I stopped it seemed like shadows were floating in the air between those willow trees which tripped me out! I suddenly became paranoid and couldn't no longer move my feet.

Coincidentally, whoever was calling me was getting closer causing me to scream out who's that calling me?' Baebae shouted it me Bae you stay right there! I did what I was told but it took her forever to get to me I started seeing more creeped out things in the air. I screamed out Auntie where are you? She said 'out of breath I'm getting closer baby'! My goodness, it seemed like I was waiting there for hours I actually don't know how long it was but it was long enough.

Finally, I saw her jogging towards me I ran towards her and asked what took so long. She said huffing 'girl what the hell you running back here for the party is back the other way'. I said 'Auntie I saw Nitta walking on this path so I followed her'. Baebae insisted to never walk back here alone especially when it's nearing night time. She said 'why you so concern with Nitta walking back here'? I made up some lie with my fingers crossed behind my back. I said 'I thought she was crying'. Baebae said 'oh no' looking in the direction she thought Nitta would be in. She grabbed my hand and said 'well we can't very well leave after running this far we got to check on her' so we continued on our way this time walking instead of running. The closer she and I got the more we heard this strange sound. It sounded weird but creepy at first Baebae stopped and patted her heart advoiding to even look at me. I thought to myself what the fuck is that! We heard it again, this time I stopped and yacked Baebae's hand and said 'maybe we shouldn't go look for her let's go back'. Baebae said 'So-soo if anything happened to me out here I want you to run back and go straight to Dadday hell he will know what to do'. I said 'ok' and thought who gone help me. What if I don't make it back my damn self causz now my legs were nearly numbed from shaking?

Finally, we made it to the lake but where was Auntie she was nowhere to be found. We stood there by the water praying she wasn't in there stuck at the bottom or something. That creepy sound was within walking distance Baebae and I stood still once again. She said 'we got to be brave out here and besides who would be brave enough to camp out on our property without anyone of us knowing about it'? I just shook my head not knowing. Baebae squeezed my hand tighter and we walked alongside the water towards these giant sequoia and magnolia trees. The deeper we went between them the more I was losing oxygen. We started seeing flickers of light more like sparkles or at less that's what it looked like to me. I looked down on the ground and it was like a trail or some sort. It looked like white pieces of crystals lined up leading somewhere deep behind these trees. At first, Baebae said 'ok So-soo get ready to take off running back towards the house and don't worry causz I'm coming with you'. Auntie Baebae was adamant but confused in whether to stay or continue in walking or turn around and run for dear life.

Somehow, I think she begun to feel safer when she started connecting the dots to this petrified scenery. I think she knew who it was in those woods because her nervousness shifted into calmness. And to my surprise I certainly was clueless to what was going on I couldn't think of anyone that would be so courageous as to want to come this far. Well I'll be a monkey's Auntie before I could say the word Auntie Baebae; beat me to the punch. It was Auntie Nitta with her split personality self. She was dressed in this black ensemble which looked like a robe or a long flared out dress. She looked like a witch with her face painted white with deep black eye liner around each of her entire eyes.

Apparently, we startled her causz she jumped straight up off the ground. Baebae said' ah shit girl you back in here chatting and performing spells'? I thought spells! I've heard that word used before in the household. Nitta said 'Bae I got to correct what I did to Karrie'. Baebae said 'huh' Nitta said 'she was supposed to leave Floyd but instead she's more in love with him and refused to let him go with her ole corroded pussy'. My mouth dropped. At that moment I just didn't care to stay in a child's place so I asked Auntie Nitta what the fuck you doing and why you dressed like a witch. She looked at me for some reason opposed to answering me. I couldn't look directly in her face because she was looking like something from Scooby doo cartoon. She said 'So-soo I only come back here when I fear something is wrong with my brothers or sisters'. I come back here to help them. I said 'to help'! Auntie Nitta I don't ever want this kind of help it's scary. Baebae said 'I'm telling Momma you know this witch craft shit is dangerous and besides Momma done told you to don't mess with this shit'. I said 'who's Momma your Momma or my Momma? Nitta said 'So-soo she talking about Gramz's'. I said 'whatttt'! my Gramz's perform this kind of stuff before? I nervously wondered who these people were that surrounded me calling themselves family. My legs really start shaking. I couldn't think of anyone I wanted to tell about this. I really tighten my grip nearly squeezing Baebae's hand to deaf. I was becoming delusional still seeing black shadows in fact, I shouted to Baebae let's go it's too many floating bodies out here. Nitta said 'So-soo it's all in your power'. Bae bae shouted stop it Nitta just stop it you scaring the hell out of her. She was right! Nitta was smiling still possessed and highly influenced that she was a miracle worker. She said 'yall interrupted me I was finishing up then she started chatting once again, slowly folding her hands up to pray and talking some foreign language. I had never witnessed anything like this before. I wondered what went wrong during her upbringing with her parents my Grandparents. I wondered why she felt performing this ritual was a safe havoc for any human being. Auntie Nitta thought she was a miracle worker who's bigger than God at least that's what I thought. I quoted a verse from the Bible out loud where it says: *God is light; in him there is no darkness at all.* Nitta said 'Red! Why you have to go and say that now I got to start all over'. Baebae smiled at me and said 'you blocked your Aunties evilness'. Nitta ran to grab Karrie's purse strap and other personal items that belong to her. She began chatting with those items. She then lite candles, and used several jokers looking cards in her hands. She slowly sat on the ground holding those items and looking ever so weird. I couldn't understand the words she was using even though I had plan on not using any of them let alone to ever come back here for my own selfish reasoning's. She blew out the incense and said some words then re-lite more. She slowly put

Karrie's articles into the lite candles still chatting. She began turning her head around in circles and for a moment I nearly jumped out my skin when she stopped rolling her head in a circle then it looked like her eyes rolled out I mean her eyes were pure white. I screamed Nitta! Baebae said 'alright bitch get your shit and let's go'! Nitta didn't move she was in a trance looking straight ahead with no eyes. Baebae said nervously with a shaken voice 'Nitta you did it you just did something I felt it'. Well whatever it was Bae's hand suddenly turned from warm to cold making me even more scared. I started backing up I was about to run and apparently so was Baebae. When I looked back from staring at Nitta, Baebae passed me up with her eyes bucked walking backwards. I heard my name being called and I know I squirted shit on myself. At first I thought it was Nitta calling me but she was still in a trance. I had enough of that shit and turned to run passing Baebae. I ran as fast as I could headed back towards the house. I took one look back and when I turned around I ran dead smack into my Daddy. He grabbed me by the shoulders looked at me then shook me. He said 'what you doing back here while taking off his belt'. He said 'didn't you hear me calling you'? You got your Gramz and Momma worried to deaf. Do you know that man whipped me right there! He said' from now on if I ever continued running when somebody calls me he would beat the life out of me'. I was too consumed with what I just saw with Auntie Nitta that I hardly felt his belt licks. I don't recall crying while being whipped because I kept trying to look into the direction that crazy ass Nitta was chanting. Daddy kept talking to me while wearing my butte out. I was more shocked then anything that I was being whipped by my Father which he rarely did. It's always been Gramz or Momma who did the disciplining and whippings to me. Moments later I saw Baebae run out the woods screaming J. W. what you whipping her for? Daddy said 'what'? Bae don't you ever question me why I'm whipping my child's ass you got that? I need to put this belt on your ass for being back here with her. Let's go now! Daddy didn't allow Baebae to baby me on the way back. He was heated with me. He fussed majority of the way back while I whimpered and sniffed all the way back scared to say anything. At that moment, I thought to myself what Granddaddy said 'Red we as a family will teach you some things'. I wondered was this stuff with Auntie Nitta included.

As a matter of fact, Daddy, Baebae and I were within walking distance from the party. Daddy noticed people were scattered into groups everywhere from what it looked like there were more people who had joined us. Baebae said 'oh my God what's happened'? Daddy said 'that's a good question Bae'. There was definitely some sort of commotion the further we three walked towards the front of the house the more screams we heard. We reached the front yard Daddy was moving through the crowd of people Baebae saw Uncle Floyd bent down on the ground and screamed Floyd! He was saying something to someone on the ambulance stretcher. I saw Eisha and charged directly towards her. I was in a dazed my damn self but managed to grab her hand. She shouted my name as if she thought that was me on that stretcher. Auntie Eisha said 'So-soo why you run off like that'? I was looking for you in this crowd of people and when I did see you, you were running towards the walking path to the lake'. I said 'Eisha I saw Nitta going into the woods' and couldn't finish because Momma saw me and pulled me by my arm. My Momma picked me up and hugged me for dear life something she hasn't done in a good long while. She said 'Sofay I had gotten so worried about you running off like that'. Don't you do that again?

Consequently, Grammy looked over and saw Momma holding me she made her way towards us. She walked right up to Momma and took me out of her arms and put me on the ground then said 'Geraldine I'm taking Sofay home with me this is no place for a child'. Oh how I wanted to say don't forget Eisha Grammy! But before I could say anything I looked at the paramedics carrying someone I couldn't make the person out at first then I saw it was Karrrie. I gasped for air. The people never stopped screaming or crying their sounds grew louder and louder. Grammy had me by the hand as she and I started walking towards her bat mobile then she stopped turned around towards Momma and said 'Geraldine I want you home with me and Sofay tonight'. Momma had tears in her eyes she hesitated at first but said 'let me find J. W. to let him know'. Grammy said 'I'll see you at the car'. She didn't wait for Momma to respond. So, Grammy and I headed for her car passing up Auntie Gwen who was crying of course. I saw Monee trying to console Gramz then Mrs. Brown was hugged up on Auntie Camille.

However, I noticed that Grammy's hand was shaking and I wondered why but I'm sure it was only a matter of moments before what was hidden inside of her would be unleashed. We were in the car maybe for several seconds and saw Momma running towards the car. Grammy said 'thank God my baby is heading towards this car'. That statement puzzled me. Momma eagerly hoped into the car and Grammy slowly drove off. As we drove away I noticed Auntie Nitta making her way towards the ambulance with what looked like a smirk on her face. Momma saw that too and said 'that bitch Nitta is up to no good'. How you gone smile when somebody just died? I screamed died! Momma who died? Grammy said 'So-soo we are not sure if Karrie is dead or not we have to wait and see poor thing'. Momma said 'I've never seen anyone laughing having a good time and the next thing you know she dropped to the ground'. Grammy said 'did she have a weak heart?' Momma said 'she didn't know'. Hell I might know is what I wanted to say because I thought about Nitta in those woods. As we drove away from my Grandparents farm I felt helpless without having Eisha in the car with us. So I asked Mommy could Eisha come with us. Grammy said' no Sofay you got to learn how to adjust being without Ms. Eisha she is not your Mother'. I whined to Grammy asking why. Grammy said 'Sofay White because I said so now hush sit back and enjoy the ride'. Grammy said' Geraldine yall keep Sofay around too much grown people business and it's not right'! She's being exposed to too much too soon when she should be in the room somewhere coloring. I don't like it and I certainly don't agree with how the White's run their household. If you had of let me helped you then Sofay would be raised the right way and not by the hand of a control freak like Olivia. And furthermore, Sofay should not be this attached to Eisha's ass like she is. Momma didn't say a word which surprised me because she didn't tolerant nothing from none of the White children or anyone who sass at her. I was good and tired as well as Momma. I wanted to hear more about Karrie I was constipating if I would share with Grammy all that's happened within the last several months inside the White's interesting life.

In the meantime, we pulled up in front of Grammy's cute little three bedrooms home. We parked on the side of the house under a shield. We all got out the car and headed for the front door. Before entering the home Grammy asked Momma and me to remove our shoes before entering her home. I ask 'how come?' Momma whispered Sofay! I hurried up to be quiet I didn't want to get popped in the mouth. Grammy went on ahead of us and Momma said to me 'Sofay I want you to be on your best behavior'. I said 'okay Mommy'. Grammy seemed excited to have us there in fact; she ran bath water without having to go outside for water. She asked if we wanted a snack I said 'no I was hunger and wanted food'. I had forgotten to eat earlier from all that I saw and hearing my stomach growling a person would have thought that I hadn't eaten in days. Luckily for me Grammy had prepared several extra plates of food from the celebration for her and her male friend. She put those plates in her car to eat later on in the day. After bathing my Grandma had a cute colorful gown for pajamas and house shoes for both Momma and I to wear. I looked at Momma in her gown and she looked like she was in Heaven. She got to twirling and smiling whereas I was frowning wearing those house shoes. My feet weren't use to those types of shoes instead I was use to walking barefoot or with socks on.

However, Grammy told me that I would have my own bed to sleep in for a change as well as Momma. It was a clever idea when she said it but I didn't think she would follow through with allowing me to sleep by myself. I have to say it was a little strange for me to adjust sleeping in that full size bed alone. Grammy assured me that she and Momma was just across the hall. She came into the room and told me to slide those house shoes off and get on my knees to pray before bed. I had no choice in the matter but to do as I was told. Grammy got on the floor with me and asked if I knew the Lord's Prayer I said 'yes Mamm' so we both said the Prayer out loud. She tucked me in and left for her immaculate bedroom. I laughed because she twirled off to her room wearing a matching gown and robe I wasn't use to that kind of attire for bed either. After she left the room I laid there listening to the sounds of cars and horns opposed to crickets or animals mating. I wondered what everyone else was doing back at the farm. I wondered how Daddy was gone sleep without Momma and I lying next to him. Actually, as the night grew I couldn't sleep so I went and got into bed with Grammy. It was like she was expecting me she threw the covers back, hit the center of the pillow and said 'come on baby'. I started dozing off but decided to go use the toilet before I wet the bed. In passing Momma's room there was a strange noise coming from it. I peeked into the room and saw Momma peacefully sleeping but making noise. When I got back into bed I told Grammy what I was hearing and she smirked and said 'So-soo your Momma is tired and haven't slept alone in many years. What she's doing is snoring. I said 'snoring how come'? Grammy said 'she's in her comfort zone in being home where she doesn't have to worry or tend to you as much because I'm here'. I hurried up to say ok because I didn't feel like hearing any of those paragraphs from that Positive minds thingy being recited. The next afternoon when I woke up it was lunch time and Grammy had already prepared lunch. Apparently, Momma woke up ate breakfast and went back to sleep something she never does on the farm. I started going into her room but Grammy told me not to bother her. So I went into the kitchen to eat I had a choice to eat the left over breakfast food or the lunch food. When I looked around I noticed Grammy's kitchen was a bit smaller than Gramz's kitchen. She had one stove compared to the three stoves I was used to. I asked her where was her other stoves. She laughed and said 'baby Grandma don't need all those stoves it's just me'. I said 'oh' and started eating the food it was a different flavor especially with the bacon and burger meat I didn't say anything and kept eating. I was admiring how so much light was in the kitchen.

In fact, I was admiring the entire house down to the shield. It was so immaculate, spacy, and colorful.

Meanwhile, I finished both breakfast mixed with lunch and

Grammy had laid this cute outfit out on the bed that had ruffled socks. I thought the socks were ribbons for my hair at the farm I wore plain white socks that I had to roll and fold down to my ankles. The socks that Grammy had laid out were actually at my ankles and not at my knees. It tripped me out that I didn't have to roll them down to my ankles. Grammy and I went to town which was within walking distance a lot closer than Granddaddy's house. She and I walked to the store; talking, laughing and enjoying each other's company. My grandmother and I were really enjoying each other's company until I mentioned what Auntie Nitta was doing in the back woods. We stopped walking as Grammy became angry with teary eyes. She said 'baby I need to permanently move you in with me'. I just can't understand why they talk around you like you're twenty one years old. There's no structure of discipline in that household. Olivia walks around like she's the queen of this earth when her kids are all dysfunctional one way or another. For peek sakes you've got to be really screwed in the head to want to bring that sort of harm to anybody through witch craft ritual. Sofay know that what Nitta was doing was the works of the devil. Baby, know to never let yourself get involve with any evil ritual because it's a sin. Our God is a jealous God who doesn't condone acts of evil. I don't ever; do you hear me Sofay ever, ever, want you to neither learn those rituals nor be around such acts'. I said 'yes mamm'. Grammy said 'my dear Lord'. I knew it struck a nerve with my grandmother because she and I ended up walking an extra mile to the ice cream parlor.

Any hoot, she and I continued back to the grocery store. I was in shocked that she purchased meat and other foods to take home to cook. I was completely out of my comfort zone and in a new world. On our way back home Grammy looked down at me licking that cone and she knew right away that I wasn't use to that. When we arrived back at Grammy's I saw Momma sitting on the porch still in her pajamas and robe which was odd. She greeted both Grammy and I with the biggest smile. We sat on the porch with her a few seconds as she said 'Momma it feels so good to be home, oh I've been so consumed with my farm life that I've forgotten about life'.

Grammy smiled and said 'well we gone have to do something about that'. Momma smiled while hugging me saying she needs to make changes in our life and that she's been thinking about how to go about it. Grammy said 'what changes are you referring to? are you considering moving back home away from those dreadful White's? She then said 'um Soo go on in the house so me and your Momma can talk'. I knew by her tone that she was trying to convince Momma into doing something she did not want to. I took the bags into the kitchen but first taking off my shoes at the door. In the kitchen all her dishes matched as well as the utensils. She had canned foods in the cabinets which was a no-no in Granddaddy's house. My mouth dropped to see three glass bottles of milk I went to the back window looking for cows. I took the foods out the bags and saw pork chops and pig ears wrapped inside clear plastic. I was puzzled because I was looking for the animals in her back yard so I went to the front porch and interrupted their conversation I had to know. I said 'excuse me Mamm but where the pigs at? Grammy fell out laughing and so did Momma. By this time both of them made their way into the house. Grammy said 'Sofay where you were living is called a farm where they fetch and kill animals to eat. Where you stand at now is called city life where I purchase everything I want to cook and eat. It's a huge difference in both lives. She said 'I want you to be able to distinguish the two'. I thought oh boy another word I'm not familiar with and my Auntie Eisha wasn't there to give me the meaning of the word so I asked Grammy what the word distinguish meant. Grammy said' baby the word distinguish means knowing the difference between the same but different situations. For example you've noticed the difference in how I live compared to how you're Gramz's live. We live in the same state but different counties we live and make different choices with taste, style, and entertainment. Gramz's and them wake up at the crack of dawn to prepare food for twenty people whereas, I get up by eight in the morning to make coffee and eat from the refrigerator whatever it is I want to eat. I work and own my clothing shop selling merchandises to people that's how I make a living for myself. Whereas, your Gramz's does not work a paying job she needs help around the house where I don't. Another example Sofay is, Olivia goes to the: shed for food that's already been hounded and killed to eat, and she gets milk from cows whereas, I go to the front porch for my milk already in the glass jars and I go to the grocery store for everything else I need. It's a difference from country life to city life. I want you to experience both lives'. Momma interrupted us by saying Mother when was the last time you spoke with Auntie Rebecca? Grammy said 'it's been awhile I was just thinking about her earlier today, I'm interested in knowing her wellbeing and what's she's doing these days'. Becca my sweet Aunt, Grammy said then she suddenly became sad reminiscing back on the old days. Momma suggested we go visit her. Grammy practically jumped into Momma's arms with excitement saying that would be a wonderful idea Geraldine. You haven't been to see her in years we will go in the morning as a surprise. Both Momma and Grammy hugged each other smiling. Grammy wasn't the type to plan anything in advance she always got up and did what she wanted to in the spare of the moment without any reservations. She said 'why plan something that far away when you could do it now'.

However, night fall arrived and both Momma and I were in the kitchen watching Grammy cook. She made spaghetti with meat which was quite tasty.

In fact, she made one meal which again I wasn't accustomed to because at Granddaddy's farm we always had a variety of food to choose from. Like I said she made spaghetti with meat, fried pork chops, fried cabbage, candied yams with marshmallows on top, homemade bread and rice pudding (I have to say the food had a different taste especially the pork chops). I didn't think I would get full from that little bit of food but I did and so did Momma.

CHAPTER 16

The next day we boarded a plane for a place called Harlem USA in New York City. We were all excited to travel even though that was my first time flying and I didn't know what to expect without having any of my Aunties to tell me ahead of time.

Anyway, we had to walk in a single file line from the terminal to the airplane to board. During the plane ride I asked Grammy why she had clothes to fit me at her house. She said 'it was already arranged for me to spend the summer with her'. She had already asked Momma weeks prior to what size I wore making it easy for her to purchase if not hand make everything from dresses to skirts. I asked did you say spend the summer with you? She said 'yes Sofay it's time you see another side of the world'. It's time for you to experience a different atmosphere around a different group of people who also love you. I asked what about Eisha Grammy? She said 'Sofay when you get back to the farm life you will be with your Auntie Eisha and the rest of them but until then I don't want to hear anything else about you being under Eisha White'. I slowly said 'yes Mamm'. Speaking of Daddy I haven't seen my Daddy nor heard from him in two days so I asked Grammy where was he? She said 'baby your Daddy is fine and he's missing both of you don't worry we will see him when we get back to Oklahoma'.

Meanwhile, the plane ride was bumpy it seemed like the plane was trying to keep from falling. My stomach dropped each time the plane suddenly took a dive dropping several feet in the air which was frightening. After six hours of flying we managed to land safely. Walking through those terminals was exciting to me because we didn't have this type of rowdiness back home. People were in rare form and everywhere in that airport either they were; standing still, walking in groups, or cussing; there were Mother's trying to quiet babies or they were telling other people to mind their own damn business.

In fact, when we retrieved our luggages from luggage claim it was more of a mess there then walking through the terminals. I enjoyed watching the array of people who were funny but weird looking to me in New York. I was standing next to my Mother as she and I were looking around the baggage claim area looking like Stamie and Olli waiting on our luggages. I pulled Momma's purse when I noticed Grammy wasn't next to us. I said 'Mommie we lost Grammy'. She said 'surely Mother isn't lost Sofay she's around here somewhere'. I looked and looked until finally I saw her near the exit door justa flirting with this distinctive dressing man. She was justa skinning and grinning in the face of a stranger at less that's what I thought. This man well dressed in a three piece suit took out a piece of paper writing something on it. Apparently whatever, he was talking about had Grammy's full attention because she started fake falling on him with laugher. I pulled Momma's arm and said 'there she go look at her, look at Grammy over there! Momma said 'what Soo' and I repeated myself. She looked over at Grammy then smiled and said 'he's an old friend of your Grandmother they're just getting re-acquainted'.

Any hoot, we finally got our luggage and headed outside. I couldn't believe it once we got outside! I said what's this shit? My mother ignored me. All these black trash bags were stacked so high with food dripping and hanging out of them that it looked so gross. I asked Grammy where was the garbage barrels to burn all of that trash. She laughed saying Sofay they don't do that here they have garbage trucks that pick up their trash. For some reason I was under the impression that all families lived like we did at my Grandparent's home boy was I mistakenly wrong. I saw how Grammy lived a very sophisticated life style nothing like Gramz's whose life style was comfort with a house full of people. Grammy worked in her clothing store whereas, Gramz's worked providing for her family inside the farm. Man what a difference in lifestyles.

Likewise, I asked Momma what kind of place was New York

because; I saw a man dressed as a lady with red lipstick on everywhere except his lips, I saw a lady dressed in a bra and skin tight shorts that revealed the inside of her butte cheeks. I saw somebody dressed as a scary looking clown, and even a man selling socks it was exciting to see that and all of this was inside the airport.

Anyway, Grammy flagged down a taxi. There were too many to choose from and a bit confusing. The drivers were; practically yelling at each other, cussing each other out, and trying to block each other from making a profit. After seeing that I knew we were in the bigger city then Oklahoma City because we rarely had taxis drivers that cussed hanging outside the driver's window. To my surprised we hoped in a taxi and went to Auntie Rebecca's house. The driver barely gave Grammy a chance to get both feet into the taxi before speeding off. Momma laughed holding on the door. We zig zag at a high speed the entire way causing me to become angry. Grammy said 'oh Sofay no need to be angry this is fun'. I looked at her and Momma put her arms around my shoulders meaning shut up'.

CHAPTER 17

Nevertheless, I expected to see this dream house for Auntie Rebecca but instead it was a three flat outdated apartment building. Strangely enough, the entire block had the same exact buildings on both sides of the streets. This was amazing to see this and I wondered how those people knew their address without getting lost because all the buildings were the exact same. The atmosphere was dark with Negros walking every which way. Some were in groups standing in front of a stoop as well as others were playing cards or dice. There were all sorts of activities; such as kids jumping rope, or they were playing hop scotch, there were board games being played and it was a sight to see from a country girl's perspective. But what was puzzling was these New Yorker's lived in a fast pace world nothing like the South where there is slowness with very few crazies walking around compared to this lifestyle.

Additionally, we got out the cab and the boys standing there in front of Auntie Becca's flat suddenly took notice of us three. Momma said 'anybody know a niggar named Tommie with a grin on her face'. Tommie slowly walked towards us pointing his one finger in disbelief. Then he shouted out what the fuck man say it ain't so and ran to Momma picking her up laughing and swinging her in circles. Grammy grabbed onto Tommie's back he turned and picked her up kissing her on the cheek nearly crying. Apparently, they were happy to see him and vice versa. He looked at me bent down to hug me then said 'what they call you cause you got a hella lot of names Shorty'. Mommy hit him on the shoulders laughing. Tommie said 'Shorty is cute as hell'! Momma said 'thank you' I looked around to see who he was talking about because I didn't have Eisha with me to translate who the hell Shorty was so I just smiled.

Likewise, out of nowhere I heard Granddaddy say 'Red I want yah to look with both your eyes and ears'. I looked at Tommie, those boys, the block and said 'ok Granddaddy I will'. I said to myself I hope Tommie and his friends are nothing like my Uncle A. J. Although, Cousin Tommie was taken back with our visit he practically carried Momma up the stairs. It was kind of funny but I didn't laughed because Momma was thrilled to be in her old stumbling grounds in New York away from the Whites.

Any hoot, Tommie had his friends bring our bags upstairs. When we got up there it was dark Tommie screamed out Grandma you ain't gone believe who's here. She said 'what boy! He repeated his self while she came out the room walking on a cane. When she saw Grammy she dropped her cane and covered her cheeks screaming Lord thank you! She reached for Grammy saying Ernestine; Ernestine baby you done finally came to visited me. I saw the joy in her but didn't grasp to why she was crying like that. Next thing I knew, Auntie Rebecca kissed Grammy all in the mouth making me say 'eeow' Momma nudged me meaning be quiet. It took several minutes of crying after Grammy helped her to sit down that's when she noticed me and Momma standing next to Tommie. She pointed at Momma to say I know that's not my baby then she started crying again. Momma walked to her to put her hand on her shoulders but instead Auntie Becca reached up for a hug. They rocked side to side for several minutes then she focused her eyes on me. Auntie Becca said 'ok I got to calm down I'm just so happy to see yall'. She blew her nose and said 'now who's this little red girl'? Grammy said' that's my Grandbaby Sofay'. Auntie Rebecca's eyes enlarged not by me but by my name. She said 'girl child she's named after you Ernestine? Lord have Mercy she reminds me of you at that age Ernestine Sofay Brown'. Grammy said 'yes Mamm'. I double looked at Grammy because I had never ever heard her refer to another woman as a yes Mamm. That tripped me out!

Meanwhile, I was trying to admire their apartment but couldn't I was distracted by the paint that was chipped on the living room walls. The front windows looked like they were hanging by a feather meaning if there was a rain storm those windows would have fallen out. The sofa had a permanent sink print in it, I was in awe. Auntie said 'Tommie move your ass out the way so Sofay can come to me'. Tommie laughed but moved out the way I walked to her she put me on her lap held me by the waist and planted a kiss on my cheek, neck, and mouth. I was a little embarrassed I guessed that was the hospitality way of city people greeting you. I asked her what happened to her walls. Auntie said 'baby when you get as old as me decorating don't matter'. Grammy said 'well decorating does not matter but being comfortable matters'. Grammy said 'we will talk later on but in the meantime Auntie Becca you been living here for ages'. She said 'yeah baby I done buried your Uncle Lester, my daughter Essabell and you know I been raising Tommie all his life'. Yes I have been here for over forty years. I always wanted to move but couldn't afford it; this neighborhood has gone through many transitions with each generation of kids. I have seen the worst and I've seen the greatest of these kids in the neighborhood'. In between Auntie Becca's life story she told Tommie I need you to go to the store for food. Grammy offered money but Auntie Becca wouldn't hear of it. Tommie said 'Grandma you got to stop crying for your eyes swell'. She said 'boy shut up I ain't seen my niece in ten years I'm just so happy to be alive to see my sister's baby'. Tommy then said 'come on Gerry we gonna go to the store'. I said Gerry! Grammy laughed and said 'So-soo that's your Momma's nickname. It's a name we shorten instead of saying Geraldine we say Gerry'.

Funny though, I've never heard Grammy calls Momma Gerry. If Gramz's were standing there she would have said 'Ernestine go sat your showing off ass down some where'...ha-ha. Now I know from listening to Gramz's conversations regarding Grammy it was true she was a piece of work. I do agree because Grammy don't flaunt her merchandise she just wears it well though she can be a bit of a show off she means no harm.

Anyway, Cousin Tommy said 'oh brother Sooo is like that where you got to explain everything to her? Grammy said 'yes we try not to hide stuff from her'. Just as I was about to sit down a young lady came inside the door with a baby on her hip and a three year old girl. Come to find out Tommie and his girlfriend Sheila along with their two kids lived there. He walked to her planted a kiss on her cheeks introduced us then told Momma lets bounce. I wanted to go with them but the baby caught my full attention. Auntie Becca said' this one here! Watch this Ernestine she said 'Sheila how was work today? She said 'fine' then existed with both kids to a bedroom in the back'. Once Auntie heard her closed the bedroom's door she said 'that whanch ain't got no damn job like Ray Charles can see and we all know he's blind'. Grammy said 'oh so how she paying rent? Auntie said 'lying on her back' then they busted up laughing. She went on to say I don't like her she half take care of those babies coming in here all hours of the night dragging those kids in here if they are not already here with me running up my blood pressure. She nasty can't clean or cook. Grammy said 'where's her peoples at? Auntie Becca said 'on the streets'. Grammy said 'Becca you can't knock her down cause she don't know no better you suppose to help and encourage her'. Auntie said 'the hell I will'! My child was grown when she died'. Well at least Essabell your child knew better she didn't throw Tommie at you she was there for him and thank God you are there for Tommie. Auntie said 'yeah well he ain't the best Child but he's respectable'. He helps out around here unlike that jazzah belle Sheila. Just then, Sheila came out the room with both kids I was drawn to the baby and I asked her could I hold him. She said 'do you know how'? I said 'yes Mamm' Sheila said 'Mamm'! You don't have to call me that Sheila will do. Grammy said 'goodness your baby ain't missing no meals' Sheila just smiled.

Whereas, the other child Kimberley who was three at the time was somewhat raggedly looking more unkempt this caught my full attention. I looked at how the baby was dressed and he looked presentable and smelled like a baby.

Whereas, little Kimberley; looked unsettled with dried up snout on her nose, hair uncombed, and she was wet wearing a soggy pamper. I told Sheila that Kimberley was wet she said 'I know I got to go get some pampers'. Little did I know Kimberley was not Cousin Tommie's daughter but baby T was his child?

Moreover, Grammy said 'come here Kimberly' then Sheila corrected her by saying no her name is Kimberley not Kimberly Grammy said 'oh I see' and looked at Becca who rolled her eyes at Sheila. From that, I knew I was gonna enjoy being around this lady she made me laugh.

In the meantime, Sheila said 'Becca I got to go get some pampers you need anything from the store'. Auntie Becca said 'beg your parten' Sheila repeated herself Becca said 'I thought that's what you said'. Haahah she went on to say since when you care anything bout me asking if I need anything. She said 'girl don't mess around up in here and get put out trying to suddenly be nice to me'. Grammy shout 'Auntie you be nice! Then Becca went on to say Tommie and Gerry went to the store for some food already. Sheila said 'then you will be waiting'. Hell I was confused and decided to sit back and ask no questions but I did ask if I could go with her to the store. Grammy damn near jumped out her skin when I asked that question. Becca said 'let her go at least I know she got to bring her ass back here tonight to be a Mother to her kids and she got to bring Sofay back'. My Grammy was extremely nervous to let me go with Sheila because she didn't know her. She felt that Sheila wouldn't watch me like she would. She even wrote Becca's number down on a piece of paper and put it in my pocket then said 'Sofay White if you are in harm's way you find a presentable adult and have them call this number'. I laughed and said 'we don't have to worry because Gramz's not here with a switch so I'm not in harm's way'. She tapped me on the stomach smiling and said 'baby be observant you in a new city with a different class of people'. I also want you to watch Sheila. I then said 'Grammy I know to look with both my eyes and ears I must not told you that Granddaddy once told me that'. She looked shocked but pleased that the old man gave me a little wisdom to go by. I looked at the front door and Sheila was waiting impatiently Grammy told her girl if anything happens to my baby you won't be able to sit for days when I get through with you! You hear me Sheila. Auntie Becca laughed and said 'did you hear her Sheila cause once she finish with you then I'm gonna help her re-beat your ass'. I laughed but Sheila didn't in fact, going down the stairs she mumbled I hate her. I said 'oowwh'!

CHAPTER 18

Nonetheless, when Sheila and I got outside the block's atmosphere changed it was more people than ever who gathered around just mingling with each other. As Sheila and I walked I reached up to grab her hand she looked at my hand and kept walking. I guess I had developed a chronic habit from being around auntie Eisha in reaching up to catch and hold somebody's hand. I had to re-look at her because she acted like I was robbing her from the way she looked at me. I didn't say anything but decided to look behind me as I walked. When I turned around walking backwards there were; kids jumping rope, men chatting and cussing up a storm, people hanging on gates as they mingled, even an ice cream truck pulled up and those kids ran straight to it. It was kind of exciting to see such an array of different activities at one time. Besides that, Sheila held a taxi down we hopped in it. This driver was crazier than the other driver that drove us from the airport.

Instead, of pulling up to the grocery store we were in front of a department store.

Miraculously, once we got out the taxi this skunk Sheila had the audacity to grab and hold my hand walking into the store. I looked at her curiously but choose to say nothing. When we got inside the store I was in heaven admiring the clothes, shoes and even the mannequins. Sheila, on the other hand, had other ulterior motives of sin. She marvel and acted like a damn fool looking at those clothes with all that laughing and holding those clothes up against her body as if she was trying them on. Next thing I knew she gathered an arm full of clothes and even had me help her with more clothes in my arms as we headed to the dressing room. In the dressing room I laid those clothes on the chair with a sign of relief due to the heaviness in carrying them. Sheila said 'So-soo go stand in front of this door and if somebody come in this dressing room I want you to cough as loud as you can okay'. I didn't know any better so I said 'ok Sheila'. All I can say is that she walked in slim but came out looking nine months pregnant. I looked and reached to touch her stomach but she blocked my hand and grabbed it as we made our exit from this store.

Actually, we practically ran out of there while she held her stomach. We ran right out to the taxi that was waiting on us which happened to be the same driver that picked us up on Auntie Becca's block. Sheila said 'So-soo I had to knock your hand out the way because I didn't want you to knock these clothes out from under my clothes'. At that time clothes censors were not implemented yet and it was semi easy to shoplift until roughly around the mid-seventies that's when people became aware that it wouldn't be as easy to steal any longer with the new beefed up security.

Any hoot, Sheila went on to say to the driver I'm starting her out young she'll know the ropes to making money real soon. The driver laughed and continued driving to the next destination which happened to be a beauty parlor. Inside this place was wall to wall ladies either sitting in a chair or they were waiting to be called to a chair to get their hair styled. That was my first time in one of those places. My goodness, I had never seen so much naps in my life. Those women really needed some type of style to their hair. My hair got washed over the sink in the kitchen whereas; here in this parlor those workers used a tiny little bowl with washing products. I was trying to memorize this entire ordeal so I could tell Eisha everything when I returned back home.

Meanwhile, Sheila told me to sit in an empty chair and then she existed into the back. When she returned those clothes were hanging on hangers and being pulled by wheels like an exhibit. She rolled that rail into the center of the floor and all those ladies got up picking and choosing through those clothes. After they chose what items they wanted Sheila started raddling off prices from the top of her head as if she actually purchased those clothes. I looked at her and shook my head from side to side knowing perfectly well I knew something was wrong with this picture. We were there for several hours it was like a rotation of ladies coming into the parlor with nappy hair but leaving the parlor with styled hair and a new piece of stolen clothes. Sheila collected a good amount of money.

By this time, I was ready to get back to my Grandmother. We got back into that same taxi which puzzled me. I had to ask Sheila why this same man keeps picking us up every time we leave a place. Sheila laughed and told the driver. See Dave I told you she would catch on. So we left the parlor and headed to the grocery store. This time Sheila's thieving ass got a basket and I was relieved because I didn't want any of that cold stolen food touching my body. She rolled the cart down several aisles choosing food but when we got to the dairy section do you know this heifer put cheese inside my pants along with biscuits in each of my pockets. She said 'Sofay be quiet and stick close by me'. I was so angry I saw stars because his brod had money but still chose to steal it didn't make sense to me. When she wasn't looking I made up my mind to find a presentable adult to help me call Grammy because this heifer had lost her everlasting mind so I made my way to the front of the store. Once I got outside I looked around at my surroundings and this time I was spell bound with the giraffe written on the walls of the store. The colors were outstanding though I couldn't make out the words I just never seen such unique artwork. While looking at the giraffe I was trying to move one of those can of biscuits out the way in my pockets so, I could pull out Auntie Becca's written number. I couldn't get to the paper for the biscuits were in my way as I began taking one can out my pocket Dave the taxi driver pulled up directly in front of me. He got out the taxi and said 'hold on little girl don't do that'. I looked up at him and said 'what'! He said 'come on and get in the taxi and wait on Sheila'. I said 'no! You a stranger' although I thought about it and truthfully speaking Sheila was a stranger as well. Dave said 'ok I'm not going to force you into the taxi because I respect your hustle'. He said 'what I don't want you to do is pull whatever it is you struggling to pull out your pocket; don't!' I said 'hustle'? He looked at me and said 'baby your Momma ought to be careful who she get to watch you.' I said 'huh'. Dave said 'Sheila is bad news and if I was your Momma I would never allow you around her you don't need to be boosting at your age'. I repeated after him like a broken record and said a booster? Dave said 'yeah that's how she makes her living by stealing goods and selling them to ordinary people to make money. You should know you been right there with her stealing. I said 'stealing but I'm not stealing'! As I turned around Sheila's stank ass was coming out the store grinning. She said 'Sofay girl why you walk off like you grown I was looking everywhere for you'. I said 'yeah, yeah, yeah and waited for her to open the taxi door without looking directly in her face'. We got into the taxi and Sheila reached in both my pockets to take those biscuits out and she put them in the grocery bags along with the other items that were either paid for or stolen. Boy I was so angry being with this thief. I blamed her for introducing me to this world of corruptness and in fact, I wish Auntie Nitta was there to whip up a spell on her ass.

However, in the taxi I didn't expect anything less for Dave the driver but to drive like someone was chasing him. I asked Sheila are we going back to Auntie Becca's house now. She said 'yes we are little one'. Before Dave pulled off Sheila gave him a hand full of money for being the driver on this apparent routine criminal spree. I sat there absorbing these last few hours up: we left Becca's place, we went to boost clothes, then went to a beauty parlor to sell the stolen goods, we also went to a grocery store for food, stole food, and to top things off we had the same taxi driver the entire ride.

Contrarily, it was night time and my first night in New York and I had become a young criminal. We pulled up to Auntie Becca's place and I looked up in the window and saw my Grandma boy I was happy to see her. I ran to my Grammy and told her Sheila is crazy. Auntie Becca laughed and said 'what took yall so long?' Before I could run it all down to both her and Grammy, Sheila opened the door with the bags of groceries. Grammy told Sheila 'I hope you got some pampers cause this girl soaked through her pamper so I put a towel on her. Sheila said to Grammy 'oh that's ok but here's her pampers'.

Anyway, I had forgotten about the cheese under my top. I pulled the cheese out and sat it on the table Grammy's eyes grew large so she asked 'girl what you doing pulling cheese out from your shirt?

Sheila jumped in saying' the grocery bags fell in the taxi so I told her to pick it up off the floor and put it in her pockets'. Grammy said 'oh' but with a hum look on her face.

Consequently, I was exhausted and looked for Momma who had not returned with Cousin Tommie. Sheila started to put the groceries away and didn't wash her hands to prepare dinner for us. I was starving and couldn't wait to eat some of this New York food. Do you know this heifer; opened cans of ravioli's for dinner, she fried butter bread on the stove, opened a can of corn, and made a pitcher of red Kool-aide. I looked down at that paper plate and said what the fuck is this? Grammy screamed Sofay White! Auntie Becca laughed then said 'yeah your little red ass is use to cooked food ain't cha'. I said 'yeah' she said 'you'll eat well after tonight'. I sat there at that moment looking at Sheila visualizing her at my Grandparents' house eating dinner with us. I said 'Sheila you shall come let my Gramz's show yah how to cook causz we don't eat like this'. Grammy said 'ok Sofay that's enough'. She then went on and said 'Auntie Becca you should think about it; think about moving in with me'. I would feel better knowing you in a better place than this. Becca said 'huh move from Harlem'! Girl you out yah mind I'm not going nowhere but here. Grammy wouldn't give up trying to convince Becca. She went on giving deep details to every nook and cranny of her apartment as to why she needed to move. Auntie Becca tuned her out by singing a hymn. Grammy paused but stared at Becca.

In any event, I asked where we sleeping at. Auntie Becca said 'hum somebody show is grown'. Grammy said 'yes I know So-soo can be out of control sometimes by not staying in a child's place but I'm working on her'. She's around adults who forgets that's she's a child sometimes they talk as if she's in the same age range as them instead of telling her to leave the room. Grammy said 'I don't want her to grow up fast but as a pace of a child her age. Becca said 'oh I see she ain't average she got sass about her'. Better you then me honey cause I'll been of broke her neck. Grammy said 'see Auntie you never had patience Momma always told you to loosen up with your rules and how you ran your house'. Becca said 'yeah you right I couldn't keep your Momma out my house she always tried to overrule what I laid down…my sister God rest her Soul'.

Any hoot, neither me nor Grammy were able to rest that night we itched all night and apparently we were not the only living things in that room. When she and I walked into the kitchen that morning Momma was sitting in the chair looking worn out. I ran to my Mother thrilled to see here. Tommie was stretching and yawning looking all but crazy. Grammy asked Sheila did she change the linens. Sheila looked at Tommie. Tommie stopped what he was doing waiting for an answer and so was Momma. Grammy said to Sheila 'the reason I asked was that I itched the entire night'. Tommie said 'Sheila what I tell your musty ass bout being nasty'. Sheila looked embarrassed. Grammy said 'its ok I'll go change the linens in a minute' then she turned to Tommie. She said 'Tommie are you comfortable living here?' He said' fo sho cuzzo why you ask'. Grammy rattled on about her dislikes and felt neither one of them needed to remain there. Tommie said 'cuzzo it never occurred to me she was unhappy Im'ma start paying more attention to Grandma'.

I mean after all, she is getting up there in age. Auntie Becca heard the end part of the conversation and said 'to Tommie who the hell you calling old you bastard'! It was funny but she continued on saying 'Ernestine I done told you I ain't going nowhere now that's the end of that'. She then said 'Sheila get your musky ass out my kitchen up here cooking ravioli and shit last night reach down there and get me those cooking pots'. Grammy offered to help but Auntie Becca wouldn't hear of it. This lady got down with breakfast it started smelling like food instead of the feet aroma that was floating in the air. She made pancakes, grits, bacon, sausage, biscuits, ham, eggs, coffee and harsh brown. I tore that food up because I was starving and thankful but really I was afraid of what Sheila was going to concur up for breakfast. After grubbing down on breakfast I sat across from Sheila. I couldn't pinpoint it but she looked pitiful almost looked out of place. Momma fed the three year old while Sheila feed her baby. Grammy asked Tommie what was on his agenda today. He laughed and said 'well cuzzo I don't plan nothing ahead of time but I just go with the float of things'. Becca asked where they went last night and Momma said to this popular Theatre. They saw the latest musicians who sing Rhythm and Blues. Momma said to Grammy 'Mother you would have had the time of your life. The music was ever so smoothing, live and full of energy. I danced, I sang, and even ran to the front of the stage. I was mesmerized and couldn't control myself. Becca laughed saying Gerry you were trying to get up on stage to sang with them huh. Tommie said 'she tried Grandma but security stopped her and whole lotta women from even touching that stage'. I thought to myself and I was worried for nothing my Mommy had a marvelous time that's always a pleasant to hear.

CHAPTER 19

Meanwhile, there was a knock at the door Sheila answered and it was the man from the airport the one Grammy was grinning with. Cousin Tommie walked up to him and greeted him with a hand shake and asked his name. I looked at Grammy who was blood shot red in the face. She asked him why he didn't call first before coming over. I couldn't make out his response because I was consumed with baby T. I nearly dropped him from my lap. I couldn't keep his head from falling forward. He wiggled too much for me so I gave him back to Sheila. When I looked over at Grammy she and her friend had scooted into a corner chatting and laughing then Grammy was off to the bedroom to change. Mr. Harold Smith which is his name extended a warm good bye but Auntie Becca told him to sit it down. She then began grilling him with all kinds of questions while I was in aww that Momma went to see live singers I wanted to hear all about it. After what seemed like several hours Grammy came into the living room looking like a glamour doll. Mr. Smith stood up holding his heart quite pleased with Grammy's appearance. He extended his hand for Grammy to take his hand and off those two went. We didn't see her until the next day. All of a sudden after Grammy left it suddenly became boring. Momma and Auntie Becca had small talk nothing like the conversation she had with Grammy. Tommie was busy telling Sheila everything that she wasn't especially being a Mother to her children. Sheila looked hurt and I felt for her because he went in on her asking all kinds of questions especially how she allowed herself to run out of pampers. He said 'what Mother gets to the last pamper and use it knowing she needed more'. Actually, he made sense I wanted to share the shop lifting spree but I feared he would have cracked her jaw so I kept that to myself for time being.

After a while, he had gotten on everybody nerves including Auntie Becca. Tommie is the type that don't leave well enough alone he take his frustrations out on others. He was so bad at bad mouthing Sheila that Momma had to intervene to make him stop. Becca said to Momma 'Nigga's like that you just leave alone'. She said 'she gets sick of Tommie's egotistic mind and if it's not his way then there's the highway'. Momma told Tommie to go out for some fresh air. He hesitated at first but took her up on her offer. He grabbed his keys looked at me and said 'Shorty come on and take a ride with your cousin'. Momma fanned both of us to leave. I wasn't expecting to go anywhere with Tommie however, I was thrilled to be in a car opposed to being in the present of Dave the taxi driver. When we got downstairs and walked towards the car I reached my hand up to Tommie. He looked at my hand and surprisingly he held it. I told him when I was with Sheila she refused to hold my hand. Tommie looked surprised to hear I was with Sheila he said 'when was you with Sheila'? I said 'last night'. Tommie said 'bet that.' I said 'huh… never mind'. As we were about to get in the car several of Tommie's friends approached us for a ride and asked where was he going. He said 'man I just got to go cool off from Sheila's ass.' Tommie said 'man yall got to chill causz I got my cousin's Shorty with me man and I'm on my best behavior'. Ray ray said 'man that's what we all gone be on our best behavior'. No sooner to driving away from Auntie Becca's place Tommie's two friends lite up a joint. It didn't bother me because Baebae and her friends usually smoke those joints near the corn field so I was use to the smoke smell.

CHAPTER 20

However, what I wasn't use to was being called Shorty so I asked Tommie why he keeps calling me that. He laughed after taking a puff off that reefer and said 'to me hold that thought'. We drove through the streets of Harlem. I realized that New York is a city that has dreams but not for me. I've been entertained as well as being afraid while being with Sheila for several hours the night before. I think if one of my Aunties were here their present would have made a difference. I was truly missing all of my kin folks especially my Daddy, Eisha and Gramz's.

For the first time, I wasn't underneath any of them and it was an awkward feeling to figure things out myself without having someone else explain to me the meaning of or why that person did that and so on. I realized I couldn't blame New York for Sheila's behavior because it's all from her upbringing. I did figure out a few things on my own regarding Sheila's innuendoes and it was scary but it turned out to be a learning experience in how having a street mentality can or will lead you in jail or twelve feet under. In Sheila's case unfortunately it was only a matter of time before she lands in jail.

CHAPTER 21

Furthermore, her chosen life style was too much with no promise or a guaranteed future. Now looking over at Tommie I pretty much predict the same type of street life mentality except he had friends of the same feather that flocked together. The guys did their best to behave but I guess the liquor and reefer took over their minds. They got to; arguing, lying and even hanging out the window whistling at women. It was entertaining for a minute until we got boxed in by four other cars. Tommie shouted Shorty get down! It all happened so fast. Ray ray shouted Nigga drive through these motherfucking cars! Tommie shouted 'how? When I slowly rose up from the floor of the car there were so many men that I stopped counting after nine. The front of Cousin Tommie's car was surrounded with those men who were threatening all of them; Tommie, Ray ray and Gerald. Tommie and his friends were standing outside pleading for their life when he saw me he said 'man I got my baby girl in the car I am a father to my kids and they need me man'.

Nevertheless, several of those men looked back inside of the car and saw me they ducked their heads in and out so fast that I thought I was seeing things. I started crying thinking that my Grandparents would die if anything happened to me. I really cried visualizing my Daddy using his pistol on these cats in retaliation if anything happened to me. After clearing my vision I looked out the window to see Ray ray get the lights beaten out of him those men didn't have any mercy or kindness. Gerald and Tommie were pinned down I didn't have time to think so I shouted let my daddy go let him go! One of those dudes turned, walked and looked inside the car and said 'man did you hear Shorty calling out for her Dad'? The big one said 'get her out the car'. Tommie's scream petrified me causing me to shake uncontrollably. Once outside the car that big man used force with his hand on my shoulders I couldn't move if I wanted too. Within minutes this stranger was stilling holding me with a strong grip when I looked up at him he wasn't there. I looked to my left then to my right and there was no citing of him making me wonder did I just imagine being pulled out that car. I know I just saw this big dark burly looking man opened the car door but where was he?

In the meantime, several yards in front of me all I heard were screams and shouting like a huge commotion of voices. Those gangster men used pipes and bats still beating Ray ray. Gerald's mouth was bleeding and so was Tommie's mouth. The fourth car door opened and some fly looking guy jumped out. He was dressed to the nines with a black derby hat, black snake shoes, and a black trench coat with matching pants. He was smoking either weed or a cigarette. He walked straight to Tommie saying now you a peppy?

Meanwhile, I was trying to memorize all of their faces but couldn't. I was trying to listen to what Mr. Trench coat was saying and what a surprise I learned. Now I know first-hand with the old saying watch the company you keep.

Apparently, Ray ray stole money from Mr. Trench's coat employee. He robbed the man that was beating his ass. At that moment, I was wondering and it made sense to why that man used every ounce of strength in his body to beat Ray ray. I mean he was making all kinds of grunting sounds. He was nearly out of breath swinging that bat up and down to beat that boy like that. I then looked towards Gerald whose mouth and nose was bleeding from screwing Mr. Trench's coat seventeen year daughter. He warned Gerald to leave his daughter alone and now she's pregnant. It seems that Gerald refuses to take responsibility in being a parent to a hustler's daughter. Mr. Trench coat managed to get in a couple of licks himself until he realized he had blood on his ring. He used Gerald's shirt to wipe it off then socked him in the nose again. Poor Gerald went to reaching for the air like he was sleep walking. He was justa waving his hand before a different man hit him from the back with a bat. My stomach fell watching this man get beat down to the ground. Then there was poor cousin Tommie who got punched around for courting and stealing a street hooker who apparently made good money for Mr. Trench coat and she was Sheila. I was flabbergasted and suddenly my tears dried up. I said to myself why am I feeling sorry for these three con artists. They played with fire now they got burned. All three of those boys knew better. You can't steal a turnip and think it will cook well-meaning they all knew what they were doing and chose to be sneaky using immature street mentality games to have their way; they didn't care about the outcome and now karma has snuck up and bit them all in the ass. Each of them was guilty in some form or matter pertaining to this crooked hustle, pimp, and weed seller Mr. Trench coat. Before I knew it I shouted out loud: *No weapons formed against thy shall prosper.* Frankly speaking, I didn't expect anything to materialize from this verse in the Bible. But it did because Mr. Trench coat and a couple of those men actually turned in my direction when I saw that I shouted leave my fucking Daddy alone. Where that came from I don't know because Mr. Trench coat walked three to four steps in my direction I guess in disbelief that a child was standing near the premises. He stood there and shouted 'niggar why didn't you say you got this kid here'. Tommie said 'I told you my daughter was in the car man'! He said 'she just saved your fucking life let him go'!

Instead of Tommie walking towards the car he fell to the ground. I was too scared to move but felt that strong hold again on my shoulders this time it pushed me towards Tommie. I stood over him saying get up Daddy I wanna go home. I don't know how often those hustlers let people go but in cousin Tommie's case two guys helped him to the car whereas, both Ray ray and Gerald were either still getting beaten or on the ground crying for mercy. My heart never stopped racing but I felt relieved for some reason. Tommie and I sat in the car and watched those four cars sped off while Tommie was wheezing for air. He looked at me with a bloody face and mouth but managed to smile through all that pain. He said 'good looking out Sofay'! I said 'Tommie are you gonna be ok'? He said 'Sofay I got no choice your Grandma would kill me if I don't bring you back'. From looking at him he appeared nearly half dead himself he didn't have to worry about Grammy doing harm because he couldn't even sit up straight in the car any way.

Even though, he was semi-conscious we sat there for a long extended time. I was looking out the window at how Gerald was trying to make his way to the car. I didn't see Ray ray anywhere. I told Tommie I wanted my Daddy. He managed to small talk but had a tough time saying words.

Consequently, he did soak up air to say the name Shorty fits you Soo. You were named using many of your Aunt's names and I figure I could give you another nick name; so I choose Shorty. Cousin Tommie said 'he was impressed by the drama that I pulled by saying leave my Daddy alone'. He said 'I was a gift from God and that my parents don't realize how gifted I am'. I heard Tommie clearly but my mind shifted to the mystery man that opened the car door. I wanted to know where he went and why he wasn't beating Tommie and his friends so I asked Tommie. He looked off into space and said 'yeah I saw you Sofay I didn't see this man you talking about who opened the car door'. I saw you jump out and run around to the driver side that's when I screamed out causz I didn't want them to hurt you. I sat there stunt knowing what I saw I made a note to myself to tell Auntie Nitta this one she'll get a kick out of trying to solve this. Miraculously, Gerald slowly crawled to the car with blood covering his mouth and upper body parts. He thought we were sitting there waiting for him but in reality we were sitting there because Tommie didn't have strength to sit up let along to start the car.

But in any event, I did jump out the front seat to run around to slam the back door shut once Gerald was all the way in the car. When I got back in the front seat Tommie said 'Sofay don't get out this car again until I get you home'. I repeated back to him home he said 'you know what I mean Grandma's house'. He tried once again to muscle up strength to start the car but was unsuccessful. Out of nowhere some man walked up to the car looking inside at all three of us then ask Cousin Tommie if he were ok. He said 'he would go get help but Tommie insisted that he would be ok'. Even though, he was far from being ok he did say after the man left that he was already beat down and all he didn't need was to get rob by a car thief. I said 'ok Tommie' I didn't think about being car jack that wasn't nowhere on my mind hell I been ready for the longest to get away from this dark abandon street that had evidence of blood and violence on the concrete. I reached over to the steering wheel because it looked like Tommie was drifting in and out. He slowly rose up and tried to smile po thing I knew he meant well but was too weak to even smile. I told him Tommie lets go I know Momma is worried and when I said that he kinda lifted his hand to turn the ignition. He moved to slow so I reached and turned the key he slowly looked at me. I said 'what the fuck man' and pushed his leg on the accelerator pad he said 'hold on wait Shorty that hurt'. Gerald was mumbling something before I knew it I said 'ah shut the fuck up' using some words I stole from Gramz. It worked because Tommie was trying to laugh which was a sign to me he was slowly pulling through all that pain.

As a result, it was obvious that Tommie was in no condition to drive let alone to be able to sit up just as I said that to myself that same man who was willing to help us earlier had returned with people in a car. He tapped on the driver's window and told Tommie man you beat up real bad there's no way you going to get your little girl home safe if you drive. Tommie wasn't up for an argument with this stranger he slowly scooted over to let this man in the car to drive. I looked in the back seat and Gerald was either knocked out from his pain or he was dead so I prayed for all three of us; me, Tommie and Gerald to make it back safely. I prayed: *Godliness guards the path of the blameless, but the evil are misled by sin*. Tommie mumbled the address and asked me to repeat what I said. This stranger waved his hand to the car behind us and we were off to Harlem. I tried to make it seem like Tommie was my Daddy by saying Daddy I love you without going in to deep with conversation because I didn't want his man to take a detour and really bring harm to us. Tommie managed to say baby I'm so proud of your courage the Bible never sounded so good to me. Then he was silent. The stranger had a creepy smile on his face that made me uncomfortable but he kept driving and listening to every word that was exchanged between Cousin Tommie and me.

Subsequently, that was a long ride back to Rebecca's when we pulled up to Becca's place I don't think I gave the stranger enough time to stop the car before I got out charging up those stairs to Momma. She was sitting on the couch I bang on that door Momma swung that door open I jumped into her arms scaring her to deaf. She screamed out Sofay, Sofay, oh dear God what's happened? I don't remembered what I said but she called for Sheila and they ran down those stairs to Tommie's car. Auntie Rebecca came out her room wanting to know what happened I told her bits and pieces before she called 911. She yelled to Momma and Sheila to leave him in the car but they had made it to the porch with Tommie. Neighbors started walking over asking if they needed help. Auntie Becca made her way down the stairs and was on the porch with Tommie, Momma, and Sheila. I told them that Gerald was in the back seat. Sheila went to the car and screamed I felled back on the porch step. Auntie walked to the car and called Gerald by his full name he didn't respond. Momma looked at me and said 'Sofay go upstairs'. I did as I was told. I went up those stairs and went straight to the window. The ambulance finally arrived with the police behind them. They took Tommie and Gerald to the hospital. There wasn't enough room for Momma, Sheila, and Becca to squeeze in so Sheila said to Momma 'we will take his car'. The police started asking questions and told Momma she couldn't drive Tommie's car to the hospital because it was under investigation.

However, Sheila got in contact with Dave the taxi driver who was at the house within a matter of minutes. He took Sheila and Momma to the hospital to be with Cousin Tommie.

Meanwhile, it took hours before things had settled down and it was me, the kids, and Auntie Becca that was left in her apartment. Baby T started crying which got on my nerves and little Kimberley was wet and wanted to be picked up. I looked at Becca who looked like she was about to tilt over from Tommie's incident. Reluctantly, I saw a bottle on the table and went to give it to the baby to quiet him. Then I carried Kimberley to the couch to change her with Becca's help. I went to the refrigerator and saw cold cuts so I made a sandwich with milk for me and Kimberley. I asked Auntie did she want a sandwich and she said yes with a smirk on her face.

After we ate I asked Becca so now what we gone do. She said 'we wait' but first I want you to tell me everything that happened. So, I did. As I talked she rocked baby T to sleep in her arms. The three year old was playing with her toys on the floor. In between talking to Auntie several neighbors came by to check on her and to see if she needed anything. Gerald's Mother also stopped by to ask what happened. Auntie was reluctant to give her the full disclosure of what happened but she did tell her she didn't have all the specifics but once she found out she'll let her know. After she left I asked Becca why you didn't tell her everything. She said 'she was being prayerful that her son would make it through to tell her what he wanted her to know'. She said 'sometimes parents are in shock when they hear the truth about their child'. They want believe what you are saying then they start spreading rumors about your character for telling the truth about their child who they didn't even know. I want no parts of it. She said 'once Gerald recuperates then he can tell her all about it'. I said 'ok' and thought damn Becca is cold hearted. From that conversation I told her about the mystery man that opened the car door. Auntie Rebecca said 'girl child that was a Guardian Angel watching over you'. Had he not appeared then everybody would have die leaving you out there all by yourself. He helped you not only to be saved but to be seen by those city slickers. Lordy, he knew some of them had a heart and by your presents it made a difference between life and deaf. We both were silent for several minutes before she asked me to go in the bedrooms for covers because she and I were sleeping on the couch and love seat till somebody came back from the hospital. The next morning, once again, I didn't sleep. It's no wonder I couldn't sleep because I kept thinking about everything that I saw being with both Sheila and Tommie's street life in a matter of a day and a half.

However, when I looked down on Auntie's floor man I swear to anybody I needed a pair of hunting boots to walk on that floor. Somebody knocked on the door and I was hoping it was Momma and

Sheila but it turns out it was Grammy. I was so over joyed to see her. I jumped on her and hugged her waist and wouldn't let go.

In fact, she walked holding on to me not letting me go I finally felt safe. My Grandma sensed something was wrong. She took her shoes off and started skipping in the air like she was double dutching rope. I laughed and said 'Grammy you so funny'. She said 'what the hell! that damn thing was longer than my foot'. I had agreed because I've been killing and stomping roaches all night on this couch. She said 'no So-soo that wasn't a roach that was a rat! I said 'I know I've been throwing marbles at those things all night long'. Grammy sat down by me and put her feet up on the couch I wanted to laugh but she was serious. She said Auntie what's going on? Auntie Becca was waking up saw Grammy and said 'child you won't believe what happened here last night'. Grammy said 'what I don't believe is that you live like this Auntie! Why do you refuse to move out of here is what I wanna know'. At first, Auntie didn't said anything then she said 'Ernestine you so persistence in my wellbeing. I know you my Sister's only child and I love you to deaf. You have always worried about me. I know I haven't kept this place up to part and have every right to make that decision but honestly Im'ma be truthful I am not comfortable here haven't been for years. I make due to keep a roof over my head. Ernestine I lost my home to Tommie. When he got older and started hanging out on them streets he started bringing anything and almost everything up in here against my wishes. I've had so many of Tommie's friends come and live here; they tear up things in here but never replaced them, they come hide here from the police, those thugs come in here to party with those hookers, baby it's been so much over the years that I can't remember them all. When I was working and come back home niggars be sitting up in here like they paid the rent. That boy is a part of me and if he wasn't I would have killed him my damn self. Like I said yesterday he's respectable but rowdy. He pay all the bills including shopping for groceries so when he started asking for a friend to stay here I gone on and say yes. Grammy was upset to hear the truth she got up from the couch and stared out the window. She said 'Auntie all these years you've been silently suffering from stress because of Tommie's ass why didn't you ever call me'? Cause I didn't want you to worry with my troubles. That boy ain't got nobody you hear me Ernestine nobody but me who tolerate his ass. I could never put him out though it nearly came close with Sheila's ass.

By this time, I jumped into their conversation saying yeah good ole Sheila with her hooker self. Both Grammy and Auntie's mouths dropped. I continued with what I had experienced with both Cousin Tommie and Sheila life styles. Grammy was mortified I think she fell into a slight coma for a second because she stood there staring at me for at least ten minutes without saying anything. Auntie said 'Ernestine don't fall apart now Sofay needs you'. It ain't nothing you can do to fix this cause it done already happened. You can't go back and make changes to what that gal done already witnessed and experienced. Grammy snapped out of her slight coma very slowly. She sat back down in dismays she couldn't believe nor comprehend how I survived what I've went through within those last two days. I said Grandma! She didn't answer I knew she was brewing something up. She said 'So-soo if I had of known any sort of this bullshit would have taken place we would have never came to New York'! She said 'baby it's ripping me apart that I wasn't here for you Sofay Camille Antoinette Gwen Faye Monee White. You mean the world to me and she existed to the bedroom. Auntie Rebecca looked at Grammy just like I looked at her as she walked back into the bedroom. When she said my full name I started folding up almost up underneath that couch. Because I knew she was about to explode. Auntie shouted out to her Ernestine no need to be angry that child is here breathing ain't she? Grammy said nothing even closed the bedroom door behind her. During, those moments of silence Becca and I just stared at one another until Baby T woke up crying. About thirty minutes later, Grammy came out the room freshly dressed with little make up on. She said 'Sofay go on in the back to bathe, and put some clothes on'. Once I returned into the living room Grammy was washing up little Kimberley in the kitchen sink and stomping roaches. Auntie Becca was coming out the other bedroom with the kid's clothes to put on then she proceeded to the bathroom to freshen up herself. My Grandma appeared to be her normal self but deep in my mind I knew she was up to something.

CHAPTER 22

Additionally, Becca came into the living room looking more settled after taking a nice hot bath. Grammy looked out the window and said 'ok everybody let's go'. Becca seemed amused but curious she got her cane and made her way downstairs while both Grammy and I held both kids. Upon reaching downstairs and to my surprise Mr. Smith was waiting on us in his big pretty black car. He hopped out his car smiling opened the car doors for us while pecking Grammy on the cheek and lips. He appeared to be gentlemen just like my Daddy he was very; suave, talkative, and polite. He started asking questions about what I told Grammy pertaining to Tommie and Sheila. Auntie Becca asked him what does, what happened to me had to do with him. Grammy jumped in and said 'because he's concerned Auntie and I wanted to hear from a man's point of view'. Initially Mr. Smith had a full day of activities for us. He took us to a restaurant to eat breakfast and it was exciting. The baby cried none stop drawing added attention from strangers while little Kimberley was having some type of shouting attack where; she out talked all of us causing Auntie to pinch her on the leg. Grammy can tolerate a lot but being embarrassed in public by a child is a no-no. She took Kimberley to the bathroom and probably spanked her though when they returned we didn't hear a peek from her. I could tell Mr. Smith was uncomfortable from the baby crying and Kimberley's loud outbursts because he started sweating and nearly chocked his self to deaf from consistently pulling on his tie. He probably wished he hadn't brought us out in public but I bet the next time he wants to impress a family he'll think twice.

Undoubtedly, the adult conversation took a turn reflecting on Auntie Becca's new place to live. This time it was Mr. Smith doing the talking. He suggested that Tommie needs to be in new surroundings with his family and that Becca needed to finally be on her own comfortably. He said 'I'm only suggesting that you make a move because those hustlers won't give up until all three of those boys are dead'. He said 'he knew of a small place a friend of his rents out'. It's a little ways from Harlem predominately white not as racist and quiet. He said 'it's comfortable you are near lots of water and it's a family oriented environment'. Grammy asked where is it and Mr. Smith said Lake Placid. Auntie shouted where you say lake who? Mr. Smith repeated his self he said 'we all will go up there once Tommie gets out the hospital to check it out'. Becca slowly said 'ok.' Grammy was delighted she felt she was breaking through to Auntie I mean who really wants to live in an apartment full of roaches that you practically got to shoot to kill and then there are the giant rats that look like a size eight shoe. It's unsettling knowing this but to have to actually experience this is alarming. Once we finished breakfast Grammy wanted to go see Tommie. So, off to the hospital we went. Upon reaching the receptionist we were surprised he was released from the hospital. Auntie had a smirk on her face over joyed knowing he was ok and at home. Although, I was ready to see Momma my Grammy wasn't ready to go back to Becca's instead Mr. Smith drove us to his place in Brooklyn. It surprised me that the three stories were entirely owned by him. He shared his place with his daughter and her kids. They lived on the first floor whereas, he had the second and third floors to himself and I must say he decorated the place like a palace. Unlike at Auntie Becca's old place in her building there were three separate families on each floor which was a little strange.

Moreover, I was impressed with Mr. Smith's neighborhood because it was cleaner with less people hanging out on their stoops.

Contrarily, we sat there a couple of hours while I, Lorraine, and Elizabeth were in their room just being kids. After running up and down the stairs playing Mr. Smith decided that we kids needed to blow off some steam then we all except for Mr. Smith's daughter Gail drove to Coney Island. We went to an amusement park where we had a ball. We kids got on rides ate junk food and were just being kids. Becca even got on a roller coaster ride with us and couldn't hang because the dives going down were too much for her heart she became dizzy afterwards. So Grammy made her sit down while she and Mr. Smith continued to walk around with us as we kids had the time of our lives.

CHAPTER 23

Nonetheless, we left there exhausted but somehow Grammy wasn't comfortable sleeping at Auntie Becca's. When we arrived back at Becca's Momma was in the window she saw us get out the car and met us downstairs.

In addition, when we all got upstairs Grammy pulled Momma and Becca to the side along with Mr. Smith. I don't know what was said but Momma packed all of our belongings. Auntie called Sheila into the living room and said something to her next thing I knew she was packing bags as well. I looked over at Tommie who was still smiling lying on the couch though his face was clear of blood but was covered with swelling in the eyes and many purple bruises all over him. He asked me to bring him his baby so I did. He and baby T baby talked while the ladies were moving around the apartment. I picked Kimberley up off the floor afraid a rat would chew her up. Mr. Smith held one Granddaughter while the other one sat in a chair next to me. We stayed at Becca's for a while as the ladies packed I was good and sleepy but stayed up to see what was going on.

Moreover, Mr. Smith looked outside then started smiling he walked to Grammy and whispered something to her then he went downstairs. Within a matter of minutes Mr. Smith along with five of his friends began moving Auntie's belonging into a moving truck. It wasn't much to move because they left the living room furniture and Tommie's bedroom set instead they took; Auntie's bedroom set, the dining room set, food, clothes, towels and several linen sets. Momma was teary eyed when I looked at her but I was too tired to ask what was wrong.

Ironically, Mr. Smith facilitated who was gone ride with whom on our way to his place. I saw three of Mr. Smith friends help Tommie down the stairs and after that my Momma had to carry me because I couldn't keep my eyes open I fell asleep.

Consequently, the next morning when I woke up I was lying next to my Mother on a couch bed. She and I woke up at the same time. I asked her where were we she said at Mr. Smith's flat. I shared with her everything while being with both Sheila and Tommie as well as my day with Grammy we laughed and Momma said 'Sofay from now on do not hold inside of me any horrific experiences but let somebody especially her and daddy know'. She kissed me than wrapped her arms around me placing her head on top of my head to say she was sorry that I experienced other people's life dramas. She said 'that my Daddy is going to have a fit when he hears all that I've gone through within those last two days in New York'. She said 'she was bracing herself cause ain't no telling what he'll do'. We laid there for a while just bonding my Momma and I.

After a while, Auntie Rebecca made her way to where we were lying saying how she will forever be Graceful with loved for Mr. Smith's hostility and unexpected help. She and Momma talked a bit before Grammy and Gail entered the room grinning. Momma rose up shouting silently Gail is that you? She said girl it's me and they hugged. Becca said 'wait a minute how yall know each other'? Grammy said 'Auntie I wondered why you grilled Harold yesterday when he came to pick me up you don't remember him'?' Becca said 'hell naw I don't remember him who is he'? Grammy said 'Auntie that's Rita's boy'! He and I went to school together and we dated off and on for years before I had Geraldine and got married. He would have been my husband had I not been chosen by Wilbert. Momma and Gail never stopped talking they were catching up with each other.

Whereas, Auntie Becca was still trying to remember who Harold Smith was. She was overwhelmed with all he had done for her. She told Grammy she started thinking that she was an undercover street woman. Grammy laughed and told Auntie she knew better to insult her like that.

Likewise, speaking of Mr. Harold Smith who happened to be standing in the door way smiling at Grammy said 'what are we going to do first today'? Gail said 'eat' and Momma agreed with her. The ladies decided to check on Tommie who was on the second floor with his family. Gail said 'she peeked in on them and saw Tommie sitting up holding his baby and little Kimberley'.

Nevertheless, Grammy, Auntie Becca, Lorraine and I remained on the first floor straightening up. I overheard Harold say to Grammy I don't know where to begin cleaning up behind everybody. His granddaughter, Lorraine was a huge help in knowing how and where to repute her Grandfather's belongings back to their original place. He was pleased that his first floor furniture was strategically placed back the way he had it.

Anyhow, as we all tried to make our way to the second floor to straighten up there the doorbell rang several times. Grammy stopped midway on the stairs to look at Mr. Smith. He immediately turned around running down the stairs not looking back at Grammy to answer the door. When I heard that voice saying excuse me sir I may have the wrong address but I'm in search of my family Ernestine Brown and Rebecca Howard. I whispered to Lorraine no it can't be who I think it is. I walked down several stairs moving my hair off my face to get closer as this gentleman continued talking. He said 'oh I'm J. W. White and this is my family'. I froze at first knowing it was an illusion I knew perfectly well it couldn't have been my dad because he was home in the country. As Mr. Smith swung open the door wide I swear before I knew it I jumped from that thirteenth step right into my father's arms. I heard Grammy scream out 'Sofay', Becca tried to grab me from falling but it was too late my Daddy caught me laughing. He and I hugged for the longest until I saw both Uncle A. J. and Floyd. I screamed out their names as loud as I could. My Daddy who was grinning but didn't put me down instead he walked over to his brothers while; they were kissing all over me, rubbing my hair, cheeks, and chin. I heard Momma running down the stairs saying Sofay! she knew by the sound of my voice something wasn't right. She came to a halt midway down the stairs completely stopping to cover her mouth and said 'J. W.' with tears in her eyes. Daddy putted me down I don't think I ever stopped holding onto both of my Uncles let alone my Dad. I tried my best to hold back those tears but couldn't

I tried to cover my face from crying until I heard someone say heeey Red. I looked and there was my heart standing right there grinning and laughing. I flipped out! And wiggled down from A. J's arms and started Jumping up and down screaming it was my Eisha. My goodness I leaped too her wrapping my legs around her. We both fell to the floor it was Auntie Antoinette who tried to pick us up with tears in her eyes. Antoinette couldn't pick us up so she bended down holding onto both me and Eisha. I looked up seeing Momma and Daddy gazing into each other's eyes then kissing. Grammy was hugging Floyd and A. J. while Auntie Rebecca had teared up and had to be helped down the stairs by Gail. Once she was on the main floor she tapped daddy on his shoulders and stepped backward while pushing herself to do a two-step dance walking towards my father grinning but saying 'boy, boy, boy my boy! What you say! Daddy instantly laughed and grabbed Becca's hand as both of them hugged one another for the longest. Those two rocked back and forth and Auntie told him it's good seeing you baby after all these years. Grammy started introducing everybody. Gail helped me, Eisha and Antoinette off the floor. We all made our way into the living room with me, Eisha and Antoinette still hugging one another walking I guess you could say we kinda looked like the three stooges attached to each other's hips. Mr. Smith was stunned for some reason he kept scratching his head frowning looking at my father then finally he said 'say man I got a question'. I'm trying to figure out how you know me. Uncle A.J. made his way into the living room after using the bathroom. He told Mr. Smith mane you got a beautiful home here. He told him thanks man. Daddy said 'Harold mane we drove up here and went directly to Rebecca's place'. We got there knocking on the door and there was no answer so we went to your neighbor Mrs. Buckner's and she told us she saw yall moving last night with a bunch of men. She didn't know where yall went but said her husband knew of you Harold. Auntie Becca said 'to Daddy who you say'? Did you say Buckner? Daddy said 'yes Mamm'. She said 'yeah that skunk is the neighborhood watch dog that don't let anything get pass her'. She's nosey as all get up and go. Antoinette laughed and said 'at first we had to wait for her husband to get home'. She then asked us was we here to help out with Tommie. Floyd said to her 'Mamm we just here for our Aunt Rebecca Howard and if you got any information to help us find her we would appreciate it'. Once I said 'Aunt' she said 'why didn't you say that in the first place that you are related to Rebecca'. She was the one that told us the area but wasn't sure of your exact address. We then went to cousin Jr. (short for junior) place to crash until now. We trailed him over here to your area. Momma said 'oh my goodness I've forgotten that Jr. lives here. How is he doing J. W.? Daddy told her he's good then interrupted Floyd by saying we started from the corner ringing bells until we got to the second house across the street. They were the ones that said to go down about six flats over across the street and thank God it was you that opened your door. My Daddy never took his arms from around Momma. He called me over to him and had me stand in front of him for the longest as he admired his seed. Daddy said smiling 'my you have grown So-soo and look at her hair'. I blushed flipping my hair off my face. My father patted his leg which meant for me to sit on it. He bear hugged me from my back with kisses all over my head. I just melted in my father's arms and did well by holding back tears that were forming in the corners of my eyes. Auntie Becca said to Daddy 'J. W. what brings you this way good lawd with cha fine self'. Grammy shouted to Becca behave yourself. Becca looked at my Aunts then my Uncles and said 'yall some fine ass kids boy J. W. if I was forty years younger'. Grammy said 'and you'll still be to old now go and sit down somewhere' we all laughed but Grammy was getting heated for some strange reason I don't know if it was from Becca lusting after Daddy or was it from the fact that my favorite Aunt was two seats away from me.

Anyhow, Gail suggested we all go out to eat because it was too many people to cook breakfast for. Me and Eisha locked eyes smirking at one another we knew from Gail's statement that she couldn't cook. Grammy caught us and I'm almost sure that she rolled her eyes at Eisha. I almost shouted stop it Grammy I saw you. But in all the excitement I literally had forgotten about Cousin Tommie and his family until Sheila came down into the living room. Floyd rose up and introduced his self and Becca hurried up to say everybody this is Sheila, Tommie's lady. Daddy said 'Tommie'! Momma said 'yeah he's upstairs'. Grammy said 'yes J. W. Tommie's upstairs but it's an entirely long story about what's happened as to why we are all here in Harold's place'. Uncle A. J. asked Grammy did Tommie's mishap have anything to do with her leaving Becca's so abruptly. She said 'not really but kind of' then A. J. rose from his seat and went near Grammy and they immediately started conversing along with Mr. Smith. My goodness it seemed like everyone was speaking at the same time. Gail asked Antoinette how long was the ride and what part of Oklahoma she's from. Sheila asked Floyd how were we all related and what brought them to New York. I looked over at Auntie Becca who never stopped flirting with Daddy she kept winking her eye at him. My father got a kick out of her he just laughed at her saying Becca you too much while still holding on to both Momma and me. Daddy said 'to Momma and I Geraldine I missed you and So-soo, sooooo much this past week and a half'! Eisha scooted her chair next to Daddy saying yeah Geraldine, J. W. has been so pitiful without yall around the house these past days he's worked everybody nerves and probably worked the animals as well. Momma laughed and asked Daddy, J. W. how did you know we were in New York? He said 'well I couldn't take it any more with my wife and baby not at home with me so I went to your Mother's house'. When I opened the screen door I saw and read the note she left. At first my heart fell because you didn't tell me you were coming here then I remembered we agreed that you would spend two nights at Ernestine's and So-soo would spend the summer'. When I made it back to the farm Momma saw my face and dropped what she was doing to ask me what happened at Ernestine's place. I couldn't muster up to say yall were in New York. Momma tried to sit me on her lap for God's sake and wanted to know why I was so sad. I busted up laughing trying to visualize that scene with Gramz's holding daddy on her lap. Daddy continued on and said 'I told her where yall was at and it was Gramz's that said 'yall got to be visiting Rebecca. So I was coming with Floyd.

We was gone fly together until Eisha got to acting a complete fool having tantrums into coming with us to see Sofay'. I turned to my Auntie Eisha and kissed her on the cheek then scooted over onto her lap. He went on to say that everybody wanted to come including my Grandparents. Tears started forming in my eyes once again when I heard my grandparents wanted to come see me and Momma. Daddy told Momma he thought he could live without us being on the farm. He admitted he couldn't. He had; sleepless nights, hardly ate, lost weight and sat many times throughout the day just staring at our family picture and wondered what she and I were doing. He said 'the first night he nearly walked to Grammy's house to come get us though he remembered that he promised Momma he would only visit and not act a fool when it was time to leave'. I waited for Momma to tell Daddy how she was missing him as well but she didn't part her mouth. I said to myself hum. Growing up all I knew from my family was love. We were a different type of family who practically did everything together with very few outsiders included. We were a family that; hugged each other, we kissed each other on the cheeks, we congratulated each other, we threw parties for each other, we worked together on the farm, we had each other's back no matter who was at fault, we didn't make anyone feel left out of a conversation no matter how silly they sounded, and we encouraged each other. The flip side of my family is that some were evil, revengeful, vindictive, and downright heartless but what can I say there's always several in the family who make it bad for everyone else.

CHAPTER 24

I on the other hand, I have seen and personally witnessed both sides of good versus evil and I have to say that I choose good at all times.

Any hoot, Daddy continued on to say that just three days ago he felt something in his Spirit that something wasn't right. He woke up in sweat then prayed that Momma and I were ok. Mommy and I looked at one another. She said 'baby you won't believe what's happened within the last three days I don't know where to start but first I want you to go say hey to Tommie'. As Daddy, Momma, Floyd, Gail, Sheila and Antoinette made their way upstairs Uncle Floyd stopped in the foyer and was in awh with the wood work. He literally bent down to touch the wood paneling and admires how it was placed on the floor. He studied the wood floors and even the banisher that went up all three floors. Next thing I knew Uncle Floyd turned back around to join in the conversation with Grammy. Some kind of way he and Mr. Harold Smith were in a deep conversation about the structure of his home.

Additionally, Lorraine came to sit next to me and Eisha to listen. Her sister Elizabeth finally woke up and came near us as well. I just couldn't get over the fact that my flesh and blood was right there with me, Daddy and his siblings. Eisha said 'Red you only been gone for a couple of days and the whole house was a wreck'. Gramz's kept calling your name especially when I cleaned the kitchen one night and poured out her moonshine she went outside looking for you. We laughed and I realized at that moment my family missed me more than I missed them. Auntie Eisha stood up to stretch her legs and I looked at her up and down then said 'dang Eisha your butte done got bigger'. She said 'Red stop it' while smiling. She then reached down to put my hair into a pony tail using her fingers as she admired the length she said "Red your hair has grown'.

Meanwhile, Auntie Becca who never left her seat said 'to Eisha 'little bit what's your name again'? She told her Eisha. Then Becca said 'goodness child you shaped just like your Mother'. My goodness Olivia had a shape like you which was rare back in those days; yeah she and I go way back. You be sure to tell her I said hello. Eisha didn't know what to say but did say to Becca why haven't you ever come down to visit us? Becca said 'she's visited Grammy over the years but got comfortable living in her own world in Harlem'. When her relatives started passing on she didn't have the passion or desire to travel anywhere. I glanced over in the corner where Grammy, A. J., Floyd and Mr. Smith were and I swear that I saw Mr. Smith quickly check out Eisha's body. I said to myself 'uh-oh' then I pulled Auntie Eisha to sit back down because I didn't want Harold Smith to continue looking at her butte. Lorraine was admiring Eisha and said 'Eisha I wish you were my Auntie'. She laughed then said 'ok I will be your pretend auntie but nobody can take my So-soo's place'. Just then, Daddy yelled downstairs for Floyd, A. J. and Eisha to come upstairs to meet Tommie. It was funny to watch Mr. Smith as he damn near broke his neck to show them how to get upstairs. Thank goodness Auntie Becca said 'Harold, Harold what you doing they don't need a tour guide let both Lorraine and Elizabeth take them upstairs'. I didn't have the heart to look back at Grammy. I can only imagine the snares that she was giving Eisha. We proceeded upstairs and I'll be damn if Tommie didn't rise up staring at Eisha. He said 'man tell me that's not the baby'. Floyd took him serious and put his arm around Eisha's neck to say yeah man this is our baby sis. Tommie said 'let me rephrased that to say nice to meet you Eisha'. She said 'yes and the same to you'. Then she grabbed my hand as I looked to my left to see Sheila who was shyly checking out Floyd. Oh brother I can feel some source of sex rundavoo taking place real soon I just didn't know when or where it would happen but I predict real soon.

Moreover, it was midday and I hadn't ate so I told Daddy that I was hungry and wouldn't you know it Tommie suddenly became hungry and out of nowhere he had enough energy to slowly get out of bed by himself. Daddy suggested that Momma and I gathered our belongings because we were going to a hotel. Tommie's eyes grew larger for some odd reason and he suggested to Sheila to do the same thing because where Momma was going he was going. Daddy said 'then it's settled we all are going to a decent hotel to rest tonight and tomorrow we will head to Lake Placid'. Momma's facial expressions started looking normal again more like a relief that the pressure was taken off of her once Daddy and them had arrived. We all headed back downstairs to tell Grammy the new sleeping arrangements. She was hesitating at first because she didn't know if Daddy wanted to include Auntie Becca and the rest of them. Daddy went on to thank Mr. Smith for his hospitality and even offered to pay for any expenses that were used to move Becca's things into a moving truck last night. Mr. Smith refused to accept any money from Daddy but suggested he wanted to help move her into her new place since it belonged to a friend of his. Floyd said 'yeah mane we not trying to take over but any friend of Ernestine is a friend of ours and is welcome into our family'. Like my big brother said mane we appreciate everything you've done on such a short notice mane. We are ever so grateful to you in fact why don't you and your family come with us to lunch. Mr. Smith stood there patting his heart quite pleased and shaking Floyd's hand. He said 'man the feeling is mutual how bout after lunch we go shoot some pool'. A. J. said 'sounds like a plan because I do want to sight see some of New York while we are here'. Auntie Antoinette ended up contacting cousin Jr. (short for junior) because we needed another car. She told him the itinerary and to be prepared to stay with us over the next two days. It took him about an hour or so to get to Brooklyn from Queens which worked out fine for all of us because we had extra time to finish straightening up all three floors and take baths to freshen up. Me and Momma shared the bathroom getting ready while Daddy, Antoinette, and Eisha were either standing outside the door or inside the bathroom with us justa talking. My family guarded me like I was some type of royalty. We all pretty much finished getting refreshed and dressed about the same time which was perfect timing because that's when cousin Jr. showed up. Once he entered Mr. Smith's home he instantly locked eyes with Sheila making me and Eisha elbow each other in the arms.

Everyone was introduced to Jr. and Auntie Becca was nearly slobbing at the mouth with Jr. looks. As funny as Becca was I wondered was she serious with all the compliments she was giving the men. It was funny enough that she was smiling and winking at Daddy but with Jr. She literally pinched his butte making him jump with buck eyes.

However, my Cousin Jr. was an unusual looking fellow. He resembled a lion to me because of his medium light skin tone and missing vampire teeth on both sides of his mouth. He had hazel colored eyes, a medium curly brown fro and a hook nose where his nose looked like it was separated from his nostrils. He was five ten in height and largely built. Jr. was a funny guy with his jokes. He was more of a moderator when it came to disputes between people. He always felt his two cents would make a difference in settling any argument. He would quotes verses from the bible if not cuss somebody out. He too had a fetish for women just like his cousins. I would try to listen to a relative as they read letters out loud that Jr. sent back home. I knew those letters were good and juicy because Jr. was always explicit describing every detail in how he scored with a woman. The men on the porch would be screaming with laughter almost like a cheering match with them agreeing in how well of a player Jr was. He relocated to New York after meeting his then girlfriend Susie whom he met in Oklahoma City while out there hanging with friends. She was visiting relatives and bumped into Jr. at the shopping mall. From that point on he and the girl established a long distant relationship for maybe six months or so before he decided to move out there to be with her. Once he got out there in New York he went buck wild and ended up losing his lady friend because he couldn't keep his pants zipped and after their relationship ended he decided to remain here in New York instead of moving back home.

CHAPTER 25

Moreover, we all started loading up into the three cars with my parents, me, Eisha and Antoinette in one car. The other car had Mr. Smith with his family and Grammy including Becca plus little Kimberley and the third car had Jr., Floyd, A. J., Tommie and his family. We trailed each other to the waffle house and we worked the hell out that waitress. I bet after that day that woman ran whenever she saw a group of blacks because with us she; huffed and puffed, sweated out her hair bun, couldn't get our orders right, had one shoe on with the other one off. Bad enough Sheila was either uncomfortable or that was her first time in a restaurant. Her whispers to Tommie were loud and rude with her saying some shit like uh huh bout time I see a white girl working and sweating out her fucking hair. Grammy caught wind of Sheila's remarks and jokingly said to her 'now Sheila do I have to take you into the bathroom Missy'. Causing majority of us to look in Sheila's direction. Eisha thought maybe those two knew one another by Sheila's childess remarks.

Surprisingly enough, Sheila didn't give a damn nor had any respect for this waitress. She found everything to complain about which drew more interest from Floyd his eyes were locked on her. Before I knew it I said 'at least she ain't the one boosting like you'. Auntie Becca shouted out 'got damn'! Tommie cheeks turned red and he whispered something into Sheila's ear that made his head shake side to side as he spoke to her. Momma said 'Sofay be quiet and stay in your place'. I looked at my father for validation but I knew to do what Momma said.

Nevertheless, Uncle Floyd made me laugh he was so intrigue with Sheila's words that he kept missing his mouth trying to drink his coffee. Auntie Antoinette grabbed my arm to say 'she's a booster'? After Cousin Tommie damn near flipped the table over speaking to Sheila she became more perturbed and excused herself from the table still mumbling something under her breath. The men watched her as she left the table and so was I. Truthfully speaking, I was trying to figure out why Uncle Floyd and Cousin Jr. were lusting over Sheila. I was not impressed with her looks I guess she was ugly to me because of how I tagged along with her that night while she boosted clothes. But really, she was an attractive woman a size twelve with a medium size brown afro and a pretty face. Her shape was in proportion with her weight. She dressed very sharp but then again she should have dressed well because she didn't spend a dime on clothes with her thieving ass. She had dark skin and black eyes. She spoke using slang words more ghetto fab. She seemed to be in competition with women by scanning them up and down as she passed by them. Sheila wasn't friendly at all and I saw that first hand at the hair parlor that night. Those women were smiling at her and she didn't return a smile or any type of greetings nor did she established any forms of conversation with any of them it was strictly business…weird! Before I knew it I rolled my eyes at her then whispered to Eisha I bet if you stand up ole Harold Smith will lock his eyes on you. Eisha laughed and said 'ok bet Red'. Everyone was in a deep conversation by the end of breakfast deciding what we were going to do next. Everyone was definitely full and nearly sleepy except Momma who kept eyeing these ladies that were drooling over Daddy and his brothers. I must say that the White men are definitely easy on the eye and women back home always gave Momma a hard time with all of that flirting they did towards my Father. The difference between here and Oklahoma is that the women here are less bold and raunchier. Though it was obvious they could care less that Daddy had a woman on his arm. What I adored about Becca is that she was a straight forward lady with honesty. She was a bit sarcastic to a point that some would say she was rude but she meant well I think. Auntie Becca said to Momma 'girl you better eat sitting up here frowning up at these skunks hell you got him what you worried for'. Momma said nothing but glazed at her coffee. I saw Antoinette nudge Eisha. Then I got to wondering why she and I were away from him all of those days. Anyway, I whispered to Eisha did she know what was going on with my parents. She said 'they are good but Momma was tired of the farm life and needed a break to get her head straight'. I looked at Momma's plate and noticed that she barely ate anything. I said 'Mommie why you ain't eating your food'? She said 'baby I'm fine this coffee is filling me up'. Daddy responded to Momma saying 'you sho is fine'. She smirked which was a sign that she was pulling through whatever it was that was weighing her down. My father reached over to kiss my Mother's cheek which put a smile on my face because I loved seeing them smooching on one another. I cut a piece of my sausage and asked momma to taste it because it was sweet. She did and ended up ordering two additional sausages with fresh scrambled eggs and toast for herself. My father winked his eye at me followed by an invisible kiss. I kinda knew where my parents were headed which was an argument and I didn't want them two to spoil breakfast for everybody so that's why I gave her a piece of sausage and besides, I heard her damn stomach growling over by me she was hungry as hell talking bout that coffee was filling her up.

However, my stomach was rumbling I had two glasses of chocolate milk plus that rich food which didn't agree with me. I had to be excused to the rest room and Eisha went with me. She and I die laughing at ole Harold Smith who tried to pretend he was blowing his nose but instead was eyeing Eisha's butte. She started switching that big ole butte and when I looked back he was stretching his arms behind Grammy's back peeking at her walk. As she and I walked to the rest room I had a flash back I said 'Eisha I've been thinking and please don't turn Mr. Smith into Mr. Johnson, Grammy would die'. She said 'ole Sofay I'm good as long as he doesn't make a move on me'. I said 'Eisha you know Daddy and them would kill him over you and besides, I like him he's been nothing but nice to all of us and keep in mind that's Grammy's boyfriend'. My Auntie just looked at the floor then said 'Red let me be honest with you your Grammy don't like me let alone your Daddy'. I knew she was telling the truth so I told her 'yeah I know she don't like you I just noticed that even more today when yall arrived in fact, I noticed her frowning at you at the celebration several weeks back'. Eisha said 'yeah I didn't like how she grabbed you then covered you up from seeing any of us'. She's always been jealous of our relationship So-soo. It pissed me off as I was walking towards yall and the next thing I saw; were you getting into her car. I was yelling to Ernestine where was she taking you and why but I was drowned out with all the ruggage that went on with Karrie. So-soo I don't know if you knew but Karrie didn't make it she died from a heart attack. I stood there stunt in disbelief. I had nearly forgotten about that day at the farm. I thought wow Auntie Nitta's spell really worked. I said 'E I got to tell you something about Nitta'. My thoughts quickly shifted on Karrie. I thought about her family and how Uncle Floyd felt about her death. I didn't expect to hear that type of sad news however; I couldn't hold my bowels and ran into the stale in the front. Eisha stood outside the door saying don't sit on the toilet without putting tissue on it. I sat there hurt really wondering if a spell could hurt people like that. Suddenly, I fell out that tranced and started hearing this weird noise. It sounded like someone scrapping the walls using their shoes followed by a howling sound. I whispered Eisha! Apparently she heard that sound also and said softly 'Sofay hurry up'. I said 'E did you hear that'? I couldn't pull my clothes up fast enough Eisha rushed me to wash my hands so she and I could get out of dodge. The sound changed as we reached the door Eisha stopped looked at me then decided we should go see what that sound was.

I on the other hand, didn't want to know which was a switch for me because I usually didn't miss out on anything. I nearly graved for drama because no two days were the same as yesterday, the drama made the day go by faster.

Likewise, as she and I tip toed towards the very back of the rest room to be nosey and what did we discover Lord and behold we were not prepared to see Uncle Floyd and Sheila in that stale getting it on. I didn't know which one was making the moaning sounds him or her. I gathered that one of the sounds were from Sheila's one shoe that was scrubbing against the wall. Eisha and I grasped for air covering our mouths in shock she and I playfully slapped each other's arms silently laughing. We started backing up walking back wards towards the bathroom's door. When we got outside that door we screamed with laughter I mean who knew! Sheila's facial expressions were like she was in pain. I mean it was a sight that I didn't need to see. The next thing we heard was Sheila screaming for dear life. Eisha told me to wait in the spot I was standing in while she went back into the bathroom. She came back out holding her stomach laughing saying she just had an orgasm. You know I know that word orgasm hell I didn't know there were levels with this thing. I said 'E what did you say to them'? She said 'she pound on the bathroom door saying Floyd, Floyd they gone call the fuzz on you'. I really tried not laugh but I did manage to say oh my goodness they're in a stale in the waffle house'. Eisha said 'I know' she said So-soo we gone go back to join everybody without saying a word'. She said 'promise me you won't say anything ok'! I said 'what'! and keep this from Momma?

Eventually, I gave in and agreed to not mention what we just witnessed in the stale to anyone. When we returned back to the tables everyone was ready to leave asking if either of us saw Sheila. Eisha said 'no she wasn't in the rest room at least I didn't see her there is what she said to Grammy' and I said 'unless she was in the back'. Eisha pulled me by the arm I was trying to keep my composure.

However, I know I was a nosey kid but inquisitive. I was raised around adults who had experienced just about everything and on most levels of life. I guess you can say I learned early on that's what's done in the dark shall come to light. I do agree with my grandmother Grammy because little does she know is I started smelling sex as early as five years old. I've seen; helpless bodies lying on the ground and heard shot fired from rifles to a nine millimeter gun. I've listened as members of my family covered up potential crimes by Uncle A. J., and even heard bodily crimes being plotted by some of my Uncles. It amazes my Father how many have suspected that country boys don't have stamina nor sense if only they knew what I've heard and seen all my life while living in the country.

Meanwhile, we started loading up into the cars and Daddy said to Grammy 'I didn't notice Floyd left the table'. Just within that moment Floyd appeared from out of nowhere pimp walking. I busted up laughing knowing very well he was just inside of Sheila's stank ass.

Eisha grabbed my hand smirking and saying come on Red lets go to the car. When I looked back at Daddy and Uncle Floyd they were doing that brotherly hand shake laughing. We all gathered into our cars headed to tour Brooklyn. We went to the popular historic spots only to be bored. Both Auntie Eisha and Antoinette wanted more excitement in a tour so Daddy flagged down Jr.'s car to ask where is some sight-seeing that's out of this world. He smiled and said 'the subway' then laughed but said 'A. J. wanted to check out Time Square'. Auntie Becca hurried up and said 'she didn't agree that it was a good idea for us kids to go there considering the high overturn in crime and pornos' so instead of walking on the strip we just cruised through during probably five miles a minute. In our car we all were Luke warm to see Time square I mean the atmosphere; was lust, the streets appeared dark, rough, and grimy looking. Quite uncleaned and over shadowed with signs for; peep shows, sex shops, porn, paraphernalia shops, theater joints, pizza joints, and including ladies of the night who resembled the ladies inside of LaGuardia airport. I was in awh whereas, Auntie Antoinette was disappointed with Time square's appearance. She said 'it wasn't what she had expected it to be; she thought it would have been more on the glamourous side'. Daddy's demeanor was hard to describe I couldn't tell if he was disgusted, irritated or just excited to see all those sex billboards. He did say that Time Square is not a place for kids. Just as Momma was about to say something Cousin Jr.'s car pulled over to the side of the street and wouldn't you know it Uncle Floyd and A. J. got out the car to walk directly towards the peep show window looking inside of it. I nudged Eisha smirking when I saw that. Harold also got out the car and walked towards us saying why we don't go to Rockefeller Center for a tour inside of the Radio City music hall. Jr. said 'that he's hung out on occasions in Time Square but he didn't remember it looking that bad' or maybe it was because he was drunk'. Antoinette said 'well shit you were real drunk not to remember this place Jr.'! My parents agreed to Harold's suggestions and suddenly we heard Auntie Becca saying yall boys get back in the car now you'll get a chance to come back out for some trim. Both my parents laughed. Auntie Antoinette said 'I'm getting sick of Becca's freaky ass'. I mean what man in this family has she not made a pass at'? Momma hurried up to speak up on Becca's behalf by saying my Aunt is just an old lady who gets her jollies out of complimenting others. Their's nothing wrong with her she's got good sense with hell of wisdom. She just loves an attractive man that's all. Maybe she's horny but she knows perfectly well it's not natural but revengeful to sleep with a family member's better half. Daddy was looking through the rear view mirror at Antoinette waiting for a response back she didn't say anything else.

Meanwhile, Eisha and I was snickering because Floyd apparently didn't get the memo about sleeping within the family because he just screwed Sheila in the restaurant's Bathroom and he knew she was Tommie's lady but then again the Whites aren't related to Momma's other side of the family. I told Eisha that adults sure can be confusing at times by judging someone else opinions instead of looking and owning up to their own faults. People really just need to be quiet sometimes and stop blaming others for their own selfish misery. And at this point I was ready to go lay down somewhere I couldn't stop yawning it seemed everywhere we drove had distance between each location if not an hour to get to A from B's location. For one I was still semi full from breakfast and was bored with all of this driving.

Additionally, we made it to Radio City music hall. We didn't expect elegant I guess because of the way Time Square looked. This building was magnificent with beautiful wall designs which caught Auntie Eisha's undivided attention. She was mesmerized with; the trickers of lines, the incredible designs with beautiful multi-colors. She studied the gigantic murals of designs; how it was painted she said 'each design told a story which was interesting for me to learn'. Eisha was hypnotized with the ceiling designs if anybody enjoyed themselves it was Eisha because she started asking; the workers the names of the Artists who implemented such beauty, she asked about the history and the creative designs of those outstanding sculptors. All along Grammy was standing a few feet away from Auntie Eisha impressed with her interest in the Arts. She walked over to Eisha to say how she never knew that she had interest in Arts. Eisha went on to explain that she use to draw and paint in school and grew fond in studying many artists, painters and Designers in the field. That explains why she fell into a moment of enthusiastic artistry. She was in her element and went on to explain in details the magnitude of how art releases and relaxes her into a comfort zone. Momma was happy to see her Mother and sister-n-law bond it was a long time coming.

Meanwhile, as excited as I was for my Auntie's dream I was ready to go. I happened to look over on the other side to see Auntie Becca's arm inside of Cousin Jr.'s arm. She was justa laughing and putting her head on his shoulders as they walked. I refused to even attempt to look over at Antoinette I just imagine what her facial expression looked like. Shortly after, Jr. asked Momma what was the sleeping arrangements because he and the fellows were going to shoot pool and Harold suggested we could go back to his place for the night. He insisted it didn't make sense to travel back from his place to Time Square just to shoot pool when there was a pool hall in his neighborhood. Momma asked Daddy what he wanted to do. He turns around and asked his brothers what they wanted to do. To no surprise Uncle A. J. said 'let's stay in the area since we are here and find a decent hotel for tonight and prepare ourselves to move Becca and Tommie into their new place in the morning'. Grammy said 'that sounded good and invited Harold and Gail to stay the night as well'. She then said 'she spotted a decent looking hotel in passing she thought it was called the Sheraton or something'. She was right and the hotel wasn't far. My parents, Grammy and Mr. Smith rented three Suites that had refrigerators in both. This was our first time in a hotel especially us kids we were excited. I was fascinated; to see families there with luggage's, I was tickled pink with the elegance of the lobby, the staff was courteous, and the fact they had a swimming pool blew my mind. I was in Heaven for sure somehow or another Sheila appeared to be distance but focused on Uncle Floyd's every move. He was no better trying to pretend she didn't exist which was weird to me and drew added attention from Auntie Antoinette. She was trying to connect the puzzle with both Floyd and Sheila causing her to pull Floyd to the side of the lobby asking him questions. Auntie Eisha didn't make it any better by telling Antoinette what we saw in the bathroom Auntie Antoinette was pissed off after speaking with Uncle Floyd she then approached me pushing me to the side while everyone else was heading up to the rooms. She said 'Sofay, Eisha told me what yall saw in the bathroom earlier today'. I want you to keep your mouth closed and know that what those two were doing is what grown people do'. I said 'I know Auntie' and hear I go being grown by saying I bet yall didn't know that Sheila is a lady of the night and she was stolen from her pimp that beat Tommie along with his friends that night I was with them. Cousin Tommie really doesn't like her. She said 'what'! I told her briefly about the boosting; the stealing, the taxi driver, and how Sheila doesn't take care of her children. Auntie's mouth was wide open she looked up and around I guess for Sheila. She said 'this shit is unbelievable but she appears to love her children Red'. I shrugged my shoulders saying well that's what Auntie Rebecca said about her. Becca came over to tell us the room numbers. I said to myself I guess Auntie Nitta wasn't the only one who couldn't hold a secret hell I was no better at keeping quiet my damn self. In reality, my family exposed me to so much so often that I felt I was grown like them. Eisha came near us to see what the hold was up and of course Antoinette was filling her in on what she heard. Eisha said 'she briefly overheard Momma telling Daddy about what I had endured with both Tommie and Sheila'. Auntie Antoinette was fuming with disgust. She asked was I ever going to tell them. I said 'yes I was when I got back home'. Both Aunties looked relieved because they had mistakenly thought Momma told me to stay quiet and do not share what I went through with Tommie or Sheila. Those two Aunties of mine were mistakenly assuming before asking. What's the old saying that says never assume anything without asking or you'll make an ass out yourself.

In any event, we headed to our rooms and prior to getting inside the rooms if anyone had walked passed them they would have thought it was some sort of party going on. Anyone could have heard an entire conversation if they stood near any of the three suites because everyone was out talking the next person. I realized then how loud and rowdy my own family was. The suites were huge and glamorous with my family including my uncles, aunties and cousin Jr. in one and Grammy with her crew in the other suite across from ours then there was Mr. Smith with his family. The suites were like replicas of a mini two bedroom house that included a living room, model floor television, mini kitchen, two bathrooms, and pull out couches. The view was good from up top until you actual stepped foot on the outside then the atmosphere changed. Auntie Antoinette was pleased as well as everyone else. At first, she was under the impression that the suite would have been a replica of Times Square's darkness and grim but thankfully it wasn't.

CHAPTER 26

Moreover, the men were preparing themselves for a night on the town. Grammy held them up a bit while she, Momma, daddy, Gail, Jr. and Mr. Smith went shopping for changing clothes for themselves. Grammy didn't want her man out with the fellows being musty or sweaty. Once they left my Aunties and I went into a bedroom and chatted up a storm. They pretty much grilled me on everything that I witnessed and had gone through. My Aunts were flabbergasted in knowing that Tommie had anger issues especially in how he treated Sheila by making a difference with her kids. Auntie Eisha had gotten so worked up from my ordeal that she went to tell A. J. in the next room. I wasn't surprise to roll over in the bed to see both my Uncles standing there in the door way looking at me along with Eisha. Both of them came at me like road runner I could barely keep up with the questions. The next thing I knew A. J. went across the hall to get Cousin Tommie to question him. Goodness gracious that poor man was either petrified or pissed off that I told my family how he got banged up by those gangsters. After giving my Uncles his depict version on his beat down by those thugs do you know this bastard had the nerves to give me an evil look.

Actually, I wasn't worried about Tommie's attitude because truthfully speaking he was in no shape nor form to even snap a green bean. Hell Auntie Eisha could have boxed with him with one arm and he had the nerves to give me a snare look. I nearly asked A. J. did he see Tommie's face when he looked at me but I didn't want A. J. to act up and jump on him. Even though, Auntie Antoinette caught Tommie eyeing me and said 'what cha looking at her like that for' he said 'huh'! Naw I got something in my eye'. I looked at Antoinette and she smiled and whispered that's why Floyd screwed your lady then she snickered which made me laugh as well.

However, I was glad to see Tommie drag his ass out our room and into his room across the hall I instantly drew a line between us even though I know it wasn't right. Tommie was family on Momma's side who just got caught up at the wrong time and became a hoodlum of the street life. Moments later I had a sudden change of heart against Tommie and decided to go to Uncle Floyd and mentioned that I forgot to tell him Sheila was a lady of the knight. I whined to Floyd saying Uncle I think Sheila is bad people. He stopped putting his shirt on and turned to me saying Sofay I gathered you went through a lot baby and I'm sorry. But I need for you to think about what you left out regarding Sheila and tell me. I tried not to laugh with my conniving little self. I really didn't want him with that hooker at all. As I talked Floyd was stiff as a board I then realized he was not only digging her but he was probably stuck on her pudgy-pie. I didn't get him. He knew she was a prostitute who boost for a living. She lived; with one of her baby's father's, she couldn't cook, and she appeared to be unhappy. I guessed her background of being unfortunate did the opposite of what I was trying to do instead of trying to move him away from her he seemed to be turned on going for her. Just then Eisha came into the room to hear the end part of our conversation then she said 'that my Dad mentioned there was something about Sheila that he couldn't pin point'. I said 'yeah he couldn't pin point that up underneath those culottes she was looser than a snake'. We laughed except Uncle Floyd. From his looks he was more infatuated with Sheila despite the fact she was Tommie's girl. He started smiling and singing in a low tone Miss Sheila causing me and Eisha to laugh out even louder. I told Eisha I thought I was deterring Floyd away from Sheila's nasty ass but from the looks of it he's generated a whole new set of lustful ideas that triggered his male hood to turn into radar for her cat. Suddenly I remembered poor Karrie. That sadden me to hear she's no longer with us but I was curious in knowing who all cried at her funeral. Eisha said 'her home going was not too sad because her family insisted that her life was a celebration. They asked everyone to try to prevent any negative distraction of crying because they had cried enough. I said 'what in the road runner request that was'! Eisha said 'that some families have their own way in burying their love ones' though Gramz's said 'she had never been to a funeral that asked such a request to not cry'. She said 'Floyd was good at the funeral he shed a tear but couldn't get pass the fact that he didn't make up with her; that waded him down for days. I always characterized him as po Floyd because he could never find the right woman. He was a hopeless romantic who was; a magnet to whores, immature ladies, ignorance, raunchy women and the list goes on. Momma always shook her head in the presence of Floyd introducing his new lady to the family. Just then, the mood changed when A. J. came out the bathroom he was full of life with his crazy ass. He popped his fingers singing and slow dancing to the music then he and Floyd started their brotherly talking about where and what shop they were going first in Time Square. Both of my Uncles were lookers very easy on the eyes. They could have passed for twins except Floyd was more muscular than A. J. Both of them had split personalities causing Gramz's to always lecture them with prayers. Uncle A. J. was more suave with wearing his shirts unbutton nearly to his navel. He always wanted to give the ladies a peek of his hairy chest and his great pearly white teeth.

Whereas, Uncle Floyd loved shopping and looking great mainly for the ladies. He always coordinated his clothes to match his shoes. Both Uncles had light brown eyes. They both worked in the field along with the other brothers but in truth they all were different in their own special way. Floyd was more business savvy in learning how to build furniture. He learned that so he didn't have to spend so much money on furniture for his new place which he also had intention to build.

On the other hand, A.J. was more of a con artist who didn't take losing to well. He was always betting in dice games or playing the numbers. Whenever, he lost he still took the winning causing innocent people to suffer because of him being a sore loser.

Consequently, Auntie Antoinette joined us in the living room with a menu of food. She was astonished that we could order food in our rooms; we all were amazed. Keep in mind we were from the County and being in New York was an all-time high for all of us because we never had this vast array of excitement nor crime except for Momma and Grammy who was born and practically raised in New York before moving and residing in the South. Our life style was limited but simple compared to the New Yorkers. What I saw in those two days would have taken years in the Country just to lift and manifest off the ground.

Meanwhile, Antoinette was excited to read out the menu and said 'get this we can charge it to the suite'! Minutes later surprisingly, guest services knocked at the door to ask if we needed towels or anything. The lady was black and rather attractive which triggered A. J. to make a move on her. Before she left the room she reminded us that the fruit bowel was free to eat and the beverages in the refrigerator were also. Eisha thanked her for her hospitality and A. J. walked out with her. What seemed like hours later the same guest service lady returned but this time she had several co-workers with her disbursing; extra towels, soaps, lotions, trays of food, additional baskets of fruits, and sodas. This lady never stopped grinning at us she said 'it's not often that colored people spent the night in any of the suites and she wanted us to be comfortable enough to come back'. Antoinette asked her how she knew we wanted food. She said 'your brother A. J.' Antoinette nudged Eisha in the arm from that I knew it was some hidden information floating in the air but I didn't care.

In addition, Auntie Becca made her way into our room excited to eat free food she came over to see if we also had food to eat. Floyd told her he was about to bring some of our food over to them Becca said 'no need' but he did take them several of the fruit bowls along with some soda and various desserts especially for Gail's kids he figured they would have enjoyed all those sweets. Antoinette was funny by saying to Floyd bruh, bruh why don't you go get one of those guest services ladies then maybe she'll give us these suites for free. Floyd smiled saying yeah right!

However, my parents made it back just in time to eat. Daddy asked where did the food and treats come from. Floyd told him from where and before he could finish speaking Eisha said 'yes J. W. Becca and them also got food to eat'. Momma was pleased to hear that her family and Mr. Smith's family wasn't left out on eating even though she looked exhausted. I asked her was she ok and she said 'yes baby I'm just a little tired'. I noticed it was always something about Daddy's presents that makes Momma's mood change and I didn't like seeing her like that. About an hour after everyone got back to the hotel the men were all groomed and ready to hit the streets. Momma asked me if I wanted to sleep with her or Eisha. I said 'huh?' because normally I don't have a choice in making decisions. I'm told what to do and how to do it so that took me completely off guard. Truthfully speaking, I didn't know how to answer Momma's question instead of giving her an answer I had decided to ask her once again if she was alright. She yawned and I knew she was on her way to bed so I followed her into the bedroom really concern with what was troubling her. I sat on the bed as she went into the bathroom to bath and freshen up. When she returned she looked semi better but still tired looking. I had a tray of smothered pork chops, mash potatoes, cabbage and soda waiting for her on the bed. Her eyes grew larger as she sat and ate then said 'Sofay why you aint with Lorraine and them'? I said 'I don't know'. As she drank her soda I laid right beside her and stared at her. Before I could say anything she said 'Sofay when you get older I want you to find a man who will love you unconditionally'. Find a man who's your equal with the same interest as you. I don't want you following behind some man losing your dreams you have strived for. I want you to be able to know what you want in life from experimenting and visiting different cities, different cultures, and perhaps different foreign countries. I don't want you to follow in my footsteps and give up your dreams just to satisfy a man or to say you are married but I want you to be satisfied within. I knew from that conversation that she and Daddy were having problems. I was so focused on being entertained with the White's that I had forgotten my Mommy had feelings let along I did not know she was going through some self-absorb situation. I moved closer to Momma as she finished eating she stretched then laid down next to me wrapping me inside her arms.

Even though, she can be a trip at times I knew my Mother could also be eccentric with multi personalities which she blamed on the

White clan but after listening to her I had a different expectation with my mommy well-being. Daddy played a major part in making Momma second guess herself continuously when she was right all alone. He played with her mind by always asking her are you sure Geraldine? After she had confronted him of being with a floozy he always made her second guess herself. He never admitted his faults but blamed her for questioning his manhood. He too was a trip! For the first time my Mother opened up to me with what was bothering her regarding my Father and his Mother my Grams.

Firstly, Momma's life was living in New York where she did anything she wanted to do. She was a city girl at heart who didn't run the streets but knew the streets. She attended Julian or should I say Juilliard Arts for dance. Her dream was to one day open her own dance studio in Manhattan. My Grandparents promised her if she saved a certain amount they would match it and use their connections to get her dream off the ground. She and her parents were hard workers in their crafts. My Granddaddy her father worked as a conductor on the transit system and ended up dying on the very track that he once worked. Whereas, Grammy endeavors was working in a department store before quitting starting her own clothing store. Momma was an only child who was spoiled and had everything other kids wished they had. She met Daddy at the height of her dream which she was implementing into fruition. She alone with other relatives went to Fresno, Texas to pay their respect for Cousin Tommie's older step brother who happened to know three of the White brothers. Momma said 'her and Daddy's eyes locked'. It was love at first sight. She said 'she should have listened to Auntie Becca's advice when she whispered to her keep it moving Gerry. You don't want any part of that good looking curly head country boy. Auntie said 'child a man like that draws too much attention from women that you don't need Gerry.' She said 'he probably have both whits and street sense which is a dangerous combination; in being slick, sneaky, charming and controlling'. Becca said all of that while they were in line viewing the body. Momma paused before continuing on she was reminiscing back to what others thought they knew about him. She said 'see Sofay you can't always believe everything you hear from others'. A part of me wanted to believe the rumors and the other part of me refused to believe them. I asked Momma did Auntie Rebecca like Daddy or any of the Whites. She said 'at first she didn't like him because she felt he was a country slickster who used his looks to manipulate women into one thing'. His looks are what drew me towards him. When I laid eyes on him at that funeral he was the finest man that I had ever seen and majority of the sisters there thought the same thing. Momma said 'Sofay when you start courting boys don't concentrate so much on looks and certainly don't go after those light skinned curly hair muscle bound men'. I want you to get somebody just a tide bit ugly he'll worship the grounds you walk on. But first find out what he's like on the inside because the outside of him is just a shell but the inside of him is the heart of the manner that counts and what's ever hidden will surely come to light. Baby it can be hard trying to decipher if a man really loves you for you because some will play games. But if he truly loves you, you will know it and feel it. Soo, I want you to find a man who has a heart of gold, a man who loves his family and who will respect you but not deter you away from your dreams. I want you to find a man Sofay Camille Antoinette Gwen Faye Monee Whiteeeee who won't try to change you. And lastly, baby try not to get a man who's a Mamma's boy.

Even though, your Gramz's was a little over powering many times with how she wanted you to be raised. When I first visited Oklahoma, Sofay I was floored at how the women were submissive in their relationship outside the White's land. The women were like zombies trailing behind their men and I vowed to myself I would never become that woman. All I have to say is to be careful when you use the word never because in the long run you will be doing what you never set out to do. When I look back, I also became one of those submissive women. I asked her what submissive means and she said 'it's when you are strictly being obedient and controlled by someone by listening and doing exactly what is ask of you'. I asked her is that what Daddy be doing to you? She said 'yes and no'. Your Grammy saw the slight change in me and she was nearly blue in the face fussing at me for letting my morals and self-dignity slowly deteriorate. From that I was able to pull through this stronghold of evil that was trying to control me. I became a regular in Church. I released all that built up stress and sadness weekly and even started to study this verse where it says: *Though you have made me see troubles many and bitter, you will restore my life again, from the depts. Of the earth you will again bring me up*. Momma paused rubbed my hair and said 'my baby I am sorry that you've seen more then you should have at such a young age'. That's why you got to stand for something or you will fall for anything. There are some good people in life but no two people are the same. We may have similarities but we are all different. Ole Sofay when you were born that was an unforgettable experience. You were the greediest little thing ever in my belly I ate and ate nonstop. You were always kicking me that's when I knew you were hungry or needed a smooth rub over my belly. You always knew your Father's hand because it felt like you were dancing when you were justa rolling throughout my womb whenever he touched me. Mother didn't believe I was feeling you in my insides each time J. W. touched my belly singing or talking to you. She said 'what I was experiencing was unheard of'. Ha-ha Mother was always superstitious in saying weird stuff like to tell J. W. to stop touching your belly before that baby come out with big hands or don't call other people kids ugly because you would come out looking like creature feature. She was a riot!

As a matter of fact, your name Sofay I know I never mentioned this to you but if J. W. hadn't fainted in the delivery room I would have never allowed him to name you. I mean come on! I was already embarrassed when he fainted. I saw his entire face suddenly change but for the life of me I never would have expected your daddy to slid down that wall like that. Shortly after he got it together when it was time to give your name to the nurse he started rattling off his sister's names I was pissed off. The only name that saved him was using Mother's name other than that we would have been feuding on the spot because the name we agreed on was Arianna La'Tress White. I was fuming as the nurse was writing all those names on paper and nearly slapped him my damn self if I could have been able to reach for him. After your birth I started regaining my confidence again. I rose up from the bed scratching my head because that was a lot for a kid to try and hone. Momma stopped for a second and said 'along the way in healing I've learned that you've got to love yourself no matter what the circumstances may be because in actuality no one in the world will take better care of you then yourself'. She's been through enough while residing under the roof of the White's and thank goodness that Grammy had been there all along to comfort her. If it wasn't for Grammy's courage and strength then my Mother would have fallen completely a part a long time ago. Grammy was an opinionated woman who tolerated my father against her better judgements. She always told Momma that if she saw daddy in action flirting with a woman believe him. Because he's telling you who he really is and regardless he's gonna get that woman in bed one way or another without your approval. Momma had paused still glazing into my eyes. She then said 'baby learn from my mistakes in forgiving'. It's easier said than done. Forgiveness is another part in all relationships but it comes to a point of letting that hurt go and forcing yourself to move on from it but do not and I mean do not forget the hurt because it's a reminder in what you won't accept if it happens again.

Anyhow, baby I have to say that I admire your relationship you have with Eisha because it reminded me of myself and your Cousin Essabell who is Becca's daughter (God rest her soul). When Essa passed away before you were born I was devastated for months. She was the only one who persuaded me to give J. W. a chance. No one else thought he was suited to be with me.

In fact, out of everyone on my side of the family it was her who said 'don't judge him by the covers from someone else's point of view seek him out first for yourself then you decide if J. W. is someone you want to spend your life with. My heart dropped than began beating a mile a minute because it all makes sense now. The reason why Momma would drift off into space a whole lot of times mid-way through a conversation is because she was lost within because Daddy couldn't keep his pants zipped up ughh! He played with her mind sort of controlling her against her wishes. And to think we three shared the same bed is what I wanted to say to Momma. Momma said 'many times throughout the day when he wasn't working in the field that she was able to feel his infidelities and sometimes smelled sex floating in the air when he was out in town'. My sweet Momma and hear I thought she was coo-coo for coco pops. She was far from insane but somehow or another other people thought she wore being unstable well. Little did they know how love and jealously had polluted her mind set. She wasn't envious of other women because all she wanted was to desperately know the skunk my father was with so she could put a hurting on her. But daddy never confessed that there was someone else he was dealing with. He thought he was slick with a hidden secret.

Anyway, many of my aunties didn't make it any better by always covering up my daddy's infidelities. I would hear my parents arguing often but I never knew some of my aunties were that way with my Mother and hear I thought we all got along as one big happy family. I asked Momma why she didn't tell Daddy she missed him at Mr. Smith's place when he poured out his heart to her. She said 'she's not a fake person and why pretend to be something that she's not so I remained quiet when your Daddy poured out his heart.' I felt he was making up for something he probably did the night before. She also said 'she hadn't missed him or the Whites in fact she was sick of them and needed a break'. The only reason she stayed on the farm was because of the genuine love and affection they all had for me. Dog gonnit, Momma has never opened up to me before in how unhappy she truly was I mean we chatted daily but not like this. Momma rubbed my face smiling saying the Mother - daughter relationship she was building with me was being slightly tarnished by the Whites interference in somehow or another they wanted to raise me their way and not allow her to raise me her way. Momma said that 'Gramz's tried to take over in how I raised you'. I felt helpless but kept this to myself and only told Glorie (one of her best friends). Your Grandparents provided everything including how they had J. W. to consistently persuade me into moving into the farmland with them after you were born. Shortly after your birth we married but prior to that I called off the original date of marrying your father because I couldn't see myself living in the country. When I first visited the farmland I was nearly devastated that they lived like that. Let me rephrased that. I wasn't accustomed to a shed of dead meat, milking a cow, watching chickens get their heads cut off for a meal. I went into a cultural shock. When I wrote Mother and told her what I was experiencing while visiting the Whites she told me to pack my bags and catch the next flight back home…ha-ha…My Mother was completely against me getting involved with your Dad's family and she was even more adamant for me to neither marry nor move on the farm after we were married. Your Grammy couldn't grasp how the White men never had motivation to move out of the farm into their own places she wanted to know what was wrong with all of them grown people. Grammy thought voodoo was used on the entire clan of White kids because none of them had any dreams to fulfill except to be under your Gramz. Grammy jokingly said 'plenty of times that I was dating your Gramz instead of J. W. because she was so caught up in our relationship that she possibly had forgotten she was his Mother'. Baby I've seen a lot happening on that farm. I've personally experienced Gramz's other side of evil when J. W. and I would quarrel. He and I would have made up but your Gramz's would still be holding a grudge with me by rolling her eyes or slamming my plate down on the table when it was time to eat. Grammy was still in New York during my courting season and pregnancy. I would write her to tell her my experiences with the Whites. The next day or so Grammy would be knocking on the front door with Auntie Rebecca, cousin Essa and a few other relatives ready to fight. From my experience along So-soo if you feel uncomfortable or sense something is not right I want you to leave that situation. I don't want you to bow down to no one because you have a voice; you have an opinion, you have a beautiful personality, you have a mind over matter and know right from wrong but never forget what I'm telling you. I said 'wow'! I told my Momma how much I loved her and there is nothing nor no one not even Eisha that could break our relationship as Mother and

Daughter. Momma slowly wiped the tears from her eyes. Somehow or another I was now pissed with the entire clan of Whites including my daddy for putting Momma in the state of mind that she was in.

Miraculously, I made up my mind that from that point on I would be Momma's eyes and ears and will no longer keep secrets from her regarding any of those got damn Whites. I wanted to share with her all those times Daddy gave me everything I wanted to not tell her that he was bumping up against another woman. But I didn't want my sweet mother to have an aneurysm. In actuality Momma has endured what it felt like to be around people who practically hated her and vice versa. From her facial expressions it ripe my heart out as she went into details from the last twelve years of living with them on the farm. She was one person who got ganged up on by eighteen other people and it's no wonder she behaves the way she does. Hum maybe I'll go back into those woods when I get back home to concur up a spell for Gramz's to stay in her place and leave my mother alone.

Any hoot, Auntie Eisha knocked on the door to ask if I wanted to go swimming with them. I said 'no'. She stood there in shock while I was snickering in the inside to myself and layed back down next to my Mother. I peeked at momma and she rose up from the bed to look at Eisha and said 'huh'. I didn't know what that meant but Eisha looked really sad closing that door.

CHAPTER 27

After that, we fell asleep until I woke up to a bunch of chaos. I saw that Momma was no longer lying beside me but in the living room. I cracked open the door to peek out to see what was happening. I saw blood on the walls with Auntie Antoinette running to the couch with wet towels. Tommie along with Mr. Smith was screaming at each other with blood dripping. Momma was just standing there not knowing what to do then there was Uncle Floyd standing there holding Sheila's hand of all things. The guest service lady was there with Uncle A. J. making me say hum. I wanted to scream out 'what the fuck is going on'! but I didn't want Daddy to turn around looking at me nor did I want him to pull off his belt to whip me. I saw Eisha slowly making her way into the living room so I did the same thing. When I got closer I saw Cousin Tommie on the couch crying from being shot in the foot. But what I didn't get and it boggled my mind was why Daddy and Mr. Smith both had blood on their foreheads, pants and shirts and where were my Uncles because they didn't have blood on them. They all were speaking at the same time making it incomprehensible to understand. Before I knew it tears started forming as I watched Momma literally checked Daddy's body for any bullet wounds. She helped him pull off his shirt as he made groaning sounds. Eisha told Mr. Smith to also take off his shirt as she and Antoinette checked for bullet wounds. Eisha and I said 'dang' at the same time because Mr. Smith had a muscular body more like a body builder type. I thought to myself geez I wonder how Grammy was able to handle all of this man.

Likewise, the guest service lady who happened to be named Helen was trying to clean Tommie's foot as he cried. I looked at Sheila wondering why she wasn't consoling Tommie but you know me by now and I said something to the effect of Sheila why you ain't over there with Tommie? Before I knew it Uncle Floyd reached over to pinch my arm causing me to shut up. I said 'ouch what you do that for'? He ignored me and proceeded to ask what happened. Of course A. J. was fired up hating he wasn't there by his brother's side. I didn't have Eisha by my side to ask any questions to what he meant by not being there but she was busy seducing Mr. Smith with those towels. Helen rose up off the couch softly asking everyone to be quiet because she didn't want other guests to become alert. She said to Daddy 'please tell us what happened out there'! Mr. Harold Smith said 'I'll tell you but first Eisha baby thank you for your kindness before putting that towel in front of his private area'. Unh huh I said to myself look at him can't keep that dick down while Eisha was standing there smirking. I shouted out where is Grammy and Harold immediately said 'she's fine Sofay we don't want to wake her up'. You don't know how it took a lot for me to keep from saying 'what the shit you mean man because Eisha is an inch away from making a move on you. You ought to want me to go wake my grandmother'. But you know I couldn't say that!

Instead, of him making a move on Eisha it was Eisha making a move on him. Man! I was too young trying to prevent adults from having sex with other people mates but I had to press on. Harold said as he sat down 'that they all were in and out of shops having a ball'. I said to myself of course there was nothing but sex and porn shops then I eyed all of the men including Daddy knowing they all had sex, probably got there penis sucked and only the Lord knows what else took place. I couldn't help it and blurred out Daddy you went to those nasty shops? Momma stopped wiping my father down eyeing him he refused to look directly at her. He said 'Sofay White you better stay in a child's place'. In fact, take your ass back in the room. I was pissed off but obeyed and said 'come on Eisha'! Now she was pissed at me. Man I couldn't win from losing I felt that my Auntie Eisha was a child like me and if I had to leave why shouldn't she have to leave. Eisha acted like she wasn't moving until my father said 'yeah both of yall go back in the bedroom'. Auntie Eisha damn near pushed me all the way back into the bedroom because she couldn't stay to be nosey and flirt with Harold. She said 'Red learn to stay fucking quiet when stuff happens that way we could stay and see what's going on'. She said 'you've got to stop being grown before someone tries to hurt you'. I ignored her cause I knew she was up to no good sitting up there rubbing on Grammy's man. She said 'be quiet' while she cracked the door to finish listening as Mr. Smith talked he said 'after about three hours or so in those shops we decided to go play some pool. We meshed in good with the other brothers in attendance; that were drinking, smoking and enjoying a game of pool. The atmosphere was cool until several hustlers entered the place. It was as if they knew Tommie was there. Tommie screamed out they were following me! Floyd said 'naw man ain't no way they were following you because they would have tried to take you out earlier today'. They had plenty of opportunities today to do that. Harold said 'they probably started following once they saw you limping on the stripe and made you a bull's eye target from that point on'. A. J. said 'wait a minute mane was one of them wearing a white suit'? Daddy said 'yeah'. Uncle A. J. said 'mane that's the brother that spotted you'. Tommie mane when that pro approached you she was the distraction while my man was making sure it was you. I thought I saw him signal his boys who were outside the pool hall. But when I saw Helen pull up me and Floyd hoped in her car and I went to go handle my business and didn't look back. Jr. was long gone with his sweet thang. My entire focused changed and fell on Helen. Eisha and I whispered those three left and went where? Harold said 'ok he had on white he's the one that's dead'. Me and Eisha both stepped back a space at the same time then we whispered to each other he's dead'? Harold said 'man like I said we were enjoying the game of pool then one of those hustler's walked up to Tommie pushing him up in a corner putting out a cigarette butte on his cheek'. I couldn't tell who was on what side because they rushed at Tommie at once causing him to scream out. When I reached the corner of the hall one of them swung a knife out on me warning me to get back. I caught his hand and tried to break it. Then I tried to move one of those guys off of him while this other brother hit him with a chair. Daddy said 'naw Harold mane that was me with the chair mane when I heard a shot being fired I wasn't trying to hit you but that brother that had Tommie on the pool table! Mane I'm sorry for that! Harold said 'J. W. man your apology is accepted'. My father continued on saying when he came out the bathroom to all this confusions he didn't know what took place. All he saw was those brothers up in the corner with Tommie screaming at them. At first Harold I didn't see you that's when I grabbed the chair to hit at least one of those mother fuckers. When I realized it was you mane you jumped up so fast off the pool table that I followed you to the corner where Tommie was. When I saw you grab for Tommie that's when I reached for him also. We both grabbed for Tommie to get the hell out of there. Daddy said 'when we landed outside the hall that's when one of them punks ran up to stabbed me in my upper shoulders I didn't feel it at first mane but then the pain creeped up on me out of nowhere'. It was chaos with folks running out side everywhere. Harold said 'yeah man we had Tommie in the middle holding him up trying to get to the car because he was shot in the foot'. Next thing one of them hustlers ran up from behind us to kick him in his back that's when J. W. pulled his pistol out and shot him causing the others to take off running. He felled to the ground as Harold and I picked Tommie up off the ground. Harold said 'man J. W. I want to thank you brother cause you fast on the trigger man'. He continued on saying we made it to the car got Tommie's ass in the back seat only to have that pimp in the white suit to pull up. He hopped out so fast to put a knife to J. W.'s neck that I froze instantly it was nothing I could do. Momma gasped for air looking at Daddy now we know why he was bleeding he was cut with a knife and stabbed on his side. Daddy said 'brother it happened so fast before I knew it I snatched my knife from my satchel and stabbed him in the neck'.

After that, we got out of dodge. We circled around for about an hour or so making sure we weren't followed by anybody. Harold was getting comfortable now he said 'he's seen a lot but never been a part of nothing that major'.

Though, Sheila was standing there apparently in shock because she didn't move from that spot she acted like she had a hard time walking towards Tommie. Momma screamed out we got to get out of here! Daddy said 'hold on Geraldine' then he asked Tommie 'mane what kind of trouble are you in with these streets thugs cause now you got me involved in this shit'. Cousin Tommie sat there with a bullet in his foot drifting in and out of conscious saying man old man slightly crying. He got it together and told them everything from his; friends being slick with those hustlers money, to being beaten by those same hustlers for stealing Sheila from the pimp in the white suit. Everybody was looking at each other silently. Helen suggested that we stay until check out time to act normal as if this scene didn't occur. She didn't want it to be obvious that something took place. She asked Daddy was he sure they weren't followed to the hotel. Mr. Smith said 'yeah I'm positive we weren't followed we drove in and out of alleyways and sat for thirty minutes at a time in different spots outside the area'. Harold asked Tommie was his life more important or the streets? Tommie said 'my life' then A. J. said 'then why in the fuck you chose to remain in the same spot without attempting to move'. You knew them motherfuckers move in that area we went too why the fuck you didn't say nothing before we went there! Mane you done put this entire family at risk to be murdered by those cats because you were proving a point to your boys. Cousin Tommie said nothing but put his head down. Eisha whispered to me that Tommie is sort of wimpy like a pee-on it's a wonder that Sheila is even with him. Uncle Floyd spoke up to say we got to get that bullet out his foot before it get affected and get some bandages for my brother and Harold. Helen slowly got up from the couch to call room service and within minutes colored men were at the door. They came in like soldiers with several containers of medical solutions. Helen briefly told them what happened several hours prior. One of those men said 'so far the coast was clear that they hadn't heard anything about any shooting in Time square'. He assured the White men and Mr. Smith that what happened out there will stay within those hotel walls.

However, Eisha and I grew tired of standing up listening so we grabbed pillows off the bed to put on the floor so we could continue on listening. As far as I'm concern those guest services men were miracle workers. They had utensils and equipment's that was used to get that bullet out of Tommie's foot. He cried like a baby causing one of those men to sock him in the chin to knock him out cold so they could finish patching his scary ass up quietly. Two of them worked on Tommie while the other two worked on both Daddy and Mr. Smith. One would burn the needle and put the thread through while the other one used red dye and other medicines to cleanse the stab wounds.

Again, it brought tears to my eyes as I watched my Mother grab a hold of my father from the back holding him as he endured that pain from the needle going through his bare skin. Looking at my Momma with her tiny self she held on to Daddy's back for dear life sqetching her eyes as if she was the one being sewn up. Despite my parents having infidelity issues Momma can't deny the fact that she loves that man. I guess she kept so much pushed down inside of her over the years that she was unable to express how she really felt even though she shared information with her besties I guess that still didn't make situations better for her and my father. After seeing my parents support one another I knew in my heart that they would work things out. Just then it was a knock on the door everybody froze but A. J. he went to the door to ask who it was. It was Cousin Jr. (short for junior) who had just finished being with a hooker. He came in dropping his mouth looking around in shock asking what the fuck happened. He said 'he went back to Time Square looking for everybody only to notice it was a desert and from the looks of things he sensed trouble had erupted and left on two wheels.

CHAPTER 28

Moreover, it was morning time and the only people that actual got some sleep were in Grammy's and Gail's room.

Nevertheless, the White brothers offered cash to the four guest services men that helped clean up their wounds only three out of four took the money while the other one refused and told my family to be careful. They left pain pills and extra bandage and advised none of the injure people to go to any hospitals for fear of the fuzz were circling around there. As the hotel workers exited the room with all the evidence of bloody towels Grammy alone with Auntie Becca and Gail was entering the suite. Grammy looked around mortified knowing something drastic took place last night. Auntie Becca walked straight to Tommie to say that they got cha again. Cousin Tommie rose up in pain saying yeah Grandma. Lord have Mercy child you got to leave that life alone you gotta family Thomas! Gail walked straight to her father to sit next to him. Momma filled them in on what took place. Harold had his arm around his daughter Gail while he held Grammy on his lap half asleep as she rubbed his arm. Auntie Becca said 'she sensed something terrible was going to happened if Tommie hung out with the fellows but she said nothing believing in her heart that everyone would be ok'. She said 'that street people always find who they're looking for in the long run and once they are found it's usually a blood bath of people being hurt'. Uncle Floyd told Grammy to go pack her bags because we were going to load the cars then go down stairs to eat breakfast and act like nothing happened. The ladies did as they were told with including Sheila, Gail and Mr. Smith who walked behind them to their rooms. I didn't know about anybody else but I was hungry and couldn't wait to eat breakfast. My two Uncles including Cousin Jr. loaded up the cars and everybody made their way downstairs to the breakfast area. We all ate as normal while Uncle A. J. was scoping the lobby for any hustlers or the fuzz. He was a funny guy but deadly. Though, it turned out that both of my Uncles had rented rooms inside the hotel that night. Uncle Floyd had a room with Sheila and Uncle A. J. had one with Helen. Now it all makes sense as to why neither of them was there when the fight broke out. Sheila still seem to have problems walking it was bad enough she was stiff as a pole a few hours ago now it looks like she can barely walk. As for me and my Aunties who had observed Sheila's appearance, Antoinette mistakenly nudged me instead of Eisha saying 'look at her Floyd done wore her out'. Eisha busted up laughing. I didn't find it funny because that poor girl was in pain so I asked her 'Sheila why you walking so funny all bended over like that' I didn't know that question caught Becca's full attention. Auntie Antoinette grabbed my arm for me to shut up while Uncle Floyd was smirking. Floyd said 'yeah Sheila why you walking like that laughing'. She didn't respond but continued on feeding her baby. I looked at Floyd who looked like he was blushing because his cheeks turned slightly red. Then I said 'wooo' it occurred to me that she and Floyd had sex and he must have knocked the bottom out of her that's why she couldn't barely walk. Back home I would often hear my Uncles and some of their friends talk how they sexed different women. They would say stuff like yeah mane when she laid on the bed her legs were closed but when she got up from me she now got a gap bigger than a quarter then they all falls out laughing. Yeah I already know my Uncles were freaks hell as a matter of fact so were several of my Aunties.

Anyway, Antoinette tried to cover up my mouth on a sly then whispered you better not say one damn thing Sofay. Hell I wasn't that slow and felt offended that I couldn't share what I thought at the table with family members. Antoinette got on my nerves with always saying don't say this, or that, to nobody. That's why I was mature for my age because when I had the chance to speak I blurred out what I needed to say sometimes causing an alarming reaction from people.

Undoubtedly, Eisha covered my ear to whisper Becca is looking at you. I refused to even look in her direction instead I drank some orange juice. And from the looks of things Helen wasn't in any better condition after being with A. J.'s crazy ass. I busted up laughing when she held onto the walls saying goodbye to everybody. I wondered why she couldn't get comfortable last night while sitting down she kept fidgeting and opening up her legs like something was stuck up in her private area. Boy I tell yah those White men were something else physically and mentally. After we checked out we all returned back into the cars we came in except that A. J. was driving our car while Floyd drove Harold's car and Jr. continued on in his car. It was a long way back to Mr. Smith's house in Brooklyn. We got back there within an hour and a half time to hook the moving truck onto Daddy's car. Those that needed to use the bathroom did while the rest of us remained in the cars. Gail decided she didn't want to go to Lake Placid so she and her girls departed but said their goodbyes and went inside of their home. It was still early roughly around ten in the morning Mr. Smith prepared everyone for the long ride ahead of us which was approximately four to five hours additional away from Brooklyn. We made two stops for everyone to use the bathroom and Momma loaded up on both food and junk food including sodas for everyone. The closer we got the more deserted it appeared to be. Uncle A. J. asked the gas attendant for directions and we were off but before leaving that gas station Momma went to check on Tommie. He was uneasy about the move because all he knew was Harlem and those rough streets. He wanted to return back to Harlem he kept drifting back to the night of his beating and thought heavenly about his two best friends but wondered if they were ok. Momma said 'she couldn't tell him anything because she didn't know but insisted that he should leave that life behind and focus on his future raising his kids and hopefully marrying Sheila'. When she got back in the car telling us what she told Tommie, Eisha said 'marrying Sheila I don't see that happening'. Momma stopped talking turned around slowly and said 'little girl what did you say'. Floyd said 'Sheila ain't marrying anybody she's not the marrying type'. Momma said 'and what type is she'? He said 'a roll over type she's good at rolling over up on her back'. I said 'and how you know Uncle Floyd'. He said 'Sofay girllll you pushing me! Just know that I know she ain't the marrying type'.

I knew he wasn't going to do nothing to me like whip me because my parents were in the car looking at him. Daddy jumped in to say 'Sofay I done told you about your sassy ass mouth'. Sass off to somebody else and Im'ma tare your ass up'. Daddy said 'baby you can't be round here arguing with adults you got to know your place as a child'. Your Daddy don't wanna have to go to jail for killing someone over you cause you being flippy at the mouth. He said 'Geraldine we got to continue to work on her, she'll be fine'. I wanted to stick my tongue out at Uncle Floyd as he shifted the rear view mirror on me but I feared my father would have reached in the back seat to yack me up into the front seat. I looked next to me at both of my Auntie's who were justta staring at me. I wasn't studding any of them in fact; I was ready to go home to be with my Grandparents because I was sick of this violent lifestyle in New York. I saw too much too soon forcing me to mature quickly in this strange city. I asked Daddy did he know I was with Tommie that night he got beaten. He turned around and said 'yeah baby I know that damn near ripped my heart out that I wasn't here for you cause you know I would have never allowed you to go with either one of them Tommie or Sheila's ass'. Tommie already knew those thugs was after his ass but he thought he was invincible. Floyd jumped in changing the subject saying I mean who knew she was a pro' then he started smiling. Auntie Antoinette said 'well Sheila and Tommie were made for each other because of their lifestyles and besides, I think what's keeping them together is that baby other than that she would have kicked him to the curb a long time ago'. Antoinette said 'Red tell me again what she used to steal those clothes'. So I told her once again. I said 'Auntie she had some type of instrument she used to cut the tags off the clothes then she quickly folded those clothes inside of a pouch that was attached to her stomach'. She stuffed those clothes inside of that pouch which made her look like she was carrying twins'. Floyd out laughed everyone in the car. Eisha said 'dag Floyd' he said 'man I'm into her! Eisha and I elbowed each other snickering. Momma said 'Floyd don't forget that Sheila is Tommie's woman' before I knew it I busted up laughing really wanting to say to Momma it's too late Floyd done got a whole of her already she ain't walking bended over for nothing. But had I said that my father would have probably flipped the car over trying to get ahold of me. So instead I pretended to zombie walk and both Aunties busted up laughing. Floyd peeked at me through the rear view mirror and had a smirk on his face but didn't laugh out loud like his sisters. The closer we got the more the atmosphere changed for the better. There were plenty of grass, trees and an ocean. When we turned that corner we were at Auntie Rebecca's new place. It was a log house that faced the ocean with very few other houses near. We country people were in awh at how clean it was compared to Harlem at Auntie Becca's old place. Grammy was quite pleased holding Mr. Smith's hand. We all stood outside the home for several minutes before entering. Tommie looked white as a ghost standing there while Sheila managed to make herself smile. Antoinette went to pick up little Kimberley and Mr. Smith was standing there proud with his chest inflated. He said 'to Auntie Becca here you are Ms. Becca the keys to your new home'. She had teared rolling down her face saying she wished her husband and child could have been there. I quickly thought geez she cries at the drop of a hat just like auntie Gwen. Man I had no chance to be happy without crying because this is on both sides of my family.

Nevertheless, Grammy told her they were there in Spirit making Sheila tear up of all people. I have to say I didn't expect Sheila to shed a tear even though she looked a bit funny crying. Cousin Jr. went to hug her to say this is your new home do well and don't bring Harlem out here to cause these white folks to panic.

CHAPTER 29

In the meantime, we slowly made our way into the log and Becca couldn't maintain herself. When she opened that door we all were blown away with how spacious and clean it was. Uncle Floyd immediately started running his fingers along the wood as if he was studying how it was fixed onto the walls. He went from room to room observing and mastering the structure of how the house was built. There were four bedrooms, a living room, three bathrooms, a spacious kitchen with a pantry, and a family room. It was really neat and warming to see Becca's facial expressions as she entered each room. She was grateful that the owner left their living room set at least the adults had something to sit on instead of the floor. They had a few items to eat which wasn't enough for all of us to eat including the little bit of food Momma had purchased back at that gas station. Auntie Antoinette asked Sheila did she like their new place. From out of nowhere she responded 'girl yeah I've already got it planned'. The big room is Ms. Becca while the middle room is for the kids and our room is this room right here and this room will be the guest room. Grammy said to Sheila 'welcome to earth'. We all laughed because the girl had been quiet as a mouse but staring at everybody.

In fact, Eisha had said those same exact words. But it was Floyd who damn near spoiled the mood by saying 'no she ain't been quiet' causing some of us to look at him.

However, Mr. Smith had a map of the city which was helpful because Cousin Jr. was hungry and wanted to eat and you know I was hungry as well. Auntie Becca didn't want to leave out for food she was still overwhelmed with being out of Harlem so Jr. and my Uncles went out looking for a restaurant to bring back food while everyone else stayed at the log home. Grammy wanted to rest a bit before leaving out to find household goods. We all sat around if not standing up watching little Kimberley and baby T do what babies do.

It seemed like the kids knew their new surrounding they were more excited than Becca and the rest of them. Cousin Tommie couldn't stand up any longer and needed more pain pills. I watched him limp to that couch with Momma holding him up and I had never seen such a whoosh in my life. He asked Momma what he was going to do out in no man's land. Out of nowhere that no nonsense Auntie of mines Antoinette walked up to Tommie and said 'what you gonna do Tommie is stop feeling sorry for yourself'. Nobody told you to be slick with those professional slicksters. You chose that life and now your Carmel has nipped you in the ass but in your case your foot. Looka here bro you put your family in danger when you stole Sheila I'm just saying to you what I heard. You can't be a punk in a thug out world but you got to know how to play the game and play it right. Hell I ought to kick your ass my damn self for jumping on Sheila as much as you have. She's not a punching bag but your woman and the Mother to your children. He blurred out children? Antoinette said 'yeah negro children! Tommie when you stole Sheila you did it for the thrill of showing off in front of your boys you didn't know she came with a package deal. When you accepted Sheila your job as a man is to accept her children as well in order for this here relationship to work out peacefully. You are almost a punk ain't you?' Auntie Becca jumped in to say now hold on Missy you don't know a damn thang about Tommie and Sheila. Grammy grabbed Becca's arm then her waist and forced her to walk towards the back to see the back yard. I think my Grandmother was pleased that somebody else other than her put Tommie in his place. Auntie wasn't finished with Cousin Tommie just yet. She continued on in saying man you got to own up that you fucked up by bringing the streets into your home. Now Sheila she turned to Sheila to say no disrespect but you knew what you did as a living and I'm pretty sure Tommie you knew too. Girl did you think you could just walk away from hooking that easy without being beaten or tracked down by your pimp? Come on girl! You should have stopped that shit after your daughter was born and got an honest job. Ok I've said my peace and I hope that you straighten up Tommie. I know we don't know each other but hearing this mess about your life got me so worked up especially knowing these two little kids are here observing this shit and who's to say that they will remember these last three nights of hell. Tommie I want you to know that I'm accepting you bro Sheila and the kids as family and if you need anything the Whites are here for you. He looked so pitiful but remorseful. Auntie said 'Tommie I'm coming down on you because I see something in you that want to do right. You just need to be around people who can help you grow and be a motivator for the times you may feel down. You need to know I don't mean any harm but I don't be around the bush with what's right is right and what's wrong is wrong. I wanted to say 'hum excuse me Auntie since you talking so much I think you should be checking your brother J. W. to keep his pants zipped up so my Momma can relax and be the good wife that she needs to be him. You know the drill by now. You know I couldn't say that! That woman would have probably had me hanging off that front banisher or some sort causing both Grammy and Momma to scratch her eyes out. But I can honestly said that cousin Tommie sure took Antoinette's hardness into consideration because he got up off that couch by himself and walked towards the front window and just stared. I might add that I didn't pay any attention to the view when we first entered the house and I didn't know how I overlooked such beauty. The view from the living room was specular! The front yard led right out into the lake, the grass was green and healthy, and it was extremely spacious. Sheila was getting comfortable she had already taken a bath and changed clothes. She called for Kimberley and I guessed she was freshening up both her kids one at a time. It was getting late and the long drive started taking a toll on everybody. I sat there hoping that my Uncles didn't get into trouble because they were taking so long to return.

Meanwhile, both Daddy and Mr. Smith pain started shifting I guessed from unloading the moving truck. They had all of us helping except for Auntie Becca, the kids, and Tommie. Their new place was slowly coming along. I heard Mr. Smith tell Daddy that Antoinette got a sharp tongue in telling Tommie off. Daddy agreed and said 'yeah mane she always got that venom to make you feel low'. Harold said 'yeah man she shoal chopped his dick off making him a boy once again in fact, don't say nothing about me'. Both men laughed shaking each other's hand. I asked Daddy how he felt because he kept rubbing his neck making sounds. He said 'I'm good baby your Daddy gone be fine'. Then he grabbed me just like old times playfully kissing me bringing a smile on my face and apparently it made Mr. Harold Smith smile also. I then climbed onto his lap as I listened to him and Mr. Smith continued on talking. Momma came from the back yawning saying she and Antoinette was going to find a grocery store for food. Just then someone was knocking on the door and Mr. Smith got up to answer it. Daddy started grinning when we realized it was A. J. coming in with bags of merchandises. He came in saying we need some help bringing in all this stuff. Daddy got up but Momma told him and Mr. Smith to have a seat because of their wounds. She kissed A. J. on the cheek and said 'I was starting to worry about yall.' Uncle A. J. said 'awh Sis you ain't got to ever worry about me cause I'm gone be alright'. Then he called out for me, Eisha, Sheila, and Antoinette to help unload the car and truck. Daddy got back up to say a truck! How the hell yall get a hold of a truck'? When we got outside it was surely a truck filled with roll away cot beds. Grammy said 'I'm speechless Floyd how yall managed this'? He laughed as I quickly squeezed him for a hug after all I didn't want him staying angry with me from our conversation in the car. You see, Floyd got a way of making a person feel scared from his angry looks alone. Once I told Granddaddy something that Floyd wasn't supposed to do which was smoking weed and I felt the rafts of his anger. He had a tooth pick in his mouth sucking his teeth making loud sounds while frowning and staring directly at me without blinking his eyes making me scared to move. I went right back to tell Granddaddy, Floyd was scaring me and he threatened Floyd that he bet not use nare finger to touch me or else. Shit I dodged him for days until he got over his anger so that's why I went for a quick hug. He looked down and quickly kissed me on the head but continued on saying when they were pulling out they were stopped by Helen's brother. He said they had been waiting all day for our arrival but didn't know how many people were in cars. He and his friend were canvassing the area in where they thought we would be and just so happened they spotted us at the stop light right here on the corner. It was all Helen's during. She contacted her people here at this popular Inn hotel asking for help for her family who was visiting from out of state. Momma said 'her family! Well I guessed she and A. J. really hit it off. Then A. J. came from the trunk of the car blushing with his chest inflated saying yeah I laid something on her that she won't forget. He said 'who knew this woman would extend a helping hand like she did last night and today'. I tell yah one thing when we get back home Im'ma send for her and show her our neck of the woods. Antoinette asked did Helen provide the food also. Floyd said 'no we went to a local store because we figured by everything happening so suddenly that Becca didn't have much to accommodate all of us and this gift was Jr. and Floyd's doing. What wasn't purchased was given to us for free. Those ladies took it upon their selves to load up on everything. We got a bunch of sheets, blankets, pillows, silverware and food. When Auntie Becca came outside to see what was going on she instantly started crying and screaming thank you Jesus! The drivers of the truck did the unloading and setting up of those sleeping cots. Once they were finished those two men briefly spoke to Daddy and Mr. Smith while everyone else was moving about. Both Daddy and Mr. Smith extended gratitude and appreciation for helping. They offered them something to eat or drink but those men refused.

In fact, they had to get back to work. Turns out one of them also moved not far from Becca's because of the trouble he got into while living in the Bronx. He said 'he'll do anything for his Sister with no questions asked because she always got their families back'. He told Daddy to keep his money because he was recovering from a drug episode. He didn't want the money for fear of relapsing back into the world of drugs. Antoinette nudged Daddy on a sly and thanked both gentlemen for helping the family at such a short notice. He said 'oh no Helen called me the moment yall left the hotel this morning asking me to do her a favor'. I got my man here who works in the local department store to get extra but new unused sleeping cots for yall.

His Uncle move people for a living as extra money so that's how we were able to get this truck. He briefly looked around and said 'yall in a prime secluded area not too much prejudices nor murders take place here you will be good'. It's not many colors that live here but yall will fit in. They don't have groups of color men walking about or standing around. The fuzz is on the lookout for anything out of the ordinary though. He looked at Tommie when he said that. Well we got to get back and it was my pleasure to assist you man. Cousin Jr. asked them how far they got to go and did small talk at the same time thanking them once again. Once the two men left it was Jr. that said 'J mane trust me when I tell you that this nice shit don't happened on a regular bases mane'. I had to pinch myself cuz to see if I was dreaming with these people being so kind. He said 'what yall won't believe is how those white women were all over us in that department store'. I don't think we paid for nothing after A J. told them he just moved in the area. Daddy said 'Jr. don't tell me mane laughing I know you didn't do what I think you did'. Jr. said 'mane they was begging for it' that's when Momma said 'um Sofay and Eisha yall go fix your beds'. Hell I wanted to hear the rest and I know Eisha wanted too as well. Moments later Momma and Auntie Becca came into the room with sheets, blankets and pillows fixing up those cot beds. Auntie Eisha and I sat there on the floor conversating and pleased that everything had turned around for Becca and them because I told Eisha how pitiful they were living before all this violence took place. Eisha left the room to return saying So-soo I'm running our bath water so we don't have to wait in line to use the bathroom when everybody starts settling down. She called out to Momma to ask for soap and towels Momma gladly handed them over to her and she was even more pleased to not have to see after me that night. After our baths we entered the front room together and came in on the last part of Cousin Jr. praying on his knees and for some reason I was astonished to hear him quote a scripture that says: *I will provide for you, don't worry.* Thank you Heavenly Father for your Glory, thank you for watching over us leading the way as you've lite the fire for light to shine in each of our paths, Lord remove all debris, traps, snares, schemes, and plots from our paths in Jesus Mighty Name Amen. Auntie Antoinette was getting emotional and grateful that she and her brothers came at a crucial time to help out the extended family. She grabbed Momma's hand and said 'Sis-n-law turn all your worries over to the Lord'. I want you to know that you were not crazy during those times you questioned us girls about J. W's other women. We didn't want to see you hurt is the reason we never confirm what you already knew about your husband. We were being selfish in not wanting Sofay to be taken away from us. We didn't want you to leave us either because through it all Geraldine we all love you tremendously. The Lord knows the battles you have faced and now it's time to heal but repent all the sins that has taken place with you, the family and J. W. Momma had a stream of tears rolling down her face and said 'Lord I seek forgiveness from you for taking the hath out my life as I wanted failure and violence to take place among my Sister-n-laws. I repent my sins Lord. You found fit for me Lord to send the Holy Spirit to help lead me into praying for forgiveness. He showed me how to not carry nor hold on to grudges against these women for covering up for their brother's way of life. Thank you Mighty Heavenly Father for your Glory. I decree and declare an increase in the Armor of light and put it on me now. Glory; increase the level of my Oils… Remove this jealous spirit from my Mind, Soul, and body now and replace it with your Glory Lord, your Salvation Lord, your Righteousness, in the Name of Jesus. *For this thing I besought the Lord thrice, that it might depart from me.* I give you the Glory Lord, I ask that you remove my pride and replace it with strength of encouragement daily in the Mighty name of Jesus sealed this prayer with a powerful Dominion…Amen. Me and Eisha looked at each other and she said out loud 'what in the Kellogg's corn flakes is this'! Mr. Smith said 'they are healing themselves with forgiveness'. Becca was still waving her hands in the air saying thank you Jesus while Tommie had tears rolling down his face looking at Momma. I walked to my Mommy and wrapped my arms around her waist and joined in with her as she was slow rocking side to side with more tears that rolled furiously down her cheeks. Antoinette had her by the shoulders wiping her eyes with tissue while Daddy was standing behind Momma. This was music to my Mother's ears because she's carried a burden of uncertainty for so long and now the truth has been validated by Auntie Antoinette. My Father was a player who played games with her mind. We all know now that my Mommy was not insane when she confronted my Dad about this hobby of bed hopping with those sluts in town. I looked behind me to see Sheila hugged up with both Jr. and Uncle Floyd and I wondered did anybody else think it was something wrong with that picture. When I thought about it I usually see the Saints in Church having a praying moment like this but it was refreshing to know that God does reside inside of each of us. The adults were Graceful to own up and release build up anxieties that caused so much friction between them. Momma can finally put it to rest that Daddy's sisters did have this back all along and she wasn't crazy. But in my Aunties minds they felt that they were protecting Momma by not exposing Daddy's infidelities. Maybe when I become an adult I can look back on this and understand more about trust and acceptance. I felt this was a start for a new beginning with my parents and family members.

CHAPTER 30

Shortly after that moment the adults went to bath and change into their pajamas while we kids were playing with each other in the living room. Jr. came out the bathroom and immediately started helping Auntie Becca warm up the food. He told her from this experience within the last two days he's joining a church and may even pack up to move back home to Oklahoma to be nearer with family. He said 'it was meant for him to be in her company because he was strike by something that told him to straighten up his life and stop being a player'. He said 'the woman that he's currently with isn't what he wanted'. She's too needy and always got her hand out begging. He said 'she likes to argue too much thinking she was controlling him by cussing at him like he was a child. Auntie Becca seemed surprised and told him to never allow a woman to pull your manhood down from you by words. She said 'words are a powerful thing that will cut you real deep with no forgiveness'. *The tongue has no bones but it's strong enough to break a head.* People can say the darness thing without any remorse causing you to feel low. Baby just pray about it like you just did here and the Lord will not only show you but he will guide you. Jr. said 'Mamm I know but she got me hooked on her thang I can't get enough of it'. Becca laughed and said 'son she's using what she got to get what she wants from yah'. When a woman finds your weakness she'll feed it to yah as a way to control you in a sense. Thangs are not always clean nor pure you've got to be careful because it's too many diseases out here. You got to get the lust out your soul and concentrate on a woman's values and worth. But mostly focus on the Lord and I'm telling you Jr. when you believe in Faith my how your life will turn for the best. You see son some of us ladies have so much to offer a man without using lust. He scratched his head frowning and looking as if Becca had been in his house with him and his girlfriend. He had a look of how you know all this.

Anyway, both Aunties were finishing up with putting the groceries into their proper places. Becca got to singing an old hymn with Cousin Jr. joining in with her singing. The food smelled good but I was dying for some biscuits and gravy so I asked Auntie Becca if I could make some biscuits. She putted her hands on her hips to say girlllll you know what you doing? Now I don't like kids playing over my food. Eisha said 'oh no Red knows what she's doing Auntie'. I went to work telling her all that I needed. Becca said 'well I'll be damn'! I asked for flour, sugar, salt, milk, butter, and baking powder. I was glad she had a big counter because I needed the space to increase the dough and use the cup rim to press and pull out each biscuit. Then I asked her for a sauce pan to cook the gravy while both Aunties had smirks on their faces. I asked Becca to put the biscuits into the stove because my Grandmother does not allow me to touch the oven. It was funny but I didn't laugh because Becca's facial expression looked astonished that a nine year girl knew her way around a kitchen. I asked her to turn the aisle on the burner to start heating the pot. I looked at Antoinette and she winked her eye and I knew I was doing well with those biscuits. I got the gravy started with using flour, milk, salt, pepper and a little bit of oil I didn't need a measuring cup I knew the amount to use from watching Gramz and Camille. Floyd and Daddy made their way into the kitchen ready to eat. My Daddy stood behind me observing what I was doing. I turned to him and asked him to taste the gravy he did and said 'add a little more pepper baby' but I couldn't because I had to check on the biscuits I didn't want them to burn. So he added the pepper. Becca was standing close by and opened the oven and we both checked on the biscuits. She took them out as I put another batch on that tray.

Additionally, everyone was out in the living room from freshening up. The food was heated and ready to be eaten. We all grabbed hands as Grammy said Grace then we started grubbing down. Becca kept staring at me still in amazement that I cooked biscuits and gravy from scratch. She told Momma, Gerry why you ain't said one word that your baby can cook! That red gal took over my kitchen! I ain't ever seen a baby cook like that before and knew what she was doing.

My parents laughed looking proud. Daddy said 'yeah well I'll like to thank my Momma for that because she believed in learning hands on'. Momma would stand next to her to explain what to do and how to do it. She started on Sofay as early as six years old in the kitchen. She made all my sisters learn that way. Becca said 'your Momma Olivia oh how I miss that lady it's been over ten years since I've seen and spoken with her last'. You be sure J. W. to tell her hello from up East. Daddy said 'yes Mamm I surely will tell her'. I asked Eisha did she like the food and she said 'it didn't taste bad but different though it was brought from a grocery store'. I told her my food experience at Grammy's and how I was amazed in the meat department in the grocery store. I told her how at Grammy's house I was looking for pigs in her back yard and wondered why the meats were wrapped in plastic. We laughed as Sheila stood up to say she had something to say. She said 'I know I'm late with this but can yall hear me out'. Tommie said 'whatttt! then got up to be near Sheila as she spoke. She apologized for showing me her way of life. She went on to speak about her upbringing at how she had no guidance as a child or adult supervision. Her household was with an alcoholic Mother who often entertained men who made passes at her. She watched as her Mother turned her cheek as one boyfriend physically molested her. Her Mother putted her out at an early age to the streets causing her to find work in a sex shop to support herself. She met Mr. Trench coat while walking inside Grand Central Union Square. He drugged her up to work for him in exchange for food, clothes and shelter. As she continued talking Uncle Floyd was practically drooling by the mouth. He was so fascinated by this woman I guess after he damn near ripped her coochie's lining out of whack he started falling for her. Sheila paused with tears forming in her eyes. She said 'Sofay please forgive me for showing you a world you had no business being exposed in'. I was being careless instead of being cautious. Floyd responded alright Sheila Im'ma pray for you she ignored him and asked me again. Hell I didn't know what to say so Eisha nudged me and whispered say yes Red. All eyes were on me I had no choice but to answer so I said 'yes Sheila'. She signed with what appeared to be a relief and continued on saying thank you Soo because that night has been messing with my head making me feel bad. Your acceptance means a big deal to me and thank you again. Floyd's eyes were damn near hanging out the socket in fact, he was starting to become ridiculous and annoying up there into Tommie's lady like him and Sheila were a couple. I looked at Uncle Floyd but before I could say anything Daddy walked next to him and stood there. I hurried up and looked at the floor I didn't want that man to tare me up!

Anyhow, the women cleaned up the kitchen while the men went outside admiring the scenery. I heard A. J. say that this place is known as a vacation spot. Harold said 'yeah man I know that and not many come here to visit I figured this would be a good spot for Tommie to settle down to raise his kids'. It's more white people than ever. Some are friendly and some are not. This town is small with little crimes and they don't need you Tommie to bring Harlem out here causing havoc. The law would love to make an example out of you.

CHAPTER 31

However, night fall had taken its toll because everyone was starting to fall asleep. Momma never played she always got her rest no matter what has taken place. The good thing about those sleeping cots was they were large enough for two people to sleep on. My Aunties were thankful to have covers and pillows. Antoinette has gotten worried for her back. She didn't want to sleep on a bare floor without having any sleeping materials. It was roughly around midnight if not one a.m. and everyone was settling down to sleep. I had forgotten to use the bathroom and woke up panicking to use it. When I looked around it was dark in the place with no noise. All I heard was different types of snoring and other noises. I constipated in whether or not to pee on the spot or to race to the bathroom. What changed my mind? was when I looked down at Auntie Eisha sleeping and knew if I had of peed she would have never let me live that down so I got up from there and raced to the bathroom. It was breezy and pleasant with the windows cracked I almost didn't make it in time. As I washed my hands I heard an unusual noise and thought oh Lordy what or who is that. It was a familiar sound I knew all too well. I tip toed into the window in the other bathroom and couldn't see a thing so I went into the kitchen window and still couldn't see. I needed to know if that was Uncle Floyd and Sheila's nasty ass because if it were I was gonna wake up my Daddy to tell him what they were doing. Her screams were getting louder hell I started sweating for some odd reason I guess from being nosey and wanting to catch Floyd and Sheila in the act. I laid back down smirking to my self-shaking my head side to side. Whomever it was started getting on my nerves with all of her yeses. I reached up to peek through the front window and still couldn't see anything so I decided to slide the glass door open and follow the sounds. Upon my surprise I couldn't hardly wait to see both Sheila and Floyd having sex because I was going to make a noise so they could have heard me. I tip toed making sure to not make a sound or step on any rocks. The sound was coming from the bushes near the window me and Eisha's cot was. I was tip toeing and laughing at the same time to reach these freaks. There they go I found them ok dang Floyd got a body out of this world. I said 'waitta minute' I looked again wiping my eyes to be sure and covered my mouth once I realized that it wasn't Uncle Floyd nor Sheila but Auntie Antoinette and Mr. Smith. Ooou I'm telling! That tripped me out! What was trippier was she was re-sighting the Lord's Prayer as Harold was going to work on her. I fell to the ground cause I wanted to see this shit. He said to Antoinette 'say it again' she slowly screamed noooo then he worked her. She moaned he repeated his self again to say, say it again and this heifer said '*our Father which art in Heaven*' then he went to work once again on her. Man, I had never nor did I have any inclines that sex was performed in so many different positions. They had my full attention now. Auntie started stuttering losing her breathe making me bust up in laughter. When I thought she saw me I fell completely on the ground stretching out my arms and legs lying flat. Goodness he acted like he was turning into a werewolf with his teeth clinching and growling hell I was waiting for fur to grow outside of his body.

Nonetheless, I wanted to see Auntie's face but his body covered hers. It was like my auntie had sank into the ground and disappeared I saw her poor little hand trying to reach up in the air that's when I crawled back to the house. I went to the bathroom with laughter to wash that grass off my legs and arms then I got back on the sleeping cot with Eisha. I laughed and hoped that there was nothing else new coming my way in watching others with this sex thingy. I mean who knew, who would have thought that my ole evil auntie Antoinette had it in her to practically steal my grandmother's man and to think I thought it was auntie Eisha that Mr. Smith wanted. I just didn't see this coming from my family. Man this family is a stone trip! I'm around a bunch of freaks. I guess well I know the only people not screwing were myself, the kids, and Auntie Becca. Everybody else was a fucking tag team waiting to get laid. I couldn't stop laughing because I was truly and honesty taken back from what I saw. I mean who knew! But then I started thinking about my Grandmother Grammy this news will devastate her about Harold and Auntie Antoinette.

Nonetheless, it was morning I laid there thinking about Antoinette and everyone else. I wondered what was up with this sex thing and why they got to have it regardless if they married or not. I looked over across at Antoinette as she slept she looked so peaceful and satisfy. Maybe now she won't be so snippy with everybody since she got her some…ha-ha. Eisha was waking up we greeted each other. I then said 'I didn't want to go out for food this morning' and Eisha agreed with me so we decided to cook breakfast for everyone just like at home. Cousin Jr. and my Uncles out did themselves at the store last night. They got everything that that was needed to cook with down to the skillets. It was early roughly around seven in the morning. Eisha and I freshened up then begin cooking breakfast. We made harsh brown with onions and chopped bell peppers though it took forever to peel those potatoes because Becca's knives were dull and nearly useless but we made do. We made pancakes, buttered grits, and sunny side up eggs, sausage, bacon, ham and buttered toast in the oven. We heated up the left over steak and sliced that up to put on the plate with the other meats. I made a side of gravy because Daddy and A. J. used gravy on just about everything. Eisha made a fruit salad using grapes, peaches, apples, oranges, and strawberry with marshmallows and sweet sauce to top it off. She then made coffee then we started setting the table. It seemed like clockwork as everybody rose up practically the same time surprised to smell and see breakfast on the table. Grammy smiled and said 'Sofay now don't be down here showing out girl cause I'm going to need a plow truck to unattached Becca from you'. Becca said 'you shoal will need that truck baby cause yall are alright with me and this little red gal can cook I'm in Heaven'! She said 'Eisha I haven't forgotten you baby cause I knew you could cook but this one here done took me by surprise'. Floyd playfully wrestled with me before high fiving me meaning he put his hand in the air so I could hit it. Grammy was itching for some coffee and I think she may have had three cups. Cousin Jr. asked Daddy when were they leaving he said 'he was gonna talk it over with his siblies first but he speck in another day or so'. Then he asked Mr. Smith when was he heading back to Brooklyn then Harold said 'in the morning because he only had a few more days left of vacation from his job'. He had to get back to spend time with his Grandkids whom he promised to take to D.C. for a couple of days. Grammy said 'oh Harold that's lovely that you will be with the girls vacationing'. He said 'Ernestine I would love for you to join us and besides with you being there it would be an unforgettable vacation'. He then playfully popped her on the butte. I immediately glazed at Antoinette who looked unsettled seeing those two interact. I really and truly wanted to say Harold I'm trying to remember if I saw you popped Auntie on her butte a couple of hours ago. I wanted to laugh but I cleared my throat to change the subject and asked Becca would she get a boat for the ocean. She said 'I don't think so sugar because I can't swim'. Jr. said 'that's what you need'. Becca said 'and what will that be Jr.'? He said 'fishing rods to fish'. Uncle Floyd said 'yell that would give us something to do today go fishing and then have a fish fry'. Jr. said 'then that's what it is we get dress and go to that store for rods, baits, and everything else we need'. Grammy said 'whoosh child it's been so long since I cleaned raw fish to cook'. Becca said 'then we got to go back to the store because I don't have any yellow corn meal'. Momma said 'we girls will go to the store because I want to look around and get a feel for this community'. As some were getting up from the table, couch and floor Daddy was looking at Mr. Smith and said 'Harold mane you bleeding did you cut yourself'? He looked down at his shirt and didn't see any blood and said where the blood is. Daddy said 'right here mane looks like your neck or something'. Grammy got a towel to wipe his neck and said 'Harold you done pulled your stitches a loose'. I almost chocked on my milk because I knew personally that he didn't pull them damn stiches a loose his self it was Auntie Antoinette's rough ass that pulled them a loose when yall was getting busy out there in the bushes. But you know yall got to know the drill by now hell I couldn't say that!

Instead, I looked at him like everyone else was screaming to myself you musty skunk. It was a little painful to watch my Grammy clean this man up telling him he got to be careful and this, that, and the other. If she only knew that Mr. Harold Smith and Auntie Antoinette were having sex hours ago I don't think she would have been receptive to help him out. I suddenly fell into a staring trance looking directly at Mr. Harold Smith. I was repulsed and nearly vomit watching how fake he was with Grammy. Momma was calling me but I didn't hear her because I wanted to blur out loud how fake both Auntie and Harold were. Momma literally walked up behind me to say Red what you thinking about that got you tuned out in space? I said 'huh Momma'. She said 'Red and looked directly into my eyes scenting something but she couldn't pin point what it was she then said 'you know what I'm going to stay here with Sofay and the babies while yall go to the store'. I refused to look at Grammy because I knew she was silencely dancing to herself knowing that I wouldn't be under Eisha for an hour or so. I was pissed and looked at Auntie Eisha to ask if she was going to the store with them. Before she could answer Grammy said 'yeah Eisha is going with us'. I whined Mommyyyy I want to go to the store with them! Momma said 'Sofay go get the comb and brush out your luggage so I can do your hair and I said we are staying here with the babies'. Auntie Becca said 'well I'm not going with yall I'm going to stay right here with you Gerry'. Then Grammy got ta saying awh why Auntie why you don't want to go? Becca said' Ernestine I got plenty of time to look around this town yall kids just go on ahead and enjoy yourself'.

Nonetheless, Sheila asked Tommie how much money he had because they needed a car and three bedroom sets; one for them and the other for the kids, then a set for the guests. Tommie said 'Sheila I got us we gone be okay'. She said 'that's not what I asked I asked how much money we got'. Floyd said 'oh shit' she said 'how much we got'? Cousin Jr. said to Floyd 'come on mane stay out their business.' Tommie gave Floyd the coldest look I guess he was getting tired of the sarcastic remarks Floyd kept dishing out. Those two played the eye ball battle game where each one stared at the other without blinking or looking away from one another. Momma said 'ok yall stop this foolishness'. She then walked to Tommie blocking Floyd's view to ask him how his wound was. He broke out his trance of staring at Floyd to ask Momma what she said. It was getting heated in there and the tension was building. Auntie Antoinette also told Floyd to stop being Peddie and go get dressed so we all could leave out almost at the same time. I have to say that my auntie was a pretty lady in fact; we all had our own unique form of beauty. In addition, Antoinette was more on the healthy side being a size eighteen. She was shapely but not like Eisha. Though she was healthy she wore her clothes skin tight drawing a lot of attention from men. She wore her hair in a pony tail that hung in length. She was a caramel color with light brown eyes which was a trade mark in the White's household. Auntie Antoinette was a realist kind of person because she sat and observed others before voicing her opinionated opinions. She had a short fuse for ignorance which caused havoc in the household with many of her brothers. She could be rough on a brother with her smart aleck way of talking causing many of her ex-men to nearly slap her in the face. My Auntie was friendly to a fault though she had friends who were just as rough on men as she was. She ran with other women in town who had similar ways as she did. Actually, Antoinette resembled James Jr. they could have passed for twins. The more I think about it she was picky in choosing men because hell she was almost like one. All she ever dated were light skin muscular men who had curly hair. That's why I was shocked that she got busy with Harold. I mean he was a good looking man who was way darker then what she was use to or at least I thought. But I have to say that many of her exes hurt her in more ways than others causing her and Nitta to go in those back woods on numerous occasions for revenge.

However, everyone was slowly moving about not really wanting to leave the log. I guess a full belly will make you tired hell I started yawning and it was only eleven in the morning. It took a minute but I got over the fact that I couldn't go with the adults. I had the comb and brush just like my Mother told me to get. She walked back to the room she and daddy slept in and flopped on the cot. She asked

Daddy to toss her a pillow to prop it on the floor so she could do my hair. He did and I sat there between her legs as she combed my hair. The adults were leaving out one by one then Mr. Smith stopped by the family room to say something on the line of Sofay I wish my Grandbabies were here to play with you they would have gotten a kick out of watching you cook those biscuits. I said 'uh-hun'. Momma whispered Sofay you better mind your manners! Then I said 'yes sir' and whispered with your fat butte. Momma heard me and used both hands to snatch my head around to face her and said 'what did you just say'? My eyes bulged I didn't realized that I had spoken loud enough for her to hear me. She repeated herself so I said 'huh'. She then pulled me up towards her by both of my arms looking into my eyes and asked did Harold do something to you? I said 'no Mamm' Momma shook me about to go hysterical thinking the worst. I had to tell her about them so she didn't go running bare foot behind those cars. I said 'Mommy he didn't touch me but I saw him and Auntie Antoinette freaking in the bushes last night'. Her eyes grew larger than a saucer. I never saw her eyes move that fast from side to side like that. She then covered my mouth with her hands as she scanned me up and down. She immediately pulled my panties down and told me to bend over on her lap as she opened my butte and coochie to look inside both of them. When I looked at her she closed her eyes tight saying a prayer then she let out a huff of air. My Momma Bless her heart was the type of woman who didn't allow me to sit near a penis as a child. Whenever any man would hold me she would tell them to put me on one leg near their knee cap; she didn't want no male scooting me up near their penis area when they sat me on their laps. Anyhow, after she re-grouped herself she called out to Grammy while Eisha and them were making their way to the cars one by one. Grammy came out her room looking like a Barbie doll with her linen colorful sun dress and matching hat on. The woman knew her fabrics as well as being one hell of a dresser. She was smiling as she stood in the door way. That one look told it all on Momma's face she may be dramatic but she was the kind that didn't sugar coat the truth. Grammy doubled looked at both of us knowing something had happened or was about to happened. She yelled to Eisha to tell them to go on without her. Her hand started trembling which meant she was able to get upset or about to explode as she walked into the room asking what it is. Momma said 'Mother it's so painful for me to tell you this'. I can't believe it'! Grammy said 'don't do that to me Geraldine just tell me baby'! Momma said 'how well do you know Harold'? Grammy screamed damn it girl! Momma gasped for needed air before saying Mother your man slept with Antoinette this morning in some bushes and your granddaughter saw them. Grammy fell up against the wall with her mouth wide opened. I was thankful that she came inside the room because had she not she would have hit that wood floor.

CHAPTER 32

Any hoot, Auntie Becca came into the family room saying oh there yall go I heard the kids and a thumb I wondered who was in here with them I thought Kimberley had fallen. Becca stopped smiling as she looked into Grammy's eyes she immediately knew something wasn't right so she said 'what's wrong'? Momma said 'Becca is everybody gone'? She said 'yes everybody but Tommie'. Momma rose up from the cot to say 'men'! You just can't trust them. Grammy was still in shock clutching her pearls looking bewildered. She then screamed damn it Harold! Becca said 'oh Lord let me sit down for this one'. Momma said 'Auntie is you sure everyone left'. Becca said 'I done told you everybody left but Tommie'. She looked at Grammy who started clutching her dress like she was having some sort of tantrum. Auntie Becca said 'Ernestine what's wrong I only know that look from something terrible that done happened'. Grammy couldn't find the words so Momma said 'Auntie my baby saw Harold and Antoinette up there in the bushes this morning having sex'. Becca said 'come again because I see your mouth moving but I didn't hear you right Gerry'. She looked at Grammy then went to grab her by the hand and guided her to sit on the cot. She then paused but said 'Ernestine now I know who Mr. Harold is, he's a Brooklyn hoe! When he stepped foot in my house that day in Harlem I couldn't remember him cause I make it a point to delete hoes from my memory bank'. Lordy so that's what I heard this morning them two making love. I'll be a monkey's Auntie unh unh. Grammy started tearing in her eyes she was devastated and angry at the same time. Little Kimberley sensed something wrong she walked to Grammy to touch her knee and just stood there looking directly at her. Auntie said 'Sofay take these kids up front we will be out there soon'. Dang that's not what I wanted to hear so I took them upfront and thankful to see Cousin Tommie sitting there in silence gazing out at the ocean. I said 'Cousin the adults are having a meeting and I need to use the bathroom'. Tommie said 'no problem Sofay I got them'. I ran and snatched that bottle off the table to give to Tommie and raced towards the back. I started tip toeing once I was near the room I came in on the part when Grammy was crying. Becca said 'Ernestine remember you two were not a couple yet you were working on it'. He done told you who he is now it's time you believe him. Grammy said 'Auntie how low can you be to fuck that bitch in some fucking bushes on a filthy ground'. Becca said 'girl would you rather they were on a sleeping cot inside this house'? It was silenced then Momma said 'and to think this wolf hid all of J. W's infidelities for years from me trying to blame it on saving my feelings from being hurt and the fear of running away with my child'. I honestly don't believe any of them like me including Olivia. Becca said 'child if you feel that then it's time to pack up and move outta there'. Don't stay in a chaotic environment Gerry with you being confused and hurt all the time while all of them are sleeping peacefully at night and you up worrying. You never show your weaknesses to nobody you hear me Gerry you never let that right hand know what the left hand is doing. She continued on saying sometimes the worst kind of woman is a religious woman who can tell you her perspectives on life using Bible verses but inside in her own Soul she's crying out for help cause nine times out of ten she's jealous of you. Child your Uncle tried that shit with me with having a secret side chick. Momma said 'and what did you do'? Becca said 'I put sugar in her car tank and a dead rat on her door step with a note that said 'it's me bitch Mrs. Howard'. This is your last warning to leave my fucking husband alone. Momma slightly laughed and said 'then what happened'. Becca said 'ole she went back telling Lester what I did but he never confronted me because if he did he would have told on himself and basically admit that he was cheating with her. He walked around for day's child slamming furniture around the house eyeing me but not once did he mention that floosy and what I did to her. I wasn't finished with her just yet. I then got my two sisters and told them next thing I knew Lucy had jumped on the girl pulling out her edges while Elizabeth was stomping here. At that time my Mother was alive. She was against my sisters whipping that bitch's ass. She came to me to say I went about handling that situation wrong. She said and I want you to listen to me both of you's. My Mommul said 'girl child why you disgracing yourself over this man'. It's him that put it in her but it was them both that fucked each other. Don't put the blame just on the woman but you blame that man as well. You put him in a corner and try to make him confess but remember men rarely admit they wrong they will dance around it and turn it around so that questioning them will make yah feel like you was the one out their fucking. Don't you believe it you hear me Becca it's not your doing. Trust me when I tell you Lester gone be mad as hell because he already know how yall whipped that bitch's ass he just waiting on you so he can trick you into thinking you were the one wrong for accusing an innocent woman in being his hoe. Trust me baby and watch his sneaky ass. She said 'the one thing is man can't be along they got to have some trim it's in them unlike us women we can go months without sex but that's not the case for a man. When you tell him no sex he'll go find that trim to satisfy his needs and he usually don't stop with one woman they got to have multiply women. The problem occurs when he gets careless but sloppy and you catch his ass out there hoeing. Mommul said 'I'm telling you baby from my own personal experience with yall stank ass Dadday'. She told me it was up to me if I wanted to continue on with a cheating man who was good for nothing or forgive him and stay with him. I've seen so many women who will do whatever it takes to hold on to a cheating man cause they don't love themselves or are afraid to be alone. The worst thing to do is use the children Rebecca. Sometimes when a woman use children as an escape goat it's in hopes of lewing that man back home regardless of the situation or she has some other arteria motive that's conniving to make that man feel guilty because of his cheating ways. You can always tell when your man fucks up cause he start doing little nick nacts around the house without you telling him. Hell I had your Dadday to repaint the whole house and buy new living room furniture. She kept my Father because she was afraid to start over. She was good at giving advice but she never took too her own advices which sadden me and my sisters. So Ernestine and Gerry I said 'that to say this'. Antoinette will get what's coming to her because how she got him is how she's gonna loose him'. Grammy said 'I hear you Auntie but Im'ma help her by beating that bitch ass when they get back'. Becca said 'no you not Ernestine you will continue on like you've been doing giving out no signs or clues'. Trust me when she get back here looking at you and Harold that guilt is gonna ripe her in two.

And furthermore, you give her ass a show without putting your hands on her you hear me! Im'ma cook dinner tonight and I'm going to set Harold's portion to the side and you can put whatever you want in his food then Becca winked one eye smiling. Oooll is what I said to myself before I knew it I busted up laughing. Momma said 'Auntie I will help you cook'. Huh! My Momma is going to cook I can't wait to see this shit! Grammy said 'Becca I like your plan but I got to slap her or do something to that fat ass slut'. Then Momma jumped in saying Mother I'm with you I'll trip her while you stump her. Becca said 'now hold on here did yall not hear me tell yall what I went through with Lester and what my Mommul went through with my Father'? Neither of you will lay hands on that child she already thinking she's carrying a secret that only she and Harold knows'. Suddenly I heard little Kimberley singing while Tommie started making his way back towards the family room with the kids. I saw him limping so I pretended to be coming out the bathroom and walked towards him. He said 'girl your stomach really acting up cause you been in there like forever'. I smiled at him and grabbed little Kimberley's hand and followed behind him to where Momma and them were. He said 'Grandma what yall in here doing'? Becca said 'talking Thomas and bring that baby over here'. She started baby talking to baby T as Tommie stood there grinning. Auntie Becca looked at me and said 'Gerry this baby of yours done been here before'. She's the needle that's keeping the White's together. She's at the wrong place at the right time observing, learning and telling. Thank goodness Sofay saw those two or else none of us would not have known right away about Harold's ass. Tommie limped back a step and said 'what the fuck! You mean to tell me Harold got busy with whom? Momma said 'Antoinette '. Wait a fucking minute you mean Ms. Holier than thou! No way man unbelievable this bitch got nerves to check me when she's an undercover hoe. Grandma you've always said to watch them Holier than thou women because they sneaky. Man and here I'm pissed off at Floyd's grinning ass. Man Gerry it's something about that man I mean he acts like Sheila is his woman. He bold as hell and flaunt all that money around in fact, they all do that shit. Grandma I have to say something to him cause he disrespectful. They act like if it wasn't for them we wouldn't be here in Lake Placid when in fact it was planned before they arrived in New York. Momma said 'calm down Tommie after all I'm still related to the Whites'. Tommie said 'yeah, yeah, yeah better you than me because I would have unrelated myself from them a long time ago'. They were all quiet for several minutes looking in different directions. Tommie said 'but you know Antoinette's hoe ass hit me deep in my bones'. She was cold as hell but in all she was right. Her mean ass helped me to get it together with a plan because come Monday morning I'm looking for a job to support my family. Becca damn near dropped the baby after Tommie said that. She smiled saying baby everything happens for a reason and no matter what Thomas you still my Grandbaby and I love you son. He said 'awh Grandma don't start getting all mushy on me and I love you more'. He said 'any way when they all leaving? Grammy said 'well Harold is getting his ass out of here tonight I don't want him around here grinning in my face'. She said 'Auntie just give me a minute to absorb all of this plus everything you've said'. I just want to get in a car to search for that little witch and stomp the shit out of her. Becca said 'Ernestine what did I just say it wasn't just that child having sex but Harold's ass played a role in it as well so if you gone get her get him too'. Grammy was fuming she practically had smoke coming out her nose and I felt some kind of way because I sat there and realized that my Dad's side of the family are ruthless people with a little dark side. I just didn't see this coming from my family! I mean I thought about Eisha's secret then I thought about Nitta's secret and now Antoinette's secret is out in the open and the only difference is that I never revealed Nitta's witchcraft secret to Momma yet. I know it will come a day in which I will reveal what I saw that day in the back woods but for now maybe it will be best that they all leave at least Tommie would be at peace. I glanced at Tommie whom seemed to be in an unsettling mood. He managed to say has anybody thought that maybe Sheila and Floyd got busy I mean something has happened between them I got a feeling but I'm not certain. Right at that moment I had already devastated my Grammy with the news with Harold now from what it looks like I might also have to devastate Tommie with what I got to say. Auntie Becca said 'Tommie don't milk the cow until you got a bucket up underneath it' meaning be sure of something before you accuse. Grammy said 'what the fuck is going on here it's too much fucking around all of us'. Becca said 'well I can assure you that I won't be screwing any of them White boys'. I get a kick out of how handsome they really are Child. When I lifted my head up from looking at the floor Momma was looking at me and said to me 'come here baby'. You don't have to be sad with what you said to me about Harold. What he and your Auntie did was bound to come out in the open sooner or later. I don't want you to feel like you are the cause of this mess with adults because you are not. You opened up our eyes about family, lies, betrayal and before she could finish Tommie said 'naw the bottom line is they had no business getting busy like that in some bushes'. It's disrespectful! They only thought about their selfish ways. Grammy said 'Tommie'! He said 'oh come on Cuz what if yall were married then what'! Auntie Becca said 'well this all stays right here in these four walls. I don't want no fighting and destroying any of these pretty walls in here.

After all of that for some reason the air was cleared up I was speechless but relieved. We all moved into the living room and carried on as usual. Shortly after that Auntie Becca wanted to finally leave her place for some fresh air so we all piled up into Harold's car headed for the store. Grammy was driving recklessly she hit the brakes so hard at the light that we all nearly flew towards the front. Auntie burst up laughing saying to my Mother hold me child this gone be a bumpy ride. I whined Grandmaaa what you have to go and do that for because I saw baby T fall out of Tommie's arms in slow motion. My Grammy was crazy as all out doors after she laughed she then said 'oopps'! Causing Tommie to hold his stomach as he damn near screamed out loud laughing I guess he sensed something that I wasn't aware of. From the looks of it people were either coming into this town or heading out with luggage's strapped on top of cars. The town was small, quiet with very few people that permanently resided there. It was almost a deserted town but Grammy said 'that's what Tommie needed to get his life together'.

However, we found a grocery store several miles away from Rebecca's place. Momma kept on laughing each time Grammy was putting things inside the basket. She put two bottles of milk of magnesium, two packs of laxatives, Pepto-Bismol, cement, aspirins, glue and other merchandises. I was stuck on the bag of cement I wanted to know what she was going to do with it but I didn't dare ask. When we returned to the car my Grandmother was going insane.

Instead, of putting the gear into drive she put it in reverse hitting the brick wall behind us. Tommie couldn't maintain his self from laughter. She had the nerves to say 'oops once again' shit I bumped my head on the back seat. Then she put the gear into drive only to intentionally run into the shopping cart. By this time I knew she was definitely destroying Mr. Smith's car. I just hoped we make it out the parking lot in one piece. From the grocery store Grammy asked Auntie where else did she want to go but first she needed to get some gas. At the gas station ha-ha Grammy some kind of way ran up on the pump's concrete causing the man who pumps gas to jump back. She started laughing which caused Momma, Becca, and Tommie to join in with her laughing. The gas pump man peep down in the driver's window knocked on it and said 'Mamm' Grammy rolled down the window and said 'five dollars of regular please'. The man said 'Mamm you just scrapped your driver's side of your car'. My Grammy was getting a kick out of destroying this man's car with her insane self she had the nerves to say to the man 'oh my' that man hadn't a clue to what was going on he really thought she couldn't drive which was far from the truth. Grammy asked the gentlemen where the nearest furniture store was. He lifted his hat to scratch his head and said 'um well uh are you the one driving over there? She just smiled at him without replying back. He said 'well you hang a right at the corner here and it's a straight shot about five miles from here in fact, you will pass Drove's road side and ask for Billy Ray and tell him that Charlie sent cha to take a look at the damage on this car. Have him look at the driver's side and that back bumper. Grammy said 'will do Charlie is it'? We left there running over a curb which wasn't funny to me anymore but weird. The further out we drove the more stores we saw. Momma wanted to stop and go inside of Sears's department store she wanted to see the different designs of furniture for Auntie Becca's new place. Grammy let us out at the door while she went searching for a parking space. Inside the store I was in awh because in the country we didn't have such a lavish store with these goods. Momma and Grammy were over there whispering among themselves while Auntie found a living room set that she practically claimed by sitting on it. She smiled and rubbed the softness in the material while I was running behind Kimberley trying to keep her from walking near the escalators. Tommie was nowhere to be found in the store while I got a whole of that little brat and nearly dragged her back towards everybody. When Kimberley and I was near Auntie for some reason she was crying while Momma was standing over her rubbing her back. I asked Momma what happened and she said 'oh baby your Grandmother and I just purchased this living room set for the family and your Auntie is just happy. Me being inquisitive asked well what will she do when she sad. Becca immediately laughed out loud saying you little busy body I told yall she been here before. Tommy and Grammy walked back over to where we were gathered he was cheesing from ear to ear holding a piece of paper. Momma said 'ok Cousin what you doing'? He said 'yall won't believe this but they gonna hire me mannnn I'm so happy I don't know what to do'. Becca stood up saying what! He said 'yell Grandma all I need is help in filling out this application you know I ain't never fill out one before. Momma went to hug him and took the paper to read it and asked him if he had an ink pen. He didn't have one but limped back to the counter and got one. Grammy said 'I'm, well I don't know how I feel because just like Jr. said yesterday we all are walking testimonies'. Evil may try to deter us but faith over rule it every time. And wouldn't you know it; it was one of the gentlemen who had moved those sleeping cots into Becca's place. He was walking pass then stopped to ask Grammy did she remember him. Both Becca and Grammy said 'yes'. He said 'he work in the docks here at Sears and came up to take his twenty minute break before seeing us'. Tommie limped back and saw him then said 'my man how you doing'? He said 'doing well my brother by the way I don't think I gave my name last night but I'm Bernard'. He said 'if I knew you all were coming today and wanted this set I would have talked it over with my Manager'. He said 'his manager was the one who gave us those cots last night'. Becca said 'baby you be sure to thank him for me you don't know how much of a blessing those beds were'. He looked at Momma who asked out loud what's today's date. He said 'it's June 21, 1965. Momma said 'thank you then she looked at him to ask how it was working there'. Bernard said 'you want to work here'? Tommie interrupted to say naw it's me who's applying. Bernard had the biggest grin on his face he went over to shake Tommie's hand and even helped with the application. He then walked with Tommie to turn the application in. The next thing we knew Tommie was both hired and interviewed on the spot.

Meanwhile, my Grandmother was more convinced that we were blessed as a family with good fortune. Momma agreed with tears in her eyes. I have to say that this summer was one of the best summers in my life and probably many of my family members would agree. Sitting in Sears I realized that family will love you but will cut you worser than an enemy. Bernard ran back to where we were sitting to say that he don't know it yet but he's hired and I explained to him that I will pick him up on my way to work for a couple of weeks until he gets a car. Auntie hoped up so fast and nearly smoother him with her bear hug. She tried not to tear up from joy but it was too late. Bernard said 'Mamm I know the feeling because I was once your Grandson years ago and had to straighten up my life. I had no choice but to get it together because I lost my Momma and a Sister from my own mistakes within a crime life of being ruthless. So I'm more than graceful to help another brother out here who's somewhat walked in my shoes. Ok yall take care because I got seven minutes left on my break. All three ladies were over joyed with excitement and here comes Tommie; walking, limping and out of breath. He was so excited that he was lost for words. He was indeed hired on the spot with a schedule, an identification badge and work duties. He said 'Bernard basically did most of the talking for him because he was stumbling with his answers'. He grabbed both of his kids saying to them we gone be alright yall.

Anyway, we all were trying to leave Sears until we smelled the aroma of popcorn. Momma shouted oh my God I haven't had this popcorn in years I've got to buy some. We followed the smell and sure enough it was a long line of people waiting to get some of that good smelling buttery popcorn.

Actually, this was my first time eating popcorn and I was delighted. I told Momma I'm finally eating something that Gramz's didn't make from scratch. I never tasted anything this good with butter and salt before I couldn't wait to tell my Gramz about this little treat. Grammy gave Becca money to pay for our treat while she existed to go get the car. When we got outside we didn't see Grammy so Auntie told us all to stay together on the side of the store. We saw this car circling around twice driving erratically Tommie said with a smirk 'naw that can't be Ernestine' until the car stopped in front of us and Grammy hoped out on one leg saying will yall come on. I was shocked that none of us recognized the car because Grammy had smashed the passage side door in where it was impossible to open up. We had to climb in on her side to get in. Momma practically helped Tommie in because he wouldn't stop laughing in fact; she had to tell him to bend and get in because he was holding up the line for everyone else. I have to admit it was quite funny. We made it back safely with a slight case of whip-blash and saw the other two cars in the drive way with the moving trailer up on the grass. Becca looked at Grammy and said 'Ernestine remember don't touch that girl'.

Grammy didn't say a word. We climbed out the car with a few bags and a new stroller for baby T that Tommie purchased at Sears. Inside the log music was playing and everybody was moving about. Eisha met us at the door to tell me she purchased a cherry Slurpee from the gas station for me. I had popcorn that I saved for her and gave her the bag. Antoinette was sitting on the sofa looking scared to death while the men were either sitting or standing around looking spiffy from their fresh haircuts and trimmed beards. Auntie Becca looked at all of them saying all shit J. W. yall know better to come back here looking this good boyah keep it up hear yall gone make Morine to start moving. It was funny I even busted up laughing. Momma went to Daddy rubbing his face and hair staring into his eyes I said 'oh Lord' there they go! Eisha snickered. Grammy took me by surprise she's so dramatic because she walked in dropped her bags and went straight to Mr. Smith sliding off her shoes to stand on top of his shoes with her arms hanging to the side glazing into his eyes but smashed up on his thang. I just shook my head from side to side but smiled. At that moment I realized that sometimes the bad outweigh the good but all in all we do have a great time as a family. Then I looked at Sheila who was standing in front of Uncle Floyd. When Tommie came through the door holding the kids his grin immediately left as he limped in the house; he gave baby T to Daddy, and then put Kimberley on the floor, he walked straight to Floyd and punched him. Floyd managed to duck but blew a knuckle hit into Tommie's face. Jr. and A. J. ran and broke them up but somehow all four of them were wrestling with Tommie on top of Floyd on the floor. The women were screaming all but Grammy who lured Harold into the back bedroom. It was several minutes before the men calmed down. When Cousin Tommie got up off the floor he walked up to Sheila and dragged her into their room. Me and my Aunties were standing in the corner looking at everyone else. Daddy said 'mane didn't I tell yah to leave that woman alone now look at this shit'. Auntie Becca said 'well that's what I wanted to hear J. W. the truth because something wasn't right with both Sheila and your brother Floyd anyway'. I had an incline that the two of them been at it but I wasn't completely sure. Daddy looked lost for words and said 'well it's all out in the open now'. Cousin Jr. said 'mane now what's gone happen'? He said 'Floyd you stay right by me mane for the rest of tonight we don't need any accidents occurring'. The next thing we heard was Sheila screaming saying stop it, stop it you hurting me followed by a loud thumb. Tommie was losing it by shaking her and calling her every name under the sun. Me and Eisha looked at each other shaking our heads. Tommie kept saying what, what, then we heard him smacking her with her screaming back saying I'm sorry it just happened. Eisha and I grabbed each other arms because we had a general idea what their topic of conversation was about. When Tommie said 'I'm gone kill him I knew that fight was about Sheila and Floyd having sex. She said 'I promise I will never fuck him again Tommie I love you'. Cousin Jr. looked at Floyd because we all were listening to them and said 'mane see what you did' then it sounded like Tommie was strangely Sheila. That's when Auntie Becca got up from the chair and said 'ok that's enough of a whipping J. W. come on back here with me to break this mess up'. When they got back there and opened the door both of them was physically fighting one another. Daddy tackled Tommie down to the ground while Sheila was bended over crying. Becca managed to wrap her arms around her and helped her walk into the bathroom where she closed the door. Daddy tried to talk to Cousin Tommy about putting his hands on Sheila but he didn't want to hear it. So Daddy told him he'll be out in the front when he was ready to talk. Moments later Tommie came out the room and said 'I want all yall mother fuckers out my fucking house now'! Then he turned around limping back into the bedroom slamming the door. Nobody saw that coming. Floyd said 'whattt' you putting us out'? Daddy said 'Floyd'! Auntie Antoinette said 'well he don't have to say it twice we will give him his wish'. Cousin Jr. said 'but we were leaving in the morning though'. He said 'mane! J mane I've been thinking and don't yall head back home just yet I want yall to trail me back to Queens so I can get my belongings mane I'm going home'. Uncle A. J. was thrilled to hear that bit of news from Jr. He said 'mane I'm glad you coming back home where you belong I've missed you more than anybody'. He said 'the handsome buddies are back together again alright yall I'm ready to go now! Antoinette asked about his lady friend. Jr. said 'cuz if she want to come to Oklahoma she's welcome but what I'm not gone do is beg her'. Eisha asked Floyd to go apologize to Tommie so they could stay. He didn't bulge nor respond back to her. Momma said 'Tommie is heated up now yall better gone on ahead and go because none of us will get any rest tonight until he get ahold of you Floyd'. Floyd said 'well that won't happen he'll be dead by morning fucking around with me'. Both Momma and my eyes grew larger after hearing that because we didn't want to see Tommie dead by the hands of Uncle Floyd. Auntie Antoinette jumped in saying Floyd man down that's the end of this we got to respect him and leave. Floyd said 'I'm not going anywhere' and then A. J. said 'oh yes you are Floyd we all are leaving here now Eisha and Antoinette go pack our bags so we can load them into the car'. I followed my Aunties into the bedroom that Momma and Daddy had shared as the girls started gathering everyone belongings. I said 'Eisha go ask A. J. if you can stay' Antoinette jumped right in saying 'no need Gramz's would have a fit if we went back home without her baby'. I went to grab my Auntie Eisha by the waist because I didn't want to see her leave. Though I was trying to train myself to pull away from this attachment that she and I had built I just wanted her to stay. As each of us had a bag heading into the front room Tommie opened his door and threw six bags one at a time including two luggage's that were full of clothes into the hallway. Antoinette told us to keep walking. She told Jr. and A. J. to get the rest of the bags from the back as she opened the front door to put her bag on the porch. As they went in the back the bathroom door opened with both Becca and Sheila existing. Sheila stopped when she noticed her bags in the hallway and started crying yelling for Tommie. She tried to go into the bedroom with Tommie but Becca blocked her telling her it was useless to even talk with Tommie. Dang Tommie is serious I said to Momma. She responded yes baby he is very serious.

However, my Father looked weary at my Mother he told her to go get our bags so we all could leave. Momma hesitated before kissing Daddy and said 'we will be home real soon J. W. Daddy then asked her when and what did he do to deserve his woman to leave him like that. She said 'ole J. W. you know perfectly well I didn't leave you'. What I left was a chaotic household where I'm almost uncomfortable and going crazy. I needed this break from you and your family. I am coming back home just not right now sweetie. He responded Geraldine who does this! Who turns an overnight visit into an entire summer I can see you spending a night or even a couple of nights but not damn near ninety days? Momma said 'J. W. please! We are not going to go through this again my love'.

Meanwhile, Eisha and I were hugged up as she and I walked towards the car. Cousin Jr. said 'mane I'm about to tear up from this'. You got my man Tommie going through something now Geraldine refuses to come home this is too much. We may have to get a bull dozer to get J out of here. Uncle A. J. laughed and agreed with Jr. about needing that dozer to make Daddy move his feet from Momma. Once they stopped laughing Jr. looked and said 'what the fuck mane! Harold's car is damn near shattered'. How he gone drive back to Brooklyn? He then asked me what happened I told him I didn't know. Truth of the matter is I wasn't telling on my Grammy even though Antoinette was one of the reasons why Harold's car was almost un-drivable I didn't part my mouth. We were all outside waiting on my Father to make his way to the car and to another surprise we saw Cousin Tommie literally carrying Sheila over his shoulders as he walked down the stairs with her then he threw her on the ground. Both my Uncles including Cousin Jr. hurried up to walk back towards the house to ask Tommie what was he doing. Tommie said 'ah Floyd she's all yours blood then he turned around and threw one bag at a time on the front grass with hate in both his eyes and heart then he slammed the front door. I grasped for extra air reaching up for Eisha's ear to whisper what about the kids and who's going to take care of them. She said 'good question So-soo'. I then looked at Sheila crying the more Floyd spoke to her the more she cried. Uncle Floyd was excited he acted like a kid in a candy store. He walked her to the car grinning from ear to ear I guess he was getting his plans in order to welcome Sheila into the family because she wasn't welcome inside Lake Placid any more.

Yet, Uncle A. J. said 'what the fuck mane! now I'm pissed he done put her out awh mane somebody go get J cause I'm not stepping foot near that log I'm ready to get the hell out of here now'. Jr. said 'mane I'll go get him' he did but ended up calling for Antoinette. My goodness my sweet Father was up in there acting a dang gone fool. His crazy self-refused to leave without Momma so he wrapped her up in some of her clothes and tried to walk down the stairs with her on his shoulders. I didn't want to laugh as they opened the front door with Momma screaming at the top of her lungs threatening Daddy to call the fuzz because he was kidnapping her. Uncle A. J. started walking back towards the house with his hands up in the air saying mane J come on mane! Put Geraldine down mane unwrap her with all of them damn shirts and bras around her neck. She's not coming J. W. not now mane let her stay and enjoy herself for a change come on mane! Auntie Becca was in the background screaming at Daddy saying J. W. White let my niece go you crazy ass bastard as she was beating him on his back with her fist! Who you thank you is let her go then she yelled for Tommie to bring his pistol.

By this time, Eisha and Floyd who was sitting next to Sheila inside my Father's car had managed to stop visionizing his new life he was implementing with her. One he heard Jr. call his name he left Sheila running towards everyone else. I peeked inside the car at Sheila I shook my head again poor thing she was justa crying. I said to myself don't come out and play if you can't hang on the playground meaning she was testing the waters before even knowing Floyd. She disregarded the fact she was in a relationship with Cousin Tommie. Sheila was lusting for Floyd for the wrong reasons because she focused; on his built, looks, and money but hadn't a clue about his lustful obsession in sex. All I have to say is that she's gone find out real soon what Uncle Floyd J. White is all about. I managed to say Sheila you will be alright. She turned to look at me like she was being arrested.

Meanwhile, I was happy that no other houses were near because someone would have definitely called the fuzz on us. I was confused to see my Father behave in this way. I mean my parents quarrel but not like this. My Father was losing it when I looked up on the porch it took five people to unattached my Mother from my Father's strong grip. I didn't know whether to cry or laugh. Jr. was screaming ok J. mane one more step down cousin just one more. Come on now let her go. Let her go J come on now we got to walk to the car mane. Eisha started crying making me tear up she didn't like to see her brother loose his grip like that. It was unimaginable to see five people walk at the same time with all of them holding either my father's neck or shoulders. I saw my poor Mother get up off the ground with her hair all over her head with tears in her eyes. Antoinette was justa cussing at Daddy as I tried to walk pass to get to my Mommy my Father somehow managed to grab me. It was like the sun evaporated I mean he grabbed me so fast and damn near rolled me up under his arms that I started screaming Mommee! Momma came charging jumping on all of them trying to reach and pull me from my father's arm. My father's strength was like Hercules because he threw me in the back seat still struggling in trying to pull away from his brothers and cousin. Tommie came out on the porch with his pistol threatening them that he was going to shoot. No one paid him any attention because they had a hand full dealing with my father. My goodness this was one hell of a mess. Auntie Eisha got into the back seat where I was and pulled me across the seat when I got out that car I hugged her for dear life trembling. Jr. walked towards us to grab me and threw me over his shoulders then walked around the car to grab Momma by the arm. He screamed twice Geraldine I got her, Geraldine I got her for you! Here is your baby yall gone on into the house Cousin and I'll see yall when you get back home. My sweet Momma oh how I wished it was reversed so I could have carried her but instead she struggled to pick me up to carry me but had forgotten how heavy I've become. Tommie ran off the porch and put me down to walk while he held Momma by her waist to help her walk. I mean after all I was a big girl who was nine years old hell my legs were almost as long as Momma's legs. Jr. yelled Geraldine hurry up now and go on inside. She did what she was told. Auntie Becca was standing on the last step reaching for both Momma and I as all four of us walked into the house. We were inside as Momma looked out the window sniffing with tears running down her cheeks. Auntie Becca was out done with my Daddy's behavior she looked exhausted but confused. She told Momma to get out the window and have a seat before he tried to come back inside. So I got up because I had to see what was going on. My Daddy I loved him to death. He was going off screaming at the top of his lungs. His curly hair looked like a wet rabbit he pulled off his belt running around the car trying to whip Eisha as Jr struggled in holding onto my father. My poor auntie looked scared to deaf as she was running around the car from my father. I screamed no Daddy don't whip her. Momma hoped back up to see what was going on she said 'he trying to whip her because she pulled you out the back seat'. Tommie limped to the window and watched them saying that mother fucker J. W. is crazy as hell look at him! then he busted up laughing. Just then Grammy came out the room with her bathing suit on looking cute with Mr. Smith following behind her. She asked what all the commotion was about. Becca started telling her and Harold the details as I watched my family finally leave. Both Grammy and Harold were shock but disappointed. Harold said 'wow my man lost it then he looked over at Momma'. I wanted to say to him 'don't be looking at my Momma because your turn is next'. It was bitter sweet when I thought about the entire situation I was more concern with Momma's condition. I didn't know if we were going to permanently live in New York after Daddy's escapade or if we would return to the country. I didn't want her to fall back into a depression I wanted her to be full of joy once again. Grammy walked to Momma and pulled her chin up to look at her. She asked her if she was ok. Momma said 'no'. She said 'ole Gerry the man is scared to deaf that you are leaving him'. Honey he loves you though his ass is stone fucking crazy but he truly loves you. Let's think about it out of all your girlfriends including mine that have fallen out of love or ended a relationship none of their husbands love is like your husband. This man came here because he felt something going wrong as sure enough something did go wrong involving Tommie. Men rarely have that kind of intuition about their mate I mean they can sense something by actually looking at you but hardly ever do they feel you through body language. J.W has faults like all of us but you got to move on if you are going to continue and stay with him. Baby you got to stop holding on to old grudges with the other woman. You said it well last night in your Prayers now it's time to walk in your Faith. Do what's in your heart and not because of hate. The man has proven his self I don't recall him admitting fully to his infidelities he still respects you, loves you, worship your daughter, and takes good care of you both. Momma allowed tears to roll down her face. She knew Grammy was telling the truth. She said 'Mother what I can't deal with any longer is living in that crowded farm'. I'm tired of looking at coochies, penises, buttes, and bare naked bodies that I don't know what to do. I can't even be comfortable to walk nude without J. W. pitching a fit. It's ok for his family to walk around nude but when it comes to me all hell freezes over he'll pull down drapes to cover me up. I feel like I'm suffocating living there. Becca jumped in to ask Momma has she ever told my father that she was suffocating. Momma said 'no she figured he already knew'. Becca said 'come here Gerry so I can slap you with my good hand'. How does he know how you feel if you don't share entirely how you actually feel he isn't a wizard child'? Momma said 'I can talk to J. W. about most things except moving out his Parents farm'. Becca said 'well I'm guessing if you mention moving into your own place now especially after today I bet he will listen to yah'. She said 'she thought my parents were having major problems but they weren't'. Daddy would creep out with another woman every so often but it wasn't on a continuous bases. Momma moved her hair off her face so I went to get my comb and brush to comb my Momma's hair because she looked like she was in a fist fight by the head. When I returned back in the front I brought baby T with me from his bedroom. I handed him to Momma as I brushed her hair into a pony tail. My Mother was extremely attractive in fact the genes were strong of good looks on both sides of my family. She looked half white with golden red hair passed her shoulders with a few freckles across her pointed nose and cheeks. She wore a size seven. She dressed casually but comfortable. Whenever she wore makeup she looked glamorous like she didn't belong in the south. She had so many women jealous of her because of her attractiveness. My mother wasn't the serious type but she always told it like it was without sugar coating the situation. She graduated from college with big hopes and dreams of dancing. She was five eight in height and carried herself like rubies. She talked slightly proper and could out slick you with just words alone. She had a few friends that visited often and they would join her in dancing, singing and having a good time. My father had a problem with Momma's dancing he didn't want her dancing around the farm he felt certain dance moves were seductive causing his blood pressure to rise up. Whenever, my mother would dance for him privately all he did was blush and grin then he sent me out the bedroom. I'm telling you once again they both were a trip and a half.

Anyway, my mother would have girl's night out where; they drank, read magazines together and painted their nails.

However, I would walk in many times to hear several friends sharing information about my father's floozies. They were precise with his where about, times and the location which had my mother's undivided attention. Momma would respond to them saying I fucking knew it wait till he brings his ass inside. My mommy I loved her to deaf but I realized early on that she could be a bit of a show off at times. She loved when certain in laws would return home to see her mingling and laughing with her friends. She would flaunt and brag making sure she was heard with how she and the girls were hanging out. Ha-ha, though, these groups of ladies were a riot they were fierce because several of them didn't associate with any of the White girls and they didn't hid it especially when Momma complained about them. What kept me laughing was when my mother would go visit a friend dressed up with makeup on my father couldn't take it causing a quarrel between the two. He felt that it was only fair to see who my mother was dressing up for and he always volunteered to take her to her friend's house to wait for her outside in his car. She wouldn't allow him to wait on her like that she felt my father was being childish and insecure which caused her to immediately cancel her plans.

In conjunction, many women were also jealous of my Mother being married to my father. They too felt that she was stuck up or high and mighty. Many of them felt that they were better suited for my father instead of my mother because they were born and raised in the south. It was always a difference being with her in town compared to my father. Several men in town flirted with her making her blush often when I was younger. I could tell she didn't mind the compliments from the fellows because her walk would change. She would put more of a bump a bump in her steps switching and all. Momma hated to see several women who would be gathered lined up along the walk way staring at her but smiling at me. Those southern women were vicious and didn't hide the fact they didn't like her which affected my mother's way of thinking and morals.

Instead, of violence she chose to tell several of her sister-n-laws and sister friends who took matters into their own hands making Momma satisfied with the end results. I also noticed that my Momma's backbone wasn't as strong as Grammy when it came to my father mistresses because she would threatened him that if she caught him with a female she would do damage to both of them. My father wasn't receptive to those threats which led to many arguments and many make ups sessions during the nights.

CHAPTER 33

In addition, we heard Tommie screaming 'Grandma, Grandma! She ripped me off. Grammy told Momma things will work out for her then patted Harold on the chest as they went out the patio door to the water. Tommie damn near ran into the living room with his money bag half full. He said 'Grandma she took my money'. Auntie said 'calm down she did what'! He repeated his self he said 'Sheila took forty thousand dollars of his money leaving ten thousand dollars behind'. See that's what I'm talking about you can't turn a hoe into a house wife man I don't believe this shit'. Tommie was angry he went to the window to look out of it then walked back to his bedroom. Momma said 'that's awful to steal from the hands that feed you'. She told Auntie that's a no-no with J. W. we don't steal from each other we leave hundreds of dollars laying around all the time and everyone knows not to touch what's not yours. But I tell you one thing let her steal from Floyd and I guarantee you he'll break several bones on her. Becca laughed and said 'that girl got a long road ahead of her because when she gets settled in I'm taking her children to her'. I ain't trying to raise no more kids my daughter was grown when she passed away'. Momma said 'I hear yah Auntie'. Moments later it was a knock at the door nearly setting panic in both Becca and Momma. Becca called for Cousin Tommie to answer the door he limped back. I said 'Momma wasn't he just walking'. She put her finger over her lip silently laughing and said 'yes'. Tommie turned to Momma and said 'Gerry was Sears delivering that set today? Momma 'said I don't think so'. Tommie opened the door to let Sears in to deliver four bedroom sets and a new dining room set. The man asked for Sheila Montgomery. He needed her signature for conformation of the delivery. It appears that Sheila purchased the sets sometime today and paid extra for an expedited delivery for that day when they were all out sight-seeing in town. The delivery men came in and swamp out both Becca's old bedroom set including the old dining room set and they replaced them with the new purchase including setting up the extra three bedroom sets. Tommie was confused but slightly happy to get off that sleeping cot and into a bed with a firm mattress. The kids had a bunk bed set; a Chester, a night stand including a matching crib for the baby. Whereas, both Becca's and Sheila's furniture had the queen size bed, a matching dresser with mirror, an amoral and night stand. The fourth bedroom just had a bed, night stand and a Chester. I have to give it to Sheila the girl got good taste. The furniture was so sharp and expensive any one could tell by the quality and heaviness of the wood. Once the men left Momma and I went to put the sheets and covers on all of their beds. We helped Tommie put their clothes in drawers. Momma was amazed to see in the bedroom corner what Sheila had purchased there was; a high chair, sheets, blankets, quits, toys, new clothes for the kids, hangers, and four lamps. Tommie said to Momma 'Cousin I'm glad she got us bed sets but I know perfectly well all of this didn't cost no forty thousand dollars'. Momma said 'I agree Cuz but honestly Tommie what made you put her out like that'. He said 'cuz after sitting down just thinking remember earlier when I said I thought something happened between her and Floyd's asses. Momma said 'yes'. He said 'well it turns out those two did fuck she admitted it to me they did it in the restaurant's bathroom and when he rented a room at the hotel'. I lost it man I threw her ass up against the wall and called her every name I could think off. Momma was shocked because she stood still and didn't move as Tommie talked. He said 'Gerry I was getting tire of Sheila's ass'. She never wanted to work a job she slept till 2 o'clock in the afternoon forcing the kids to lay there with her. She always complained about nothing but stole everything under the sun. Whereas, the streets were how I made my money. I know I was just as at fault by not loving her the way she needed to be but I tried. Now I gots no respect for her that was building up even before Floyd and them arrived. It's not right but I'm not the type to get up every morning to go to work or at least I thought it but now I got no choice but to work. Don't get me wrong cuz but this is my first real job I'm kinda of nervous man I can't fuck up. Momma assured him everything will work out for the best. Momma told him he made his choice when he putted her out and she asked him if he would go get her and bring her back home to make things work out. He said 'naw he can have her I'm done'. Momma asked him what will he do with the kids. He said he'll send them down South for a while but they got to come back. Momma picked up his money bag and placed it on a shelf in the closet. She turned to him to say at least she didn't take it all Tommie. He said 'Gerry stop trying to find ways to take up for Sheila we just wasn't meant to be together'. I stole her off the streets to satisfy my male ego. I felt like I was stuck with her cause she was in no hurry to leave me. He said 'yeah but she knew I was saving that money for us to move out and get a new ride'. Momma said 'really'! Family was what I was thinking. We all have issues some can be solved whereas other issues linger on. I am definitely walking the path among wolves. I mean who knew all of this would take place. This summer has been; joyous, sad, unbelievable, and life changing. I've seen the inside of lust mixed with insecurity that led to betrayal and it's still another two months before the summer ends and school starts back up. After looking at Momma I left the room to run her some bath water and even went into the bedroom to get her underwear along with some fresh pajamas and her house shoes. We had moved all the sleeping cots into the fourth bedroom for time being because they were in the way. It was tight in that fourth bedroom but we put as many of them sleeping cots in the closets then the remainder cots were standing near the corner walls. Everyone's room was in perfect order and Auntie Becca was so pleased she grabbed a whole of my Mother's waist and thanked her once again for everything that she had done. She did well by not crying but the tears were frozen in the corners of her eyes I could tell she was holding them from running down her cheeks. It was a special moment.

CHAPTER 34

In addition, it was almost night fall and I couldn't wait to take a bath and go to sleep my damn self. Auntie was in the kitchen preparing food. I saw the fish and asked where it came from. She said 'they brought it because there was no way they went fishing today with some much that happened'. I noticed she had an entire fish set to the side but I didn't ask why knowing there was a reason behind it. Grammy and Harold came in from viewing the water. I told her how pretty she looked and she said thank you. Then Grammy turned to ask Becca what was she cooking she told her fried fish, fried green tomatoes, boiled okras, potato salad, spaghetti, and coleslaw. Becca said 'I put yours and Harold's to the side because I didn't know how long you were going to be outside'. Speaking of Harold he was looking unusual by the face, but I got to say he's a good looking man. He's about six feet two in height like my Daddy. He was a well-groomed man. Though I can't help but wondered was he heavy when he lay on top of Auntie Antoinette last night. I guess I'll ask her one day.

In addition, Mr. Harold Smith was a dresser who wore a gold long chain that hung from his pants hoop. His voice was slightly deep more of a base tone that could carry over most conversations. He was very polite, observant, and humble. He did well for himself financially because he owned his property and worked a good job in the metropolitan area.

In fact, his friends that helped moved my relatives pretty much resembled him or one another. I saw my mother checking a couple of them out. Harold is a family man who was divorce but kept his daughter Gail to raise her. The man has a good heart despite being a bed hopper.

However, I wanted to ask was he ok but choose to continue holding the baby. Grammy said 'oh thanks Auntie let me wash my hands to help you'. I looked up just in time because I saw Auntie Becca slide to Grammy the laxatives along with the milk of magnesium. They continued talking and slightly laughing even though those two were up to no good. Tommie made his way up front then stopped to look at Grammy. He said 'damn Ernestine laughing but umm can somebody go find Ernestine'. Grammy blushed as Tommie continued on by saying 'Cuz if we weren't related girl but seriously I got to give it to you because you wearing that bathing suit like a model'. Harold turned around to look at Grammy but said not one word.

Consequently, my Grandmother said 'hold up Auntie I left something and ran out the front door she did it so fast that I didn't get a chance to get up to look out the window to see what she was doing. She came back in turned up the corner of her lip and snared at Harold. I said 'uh-oh'. Momma came out the bathroom looking ever so refreshed. She smiled as she observed the food and told me my bath water was ready. She set the table as she observed Mr. Smith putting the high chair together for baby T. Becca turned around to say 'Harold you don't have to put that chair together baby Thomas can do it'. He didn't respond back making Auntie snicker with covering up her mouth. The food was ready and we all sat down on the new chic dining room set to eat as I watched Grammy. She was more cheerful then usual she sat next to Harold rubbing his face, then his chest and she didn't even take a bath to change her clothes which was highly unusual for her. During dinner the table kept moving from up under. Harold's knee kept hitting the table come to find out it was from Grammy tickling his thang. Tommie kept laughing out loud saying this has been an unforgettable day for me while grinning. He was tickled pink. Auntie said 'yeah baby this certainly has been a day and from it Im'ma have to get out here and find me two men to satisfy my needs with all of this sex business going on up in here baby because they done set off Morine'. She ain't stop jumping and thumbing I'm about to lose control of her'. All the adults laughed then Grammy stood up and threw her drink in Harold's face. Everybody stopped laughing but me I was practically on the floor because I saw it coming. She said 'ooou ah baby say a prayer again so I can give it to you then she spit in his face'. Tommie said 'alright yall' he got both his kids and said 'come on Shortie' I said 'uh uh no I'm staying' I watched Tommie bended over laughing as they went into the back room. Harold said 'what the hell are you doing Ernestine as calmed as he wanted to be'. She said bringing back memories from last night you son of a bitch how could you Harold how could you fuck that fat bitch outside on the ground, the ground Harold! I saw him drifting in and out I didn't think he was the type to practically faint I mean he instantly put his head down on his chest closing his eyes real tight shaking his head side to side while Grammy continued to go off on him. She told him to get his fucky ass up and get the fuck up out of there. I said 'funky! I didn't smell a stench on him hum'. Harold dragged his self-up very slowly from the table like a robot that's running out of batteries you know at a slow pace as Momma told Grammy to calm down. As he got up Grammy got to hitting him on his back, head, and even poured spaghetti on his head before Becca and Momma pulled her off of him. He was like a zombie! Just like that! He even turned around slowly speaking in a slur by this time I was literally on the floor laughing and kicking my legs up in the air because it was so damn hilarious. Both Momma and Becca were in pain holding their sides from laughing as well. Grammy didn't give up as she was pushing Mr. Smith towards the front door he managed to say wait, wait Ernestine wait I got to go to the bathroom can I use the bathroom please Ernestine while still squeezing his eyes shut and shaking his head from side to side. She said as loud as she could 'what! Hell naw nigger shit on your way home! My goodness I was absolutely impressed with my Grandmother's revenge I mean who knew, who knew this woman was a fire cracker I had never witnessed nothing like that in my life. Again, I didn't see this coming from my family! Grammy quickly ran to the back to return with Mr. Smith's luggage I mean she was stomping and walking extremely fast as if she was about to miss a train. She opened the front door and just threw his luggage outside without looking to see where it landed. Then she turned to Auntie Becca to grab her by the shoulders and fell out laughing herself. Auntie was wiping tears away from her eyes from laughing and Momma was still holding her side. I was still on the floor but rolled over onto my stomach once she closed the front door. Tommie came out the room to say Im'ma need some type of surgery caused yall done ripped my kidneys apart with this shit. He said 'man Ernestine that was as clever as hell how you did that'. Now when you got Grandma laughing into tears you are funny as hell. Auntie said 'yes indeed I'm gonna have to write this one in the books she said 'Ernestine girl you was smooth with it'! Grammy said 'well I learned from the best Auntie and that's you'. Momma said 'Mother you've been so calm all evening not having or showing any expressions of an attitude or anything how did you do that? I know he didn't see this coming. Grammy was a shade lighter like she was relieved to get rid of Harold and his shenanigans. She went on to say Auntie it took an enormous amount of strength in not to beat Antoinette's ass today as I pondered with this sex thing between her and Harold. But I'll tell you one thing his ass won't even make it to the nearest gas station because he's full of twelve laxatives pills and a half bottle of milk of magnesium in his system. Talking bout can I, can I use your bathroom ole fucker! Coming up in here putting baby T's high chair together. Her voice was loud as she asked Tommie did you ask him to do that. He said 'noooo' still laughing. She went on to say she purposely went to the spot outside where he and Auntie Antoinette made love before coming inside the house. She said 'I maneuvered my way holding his hand as he looked shocked but speechless'. I went directly to that spot acting like I dropped my bracelet there and looked him in his eyes and asked him to help me look for my bracelet. Hell his ass was as white as a sheet. I moved the flowers and sure enough it's a body print so I said to him looking directly in his eyes while tilting my head I said 'Harold what do you supposed happened here'. Tommie busted up laughing holding his stomach. Auntie said 'oh that's why he looked so funny when you came in here'. I knew you said something to him. Grammy said 'ha-ha Auntie I love the fact you had everything lined up for me to use in his food'. As you passed it I used it on the entire plate. Auntie said 'yeah baby I'm a bad influence on you shame on me' before she started laughing again. Grammy said 'when I ran outside I slide some cement into his gas tank all I got to say is he'll be stopping for both gas and to shit about every five to ten minutes all the way back to Brooklyn. He won't have any changing draws because his entire luggage is filled with bleach and mud' then she held her own stomach laughing. I couldn't stop smiling when I looked at my Grandmother she was a looker very pretty in the face. She was a size fourteen. She was five, five in height with shoulder length brown curly hair. My Grammy could have passed for a white woman but she had too much nigger in her to be completely white. She knew the streets but hung in them as a youth. Being light skin in New York during the fifties and sixties was somewhat easy for her making her pretty much excluded from the life of being discriminated against. She was blessed to not have been a maid but was able to choose pertinent jobs and places to live before her marriage. Grammy was strong in communication and if need be she could have out slick you with her eye closed. She was light skinned with a white woman's pointy nose. Her eyes were hazel colored and she carried herself very sophisticated.

Ironically, my Grandfather Wilbur (God rest his Soul), was Grammy's late husband he was nearly scared of her. He said 'she continuously threatened him if she ever caught him with another woman that he wouldn't pee right for three weeks'. My Grandmother definitely had an evil streak about her if you got on her bad side. She grew up around strong women who went toe to toe with their men in standing up for their dignity and strength. Then I observed Auntie Rebecca my goodness who was a size twenty. She wore her hair in a short neat curly brown afro that had a trail of grey lined up around her edges and front hair line. She was brown skinned with hazel eyes. She was five four in height and was a devil in disguised. Auntie Rebecca yearned for revenge in any shape or form. She felt it wasn't right to not be treated as a queen by your man. She definitely ran the streets of Harlem back in the day while advoiding the life of prostituting. Auntie was a no nonsense type of person who was quick to butt into other people conversations. Her husband Uncle Lester (rest in peace) thought she was nuts especially when he was caught out there with his many floozies. She once remembered her vow when she and Uncle Lester were married but she revised it to him as she cooked his food using everything except rat poison to try to make him stop creeping out on her. I know he had to eventually put two and two together especially after those meals because he was up all night with direahea runs.

Lastly, Cousin Thomas aka-Tommie hum, he had a look going on rather on the rough side a bit. I'm not sure where his looks came from because it wasn't from the Howard's side of the family. He was dark skinned with black beady eyes. He was five eight in height and dressed simple wearing jeans and a tee shirt. He kept a pick in his hair the entire day. You know the one with the black balled up fist. Tommie lost his Mother to a fatal illness and never really got over her death. His father disowned him as a child causing much resistance and angry from his mother and other members of the Brown/Howard side of the family. He felt that street life was the best way to make money instead of working a real job. Auntie Rebecca was evil in her own way causing Tommie to miss out on what love really is. That's why he couldn't love Sheila correctly because he didn't know how. My family I loved them to deaf regardless of the many faults that we all encounter. After that night everybody slept well including the kids we all got up late the next morning to start a new day without any drama until Becca looked outside and saw Harold's luggage still on the ground. She said 'she didn't think he could bend down to pick it up so he left the luggage where it was thrown'.

However, we stayed with Auntie for an additional week or so before returning back to Oklahoma. Grammy made sure before leaving them that those two Becca, Tommie, and the kids didn't want for nothing. It was tearful when we left even Tommie tried to man up from crying. Both Auntie Rebecca and Cousin Tommie were ever so graceful for everything that both Grammy and my Mother did for them.

CHAPTER 35

Finally, we were headed back home and I was good and ready to be back. Grammy had to get back to her clothing store to recoup all the money that she spent in New York. We made it back to Grammy's safely. Momma and I still had to take our shoes off at the front door. She had mail everywhere including two notes from the Whites that said let us know when you arrive back home with a happy face on it. Grammy immediately balled those notes up without even telling Momma. She waited after two weeks to tell Momma she got a note from Daddy saying to let him know when we are back in Oklahoma. She only mentioned it because Cousin Jr. visited her store and stay a bit to chit chat with her. Other than that we still wouldn't have known that the Whites were waiting on us to return home. Momma and I spent our day's conversating; we watched black and white television. We watched shows like Rifleman, Daniel Boone, Frankenstein, Abbott and Castillo. We ate yellow watermelon from Grammy's garden on the front porch. Grammy would say before leaving for work don't yall play over my watermelons you either eat the yellow one or the green one but don't waste neither. Ha-ha she was definitely a fire cracker.

Actually, it was the greatest thing seeing my Mother smiling and laughing with me. I desperately wanted to ask when were we going home but I didn't want her to get upset so I stayed in a child's place and never asked that question. Momma kept us occupied daily along with Grammy's neighbors Esmerelda and her daughter Moochie who was my age she and I hit it right off the ground. The four of us would drive to Grammy's shop to visit her occasionally and even drove to Oklahoma City to go to the movies and shop for clothes. Moochie and I played marbles, hop-scotch, and double-dutch. We used the front porch rails to tie the rope to it as though it was another person who was turning the rope we had a blast. Moochie and I even walked to the corner store for junk food. We would go in there with fifty cents and come out with two bags full of treats such as; penny strawberry cookies, sour pickles that had to have a green jolly ranchers sticks to put inside of it, we brought cigarette gum, hot corn chips, Chico sticks, and candy apples where it was a hard crunchy red candy coated outside of an apple. Those were some of the best junk foods around.

Additionally, we were enjoying our new friends but Momma took me by surprise one afternoon when she asked me if I was ready to go back to the farmland. I damn near wanted to pick her up but I remained cool and responded back by saying Mommy whatever you want to do I'm ready when you are. She said 'ok baby come and lets go pack our bags we're going home Sofay'. That was music to my ears. She said 'we will leave when your Grammy get off of work this evening'. I hid my excitement because little did she know I've been ready for about two months to get back home now its official we are headed back. My Grammy couldn't get home quick enough I was guarded that clock from the front porch. I wasn't mad or anything when Grammy tried her best to stop Momma and I from returning to the farm. She pleaded and told Momma she would buy her a car whatever she wanted to keep her from returning there. Momma was adamant and stern with wanting to go home. I was getting worried at first because Momma seemed to have weakened a bit going up against her Mother. Grammy realized it was a losing battle she looked devastated. My heart sank watching her but I still wanted to go home. Grammy took her sweet time changing from her work clothes to house clothes. Both Momma and I were getting impatience with her movements she and I had been sitting on the front porch for nearly two point five hours. Just as Momma rose up from the chair on the front porch to go inside to get my grandmother, Grammy came out looking at both of us. She looked suspicious as though she intentionally took her sweet time in stalling by making momma and I wait for her. Momma said 'Mother this is not our final visit with you stop acting like that'. I told Sofay that from now on instead of a few hours in visiting you, she and I would spend a weekend with you once a month'. That putted a smile on her face she quickly snapped back by saying ok baby sounds like a plan well come on what yall waiting for. We got into the car I couldn't maintain myself from excitement and apparently Momma was just as excited as I was. As we approached the farmland I thought Grammy took a wrong turn and apparently so did Momma. We all looked at the new renovations that took place on the land. There were four newly built houses behind my Grandparents home and two trailer homes that sat on the side of the barn. There was a sixteen wheeler Wiggly's Foods truck backed up near the fields which now had black tar going all the way back near the fields instead of the usual dirt. And also we saw an ambulance van with the sirens spinning sitting on the road. Grammy turned and looked at both of us and said 'welcome back home White girls'. before we all got out the car. I ignored her as the first person we saw was Uncle Chester he was looking at the ground Momma called his name. He looked up and almost ran to us but I ran to him jumping up in his arms boy my Uncle swung me around in his arms but never put me down. He grabbed Momma kissed her on the cheek then bear hugged her he also pecked Grammy on her cheek. He said 'baby girl I'm so happy you and Red are finally back home I won't even tell you how your man has been acting'. Next we saw Uncle Earl he looked but first dropped his tooth pick out his mouth and yelled out somebody go get J. he walked to us grinning I left Chester's arms for his arms and he did the same thing as Chester. Before I could get a grip on his neck I saw Baebae and I screamed Baeeeee she looked and grabbed Auntie Camille and they ran to us it was so good seeing my family. When I heard my Grandmother Gramz's calling my name I started tearing up she was saying to the people standing near the ambulance move outta my way then started calling my name she said 'Soo-so baby where you at baby'! Sofay! Lord have Mercy where's my baby! Sofayyyyy when we locked eyes she was the most beautiful chucky woman that I had ever seen with Auntie Nitta and Uncle R.L. both walking on each side of her. Earl had put me down the closer Gramz was getting towards us. Finally the woman who practically raised me was less than inches from me I froze I couldn't move my legs I was so excited to feel my Grandmother's arms wrapped around my waist. She said 'baby Grandmamma is coming to get you baby Lord thank you Jesus! When she was within inches from us she said 'R. L. would yall look at her'! My Gramz's was standing right in front of me teary eyed ignoring Momma and Grammy. She took a breath and stretched out her short arms wide I jumped right into them. My Gramz hugged me so tight I nearly became unconscious. She too swung me around in the air I closed my eyes enjoying the moment. I felt her crying as she stopped walking in circles. I felt her moving when I opened my eyes she was reaching for Momma whom she planted a kiss on her cheek as well as Grammy's cheeks. My goodness Gramz's was a short plugy woman who wore a size twenty two. Her hair was shoulders length salt and pepper which she kept up in a bun with Barbie pins. When she took her hair down at bed time it drove my grandfather crazy. Granddaddy was probably heard across town with his excitement as Gramz's put her night clothes on. Granddaddy said 'no matter her size she was still finer then moonshine' and on most nights we all heard them in their bedroom freaking causing Camille and them to bang on the walls for them two to keep it down. They too were a trip! I told yall I grew up arounds freaks.

Even though, my grandmother was a little devious at times she demanded everything to go her way. She was selfish to a fault and didn't hide her selfish ways. She was an advocate for control. She felt that if it wasn't for her then my parents wouldn't be happy. I'm not saying anything negative about my grandma. Though, she attended church on a regular bases including Bible study she really went not to just pray for the family but to pray the hardest for the children that were giving her the most hell with their daily lives. But in actuality if my grandmother had of stayed out her children lives I'm almost certain we wouldn't be living with her as well as many other of her children. Her pride and joy was her family. She enjoyed rising; teaching, cooking and watching each child grow up into their own person with her guidance.

In addition, Gramz's playfully hit Grammy's arm saying they were gone away from here to many days gul. I started seeing all my family except Granddaddy and Daddy. My Gramz didn't put me down as she walked I knew I was heavy because she kept swinging me from her left to her right hip without allowing anybody else to touch me. I saw Eisha and she jumped up trying to kiss me while I was still in Gramz's arms. I had my legs wrapped around her hips holding on tightly around her neck. I looked back and saw Auntie Faye and Monee who were walking and each one holding Momma's arms and grinning but talking. As we all walked I heard Momma ask Faye what's with the ambulance and what happened. She said 'Mr. Johnson got hurt' I looked at the ambulance and said 'Mr. Johnson what he doing here! Awl naw did he mess with Eisha again? My Aunties intentionally laughed out louder trying to cover up what I just said. I noticed Gramz immediately stopped walking and putted me down. She looked at me then said 'Grandmamma so glad you home Sofay I have missed you so much'. She turned and asked R.L. where was Granddaddy. He said 'he coming' just then I heard his voice. He started smiling when he saw Grammy and told her Ernestine what you been doing out in New York cause you done aged backwards. Grammy said 'ol James cut it out' laughing before she hugged him. He looked at Momma and hugged her then said 'welcome back home baby I missed yah round here' then he got to me while he played like he was dancing saying where's that little rascal at where is my baby I said 'here I am Granddaddy grinning'! He said 'well come here than before he picked me up he studied my face first then picked me up for a bear hug. I tell yah family knows how to show love and make you feel good and welcomed. I looked around because there were still Aunties and Uncles that I hadn't seen yet. I looked out at all those people and said 'Granddaddy I thought yall was gone stop all of these people from coming over here'. He said 'got damn'! My baby is back up in this farm'. Then he went and put his arms around Gramz's shoulders then stood next to her as Eisha came next to me to hold my hand. If my Auntie only knew how much I missed her she would have cried even though, I couldn't control the tears from rolling down my own face and to think I had nerves to talk about auntie Rebecca with all her crying hell I was no better in holding back my own tears of joy. Momma had tears in her eyes as she looked at me. I don't think my Momma realized the impact it had on everybody with us leaving the farm for the summer. But it hit her at that very moment now she knows that the Whites do love her as being one of them.

Nevertheless, Grammy asked Gramz what was that Wiggly's Foods truck doing out back. She said 'Ernestine, James got that contract deal with the grocery store'. Gul remember I had wanted you to come by here to help him understand what he was signing and reading'. Grammy said 'yea I remember'. Gramz went on saying that they hired an attorney whose specialty was in contracts he helped us by going over single word. He gave us the ok to go on ahead and sign off with the stipulations being they send a truck for the goods and James is paid on every delivery. This is the most we been paid without being cheated out of our money that's owed to us. James didn't sign off right away because he isn't too quick to trust everything he hears regardless of their title and whose during the talking. But it's been working out just fine with less work for him and the boys'. Grammy hugged Gramz's saying that Blessing was a long time coming Olivia. We all were still standing in the same spot until I looked up on the porch and saw both Sheila and Helen. I said 'Momma look there go Helen she turned and looked and said the same thing I said Helen! Chester said 'yall know her? Grammy said 'we met her in New York'. She and A. J. hit it off real good. Bae laughed and said 'yeah we heard a lot went on up in New York'. Momma said 'yeah some things took place'. After several seconds we started hearing a commotion from behind us and wouldn't you know it, it was Daddy, A.J., Gwen, Floyd, Monee, James Jr., Marshal, and Cousin Jr. walking towards us. I couldn't maintain myself after seeing all of them walking I mean I started grinning and laughing at the same time. Granddaddy said 'oh Lord here comes my boy alright yall move outta of J. W.'s way'. Grammy started laughing whereas I couldn't be still and for one Gramz had me by the shoulders I didn't figure that one out yet but any hoot; Uncle Marshal picked me up kissing me. I hugged my Uncles while watching Daddy walk straight up to Momma picking her up off the ground. He hugged her so long hell I was getting jealous even though I went from arm to arm with my family members I still needed that hug from my Father. He finally put Momma down and reached for me. My Father had tears in his eyes making me cry immediately. He kissed me. Normally I would have been like ugg Daddy but this time I didn't mind at all. He then picked me up grabbed Momma by the waist kissed Grammy on her cheek and told her to follow me. I heard Cousin Jr. Say 'mane how long this ambulance gone be here? Then he and Chester started talking but walking behind everybody. We all walked including my Grandparents towards those two story homes. I was in disbelief at how well they were built and I was clueless as to why we all were headed in that directions. My Grandparent's home also improved with new siding and grey paneling going all the way around it. For once the home was one color with a newly built front porch including stairs. The closer we got to those homes I suddenly started trembling and I couldn't explain why but my Father looked at me saying 'it's ok baby' we reached the first home and Daddy said 'welcome to our new home Geraldine and Sofay White'. Grammy grasped for air patting her heart. Momma said 'what'! With eyes wider than a saucer Daddy never stopped grinning. He said 'yell baby this is our very own home'. He said 'I refused to move in here fully until my family returned back home'. Momma said with tears now rolling down her face 'but, but, Daddy stopped her before she continued and said 'well Mrs. White are we just gone stand here or are we gonna go inside our home'. Before Momma said a word Daddy put me down to literally picked her up and carried her up the front stairs. Momma was overwhelmed she couldn't even turn the door knob so Daddy opened the door for her. There were two front doors resembling Mr. Smith's front entrance at his flat out in New York. When we walked through the second door it was like paradise it was the most beautiful space that I had ever seen. Grammy walked in saying oh my!' as I stood in the foyer Auntie Gwen patted me on the shoulders saying 'hey baby girl look how you've grown' I said' hey Auntie Gwen' grabbing her by the waist hugging her'. She said 'Sofay' then started crying. Gramz's shouted out 'Gwen did you forget to take your nerve pill today? She said 'yes Mamm I did but I'm going to do it now' I looked at my father and asked what a nerve pill is? Daddy said 'well Soo your Auntie nerves are shot so the doctor prescribe her those pills to keep her calm and help her stop all that crying she's been doing'. Right! I said 'I had almost forgotten how Gwen cried at the drop of a hat getting on everybody's last nerves'.

Anyhow, my Father went out his way to prepare this home for all of us. This was a gift Momma wasn't prepared for. I remember her talking about having our own space with Becca and Grammy and all along Daddy did listen to her during those argumentative times. He had planned this without letting her know because he wanted his woman surprised but happy. Come to find out through Gramz the day Momma and I left for Grammy's Daddy had already arranged a meeting the next day with contractors to build our home. He just knew Momma would have been there to not only meet with the guys but to give her input in how she wanted the house designed. After Daddy's trip to New York he had changed his original design for a more fancier but lavish appeal. Our home was a combination of Mr. Smith's three flat as well as Auntie Rebecca's log cabin home.

In addition, the wood floors were oak; the foyer had a round oak table in the center that had a huge vase with flowers in it. Next to the foyer was the the living room across from there was a sitting room. It was a four bedroom four bath room home which my Father turned one room into a dance studio for Momma. The other bedrooms were for me, my parents, and a guest room. We all walked through this spacious house in amazement. Further back was the dance studio and a tiny bathroom with just a toilet and sink. Upstairs were the other three bedrooms with adjacent bathrooms. When we got to my room I was floored I didn't see that coming.

After all, I've slept with other people including my parents all my life that I didn't know how to re-act now that I had my own room. When Momma opened the door it was like I heard Angels sing. My bedroom set was white with light pink walls and white and pink curtains. There were huge stuffed animals on the bed as well as the floor. I had toys and even a white rocking chair. I ran and jumped on that bed rolling back and forth grinning from ear to ear. I blocked everybody out during that moment I grabbed that soft pillow and just laid there. Next thing I heard was my bedroom door closing then Gramz's said 'baby'. I looked up and there were my Grandparents standing next to my bed looking directly at me. I swallowed hard not knowing what to expect. They sat on each side of me with Gramz's reaching for my hand while Granddaddy put his arm around my shoulders. I took a deep breath. Gramz's said 'baby I want you to repeat to James what you said outside about Georgeis' I said 'ol no I'm in trouble' Gramz said 'no, no, no you not in trouble baby I just need for you to tell us everything about Georgeis messing with Eisha'. Granddaddy said 'Red I'm counting on yah to tell your Granddaddy the truth baby'. You know I'm not gone let nothing happen to yah sugar'. I paused then looked at both of them and started telling them everything that happened between Eisha and Mr. Johnson. They were silence with Gramz's tearing up. Granddaddy kept repeating to his self-saying I can't believe it, I just can't believe it Olivia'. Just then Eisha opened the door bended over laughing. She said 'Mommy and Dadday yall got to come see Geraldine she almost fainted on the floor after stepping into her dance studio'. Marshal caught her before she hit the floor. Granddaddy said 'Alright baby girl we'll be down shorty' he said Eissh you make sure to tell everybody don't come near this door until we come out you herr'. Eisha slowly stopped laughing and said 'yes sir'. I looked at Granddaddy and asked him if Momma was ok he said 'yeah baby it just sounds like she got a little excited'. We were all quiet while they were thinking about Eisha and Georgeis I was thinking about my Mother but remembered Grammy was down there with her. I looked at both of them while Gramz had tears streaming down her cheeks now but Granddaddy was teary eyed but nothing rolled down his face. He said 'now Red go back to the shed' so I did as I talked he stood up on that part and walked towards the window as Gramz followed him with her eyes. He said 'now it all makes sense my chillren didn't want us upset Olivia they kept it among themselves but they whipped his ass for it'. Granddaddy said

'Red that day I went to visit him'. I interrupted him and said 'yes sir it was Daddy and them that whupped Mr. Johnson and put him in the hospital'. Then he said 'what about that day you spit at Georgeis baby because I tried everything in me to figure out where that behavior came from'. It was out of the clear blue sky you did that now I'm guessing you did that from your Auntie and Mr. Johnson. He looked at me and I said 'yes Granddaddy'. He said 'damn baby! When you get older Red and start having your own chillrens you will have a better understanding in how this type of news is one of a parent's worst nightmares. As a parent you never want anybody knocking on your door to tell you your child has been murdered, or rape, or in jail, or in a deadly accident. The feeling from that kind of news is unexplainable it makes you go numb. A parent wants every detail to what happened to that child then the plotting for revenge surfaces. Some would say forgive the perpetrator but baby it's easier said than done because you still want to rip that person or people to pieces. Gramz's interrupted to said 'So-soo when you said 'ah did he lick Eisha again I almost wet myself'. I couldn't pick my heart back up that's why I held you down by your shoulders I wasn't letting you out my sight until I got to the bottom of this. Lord have Mercy why my chillren thought it was best to handle this themselves without saying one fucking word is what I don't understand. I said 'we all were told by the boys not to say one word to either of you'. Marshal said 'that if you knew Granddaddy you would kill him'. He looked back from the window and said 'he be right'! Then he said 'see Olivia my friend of over forty years wasn't a friend after all'. I trusted this man with my life do I need to remind you he was the only one to come through for us and helped us during our time of need. I would have never suspected him to hit on my baby girl out of all the low down shit he's done over the years. But you know that's why his ass got a blade right there in the chest because of A. J. I asked Granddaddy what happened with the ambulance being outside on the road. Gramz's jumped in to say Georgeis just recently started back visiting us again. But wait James! now it all makes sense. Every accident that has occurred with Johnson has happened on our property. Let me see, he done got his finger sawed off, he fell on a trap twisting his ankles, he got an arrow shot in his hand and now he's in ambulance headed back to the hospital with a blade in his chest. Gramz's slightly laughed after repeating what A. J. said to her. He said 'Momma he was already standing there so I went to sharpen my blade and lost control of it'. Gramz's said 'James isn't there a chain in between bricks holding that saw from flying blades? He said 'yeah Olivia'. Granddaddy said 'dog go nit why continue to still come over here when you know you molested my baby'. Because he knew neither of yall knew what he did to Eisha is what I said and furthermore, I felt it was time to change conversation from my sweet Auntie Eisha and focus now on something else. I said' I think yall should also know that Auntie Antoinette slept with Grammy's boyfriend Mr. Smith; Gramz's fell back on my bed. Granddaddy ran to her side saying Olivia, Olivia get up'! She said 'James I can't' so he pulled her up with one arm she grabbed a whole of his waist and sobbed'. Granddaddy said 'Sofay you got too much balled up in yah child'. Lord help my family Jesus! He looked down at Gramz and said 'Olivia get yourself together now here! She said 'James I can't I'm about to fall to pieces our baby has been molested and now we got a slut of a daughter'. He said 'Lord Sofay what took place out there in New York because Jr. done came back here sugar coating everything which cause me to suspect something didn't go as planned'. So I did tell them but first I looked at my Grandmother who started looking darker in the face. I said 'Gramz you got to stop crying (I stole that phrase from Cousin Tommie when Auntie Becca was crying) then I got up cause I was curious what those other two doors were in my room. I got up to open the first door it was a closet full of clothes and shoes. The second door was my God a bathroom I screamed to my Grandparents I got my own bathroom! Granddaddy tried to smile and said 'yeah baby it's time you got everything that you should have had a long time ago'. J. W. didn't care about the price and went all out he wanted you and Geraldine happy but comfortable. Hell I was becoming overwhelmed myself and needed to sit down. Yet I was still upstairs telling Auntie Eisha's business to her parents even though I was missing out on the fun downstairs I should have kept my big mouth closed. But I marveled at how everything was so well put together I was almost scared to touch the towels. My Daddy is what I said slightly smiling; however, I got two towels for my Grandmother's eyes as well as one for my Grandfather I hated to see both of them sad'. I sat back down between them glad to see my Gramz's was slowly coming around while Granddaddy put his arms back around me this time he scooped me into his lap and hugged me real tight while Gramz scooted closer to him. He said 'Sofay this was too much to handle even for somebody that's crazy. You've seen too much child heard too much and learned too much all at a young age. Baby I want you to get on your knees and pray every night that the good Lord will continue to give you strength. When I think about all of this I didn't start seeing this type of stuff until I was in my twenties. Dog gone it; you done seen your Daddy out there trying to kidnap your Momma, Tommie getting beaten by thugs, there's Tommie stealing Sheila from hustlers and Sheila stealing both money and clothes. Becca done got horny and then theirs Antoinette in the bushes with your Grammy's boyfriend Harold. He said 'my sweet baby Jesus - Heavenly Father I decree and declare that you continue watching over my family. Lift these wicked demon spirits off all my chillren and replace it with brightness of light, a clear but clean path, a clean spirit over matters and put the Armour of the Mighty Word of God in them. Hallelujah I ask you Heavenly Father to create a renewed Mind, Body, Soul, and Spirit for all of us, In the name of Jesus Amen. And no weapon formed against thy shall prosper is what I said proudly. Gramz's said 'you go head girl' before kissing both Granddaddy and I. Silence again, but he said 'well Olivia I'm making major changes around here effective now'. We are officially stopping all these men folk from visiting our home since now Camille, Floyd, and Jr. also got their own houses right here they should have their company on their own property'. I said 'wait so these other houses are for Camille and them? Gramz's said 'yes and those trailers belong to A. J. and Faye. Granddaddy went on saying Olivia I'm going to the hospital and I'm gonna try not to take my pistol with me to speak with Johnson. It's gonna be finalized once I leave there we will no longer associate ourselves with him. He said 'got dog it! it's killing me Olivia that my baby thought it was fun to do something like that with one of my best friends who knew better. I know he lured her cause that's what he does to them girls. She got to be scared and hating him for returning back here. I can't imagine how our child is feeling these days. Well I tell you one thing my baby girl ain't got to ever worry about this bastard stepping foot on these here grounds'. I looked at my Granddaddy sad face and it was painful to look at him. Then suddenly I got nervous because I didn't want any whippings for telling my Grandparents everything. I just stared at Gramz's. She asks what was wrong before I could say it my Grandfather said 'well-baby and patted me on the shoulders to say don't worry yourself Red Granddaddy is right here and I guaranteed you J. W. won't lay hands on you or any of the rest of them. He said 'Olivia is you ready to join our family and she said 'yes James'. Alright Red lets go on down stairs'. I didn't want to run and leave them behind so I walked as they walked and we entered the dance room. I saw Simon and walked to him hugging him. I asked him what he was doing there. He said 'he was visiting Auntie Camille she needed help putting up her new drapes'. I said 'huh' then he said 'she needed me' causing Jr. to laugh out loud. I left him looking for Momma I found her sitting on top of Daddy's lap which I hadn't seen in like forever. They were in the living room sitting on the sofa so I went and climbed on top of my Momma's lap. Gramz's came into the living room looking at us and immediately started crying. Camille grabbed Gramz's by her shoulders kissing her saying 'awh Momma' she looked at Camille and repeated back awh Momma when you and Simon gone get married and settled down sitting up here calling him to hang up some drapes'. Camille left the living room with Gramz walking behind her fussing. It was funny. I looked at my parents and asked Daddy was he happy. He said 'Sofay, Camille I'm about to do a dance for you and your Momma in a minute to show both of you how much I've missed you'. Momma laughed telling him she believed him but he didn't need to dance with his two left feet. Daddy laughed saying he was a better dancer then any man Momma knew. My father suggested a dance contest to see who the best dancer was and that's just what those two did. We headed to the dance studio as Daddy was high fiving his brothers and cousin pumping his self- up. While Momma had the ladies to cheer her on. My Grandfather plugged in the radio and wouldn't you know it my father's favorite song was playing and he immediately broke out doing the mash potato. Everybody started cheering while Momma was like oh uh-uh then she broke it down doing the twist of course the older ones went crazy but Daddy wasn't finished just yet he stopped looked at Momma and said 'alright Geraldine but what about this move' it was the funky chicken. My Granddaddy couldn't maintain his self so he joined in with Daddy and did the chicken dance. Ha-ha my Mother wasn't going to let my Daddy win so she called Grammy, Gramz, Camille, Gwen and Helen and they broke it down doing both the swim and the loco motion we had a blast during that moment and of course the ladies won against my Father's better judgement because in his eyes he was the winner. It was definitely a celebration in celebrating life, love, joy, and family. Cousin Jr. left and came back with beer, moonshine, and cigars for the fellows. Granddaddy's friend Mr. Martin came in looking for him. He was impressed in how I grew several inches in height over the summer as he talked I was eyeing Auntie Eisha to see if she had that lustful look in her eyes.

In addition, both my Grandmothers were out of breath from dancing and existed off into the living room to sit down. Eisha and I were on the floor playing jacks as Uncle Earl walked on a jack with his bare foot and started shouting all shit! Gramz's yelled out alright Earl didn't nobody tell you to walk without your shoes on. Eisha said 'Earl now you made us lose the ball how we go finish playing jacks? He said 'E did you see where the ball went and besides get your butte up and get the ball yourself'. He kept walking to catch up with the men. I have to say many times all of them got on my last nerves with being stubborn and mean. Moments later Auntie Monee, Gwen, and Nitta came in with pots of green tomatoes, corn, and okras. My Grandmothers got up to help cook as I looked at my parents slow dancing as both of them walked into the kitchen they were funny to me. My father popped my Mother's butte before leaving the kitchen to join the fellows outside on the front porch. Grammy never stopped smiling as she observed my parents. As he walked passed me, Eisha and Camille teased him about his dancing. He said 'hold up did yall not see me getting down with my moves yall know I beat the ladies I'm the king of dancing'. E said 'yeah, yeah, yeah brother' then he high fived all of us before walking onto the front porch.

Consequently, Sheila walked in looking all but friendly. Auntie Eisha got up off the floor to greet her and then sat back down. I didn't speak to her but eyed her as she walked passed us and into the kitchen. I whispered to E saying I didn't see her arm in that sling earlier what happened. Auntie E whispered back smirking she said 'she came down here stealing money laying around the house'. She did it the first time and nobody said anything we acted like we normally do. It was Earl that told Floyd we got a thief in the house. Floyd told her we don't steal from each other and if it's something she wants he told her to tell him and he'll go buy it. This knuckled head ignored him with her thieving ass. Earl wouldn't let up and set up a bait leaving four hundred dollars lying around once again she stole that. Floyd flipped out springing her wrest. Their argument turned into them shoveling each other until she slapped him across the face then he grabbed her arm just a little too hard. She's been in a sling for about three weeks. I said 'wow she took the bait and still stole I wonder what she was thinking. Then I shared with both Camille and E how Sheila stole forty thousand dollars from Tommie the day he put her out. Camille slide on the floor to say come again! Then she looked into the kitchen like she was looking for Sheila. She wondered why she needed all of that money when Floyd has been spending nothing but money on her ever since she came down here. It seems like she has a bag of goods every day when she comes back home. Camille continued on saying she gives me the creeps because she stares too much with the little bit of talking she does around everyone. Eisha jumped in to agree with Camille she said 'she also had notice Sheila does an excessive amount of staring but she ignores her'. We three sat there for hours chatting and then the real party had started outside with the men. You could hear them from blocks away because they were so loud and full of moonshine. At least Uncle R. L. was sober because he brought in ribs, chicken, and links that somebody was cooking but forgot about. Simon came in looking for Camille to tell her he was leaving to go pick up his nephew from the city. He asked her if she wanted to go with him and she said 'no she wanted to stay but ask him to come back to spend the night with her'. He blushed and told her he would. As Simon left out boy the men were on fire I mean that beer and moonshine took the best of some of them because they were so loud arguing and cussing. When I walked to the second front door I saw Mr. Martin, Jr., James Jr. and Granddaddy wobbling trying to stand up straight. I went to tell Momma who was sitting at the table talking and sampling the food but I ended up doing the same thing in fact, Gramz's made both Eisha and I a plate and we sat on the floor to eat. I was eating and admiring how the kitchen was put so neatly together. It was a lite beige color with decorations from curtains to pictures. The cabinets were oak and rather fancy. I got up from the floor to open all the doors to look inside of them. Each cabinet had; plates, cups, glasses, can foods or seasonings. I looked at Grammy saying now I know Daddy didn't choose all this fine decorations by himself. Auntie Nitta hugged me from the back to say naw J was confused in what to choose for the designing of your house. It was me, Camille, Antoinette, Floyd and the contractor's assistant who pitched in ideas. Momma thanked them for helping my Father. Truth of the matter is my father could barely coordinate colors let alone comb my hair. Many days when Momma was sick in bed he would comb my hair having me looking like Pippi long stocking by the head bless his heart. It was Auntie Eisha who would sit me down to re-do my hair the right way while my Daddy always thought it was nothing wrong with the way he did my hair.

Anyhow, Eisha asked Nitta did she see my bathroom and she stood with her hand on her hip saying wait a minute you got a bathroom Red? I grinned from ear to ear saying yes Auntie. She said 'well you just gonna have to show me then'. I did and she was more pleased knowing I loved both my new bedroom with a bathroom. When I got through showing some of my Aunties and Helen my new room I asked them what happened to Mr. Johnson. Auntie Gwen didn't want Helen to hear the conversation so she exist the room with Helen in tote. Nitta said 'baby he brought his ass back here out of nowhere'. He walked on the porch acting like he was trying to surprise Dadday and shit. I was the first one to see him so I ran to tell J. W., Chester, Floyd, and Marshal who practically ran off the field to the porch. When we saw him he looked uneasy but managed to greet us one by one. He stayed for some hours but before he left Bae bae walked with him to the road while Dadday went into the house happy that his friend resurfaced. Marshal got his bow and arrow to shoot him in the ass but it missed and landed in his hand.

As a matter of fact, he's had a few accidents here but he kept coming back over here. I guess his pride got the best of him because he acted like he refused to be run off from around here. I didn't want anyone to know but I felt sorry for Mr. Johnson I listened how my family welcomed him with a lukewarm greeting but in the inside they were honing plots and mischief to pull his Soul out of him. Camille jumped in to say as much as we set traps to harm him he still brought his silly ass back here.

Meanwhile, as the evening grew into night I started feeling settled in our new house. My parents and I walked everyone out except the men on the porch that was planted in their seats or sitting on the banisher my Father laughed looking at his brothers. He said 'it brought so much joy to him seeing the family getting along without any drama'. Momma asked Daddy who will walk Mr. Martin home he said 'he would if everybody else was too intoxicated'. My father left the two front doors open for them in case someone had to use the bathroom then he headed for his room. I went into the kitchen to check on Grammy who was moving around straightening things up. She turned around to say what a surprise Sofay I'm so proud and graceful that your Daddie built this beautiful home for you all. She said 'she would not have missed an opportunity to see Daddy's reaction when we returned home earlier that day'. I didn't realize that my parents were standing behind me as I talked. I told her Grammy I'm happy you stayed with Mommie and me. I was so happy my daddy built me a bathroom let alone this pretty house. I said I'm so happy to be back home with my father because he don't know how I missed him. My Father came to me and bend down to say 'you make me so proud Sofay and if there is anything we need to talk about you know that I will have both ears open for you at any time alright baby'. I grinned back at him and said 'I got something to say he said what is it then I asked him if Grammy could come and live with us'. Momma made her way all the way into the kitchen staring directly at her Mother. My parents and I looked at Grammy at the same time.

CHAPTER 36

Instead, of an answer she sat down and just stared back at all three of us. My Mommy said 'well Mother is you going to answer your Granddaughter'? She couldn't because she was taken back with the question. Daddy said 'Ernestine I know you and I got this love hate relationship but my baby asked you a question'. She still said nothing but continued to stare at us. Daddy said 'ok Ernestine then know that you are always welcomed here at any time in fact the least you can do is spent tonight with us and besides it's too late for you to be driving alone out here at this time'. Gee if I was forewarn to not ask that question I would of not parted my mouth because my Grandmother either wanted to cuss me out or she was really taken by surprise. Momma walked to Grammy kissing her on the cheek while sticking her hand out to her as we all walked from room to room touring our home and listening to my Father as he gave us the reasons why he choose this, that, and the other. Grammy did spend the night with us that night and slept in the guest room which was really her room. Her room was completely tan and white with fancy drapes that matched her bedspread. She had a storage bench at the foot of her bed with a tan rocking chair in her room. She also had her own bathroom with tan and white towels. She was pleased at the color coordination that was perfect.

Meanwhile, my Father assumed I would be afraid to sleep alone he was further from the truth. I had no problem sleeping in my own bed after all it was my Grammy that introduced me into learning how to sleep by myself when Momma and I spent the summer with her. My Father was getting on my nerves about sleeping alone. He offered the choice of sleeping with them or to sleep on the two seated sofa that was in their room for decoration. I told him that I was a big girl truthfully I was holding my breath after I said that because I didn't know how he would respond. His response was well alright then big girl but if you then Momma pulled him out my room and slightly closed the door. I heard him say now wait Geraldine I'm not gone have then their door closed. I laughed and rolled over but hopped back up to use the bathroom because I didn't want an accident in my new bed I even left the light on. I slept well my first night. The next morning when I woke up I laid there and got up to turn on the radio but there was no air wave it was too early for the VJ's to start work. I then decided what I was doing for that day. I went to wash my face and brushed my teeth. I slide my house shoes on and walked and cracked open Grammy's door she was snoring laying on her back I laughed then I walked to my parents room to peek in their room and noticed both of my parents were naked I said to myself 'dang Daddy' so I tipped-toed in to picked the covers up off the floor and covered him and Momma up then I closed their door. I laughed as I went down those stairs saying my parents are officially husband and wife again. I went across to my Grandparents house I knew they would be up and sure enough they were. They were in the kitchen drinking coffee and talking. I said 'good morning to them' they responded and it wouldn't be a morning without Gramz's sarcastic remarks. She looked at my pajama's and house shoes saying well aren't you pretty you see James she ran off with that damn Ernestine now my baby is high and mighty with house shoes on looking like a Barbie doll. I said 'Gramz's'! Granddaddy said nothing but looked sadden. I scooted my chair next to him and asked what's wrong. He didn't get any sleep from yesterday's news regarding Mr. Johnson. Gramz's said 'James it was the right thing to do no need to beat yourself up'. He said 'I know Olivia but this here done damn near ripped my heart out'. He looked at me to say baby I went to see Georgeis last night in the hospital. I sat in my car for the longest and made another stop before I went inside to see him. I left my pistol in the car because I knew had I took it they would have rolled him down to the morgue especially with the moon shine inside of me. I went in there he was laying there wrapped up and looking dazed. He rose up trying to smile but I didn't smile back. I sat down next to him and just stared at him saying nothing. He asked was I okay I told him naw man. He sat up fully alert now I said 'Georgeis you been my friend for how long man'. He looked wide eyed and confused. I said 'I done watched and listened to you sexing all these women and girls but now you got to pay for what you did'. He said 'what'! I said 'man I know you been up in my baby and out of all the fucking females you done stoop so fucking low is to molest her right there on my property man'. Georgeis you been there for all of my sixteen chillren and for you to touch my fourteen year old baby I can't accept that nor your friendship ever again. He said 'hear me out James'. I told him naw man I need for you to admit what you did to Eisha White on February 14, 1965. Admit it man so I can move on from here. He stalled briefly then said 'alright my buddy I'll admit to having oral sex with Eisha'. I said 'naw man that won't do say her name and the date so I can go on home to my family'. He stopped crying stared directly in my eyes and said 'I admit to having oral sex with James and Olivia fourteen year old baby girl Eisha White on February 14, 1965'. Officer May and three other Officers on the force walked in the room with a camera to take his picture. There was a reporter and a recorder who recorded the conversation. Gramz's said 'James' and she got up to kiss his forehead then she stood next to him rubbing his back. I touched his hand my Grandfather squeezed my hand and said 'baby that was one of the toughest thing to do to one of my best friends'. I rose up but stood there looking at how he was about to break down even further. I socked him in his jaw as hard as I could and walked out of there. They handcuffed him in that bed to take him to jail. I didn't know what to say but managed to say Granddaddy is this my fault? Both my Grandparents said 'no Sofay it's not your fault'. Granddaddy said 'but I blame myself for not putting this puzzle together'. Gramz's said 'now hold on James we are parents and we cannot be with our chillrens at all times throughout the day'. We can only hope before she started crying. Granddaddy grabbed her hand to kiss it. I got up to wrap my arm around my Grandfather's neck and used the other arm for Gramz's waist. He said 'well I put my friend away for some time'. But before the hospital visit I stopped in the Sherriff's office. I told both Officer May and Shelby that if they wanted a dead man they needed to arrest him. I explained what he did to Eisha and they were floored but discusstate. I told them to keep her out the papers but make sure Georgeis is in the papers for what he did. Shelby wanted me to get him to confess what he did to Eisha for a stronger charge against him and that's what I did. Later on today Im'ma go tell Gertrude what happened. He said 'Olivia we gone have a talk with our daughter and after that we will buried this thang for good'. I said to myself man that damn Eisha with that big ole booty better not do this shit again.

CHAPTER 37

Nevertheless, about thirty minutes later I left there feeling awkward and went back home to cook. But before leaving I told Gramz's I was gone cook breakfast and she asked if I wanted her to help. I said 'no mamm'. She reminded me how to turn the stove on without burning up the stove towel and said to yell out the window if I needed her. Once I got in the kitchen I prayed to be able to turn both the stove and oven on without being afraid or having to wake my father up. After I prayed I gathered fifteen oranges and squeezed them into four glasses after using the old fashion juicer. You know it's the little white cup that looks like a balled up hand with ridges where you slice the oranges in half and pressed and turn.

Any hoot, I made coffee. After that I peeled and sliced the potatoes for harsh brown I rinsed them off and putted them in the pot to cook using oil, salt, pepper, onions, and green peppers. Then I made both homemade biscuits with gravy. For the gravy I used flour with chopped onions, milk, chopped up green peppers, and a little seasoning. I was deciding what else to cook for breakfast so I cooked those left over green tomatoes, I made sunny side up eggs, I fried slap bacon, and I fried some skin, along with grits. Man I was exhausted! I'm not sure how long it took to cook but my parents and Grammy were still asleep. I saw eating trays in the pantry which was perfect for me to carry the food upstairs. I liked how the dishes matched the trays it was such a neat little combo. I had to make two trips to the kitchen. I placed each tray on the floor at the top of the stairs hell I almost got back in my own bed I was exhausted from cooking. I knocked on my parents' door no one answered so I opened it and said Mommy, Daddy wake up, wake up while carrying the tray. No one moved I had to put the tray down to shake both of them to wake up. My father woke up kicking and reaching for the covers I jumped back and said 'dang Daddy what you doing! He said nothing but made sure he was covered up I smirked and said 'here's breakfast'. Momma sat up in the bed stretching her arms smiling and said 'Sofay now don't go spoiling me and your Daddy with all this cooking'. Daddy smiled eyeing those biscuits and gravy saying oh no spoil your Daddy I love it pumpkin. I said to myself 'pumpkin'! dang he real happy. Daddy said 'where's your tray'? I said 'with Grammy's I'm going to take her food before it gets cold'. As I walked out Momma said 'wait this girl done made both of our favorites baby I hadn't had fried skin in like forever. She bit down into it moaning I tried not to laugh as I opened Grammy's door. She was getting up and smiled as I walked to her bed with the food. She said 'Soo don't you be bribing me to live with yall'. She looked at the food and grabbed the coffee cup. She had a fetish for coffee I had two cups with milk and sugar along with orange juice for both of us including the food. I sat on her bed as we ate and chatted up a storm. I was disappointed that she chose not to live with us. She explained why but being a kid I didn't agree with her reasoning because regardless I would have love waking up to my grandmother being in the next room. My Momma came into the room with just her underwear's on feeling free to be able to walk as she pleases. She asked Grammy to hang out with us today and not go to work she acted like she didn't want to at first but she gave in to saying okay. As we were leaving Jr. was seating on his porch in his underwear's and t shirt. He said 'morning yall' we spoke back then Momma stopped and asked him what he was doing this a.m. He said 'nothing so far cousin' she said 'come on and join us we're going to hang out in the city today'. He obliged went into his house then came out running to the car. As we passed my Grandparents home Helen and A. J. was sitting on the porch and Momma invited them to come along. We all piled into the car headed for the city we all talked the hour ride and had good conversation. We went to the shooting ranch where we rode bumping cars; the men played horse shoes, threw darts, and practiced their shooting. We all played games inside the game room and rode the hay ride. It was still early so we went to the movies to watch Black Dracula and it was scary. I just hoped I could sleep that night without being scared or there would surely be a urine accident in my new bed. Before we left Oklahoma City we stopped in both the ice cream parlor and a popular cigar shop. My father purchased gifts for my grandfather such as a new pipe, some snuff, many different flavors of tobacco, and various brands of cigars. Cousin Jr. was in his elements of joy in purchasing a cigar humidor as well as vintage and popular cigars. Uncle A.J. also purchased many different cigars for his guests that often visited his new home in one of those trailers that sat beside the barn. As the men were leaving the shop Jr. noticed the local newspaper and it blew his mind once he read the caption. It said 'man molested an innocent fourteen year old girl'. The paper showed a picture of Mr. Georgeis Johnson being handcuffed in a hospital bed. Cousin Jr.'s mouth dropped as he showed the paper to the adults. He purchased the paper and read the article out loud as we headed back to the country. Uncle A. J. said 'J should we mention this to Momma and Dadday? Daddy said 'wow he done finally got caught'. I would like to know what innocent man's daughter they talking about. Jr. said 'mane they didn't print her information because she a minor hum I can respect her family's privacy'. I said 'nothing but looked out the window and wished I had gotten a larger ice cream cone'. Grammy was tired and asked Daddy to drop her off at home. Helen asked about her car. Momma said 'well Helen if you not busy in the morning would you trail me over to my Mother's? She said 'sure'. We made it back home and we couldn't park fast enough without Auntie Eisha and Monee saying why yall didn't tell nobody you were going to hang out we wanted to go. Cousin Jr. told them to move big heads and it was no more room. Monee said 'alright Jr. don't make me bust out a window in that fine pretty house of yours then she took off running with both Jr. and A. J. running behind her. Daddy told Momma and Helen to gone on in the house while he talked to his parents. I asked Daddy if I could come he said 'gone on in with your Momma and Eisha'. Man I wanted to go and be nosey but oh well I got to do what I'm told because my Father is half crazy. I watched him walk to his parents' house holding the newspaper under his arms and his gifts to granddaddy in his other arm. My Father the head man in my life was a well-built man I guess from working shirtless in the field with all that lifting and bending that he did. His walk is something like a pimp walk to me the kind of walk that makes you say ok who is this with his bow legged self! He's stands at six one in height with medium caramel tone skin and hazel nut eyes. His beard and mustache was faded almost invisible but lined up neatly on his face. He's a no none sense type of fellow majority of the times but will laugh if it's something really funny. He genuinely gives love and affection to his family and does not hesitate to correct any of his siblings if they are being belligerent or foolish. He's a talker who will talk your head off causing Momma to tell him many times to shut the hell up from talking to her because he gave her a headache.

Undoubtedly, my father was the eldest child making him have added pressure of always being pulled in between his sibling's rivalries. My grandparents were no better in always relying on him for almost everything beyond a son's duties. He was under pressure to please his parents who at times had forgotten they had other sons to help them. He was grown with a family still living under his parents' house which took a toll and started affecting him. He once told my mother he didn't know how to escape from my grandmother because she had a whole on him and the other children until he came up with an idea to build our home on his parent's property to keep peace. I tell yah the pressure of control!

As a matter of fact, when I was younger God forbid me to be with my Father in town with those vultures of women. They would have tried anything just to break my parent's relationship apart. I could tell the ones he liked because of the actions he gave out to them. Oh yeah I saw him in action when I was younger he always bribed me with sweets to keep me quiet whenever we returned home. As I've gotten older and observant he tries his damn-ness to ignore those women sometimes it work while other times he would shrug up his shoulders sticking his hands in the air. I mean he's a good looking man as well as his brothers including my Granddaddy. Now my Grandfather is the main man that I loved. He was a true man of standards. He too had a distinguish walk and bow leg as my father. He was a small built man five eight in height. Brown skin with those same colored eyes as my Father and I. He's wasn't a dresser but loved wearing his jumpsuit overalls which he nearly had all colors. He loved smoking his pipes and drinking the homemade moonshine that he could make with his eyes closed. My Grandfather came from humble beginnings as a youth in the South. He was a part of segregation where he picked cotton and worked on the railroads. He saw many friends being hung on trees for various reasons. His life was limited with many trials and errors. While his parents kept him and his two brothers busy on the farm he had dreams of one day owning the land with expansions. It was rough for him in those days but through his parent's perseverance they helped make a man out of him. His parents eventually wanted the mortgage in his name because they were afraid to put the far in their names. Granddaddy fought long and hard to become the owner of the property that we reside on. He fulfilled his childhood dream and it took many years to do so. My Granddaddy once had a trail of women whom he tested to see who had what it took to be his woman. He would have them cook and clean his place and somewhere along the way my grandmother won the prize in beating out those other ladies in cooking and cleaning. How weird is this? my Gramz's once dated granddaddy's brother J. C. He said 'she was too much woman for him always sassing off at the mouth and controlling his every move'. Granddaddy said the same thing about Gramz's. He said 'he had to tell her that his mother was dead and he wasn't looking for a replacement of her'. He said he really didn't want her because she had been with his brother but sparks fell somewhere between those two and they been together ever since. He said before he made his decision in what woman he wanted that Gramz's nearly threatened him into moving in with him which got him charged up because no other woman was bold like my grandmother.

Besides, Granddaddy always had a good story to tell especially if it didn't make sense as to why one of his kids did or said something stupid. He always told A. J. mainly after he was in trouble that what he was doing out there was nothing but a repeat of what he did himself at that age. He said the only difference is the day and age but it was still the same bull crap.

Likewise, as Eisha and I walked to our house we passed a small group of people standing near the porch whispering about Mr. Johnson being on the front of the newspaper. When she and I walked inside Momma was in there with Helen asking her how has Uncle A. J. been treating her. She said 'so far okay but it was some little tramp that was drooling over him when they were in town'. She said 'he was different from the usual guys that she has dated in the past'. My Uncle sent a round trip ticket to her which floored her. She said 'he's been nothing but a gentlemen but she don't care for the attention he gets from women'. I wanted to say you haven't seen anything yet wait until you two run into one of his many obsessed exes'.

Anyway, my Auntie Eisha and I hung out in my bedroom for the night. She spent the night and I was glad because I had a nightmare that Dracula was hiding under my bed flying from side to side with that cape on causing me to shake uncontrollably when I woke up. I thought to myself don't tell Daddy he would try to sleep under my bed until I became less afraid ha-ha. Eisha and I got dressed as I stopped and looked in the mirror at myself. Hum I had a look going on rather on the cute side at least I thought that. I was short at four six in height. My thick red hair was shoulder length. My eyes were the same color as my Father's. I too had that pointed shaped nose just like Grammy and my Mommy. I had a small pot belly that was filled with hog maul, chitterlings and every other type of animal. People always stared at me sometimes making me uncomfortable especially when I smiled my dimples were deep in my cheeks. Gramz's always said 'mighty funny how so many are jealous of my baby's fine hair and good looks'. She would often put her finger into a dimple as she watched me talk causing me to laugh. I was always around family leaving hardly any room for friends. I didn't have a hobby except being nosey and inquisitive but then again I was around nineteen other people daily who had some form of drama that took place causing me to be nosey. I dressed cute my mother made sure I had every color ribbon and burettes there were. Funny though, whenever

I went back to the farm from visiting Grammy I had on new clothes; which infuriated Gramz's. She felt that my other grandmother was showing off because she had good taste in clothing. Boy I tell yah Granddaddy was absolutely right when he said those two were like mud and water. Because truthfully speaking they both talked about what the other didn't do right as a grandmother leaving me confused most times.

CHAPTER 38

Likewise, I hadn't seen the inside of the other new homes so Eisha and I started by visiting Cousin Jr.'s place first. His place was designed differently with having; three bedrooms and two bath rooms which were on the first floor as the living room, kitchen, then his sitting room was up on the second floor with only a toilet and sink. Cousin Jr. was so excited to be back in the country with family that he was still beaming. He was preparing a pig to roast for his parents who were coming over to visit him. I asked him about his girlfriend back in New York. He briefly talked negative about her before asking what happened after they left that day. I told him. He laughed and said 'Red I've always loved Ernestine she's my kind of woman'. We left Jr.'s for our next stop at Uncle Floyd's who wasn't home so we went next door to briefly visit Auntie Camille's place. She was in the kitchen cooking thrilled to be on her own. Her place was four bedrooms with two upstairs and the other two bedrooms and bathrooms downstairs. Her living room was a size of two rooms together. Her kitchen was also gigantic with two different sets of table.

Instead, of her having the two front doors she chose one door. She preferred an indoor patio instead of being seen sitting outside on her front porch. I said 'hey Auntie what cha cooking? She said 'hey baby I'm cooking smothered pork chops, mashed potato with gravy, black eye peas, corn bread and cherry pie'. She stopped to look at me. She said 'girl you looking more like Ernestine'. I smiled and asked her if she's marrying Simon. She smiled and said 'hopefully! I'm trying to get him to move in with me but….' I looked at Auntie Eisha who was looking out the window and saw the Wiggly's Foods truck backing up near the field as we also saw another group of men with a loading truck. Auntie Camille said 'those were the same men from last week who installed her telephone services. They returned to finish the job by installing services in everyone else home including my grandparents'. I was admiring my auntie the oldest girl next to my father. Auntie Camille was educated studying to become a nurse. She said she's seen so much blood coming from her brother's wounds over the years that she decided to study the human body to see how we operate. Camille was a size fourteen with a bit of an unusual shape. I use to see her wiggle into her clothes like she was stuffing sausage into a wrap. Her skin tone was light with short black hair and black eyes. Her smile was incredible and she praised her pearly white teeth. Unlike her sisters Camille didn't have a flock of men running after her because she chooses books over men until she met Simon. Those two seemed opposite but somehow they meshed well and been together ever since. Honestly, I was surprised that auntie had her own house built because she was always up underneath Gramz's. She was so attached to her that Granddaddy would tell her Camille get up and stop being up underneath Olivia so much and go find something constructive to do. Funny though, at first granddaddy didn't like Simon for Camille then suddenly it seemed like he was contacting Simon more than Camille. Momma insisted that granddaddy paid Simon to court Camille because she was a home body who never liked to venture out in town for fun. Simon would come by unexpectedly just to take her to town to have a little fun which brought a smile on Granddaddy's face.

Meanwhile, Eisha was bored at Camille's so we left heading outside to watch those men finish positioning that tall pole. I told E let's go to Uncle A. J. and Auntie Faye's trailer home but she was against it and wanted to go feed the horses but Gramz's called for Eisha to help clean those chickens for dinner. I would have helped but I decided to go to my new room. I went in there kicked off my shoes and got a blanket from the closet to lie across my bed and laid there listening to the music on the radio. I must have dozed off because next thing I knew Auntie Eisha was in my room shaking me to wake up. I woke up to see she didn't have on any bottoms. I re-looked again and said 'Eisha where's your panties at? She walked to the window peeking out and when she turned to face me she was crying with whaps on her legs and butte. I was confused and nervous not knowing what was going on. I asked her again. This time she walked to my bed and bended down to sit her wet naked butte on my bed. She looked at me to say Red I got caught with Sheila messing with me. I saw her lips moving but couldn't hear the sound as she spoke. She shook me by the shoulders as I tried to imagine Sheila and her freaking. I asked her how that happened. She explained how it started with Sheila. Eisha ugg! Is what I said. My Auntie was young and curious and wanted to experience just a little more with a female. I asked how she even knew about that. She said 'from the magazines in town that she saw'. As she talked I thought about my Grandparents and Uncle Floyd what will their reaction be when they found out. Eisha was either smiling or cracking up when she told explicit details about this shit. I prepared myself to hear her out as she was dying to tell me. She said 'after helping Gramz earlier today Sheila was parking her car. She called her over and asked her if she's seen Floyd. Eisha told her she saw him earlier and didn't know if he was home. Sheila asked Eisha to help her with the bags into the house and she did. Once inside all sorts of hell exploded between the two. I said 'Eisha and hear I thought it was Mr. Harold Smith who was after you when the whole time it was that prostitute Sheila'. She smiled and from that I knew something wasn't quite right with my Auntie. We were quiet for a moment. I was numb as I looked at her excitement in wanting another woman's thang to touch hers. As they were in the act Uncle Floyd walked in the house and caught them. He freaked out! He dropped the flowers he had for Sheila and took off his belt to beat Eisha and Sheila. That explains the whaps on her legs and butte. She said 'he grabbed Sheila by her hair and dragged her in the kitchen that's when she took off running to our house'. I was floored and had not a clue that females do it to each other. I knew well about a man and a woman because of my parents, grandparents, and Antoinette with Harold but two women having sex was unheard of in those days to me. My Grammy will literally have a heart attack when I share this news with her. I didn't know what to say nor do but needed my Auntie's naked tale off my new bed. I went to my drawer to find something for her to put on because she actually smelled. I couldn't bear to see her sneak in the house looking like that so I ran her some bath water and told her I would go get her clothes from her room. I told my Auntie to not leave my room until I came back with her clothes. She went into the bathroom I closed both the bathroom door and my bedroom door and charged down those stairs to my Grandparents home. It was the usual noise atmosphere outside with the coast being clear to enter their house using the back door. I fly straight to Eisha's room. There was a basket of clean unfolded clothes I dumped all those clothes out and found some of Eisha's panties and shorts. As I was leaving out I had to run back and put those clothes back into the basket then I wrap her things around my waist and charged back home. I stopped on our porch after hearing Sheila scream out ouch Floyd you're hurting me. I wanted to go next door but I felt my Auntie was more important. As I charged up those stairs Momma was opening up my door calling my name. I said 'Mommy' she turned around and asked why was the door closed. She said 'Sofay we are not going to have closed doors around here ok'. I froze not wanting to disclose what happened to Eisha. Momma walked towards me saying girl is you alright? I teared up saying Mommy I'm scared. She lifted my chin higher and asked why. I told her briefly who was in my room and why. My mother grasped for air patting her heart and walked into my room. Eisha was sitting on my bed wrapped in a towel eyeing my mother. My mother putted her hands on her hips saying to Eisha what have you done this time little girl. She pleaded with Momma saying she had to see what she felt like. Momma said 'what! girl damn it'! She then asked was she satisfied. E just put her head down. Momma said 'sis I don't believe you realize what's about to happen to you with your family'. Eisha said 'no mamm' almost embarrassed. I pulled her clothes out from inside my clothes to give to her. She dressed as Momma got the comb and brush to comb her hair. Momma looked at her hair then smelled it and said come on down stairs so I can wash your hair

Eisha. We all went down in the kitchen as Momma tried to talk some sense in this beaded head girl. She said 'baby you are fourteen years old and you have your entire life ahead of you'. You have to start taking responsibility for your own actions Eisha. Sister n law I held my peace regarding Johnson but you were scold enough leaving me to stay quiet. But this time, I have to say something because now from what you did with Sheila her relationship with Floyd will never be the same again. You have to stand for something or you're fall for anything and I don't want that happening to you. Momma said 'Eisha you were so caught up with Sheila that you've forgotten that is Floyd's home whom he shares with her'. She said baby I am out done! Eisha said 'she didn't think about being caught by Floyd'. Her entire existence was on Sheila during those moments. Momma said 'baby alley cats will use you as a litter box if you let them pee on you and that's what Sheila did to you'. I can't blame Sheila fully but I blame you also because you've been down this road before. The only difference is this time you sexed with a thirty six year old woman with two kids. Momma sat Eisha down in the chair to dry off her hair she was disappointed. She sat next to her too grab her hand to say I hope you make better decisions as time goes on. Don't be ashamed for what you like or who you like because you've got to be happy in life Eisha. Really I don't know how you should feel but don't let this effect who you are as a person. All I'm asking you E is that you don't make a move on Sofay cause J and I both will harm you. She said 'dear God'! this family will explode with all kinds of fireworks because of what you and Sheila did. I just feel none of them will be nice to you for what you've done E. This is not something that no one is prepared for nor do they know how to deal with. My God Eisha your mother might well I don't really know how all of them will react I'm just speculating. Momma said 'Eisha know that I am here for you baby it's killing me my heart is aching sweetie because all hell will break loose soon sweet heart'. Momma had tears in her eyes looking at Auntie Eisha. She said 'honestly E I still have high hopes to see you with a boy courting, getting married and having kids. I want the same for my baby'. I'm not gone beat you up for this because I've said enough and I got a feeling that your brothers and sisters are going to do more because Floyd is going to share this with them so be prepared. She said 'Geraldine my brother already whipped both of us with his belt'. He got me real good. You see these whaps!

CHAPTER 39

Meanwhile, I was making her a roast sandwich with chips and Kool-Aid while Momma did her hair in pony tales. My Auntie looked so pitiful as she looked at Momma and asked her did she want to know what happened. She said 'not really baby but if you want to share it with me then go ahead'. My Mother eyes were larger than my mines as Eisha talked. Momma told her that from now to don't be so quick to let someone pull her underwear's down. Try to get to know them first before going all the way in sexing them. She said 'Eisha you are a minor meaning you are a whole lot younger than Sheila's ass'. She told her, that her body is her prize possession and it needed guarded twenty four hours a day. She told her she would help guard her because honestly two women together in the South during that era was a forbidden taboo that would led to death. Just then there was shouting and cussing then Gramz's and them stormed in calling for Eisha. She walked right up to Eisha and slapped her out that chair. Granddaddy was taking off his belt cussing up a freaking storm saying you done lost your everlasting mind that the good Lord gave yah. I watched as my Uncles and Camille had their belts off waiting in line to beat my Auntie. Everybody was talking and shouting at once that it sent me into a another place especially after watching my grandfather fall to his knees holding his heart screaming at the top of his lungs. I looked and saw my Mother try to restrain Gramz's from choking Eisha that she gave up screaming at all of them her damn self. Suddenly I felt sick like my stomach wanted to release itself but instead the room started spinning I felt like I was being lifted off the ground and I couldn't control my eyes everything became blur I was losing my balance reaching for the air and couldn't stand any longer it was like both a sick and weak feeling at the same time I was drifting off then it was completely black. I heard my mother and gramz's screaming then I drifted into darkness.

I'm not sure how long I was out but I woke up with a cold towel on my head in my parent's bed. It was even more commotions than ever this time everybody was inside our home including my father who was screaming at the top of his lungs saying to James Jr. to get that bull dike off this property. I tried to rise up off the pillow but both Auntie Camille and Faye made me stay still. My head was pounding with pain I asked Faye what happened and she said 'shhh baby don't talk you hit your head when you fainted'. Camille was yelling out to whoever was listening to her saying somebody send momma home I'm getting sick of her, send that woman home now! I tried to look in the hallway and saw men on top of men talking if not screaming. Then one of my Granddaddy's brothers Uncle Junior Senior came into the room. He removed the towel off my head to look at it then he put more ice inside the towel before putting it back on my head. He kissed my forehead and said 'baby you gone be just fine got damn it'. He stood there looking at all of us and said 'J. W. what did my brother just tell you man'? Daddy said 'Unk not now mane I'm gone beat the hell out of both of them'. Granddaddy came into the room pushing James Jr. out the way to say Jr.-Sr. man these damn kids of mine gone give me a heart attack. Granddaddy's other brother Uncle J. C. came in the room behind him to say James man don't be round here asking for a fucking heart attack man what's wrong with you man and who is this Sheila brod? Uncle R. L. came in the room saying Dadday mane look how you looking come on and let's go home. Granddaddy said 'R. L. this ain't the time now son leave me the fuck alone'. He said 'Dadday look how you sweating and out of breathe'. Faye said 'Dadday listen to me Uncle J. C. help him to the couch over there'. Gramz's was making her way up the stairs she too was still cussing and Camille got up off the bed to stop her from entering my parents' bedroom. Gramz's was looking and yelling for Eisha but Camille blocked her from entering the room and asked Simon and Uncle Chester to take her home. She tried to resist but Granddaddy yelled to her to gone on ahead home Olivia. I listened as Uncle J. C. couldn't believe my Grandfather as he went into details about Georgeis and Eisha. He said 'brother now I done told you man for years just cause he smiling at yah don't mean he like yah'. Look what he's done to my niece now that girl is ruin about relationships!

Meanwhile, I was searching for my Mother and didn't see her. I didn't say anything but my family was making my headache even worst with all of this commotion of voices. Cousin Jr. flopped on my parent's bed asking me where it hurts. His father Uncle Jr.-Sr. looked out the window and shouted oh lord Jr. your pig on fire! Cousin Jr. took off running with R. L., James Jr., and Marshal running behind him. Gwen came into the room saying Red let Auntie see that bump on your head. Next thing we heard was my father screaming I don't want to hear it I want her off this property before she bump bush with another one of my sisters. Tears started slowly rolling down my face because this was such a terrible situation. Every adult in this room was losing it and apparently so was Uncle Floyd he barricaded his front and back door for fear that his brothers were going to harm Sheila. Baebae came in the room fired up screaming and apparently high from smoking weed because you could smell it on her. She shouted using her hands as sign language saying lets go kick his back door in. She continued on acting like some sort of cheerleader still shouting yell Unk that's right what grown ass woman would do such a thing to a child'? Uncle Jr.-Sr said 'naw man you can't lock Eisha up in the barn man make some sense James Senior'. This was passed a mess and even a hot mess is there something called an enormous mess? I just looked from person to person as they plotted revenge on Sheila and planning ways in how they would punish Eisha. Uncle Earl said 'ah J mane the side window is open in Floyd's place I'll go get a ladder from the barn so we all can climb in'. My father agreed and tried to go outside to do just that until both of Granddaddy's brothers stopped him in his tracks.

In addition, I asked Auntie Faye where was Eisha she said again 'shhh'! Just then Antoinette flopped next to me saying look at you Red my poor baby. Camille came back to sit in her same spot to say leave her alone Antoinette. She said 'all I'm saying is Eisha should be ashamed with all that butte going to waste'. Gwen rose up to say what the fuck you mean Antoinette she's our baby sister. Antoinette said 'who would have suspected such a thing I mean two females'! she said 'we don't even know no females nor condone that type of sex act. Sheila done came down here and set the population to an all new high and it's not even drugs. Camille charmed in to say you know sis you need to be dragged behind Dadday's truck for saying something so stupid. Then I managed to say Antoinette I know you ain't talking. She looked dumb found and said 'excuse you Miss-Missy'. I constipated if I was gone bust her out or not but she pissed me off talking about Eisha so I said 'at least Eisha didn't sleep with Harold like you did'. Antoinette stood up covered her mouth shocked that I knew and said 'he wrote me to say stay far away from him in this life time'. Then she looked at her sisters. Gwen asked Harold whose Harold? I said 'my Grammy's boyfriend'. Gwen, Faye, and Camille froze looking at Antoinette in disbelief. Faye said 'you bitch you gone talk about Sheila when your goat ass done fuck Ernestine's man! Ha-ha Antoinette took off running with all her sisters running behind her. I was glad to see them leave now I needed all of them out of our house for peace and quiet. I see now what Cousin Tommie was talking about that day he put the White's off his property. My family shole can be worrisome and this was one of those times.

Contrarily, I started whining to my Father saying Daddyyyyy kicking my legs on their bed pouting and hitting their bed with my fist as he walked to me saying what is it baby so I kicked the bed again and looked at him my poor father didn't know what that meant so instead of putting all of them out the room he yelled for Camille accusing her of putting too much covers on me. I was dumb founded but thank goodness not even a minute later Doctor Bryson was making his way into the room he asked everyone to leave but my parents. My Father finally put everybody out of our house. He helped granddaddy and Uncle J. C. down the stairs then he went to the guest room for my mother. I sat up watching my Mother walk to their bed to look at the bump on my head. I asked her why was she crying and she said 'it was just too much for her to handle with Eisha'. She was in the guest room consoling Eisha who was a wreck from being whipped. Doc opened his black bag and pulled out a statoscope, a tongue board, and a blood pressure tool. He examined me thoroughly. He checked my glands, my anodes, my forehead, throat, and ears. He looked for signs of yellow fever disease and tuberculosis. Then he checked my blood pressure, nose, and mouth and even had me walk to and from the dresser several times. He said 'I didn't show any signs of any fatal diseases or dehydration which was a plus. My father asked then how did a perfectly healthy girl just faint Doc. He said 'son exactly what took place round here today'. Daddy was careful in not exposing Eisha's current situation he danced around that sex encounter with both girls but he did elaborate but exaggerated on me walking upon grown folks in the act. Doc said 'I yi-yi I see well from the looks of it when your nerves are continuously triggered it sets off symptoms of many ailments including fainting J. W. You see J too much has happened to her little mind in such a short period of time she's adjusting to change at a rapid pace and she just can't handle it. She needs time to adjust in accepting new changes that's all. Sofay is at a level of not accepting change at a rapid pace which can also trigger a pattern of stuttering, uncontrolled shaking and other symptoms. For example, this house was a shock to her, she traveled for the first time, she's experience another family's way of living out there in Harlem, and then she walked in on grown folks all of these circumstances are shock factors which her little body hasn't adjusted to. I'll leave some aspirins for her head and body ache. She needs plenty of rest. That bump will slowly fade away in a day or so no need to worry. But if she faints again you rush her to the emergency room call me and I'll meet you over there. Daddy said 'ok Doc'. Doctor Bryson looked and said 'Geraldine why are you crying my love? Sofay will be just fine'. Momma said 'Doc I've suddenly experienced shortness of breath'. He said 'is that right well let me give you a pregnancy test and check you out'. Daddy shouted pregnancy! Doctor Bryson pushed his glasses back on his nose and proceeded to check my mother out. He examined her and found nothing out of the ordinary and she wasn't pregnant. He left some volume pills for her to take so she could rest that night. Then Doc was about to put his Instruments back into his bag until

Momma said 'Doctor Bryson can you please check J'. He looked at my father who was almost resistance but gave in. It's a good thing he got checked because daddy's blood pressure was elevated being on the border line for the sugar. Doc said 'now son I'm going to need for you to rest you're doing too much around here'. Your pressure is high so I'm going to leave you these seven pills that you are to take daily starting now. I'll wait while you gone on in the bathroom to take this pill son. Momma said 'no wait I'll get a cup of water so I can see him take the pill'. Daddy got offended and started talking then got quiet. Momma did what she said and came back into the bedroom and asked Doc to put the pill in her hand so she could give it to my father. Doc slightly laughed as he started putting his equipment's back in their bags. Doctor Bryson said 'Geraldine you a damn good woman and I wish it was more women like you around here'. Daddy asked Doc one last thing do you got any pills for Eisha's butte to make it go down. Momma whispered J. W.! Doc looked shocked as his glasses were at the tip of his nose but said 'J if I had that answer I would be a billionaire and no son no sucha thing'. He advised us all to get plenty of rest and liquors. He told daddy to stay away from salt, sugar, and stress then he left for my grandparents' house.

CHAPTER 40

Moreover, Momma walked the doctor out and daddy stretched and lay next to me with his hands behind his head. We looked at each other and I said 'mane it's hard out here for a colored man'. My father laughed saying baby it shole is you just don't know what your daddy goes through on a day to day. I rose up to peck my father's cheek he smiled and wrapped me in his arms. Momma came back in the room and went straight in their bathroom to run daddy some bath water. He and I watched her as she moved around the room. The next thing I saw was her standing on the side of the bed just staring into daddy's eyes. Daddy said 'you know what hurts me about this shit Geraldine?' Momma said 'what J'? He said' it ain't no need for us to teach our daughter about the birds and the bees cause these mother fuckers done built a fucking nest around her already'. Momma said nothing but continued staring at daddy sideways making him say what is it Geraldine. She said 'J you can't leave Eisha in there forever'. Daddy said 'now Geraldine, Eisha needs to be taught a lesson up here bumping bush with another female'. I mean and Mommy stopped him from talking by bending down to put her finger on the lips then said 'what did Doc just say to you J you on the border line of sugar and high blood pressure baby'. She said 'do you trust me J'? He rose up further to say you know I do why you ask that question baby. Then go get in that tub Mr. She pulled him off the bed to pop him on his butte smiling. He told her alright don't start nothing! Once he was in the bathroom she walked passed me winking her eye. She came back in the room holding hands with Auntie Eisha. I lite up like a tree and got on my knees in the bed. I watched my auntie who looked like she had aged ten years older. Her eyes were nearly swelled shut and her smile wasn't right. She walked to me and I hugged my favorite Auntie and didn't let her go for the longest. When I looked into her eyes she said 'Red they beat me'? I said 'Auntie' then she slowly tried her best to hold those tears from falling. Hell I didn't know what to say but hugged her again. She whimpered on my shoulders oh how I wished I could have removed that pain away from her but I didn't know how to. All I could say was Eishaaaa with my bottom lip poked out. She sweated her hair out and showed me new whaps, blisters and redness on her legs. She was devastated that granddaddy and them actually hit her with a belt and some of the brothers used a switch. I couldn't think of anything to say but was relieved when my momma came back in the room with two bowls of popcorn and soda pops on a tray. She had a bowl of witch hazel with towels as well as clean linens and a new bedspread for the bed. She said 'it was too many bodies on their bed and she wanted to be comfortable while sleeping'. Momma gave Eisha some of my pain pills for her whaps and I also helped in rubbing towels on her wounds which was everywhere on her body. Eisha was relived as Momma and I gently wiped her body down for comfort. When I looked at my auntie she was two sizes an sixteen at the bottom and a size medium at the top. Eisha was beautiful to me she was a girl who always smiled no matter what. She had a soft spoken voice almost like a baby. She was light skin with hazel eyes. Her hair was longer than her ear lobes but not reaching her shoulders which she kept into two pony tails parted down the middle. Like I said earlier her shape was that of a grown woman. My Auntie had a heart of gold always being my shadow. She truly had patience with me with always having an inquiring mind. She loved the arts everything to do with a pencil, paper, ink and other materials. She dressed ok but loved everything to be skin tight on her causing my grandparents to have fits and making her go back in the house to change clothes. Eisha was the baby and some of her siblings treated her as such while a couple of her sisters would almost be in competition with her body for some reason. She was a straight B student who rarely missed a day of school. Some of the boys in school would deliberately bump into her butte making her threatened them by going to get a brother. Those boys quickly got back in their place and left Auntie alone. Though several tried to court her by asking to take her to the candy store Eisha always found some excuse to not be bothered with them boys.

Any hoot, my father came out the bathroom singing until he saw Eisha sitting on his bed. He stopped and stood there looking at her. Hell he was making me uncomfortable looking at her. I cleared my throat looking at my mother who was changing her linens. I started nodding my head towards daddy she then looked at me as I moved my eyes towards my father. My mother followed my eyes and turned to smile at my father who wasn't even looking at either of us but he was staring at his baby sister. Momma finished making the bed and turned to my father to ask him if he was hungry. He didn't answer her but continued staring at Auntie while putting on his under shirt. Momma said 'J. W. not now and please stop staring'. He didn't but was still standing still so momma got her some changing clothes and panties and practically pushed my father back into the bathroom with her. Eisha and I heard them arguing as she teared up. I grabbed her by the shoulders bumping my head against hers. I said 'Auntie don't cry cause you know you'll get to sliding on the floor'. She slightly laughed and tried to dry up her tears. Moments later, Eisha was loosening up a little she went to the window to look out and I asked her to come back over to the bed to sit with me. Because so many were walking back and forth passing our house to either go to Camille's or Jr.'s place and I didn't want to see anybody else that night except Eisha and my parents.

Instead, she went to turn the channels on the television then my parents entered the bedroom making Eisha nearly run back to their bed. I had to give it to my mother because she made it a priority in keeping my auntie comfortable despite what took place. My father wouldn't stop staring at her as he lay in the bed. Momma climbed into bed asking what was on television reaching for the popcorn. Eisha found comedies with mom Mable and we watched that while my father was in his own world. Auntie asked where was she sleeping and my father told her the floor. Mommas hurried up to say ignore your brother Sis. You can sleep with Sofay or in the guest room which ever you like. Daddy said 'naw Gerryyyy they will both sleep right here in this beddddd'. Momma repeated back Gerry! Before she busted up laughing. Eisha's body was aching really badly so my mother ran her some bath water putting Epsom salt in the water along with some green alcohol. She soaked awhile as momma and I went to check on her. She was silently crying so my mother bends down next to the tub to wipe her eyes and told her that she got to stay strong. She said 'she never thought her family of all the people in the world would turn on her for bumping with Sheila'. It was the beating from my grandfather that nearly ripped her apart because like me he's never whipped neither of us. My sweet mother was lost for words. She did say Eisha sometimes your very own family can be the worst at letting you down when you need them the most. She said 'baby give them time to get over this before things get back to being normal'. Momma got one of daddy's t-shirt for E to sleep in. We three slept in my parent's bed as my father sat on the couch the entire night probably staring at auntie E. The next morning my father was sitting up on the sofa looking drained. He didn't sleep a wink from probably watching his bed all night. He decided he wasn't working in the field that morning my mother was pleased because he needed to start doing for himself and rest more. He went downstairs to made breakfast for us. He made pancakes, sausage, fried skin and eggs. Daddy was still in disbelief with E and Sheila that instead of eating he was boldly staring at E forcing momma to nudge him in the arm to stop staring at her. He looked away for a second but started back up staring making all of us uncomfortable. Momma said 'alright my dear husband did you forget that this is your baby sweet sis'? She said how about you look at me J. Daddy said nothing but sucked his front teeth then put a tooth pick in his mouth. My mother told us to hurry up eating then looked at daddy to ask him was it ok for us girls to hang out at Grammy's shop. He said 'it would be fine'. Auntie and I went back upstairs to change into more appropriate clothing but Auntie's clothes were all at home at my grandparents' home. I changed and wished E could fit my clothes because neither of us really wanted to go to her house. As we were heading out the house my father's stares seemed to turn to hath so I said 'stop it daddy you scaring me'. Momma tried to warm up to him by saying ok J, Gerry has spoken and she says it's ok to leave baby sis along come on now enough is enough husband. She had to literally pull my father's chin down to kiss him other than that he watched us I mean he watched Eisha as she walked with us. Auntie Ruby was sitting on Jr.'s porch along with Jr.-Sr. She walked off the porch to greet mainly Eisha. She said 'hey Eisha baby with a warm smile it's been awhile since I saw you last'. She said 'Eisha can you believe Miss Sofay here got her own room plus bathroom'? Eisha said 'hey Auntie and no I can't believe it'. She small talked but really she was fishing for a more in depth conversation with her regarding Sheila. Momma interrupted them by saying Aunt Ruby we got to be going. As we walked over to my grandparents place it was like everyone was waiting on Eisha to arrive including Floyd. Many of them were sitting on the porch staring directly at her including Gramz. She put her head down as Momma told her to pick it back up again. I couldn't tell which one was the coldest with hatred in their hearts because they all frowned at her making Momma and I uncomfortable. Nitta and Monee didn't make it any better with their boldness in whispering out loud saying it that fish! Momma said 'yall so rude'! Then she said 'Olivia me and the girls are going to visit my mother and spend the day out'. My Gramz's disappointed me because she didn't respond back to my mother instead she stared at Eisha as she and I walked into the house. In the house the men weren't any better. James Jr. spoke to us but intentionally hugged me and not Eisha even though she reached out to hug her brother. My heart fell because I couldn't believe how my family was acting with the baby of the family. While Earl, Chester and A. J. were just standing there staring and not moving we had to literally walk around them. Uncle Chester was the only one who walked behind us to hug Eisha and asked her how was she doing. I asked Uncle what's wrong with everybody. He said 'baby I couldn't tell yah'. But what I do know is this is a life changing experience that we were not prepared for Sofay while staring back at Eisha.

In fact, Eisha and I proceeded to her room for changing clothes as Antoinette saw us and left the room snickering. Oh how I wanted to kick her. By this time I was getting angry with blood shot cheeks. I looked at Faye as she stopped to look at my bump on my head. She looked but started staring at E. I was toooo uncomfortable and demanded Eisha to hurry up to change so we could get out of there. Eisha changed and was lukewarm as she saw granddaddy. She didn't even attempt to get a hug from him and vice verses. He looked at her fanned his hand in the air and walked the opposite way from us. That sent her flying to the bathroom to vomit. I ran behind her wrapping my arms around her waist as she vomited which made me start crying. I helped her grabbing tissue to wipe her mouth as I kissed her repeatedly on her cheeks. Man! I Didn't See This Coming From My Family! As she and I left the bathroom Uncle Floyd was standing there against the wall staring directly at E. My heart was beating a mile a minute as he tried to say something. E froze in her steps I couldn't bare seeing Floyd to be mean to her so I pulled her as hard as I could to move so we could leave. She tried to walk straight to the car though she stopped to say something to Gramz's. She couldn't find any words then Nitta said 'what's wrong a cat got your tongue or is it a tongue got your cat'. Momma hopped up saying Nitta burn in hell while the rest of them laughed out loud. She yanked both E and I arms and we walked towards the car. Auntie Nitta was still talking smack saying good bye Geraldine and Red then Momma turned around to say and Eisha too. My Auntie's little heart was shattered in fact she broke down crying in the car. Momma stopped the car in the drive way and wiped Eisha's eyes and told her don't ever let people pull your soul away from you because nine times out of ten those same people judging you are just as miserable as you. My goodness it's one thing to hear other people rip you apart but when it's your very own family it's a tremendous let down of pain. Momma told her we gone get through this, we gone get through this! Lordy I never thought it would be a day that the White's would be divided up. Then Momma was silence all the way to town while Eisha and I small talked. Our first stop was to Annie Linens a store that carried art supplies, toys, tools, and hunting supplies. Momma told us both to get only four things each to purchase. That brought a smile on my Auntie's face I went down one aisle while Eisha just stood there. When I looked back at her she waved at me to come back to her I did she said 'Sofay please don't leave me I want to walk with you'. We walked together of course holding hands. I didn't know at the time that my Auntie had been scared just about all her life. She shared with me how her sisters had always picked and taunted her regarding her butte. I do recall many of those joke days but it seemed to not have an effect on her morals because all she did was laughed at those criticisms but deep down in the inside she was hurt. She latched onto me because I never criticized her but took up for her hell I was too young to joke about somebody's butte. My mother would have popped my lips purple. She shared that information as she and I were walking down those aisles. She said 'Sofay you are my only friend who I love unconditionally'. You stood by me even when I played with your thang that day in the bathroom. I knew in my heart that you would tell that part but to my surprise no one to this day knows what took place and Sofay I love you even more for that. I said 'E you were already in trouble and if I had mentioned that you would be walking crooked forever'. She said 'when I was a baby some of her sisters acted funny with me because I looked white'. But not Eisha she didn't agree with their logic as she grew older because I reminded her of a Barbie doll with red hair. I asked her my Aunties didn't like me? She said 'they were hesitating at first to touch you instead; they would eye and nudge each other'. They would be mean to you Red by purposely hitting you for no reason when Geraldine asked them to baby sit you. They did that for many years being fake. Some of them would sit there and let you cry but when Geraldine came back home they would run to pick you up pretending to baby talk to you making sure she heard them. My sisters were ruthless even to me. As I got older and realized how they were treating you I told J. W. He jumped on Nitta, Antoinette, Monee and Faye and I mean he beat them really good. Gramz's was heartbroken in hearing that her girls were being mean to the first grandchild. Hearing that news made me feel some kind of way about my family. I wanted to cry but what good would that have done because the damage had already been done. So I hurried up to change the conversation to say Auntie, Momma said 'for us to get four things each I want you to buy everything for yourself it eight things instead of four'. She grinned so hard that I started tearing up. I was really hurt learning how my aunts treated me because I looked mixed. Now it makes sense to me as to why everything I did or said my aunties are always replying back with those famous words oh my baby! It's because they are guilty of mistreating me as a baby and I guess to make up to my father they programmed themselves to connect with me regardless of my skin color. I really can't elaborate on how my aunties really feel about me because this is shocking news to hear.

However, Eisha was in her element with artwork. We had to get a basket as she got; paint brushes, paint, an easel, art paper, pencils, drawing pencils, an apron and glitter. I counted her things and said E you need one more she was so overwhelmed with what she already had that I left her alone and put a package of jacks and a yo-yo in the basket. As we headed searching for Momma we found her talking with Grammy's neighbor Esmeralda. I spoke and asked where was her daughter Moochie. She said 'at her sister's house for two weeks'. Then Momma introduced Eisha, Esmeralda looked shocked saying no that's not the baby girl looking her up and down. She said 'look how pretty you are'. She said 'the last time she saw Eisha she was six years old or younger'. She shook E's hand saying hello little one and told momma she had to get going. Momma said 'see Eisha it's not always about your butte Esmeralda was impress in how beautiful you are becoming'. She just blushed and then said 'Geraldine it was Sofay's ideal for me to use her four gifts making me have eight items'. Momma fanned her off but looked in the basket and smiled. We left there and went to the grocery store. I said 'Momma we buying food now because I saw all those can goods in the cabinet and those meats in the freezer. She said 'well baby we need to catch up with others because now days not many are hunting for food but they are purchasing parts of the cow, chicken, pig and other meats'.

In addition, Eisha was dying for some strawberry powered milk so Momma got it for her. We left there and headed to Grammy's shop. This was Eisha's first time visiting my grandmother and I prayed that she was receptive in seeing her with Momma and I. There were several ladies in the shop with their small children I saw Glenda who was Grammy's assistant standing in the middle of the floor watching the crowd. My grandmother was in the back office doing paperwork. We entered in and she stood up walking to greet us including Eisha. She asked were we just out and about or sliding through to see her. Momma said 'yeah we were passing through but she needed to talk with her'. Grammy told us kids to go to the break room for refreshments as she and momma talked. We got back there and it looked like a candy store. I immediately went for the candy apple and insisted that Eisha bit into it. She's never tasted anything like it before her face told it all. I told her my reaction was the same as hers when I first tasted that great treat. I looked over and saw a plate of skins with bottles of hot sauce. I immediately grabbed two skins and poured hot sauce on top and shot to Grammy's office to give it to my mother. Upon reaching the crack door I was floored to hear my mother crying. She was upset that Sheila touched Eisha more like she turned her out causing a riff among the family. Momma pleaded that Eisha is a baby who was experimenting. Grammy was silent but kept saying un un unh that stank skunk done brought that dike shit down here? No wonder Tommie got rid of her up there rubbing some child's cunt with hers. I was peeking behind me making sure Eisha wasn't opening the door nor walking out of it. Grammy said 'these people in the south are not fully knowledgeable about the same sex life as we are being from New York'. Down here they react by beating a person thinking those belt licks would pull that way of life out of them. Momma said 'that's what they did took turns beating her I couldn't take it Mother her cries changed each time a different person whipped her'. I know she was having a nervous breakdown or some sort she wasn't right at all. It's like she was crying with her eyes rolling in the back of her head. Looking at that damn near ripped my heart out mother then Nitta's bitch ass was yelling for me to move out the way and if I didn't then they should hit me as well. Grammy said 'did they hit you Geraldine; did they put their hands on you'? She said 'no mamm they know J. W. would have cleaned house had any of them laid a hand on me'. Grammy made a sound of relief and asked where my father was'. Momma said 'working in the field'. Grammy said 'Lordy, Geraldine! baby they could have turned to bring harm to you for interfering. What were you thinking baby'? She said 'Mother no one deserves a beaten by ten different people at the same time like that'. That's a child no matter what! Grammy said 'my God! No wonder she's looking funny in the face. I could tell it was something going on with Miss Eisha. Geraldine what happened to Sheila? Momma said 'Floyd raped her thinking he was removing the spirit from her body'. Grammy said 'now you got to be a fucking idiot to think you can move a spirit using sex'. She said 'I've been telling you for years them damn Whites are bad people in their own little world'. Grammy said 'I can't believe this shit'! Momma nervously said 'Mother my baby fainted'. Grammy screamed 'what'! She said 'Lord have Mercy Gerry what will it take for you to come to your senses and move your family off that damn plantation of insane mother fuckers'? Momma was silent but said 'Mother move and go where because J.W. isn't going anywhere'. I love that man's dirty draws I can't bare living without him in our lives. My heart fell saying live without my father! Grammy said 'Geraldine this is serious that child is lost and confused because she's never been physically beaten like that by her people. I know Olivia's ass ran with this in being the center of attraction with her flippy mouth ass. Momma said 'yes she did change in fact all of them have' then she told her about our earlier experience at my grandparents' home. Grammy repeated herself three times by saying Lord have mercy! Grammy said 'Geraldine as much as I dislike Eisha and many of those Whites I don't want her going back there tonight'. My goodness Gerry! Being secluded on that land unaware that there's a real world out here has fucked Olivia and James Sr's minds'. Momma said 'you know I know first-hand how it feels to be excluded and feeling left out of place with the White's they make you feel uncomfortable and none of them hide it with all that damn; giggling, whispering, sarcastic out bursts and nudging one another'. I never thought they would turn on Eisha like that. All I know is that I won't turn my back on her and they don't have to worry about my baby because she loves her Auntie to death. Grammy said 'naw baby she also got me too I'm here for her'. So it's final then both girls will stay with me until this thing calms down. Lordy, that poor baby!

In fact, momma said 'let me ask J. W. to see what he says'. Grammy became so angry and called momma's full name to say Geraldine Lynn Brown White he is not your got damn father. Stop this shit of asking for permission to do things you are a grown ass woman girl. You share with him your plans but stop fucking asking this man what you can and cannot do. Momma was quiet that's when I tip toed back into the break room. Eisha said 'what took you so long I almost came out looking for you'.

Frankly speaking, we ended up staying with my grandmother Grammy for the next month or so missing the first two weeks of school. My parents with Gwen and cousin Jr. had visited us at my grandmother's house but no one else came by. The first few days were a little rough with my auntie having crying spells from being away from home for the first time but we got through it with Grammy's help. She kept us occupied alone with Moochie her neighbor's daughter. One of the excitements was spending a weekend that included Grammy, Momma, Gwen and Faye, Eisha, me and Moochie we drove to an amusement park in Grand Prairie, Texas. My Aunts were more excited than us kids because for the first time they left the country. My grandmother speared no mercy and showed us all a dynamic time. But, it didn't stop there because we also spent a different weekend in Dallas to attend the County fair which was a sensational time. That time it was just us with Momma and two of her best friends with their children. Every time I looked at my Auntie her mouth was moving with eating almost everything in sight. It was funny watching her facial expressions when she ate; giant size pretzels with cheese, popcorns, corn dogs, cotton candy, fried hot dogs I got a kick out of watching her. It felt good seeing Eisha slowly returning back into herself but she seemed to get better and better as the days went by. Grammy noticed it also and told her she was happy she was enjoying herself. Once we returned back to

Grammy's house our healing continued on with us splurging on junk food and candy like never before. Eisha was back to herself by talking none stop causing Grammy to whisper to me does she ever shut up damn! E started recognizing that the world does not revolve around and inside the farm. She noticed Grammy's life style especially her demeanor in how my grandmother; walked, talked, dressed, and how she carried herself as a lady. My grandmother taught us etiquette; in how to communicate, walk, speak and eat at the table. Grammy was a stickler in not being embarrassed out in public. She had us at work with her many days as Eisha wanted to learn about fashion. That made my grandmother's day to hear that. She first taught her how to use a cash register and even gave her the opportunity to ring up clothes. She let Eisha measure customer's body frames for their custom clothing's she was tickled pink. She had us observing how she does inventory and payroll. We were unloading boxes of newly arrival of clothes, shoes, belts, and fake jewelry. Glenda enjoyed delegating duties to us kids which gave her a break in handling the store alone. Eisha mentioned to Grammy that retail was something she would like to pursue when she gets older. Grammy told her that's good and all but to also have something else to fall back on. She told her to stick with her love for art because she's good at it and use retail as a secondary skill.

CHAPTER 41

However, the days were narrowing down and it seemed like the month stay flew pass. When it was time to go back to the farm my grandmother had designed clothes especially for Eisha's built. She had beautiful long dresses, skirts, and loose shorts with tops that didn't reveal her shape. I got a couple of outfits myself including several pairs of shoes. Grammy told us we were set for school at least for the first two weeks once she and I started. Well it was time to leave and my grandmother was with her latest man who took us back home. I was proud of my auntie once she met Herman she stayed in her place and didn't try to provoke his manhood to rise by wiggling that butte of hers. She and I were both nervous not knowing the reaction that we were going to receive from the family. When we pulled up on the road my Auntie grabbed my hand. Now I know when she does that it's from a nervous reaction. It's so her hands don't start shaking.

In addition, there were quite a few people on my grandparents porch as we walked passed. Neither of us looked up on the porch. I asked her did she want to go inside to say hello and she said 'no' so we continued walking to my house. My parents, Uncle Chester and Auntie Gwen were on the porch grinning as we were also. Surprisingly my father picked his baby sister up with the warmest hug which brought tears to her eyes. Chester did the same as Gwen kissed her on the cheek. Mr. Herman was carrying our bags Momma was pleased knowing that Grammy went out her way for Eisha and also having a new man in her life. As we entered our home I noticed the sitting room now had furniture in it with a floor model television set. My father cooked dinner and invited Grammy and Herman to stay. They couldn't due to their own plans. Momma told us to take our bags upstairs to our rooms. Eisha's mouth dropped and so did mines as Momma playfully marched towards us saying hunt two, three, and four who's at Sofay and Eisha's door. It was corny but she meant well causing us to bust up laughing including Daddy.

In addition, as Eisha walked into her new room she screamed. My mother had gone to the barn to retrieve some of Eisha's artwork and hung the pictures in her new room. Her easel was put together and stood in the corner with a new art chair. She marveled and touched everything in amazement covering her mouth. I knew she was beyond thrilled. I said 'E did you hear momma when she said 'yall rooms'. She said 'yes I did' then she looked around the room as if it was her first time there. I asked her do you want to stay here with us E and she said 'more than anything because I don't want to live with momma's no longer they all are mean'. I assured her that her parents wanted her but needed more time to heal. She said 'now Red we are together forever'. I just smiled not knowing if my grandparents really did turn their backs on her.

Anyway, my father called for us to come down to eat and we did. My dad got down with his famous ribs, chicken, hot dogs, polishes, hamburger, potato salad, cole slaw, spaghetti and seven up cake. He too was an excellent cook like Gramz's and Grammy and I was shocked hearing Momma actually touched a spoon to help my father cook. Gwen teased momma's cooking while reaching for Eisha's shoulders to hold on to her. Uncle Chester sat next to E as he held her hand and smiled at her. It was re-assuring to see three of the eighteen children trying to soften up to E.

In fact, Uncle Chester asked E what was she doing within the next couple of days because he wanted to spend quality time with her. She didn't respond back but smiled looking down at her plate. Momma interrupted by exaggerating how she made the potato salad which took the slight pressure off of E while Chester patiently waited for a response. After dinner my father's kin folk left as we all went upstairs to freshen up. My father cut up watermelons and found something to watch on television. We sat in the sitting room enjoying each other's company except momma as E and I shared our visit with Grammy to my father. Daddy looked at Eisha and said 'E, Geraldine and I have been thinking and decided that we would love for you to live with us'. We feel you would be better here growing up into your preteen years and beyond. But first sis let me apologize in how I acted towards you that day. I should have handled you differently but better than that. I left the room so those two could talk with each other. I went to my parent's room to sit with my mother as she was reading the newspaper. I was telling her what daddy was saying to Eisha. Momma looked in the door way and told me to never revealed this but Eisha wasn't welcome back home and neither was Floyd. They've written her off for being with Sheila. Daddy and Chester were indecisive in who would take her in I was going numb hearing this. I ask momma why would they do that to her. She said 'instead of the past month of things getting better around here things had gotten worst'. She said Floyd had stopped working completely. He threatened to kill himself if any of them harmed Sheila. He insisted that it was Eisha's butte that provoked Sheila to sex her. Momma said 'baby your Uncle Floyd is in denial and has become possessive whenever Sheila leaves the house'. She leaves and returns with several looking street women. They are having all sorts of parties almost daily. Sofay it's been awful around here. What was shocking to me was to hear Olivia tell her children to do any means necessary in getting Sheila off the property. When your Uncles went to Floyd's house to board it up he fainted. He stayed with Jr. for three days acting a damn fool because Sheila wasn't welcome there. Floyd went ballistic in tracking Sheila down to bring her back home. Momma silently laughed and said 'when he found Sheila and tried to bring her back home they couldn't park quick enough before the brothers jumped on him and your aunties tore Sheila's ass up'. Sheila's leg was fracture as she and Floyd slept in the barn for several days. It was James Sr. who told his boys to un-board Floyd's house so he could go inside. They did but the tragedies didn't stop because Cousin Jr. set up traps where Sheila walked into nearly ripping her ankles apart causing Floyd to faint once again. He knew damn well he wasn't capable to handle his crazy ass brothers. After that, that's when he threatened to kill his self if another accident happened to Sheila. Soo-so it was awful baby I nearly packed up to go stay with you all at Mother's but J assured me that things would calm down soon. I'm just so thankful you were not here to see any of that. I said 'wow' I guess Uncle Floyd is thrilled to have a lady that he'll do anything to keep her'. Momma said 'yeah it seems that way'. I then shared with her the conversation that E and I had regarding how my aunties treated me as a baby. My mother sat all the way up in the bed saying you've got to be kidding me! I also shared with her what Nitta did in those back woods that day. Momma was infuriated with disgust she couldn't believe what she was hearing. She said 'those bitches are no good that's why none of them are married with children'. She said 'those bitches were worser than my grandmother Gramz whenever her and my father quarreled they were always in between us just like Olivia until momma brought it to daddy's attention'. That's when envy really surfaced inside of that farm house against my mother. My aunts had gotten away with mistreating her for so long that it was a routine habit for them and none of them expected nor was aware that my father suddenly got wind of what they were doing. He immediately addressed each of his sisters who were involved before kicking their buttes for mistreating my mommy. My father didn't stand for it and from that moment it caused a division among the sisters and nearly a gang fight to break out among them all. That's a main reason my father is so protective of momma and I because she knows how low down his family really is. Momma said' Nitta was only doing witch craft because that's what was taught to her by her mother'. She said for me to not believe that stuff because 'those rituals are all in your imagination and if you think it's real then it will be real'. Sofay you have to always protect your heart and say I bind the enemies attack and turn it over to the Lord and say in the name of Jesus. And besides when a mother turns on her child because of the choice that child makes really speaks volume in the type of person she really is. Momma said 'she always believed that Gramz's used voodoo to keep her kids right where she wanted them to be right under her'. She often saw her walking from those back woods looking scary. Goodness Mother has been right all along in saying the Whites are insane. She also said also: *Sometimes people pretend you're a bad person so they don't feel guilty about things they did to you.* I just didn't know how we all were going to survive on the farm with all of them disliking Eisha, Sheila, and Floyd. I told my mother all this time I thought Eisha was special when in fact I was further away from the truth and momma agreed. That night I slept with my Auntie I wanted her to know that she was welcome in our house but I will never share with her she was definitely put out of her own house at the age of fourteen. It wasn't my place to say anything it was my grandparents responsibility to inform her. Though, Uncle Floyd was out of control with keeping Sheila around against everyone else approval she not only introduced same sex to Eisha but she also brought threesomes onto the farm. Floyd was unattainable in sexing two women at the same time. His appearance changed. He was losing his muscles and when I saw him I just looked the other way.

In fact, granddaddy was patiently sitting back watching Floyd's every move before he made his move. Floyd had more male friends over more than ever Momma called it sex parties it pissed me off that the White's continued to; watch, look and listen as Floyd entertain city hookers and maybe even pimps inside his home with his simply ass. The next day I saw my Granddaddy, Uncle J. C. and daddy heading towards the lake with fishing rods in their hands. That brought a smile on my face I also loved seeing my father happy just like my mother. They were having a good time with smoking those cigars, talking and walking with their fishing gears. Then there was auntie Monee and Faye picking peaches as I went to the barn for my bike. Gramz's called me over to the porch to ask why I haven't visited her since returning back from Grammy's with Eisha. I told her I didn't know. I heard Eisha calling me so I told Gramz I would be back. I ran home to see what she wanted. She said 'she checked my room and didn't see me'. She asked me if I did my homework and I told her yes. Cousin Jr. came out on his porch and called Eisha over to tell her he was proud of how she ignores Sheila and her camp of hooker friends. He told her one day all of this mess will be over for good and not to worry. He also told her he wanted her to draw for him two pictures so he could hang it up in his living room and in his kitchen. Auntie jumped up and down nearly kicking him with excitement. He told her he wanted something dealing with fruits or food painted for his kitchen and the other picture he wanted her to use her imagination to draw something grand and pretty. E ran home to tell momma the exciting news.

Meanwhile, as I was heading back to my grandparents to retrieve my bike that bitch Sheila pulled up in a new Cadillac with three hooker friends. I got so heated up that I waited for them to walk towards Uncle Floyd's home. I rode my bike where they had no other choice but to walk by hell I dared her to try to do anything to me I was far from worrying. The closer they walked looking confused the more I had rage in me I started counting to myself and when I reached number five I took off peddling as fast as I could running and knocking those bitches bags to the ground and running over their feet. I hadn't a clue that Uncle Floyd was standing on his back porch because I heard him calling me and I said 'shut up Floyd' and peddled and peddled not realizing that I was riding directly by the shed my mind was set on turning back around to re-ride over Sheila's feet. Before I knew it I ran dead smack up on those fucking pipes destroying my bike. You know the pipes that granddaddy had the sign on saying watch the pipes any how it was too late I must have hit the pipe line because black gooey liquids shot up into the air landing all over me. I have to admit I was a little frightened because I knew James Sr was going to have a two fits and a half. I got up off the ground looking at this mess of black stuff. I tried sitting on it to stop it from shooting up in the air but my butte didn't do anything so I got back up off the ground to head back home.

In conclusion, when I looked back the entire shed was covered with this black stuff and was still shooting up in the air I thought oh brother they gone hit the roof after this one here. So I prepared myself to walk this long walk back home without my bike. The closer I got home the more I saw lights. But goodness gracious this black stuff was on my entire body running into my eyes and ears. I kept shaking my ears because I couldn't hear anything. I don't know how long it took me but I finally made it home to see three police cars up on the grass. Officer May, Shelby and Goldberg's were walking Uncle Floyd and his company out in hand cuffs to the squad cars. Everyone was outside as I walked passed them. I had to stop and bend my head sideways so that gooey stuff could run out my ear once again. My grandparents and Uncle J. C, who I thought had gone fishing with my father looked with their mouths wide opened as I continued walking to my house. Daddy walked to me smiling at least I thought but turns out he was crying. He had tears running down his cheeks. He walked up to me using his shirt to wipe my eyes then looked at his shirt letting out a loud a scream. I said 'dang daddy'. My father bends down to my level staring directing in my eyes but he was lost for words. He kept touching me and looking at his hands. He said Sofay, Soo-soo-sooooo Sofay I said 'huh daddy' he repeated my name once again I could barely hear him because that stuff was clogging my ears. My father damn near ripped my ear lining loose when he called his self-unclogging my ears with his finger. He kept wiping this stuff on his shirt looking at it crying. Then Jr. walked towards us dropping the toothpick that was in his mouth. He rubbed me looked at his hands and screamed out no fucking way mane while laughing. My father couldn't get passed my name he looked at Jr. and stuttered my name again so I said 'daddy why you crying and stuttering my name' He did it again so I said 'daddy you gone be mad at me'. He said 'no pumpkin I am not going to be angry with you' he was still wiping my eyes and nearly having a heart attack at the same time. I said 'daddy I ran over those damn pipes by the shed' when I got up off the ground all I saw were people running towards the shed. I looked up as Eisha and Momma slowly walked off the porch smiling. I said 'mommy daddy and Jr. knocked me down running to the shed'. She smiled and said 'come on Sofay so I can save this oil off of you little one because you stuck gold baby we are rich'! I said 'huh mommy' She said 'baby I'm about to have a heart attack like everyone else who ran to the shed' as she and Auntie Eisha each grab my hands we walked up the stairs to our house. I asked why was the fuzz there on the grass and Momma said 'oh they arrested a prostitution ring at Floyd's place'. I said 'I be damn' Eisha busted up laughing and so did momma.

Boyah family! I know some of yall thinking my family is fucked up but what can I say except don't judge us cause some of yall got jacked up family members too.

ANNOTATIONS

Giant Print Holy Bible Reference; King James Version Giant Print- The book of the Old Testament-No weapon that is formed against thee shall prosper: and every tongue that shall rise against thee in judgement thou shalt condemn. Isaiah Chapter 54:17 pages 1015. Zondervan 1994 Grand Rapids, Michigan.

[Electronic] Daily wisdom; Blessed and Unstoppable-To change a behavioral, we must address the thinking that produces it.

[Electronic] New International version-1John1:5-God is light; in him there is no darkness.

[Electronic]Power of Positivity-Social media–Instagram-A good life is when you assume nothing do more, need less smile often dream big laugh a lot and realize how blessed you are.

[Electronic] Bible hub-Parallel verse-Godliness guards the path of the blameless but the evil are misled by sin. Proverbs 13:6-New living Translation(NLT)Tyndale House Publishers, Incorporate, carol stream Il 1994, 2004, 2007.

[Electronic] Bible gateway-Our father which art in heaven hallowed be thy name.Chapter Matthew 6:9-13. New International version (NIV)-Bibilica 1973,1978,1984,2011.

[Electronic] Pinterest-I will provide for you. Don't worry-Luke 12:22-34-www.purposefullhomemaking.com.

[Electronic] Power of Positivity-Social media –Instagram-Sometimes people pretend you're a bad person. So they don't feel guilty about the things they did to you.

[Electronic] Bible hub-Parallel verse-For this thing I besought the Lord thrice that it might depart from me. 2 Corinthians 12:8-King James Versions(KJV)Tyndale House Publishers, Incorporate, carol stream Il 1994, 2004, 2007.

[Electronic] Quotesuu-The tongue has no bones but it's strong enough to break a heart-motivational.

[Electronic] New International version-Though you have made me see troubles many and bitter you will restore my life again from the depts. Of the earth you will bring again me up-Chapter Psalms 71:20.

Printed in the United States
By Bookmasters